"*The Big Gumbo* is a moving narrative about a European family settling on the lonesome shortgrass plains west of the Missouri River. It reminded me of *My Antonia* by Willa Cather and *Old Jules* by Mari Sanduz—two classic stories about survival and final success. Terrific read!"

William Kittredge, *Hole in the Sky* and *The Last Best Place*

"A story of place, *The Big Gumbo*, explores the different ways passionate people respond to living in a harsh and isolated land. ...Winthers knows the importance of these topics and she weaves them skillfully through her characters' actions and reactions. She also knows intimately this harsh land suitable only for raising sheep. ... Readers of this fine novel will not only be entertained by a story that needs telling, they will come away knowing more about Norwegian culture, the power of love, loneliness, and the revealing, unforgiving, impact a place can have upon people's lives.

Robert Lee, *Guiding Elliott*

"I was riveted by this poignant story of young homesteaders struggling for survival and identity in the relentless prairie landscape of 1890's South Dakota. Jean Winthers immerses us not only in the realities of pioneer life and the unexpectedly fascinating details of sheep ranching, but also in the human drama of three young people loving, suffering, and growing together. Please, Jean Winthers, give us another book and continue the story!"

Jane M. Healy, Ph.D. Author of *Your Child's Growing Mind*

THE
BIG
GUMBO

Published by Bitterroot Press, www.bitterrootpress.com

Cover by Mariah Sinclair.

Paperback ISBN: 978-1-947234-12-3

Ebook ISBN: 978-1-947234-13-0

Hardbound ISBN: 978-1-947234-14-7

THE BIG GUMBO

JEAN HERBERT WINTHERS

"There was nothing but land; not a country at all, but the material out of which countries are made."

Willa Cather, *My Antonia*

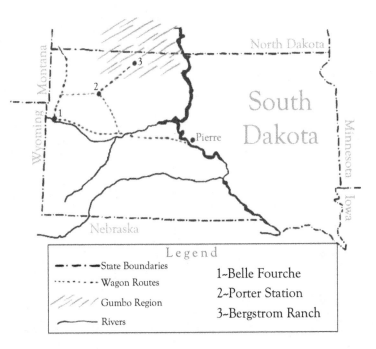

North Dakota

Montana

Wyoming

• 3

2 •

1 •

• Pierre

South

Dakota

Minnesota

Iowa

Nebraska

Legend

State Boundaries
Wagon Routes
Gumbo Region
Rivers

1~Belle Fourche
2~Porter Station
3~Bergstrom Ranch

Chapter One

*R*annei knew Arne was eager to be on his way West, but this first glimpse of New York City from the deck of the steamer *den Norge* filled her with awe and an eagerness to see this grand city. As they steamed into New York harbor that spring day of 1891, Rannei and Arne Bergstrom, newly wedded immigrants from Bergen, Norway, had come to the deck early to claim a good viewing spot. It was well they'd done so, for every passenger on the boat – almost all Norwegians, with some Danes and Swedes and a few Finns – crowded the decks too. At her first sight of that famous lady, the Statue of Liberty, a shiver of excitement ran through Rannei. The gleaming statue, torch upraised, was her assurance that after such a long voyage, they'd finally arrived.

The weather had been for the most part calm, and *den Norge* had made good speed, completing the passage in twenty days; a very respectable time, the captain had told them.

Among the thousands of newly arrived immigrants who streamed into New York harbor daily, Rannei and Arne were more fortunate than many. The Bergstroms had purchased tickets for second-class cabins, so were spared the unpleasantness of the steerage decks, where emigrants crowded together with little privacy and nothing to do but endure.

Rannei had brought along a good supply of homespun yarn and spent the long, largely uneventful days knitting a sweater for Arne. The design was a traditional Norwegian pattern, one she had made many times before, so she had no trouble following it while chatting to her fellow passengers.

In Norway, Arne had worked as a fisherman on sailing vessels, so was at first intensely curious as to how the steamer propelled itself through the water without sails or oars.

"Not as much work for the men, true, but the noise! It is no good for fishing," he predicted to Rannei. "It scares the fish."

Early on in the voyage, Arne had discovered several fishermen friends he knew, who were also immigrating to America with their families. They, too, were headed for the Dakotas to find free land. He began spending time below decks with them, and Rannei came along, much to the dismay of the captain, who did not like the classes to mingle. She'd brought her guitar with her, and many knew the songs Rannei played, and sang along with her.

Soon, Rannei was in great demand as an entertainer. On fine days, she would gather a crowd around her on the deck, or if the weather was cool or rainy, in the dining room the passengers used between meals for reading and recreation.

Although the newlyweds had enjoyed their second-class accommodations, the rooms were not luxurious. The partitions between the tiny cabins were so thin that those in the cabin next door could hear every sound. The bunks were not built to accommodate a man of Arne's size, but Rannei and Arne, in the first flush of married ardor, managed to sleep together at least the first part of every night before Rannei would have to crawl into the upper bunk to get a restful sleep.

But those restless nights in narrow beds had finally come to an end. Now, with New York City spread out before them, Rannei and Arne and all the other immigrants were soon streaming off den Norge and into customs inspections at Ellis Island. As second-class passengers, the Bergstroms had already passed customs in their cabin and did not have to stand in line at Ellis Island. Rannei wondered how Arne's friends in steerage had fared, but in the confusion of disembarking she'd not had a chance to find them. As many of them were also headed for the Dakotas to find free land, she hoped she might see at least a few of them on the train west.

Soon enough, Rannei and Arne were standing on the docks of New York, blinking in the late afternoon sunshine. The Lady loomed so near them it seemed they could almost touch her. From the harbor's edge, New York looked much like Bergen, with ships at anchor dotting the water to the horizon. Rannei and Arne tore their gazes from the harbor to a mountain of luggage piled on the dock, from which their next task was to reclaim their possessions.

All stacked together, their own luggage resembled a small hill. Arne's Uncle Jens, who had returned from America back to Norway the previous year, had made lists for the newlyweds of what they must take along, such as a bedstead, small farm tools and household goods. Larger farm implements, Uncle Jens assured them, could be bought once they arrived. It would be much too expensive to buy such things in Norway and ship them over, and they were sure to be cheaper and more modern in America, said Uncle Jens. The items from his list had been duly packed in crates that now formed the bottom layer of their luggage pile.

Atop the layer of crates stood Rannei's dowry chest. Rannei's grandfather had been a sailor earlier in his life, and long ago had purchased the special chest from a fellow sailor. Made of teak, the heavy wood chest was beautifully and intricately carved with strange designs and even words, although no one so far had been able to decipher them, not even the sailor who'd sold it to him. Grandfather Engels had given the chest to his daughter Kristin when she'd married.

Now, Kristin had passed the chest along to her daughter Rannei on the occasion of her marriage to Arne. It contained Rannei's dowry, including bedcovers, pillows, linens, a coverlet made of eiderdown, table covers and napkins, pewter mugs and bowls, silver spoons and knives, carved wooden candlesticks and candles, and an heirloom from Rannei's grandmother, a candlestick of beaten silver. When the chest was full, it took two strong men to carry it, or four lesser ones.

After the wedding, Rannei had added to the chest a small leather midwife's case, with silver scissors, waxed thread, clean soft cloths, and little tins of herb leaves and ointments, all compounded by Rannei and Kristin. Inside the smooth brown cover of the case her mother had written, in her clear hand, instructions on child birthing in English and Norwegian. So far, Rannei had had no cause to review the contents of the little case. She and Arne had been married but one month, and she'd experienced no symptoms of pregnancy.

On the top of their luggage pile were several valises containing clothes to last them two years. Besides all this, Arne kept their savings in American bank notes securely wrapped in a money belt around his sturdy waist. Rannei's dowry money she carried herself, tucked into a soft bag of chamois leather and pinned inside her chemise. With all these belongings, Rannei and Arne were as well equipped and hopeful a pair as any immigrants arriving on American shores.

Arne left Rannei momentarily with their things, navigating the crowd of other new arrivals to locate a dray. He soon returned with two men he'd hired to take them and their belongings directly to the railroad station, their departure point for this new country's interior. Uncle Jens had advised them to do this and to secure tickets right away for their train journey to Chicago.

Arne purchased the tickets with Rannei by his side to assist with any difficulties in translation. When the ticket agent said the train journey to Chicago and beyond would last several days, the thought made Rannei feel utterly exhausted. Leaving the ticket window, she summoned the courage to speak her mind.

"Arne, it has been such a long ocean journey, I hate the thought of getting in a train car so soon. Can't we at least rest here one extra day? I would really like to see this place. When will we ever have the chance again?"

Arne gazed at her with a thoughtful expression, then turned back to the man who'd sold him the tickets. "These tickets are good for next day, also?"

The ticket booth man looked confused.

"We may want to stay an extra day and see the sights," Rannei explained, silently thanking her mother for making her learn English from childhood on. Otherwise, she and Arne would have been completely lost.

The ticket booth man gave her a friendly nod. "Of course, the tickets are good the day after tomorrow, if you prefer. Your luggage will be quite safe in our baggage room until you board. I also have a hotel recommendation for such a fine couple as yourselves. Would that be of interest?"

Arne said it was, and the man looked pleased. The hotel was quite nearby, he told them, and they were sure to find it. He even drew a little map on a piece of paper, which named the streets in English. Carrying a small case each, they went in search of it.

Arne knew what English Rannei had taught him, but he had never mastered tenses, and so put everything into the present. Since he had never learned to read in English, it was Rannei who had to interpret the written signs. Nevertheless, despite the map and Rannei's English, once they returned to the streets, they quickly became overwhelmed.

Little that Rannei and Arne had seen in their lives, even on their honeymoon in Bergen, had prepared them for the rush and stench and confusion of New York. Such a hubbub of ringing streetcar bells, clopping horses' hooves and creaking wagons, the deep booming of ships' horns and sharp toot-toots of tug boats. Everyone seemed in a hurry, and when Rannei tried to request directions in her slow but correct English, no one had time to answer.

Horse-drawn vehicles of all kinds clattered through the thronged streets, their drivers impervious to lowly pedestrians. On their first attempt at crossing the street, Arne just missed being run over by a contraption that looked like a railway car on iron wheels, propelling itself, as if by magic, along two iron rails. Rannei, seeing it bear down on them, pulled him out of the way just in time. The driver did not even look at them, and the people in the car stared vacantly at them out the windows.

Finally, they found the Grand Hotel recommended by the ticket agent, its faded gilt sign above a rickety-looking entrance belying its name. If it was not the best one in New York, its rates made up for it. Rannei was sure they were cheated, but she knew little about the American money, and Arne himself was still trying to figure it out. They paid the price asked, too relieved to have found it to protest. But before Arne paid, Rannei made sure the price included hot water for two baths, to be sent up immediately.

The next morning, rested and sated after a night of love-making on a lumpy, sagging, but wide bed, Rannei and Arne were up early, feeling quite famished. Outside the hotel, they found a small restaurant on the corner, where they ate a "farmer's breakfast" of eggs, sausage and fried potatoes — "all you can eat for fifty cents." Restored by the meal, the young couple set out to see New York, Rannei's hand tucked decorously into Arne's crooked elbow.

Rannei was wearing her town clothes for the occasion, one that her grandmother's seamstress had made for her from the latest fashion book. The jacket of her blue serge suit had sleeves that were puffed at the top. Under it she wore a snowy-white blouse of softest cotton, with a high collar and bands of yellow and blue Bergstromer embroidery down the front.

The nipped-in waist showed off Rannei's trim figure, her waist tiny even without the corset. Rannei had given her corset away on the boat to a woman who was sure it was the "latest thing from America." Rannei was just as glad to be rid of the pinching thing, and resolved never to wear one again. Her straight skirt, worn with only one narrow petticoat, reached her ankles, falling just below the tops of her high-buttoned walking boots. A black felt toque perched on her coronet of black braids, the veil covering part of her forehead, and tied behind the hat in a stylish bow.

She felt proud to walk beside Arne, who was also fashionably dressed in his "good" clothes. He wore a loose sack coat of dark blue worn over a soft white shirt closed at the neck with a black string tie. Red suspenders and soft felt hat completed the outfit. They made a striking couple, Rannei thought, catching a glimpse in a big shop window; Arne with his golden, brawny good looks, and Rannei herself, slim and dark. Although they looked unlike the average immigrants, they were obviously not New Yorkers either, she knew. Her braids and the embroidery on her blouse, Arne's baggy clothing and soft felt hat, as well as the way both of them gaped in wondering delight at everything around them marked them instantly as foreigners.

It did not occur to Rannei and Arne to wonder what people thought of them. They were enjoying the day, themselves, each other, and the wonderful new world in which they found themselves. The streets of New York were crowded with people wearing clothes of all descriptions, from satins to rags, furs to tatters. Rannei heard conversations voiced in accents and languages she had never heard before. Everywhere they went, people whistled and sang, shouted and laughed, and clamored and begged, filling the air with unintelligible sounds.

As they turned down a street near their hotel, one of those magical cars that had almost run Arne over the previous day clanged past on its iron rails, stopping at almost every corner for people to get off and on.

"See, Ran, it's like a little train," Arne exclaimed in delight. "People use it to travel about the city. Let's try it!"

Rannei was willing, though the speed and hugeness of the car frightened her. She could see that they were too late to catch that one, so she suggested they watch it for a while to see how it worked. It was a fine May morning, so they sat in a sidewalk cafe, drank coffee, and watched the life of New York hurry by. Rannei asked the waiter when he came to refill their cups if anyone could ride the iron cars.

"You bet, sis," said the waiter, a big burly man with an apron around his waist and sleeves rolled up to his elbows. These street cars were the very latest in city transportation. Some cities, he said, still used horse-drawn cars, but here in the city center they used modern electricity. All one had to do was pay a token fee as one entered and one could go as far as the line went or get off anywhere in between.

"Saves a lot of walking," the waiter said. He stuck a hairy hand into his pocket and produced a few coins, showing them the exact fare to put in the fee box.

"Just go down to the corner there, and the car will come in, oh, half an hour. Ride it from one end to the other and see the sights. Down by the Battery, at the end of the Island, you can get a look at the Statue of Liberty, or even take the ferry to the island if you want, and climb right up inside her. Along the Hudson River waterfront, you can see some of the biggest ships in the world. Or maybe you'd like to go to Central Park and ride through it in a hansom cab. It is beautiful this time of year, and lots of rich people go there. And always it is most interesting to walk along the streets and see the fine shops and the beautiful buildings."

The ebullient waiter told them he had come from Italy three years before, and now here he was, earning a fine living as a waiter in this cafe. "Someday I will own a finer cafe than this one, too," he said proudly. "I save all my money and soon it will be enough. Here in America, everything is possible."

Rannei listened, fascinated. To think of a poor man earning enough to dream of owning his own restaurant! That would never be possible in Norway. "Maybe it is here in the cities where the opportunities are," she said to Arne, after they had taken their leave of the friendly waiter and were strolling down the street to try the electric streetcar.

Arne laughed. "He dreams of a little building and to cook food for people," he said. "You and I, we will own ten times what that man has. We can buy hundreds of acres of land—that is how they measure land here, Rannei, in acres, Uncle Jens tells me."

"Yes," Rannei said, fired anew by his enthusiasm. "We'll have hundreds of acres, and hundreds of trees to grow fruit, and hundreds of fields to grow corn. And we will earn hundreds of krone, dollars, too!"

Arne looked thoughtful for a moment, almost hesitant, but then his lips creased into a smile. "You bet, Rannei," Arne said, trying out the new English expression he had learned from the waiter. "You bet!"

They spent the rest of the day seeing many of the sights suggested by the Italian waiter, although they did not take the ferry over to Bedloe's Island and climb up inside the Statue of Liberty, choosing instead to admire the statue from the Battery. Somehow it did not seem right to either of them to go inside the Lady.

"I'd rather remember her as we see her now," Rannei said. "She looks like a goddess. Frigga maybe, or even Freya."

"She looks more like one of the Valkyries to me," Arne teased. "Look at that torch she holds. And that stern look on her face. She looks as if she is ready to ride into battle."

"Never!" Rannei cried passionately. She did not like to be teased about her gods and goddesses. "She is too beautiful for that, too kind. She welcomes men and women, and children too, into America. She would never hurt them."

"I guess you're right, Ran," Arne said. Rannei knew he was placating her. He'd teased her before about how serious she was about the Old Norse gods. Arne was not a religious man himself.

After viewing the Lady, Rannei and Arne walked along the wharves of the Hudson River, admiring the ships from all over the world docked there. As Arne described the features of the different boats to her, Rannei was reminded again of what Arne had told her, how he'd seen enough while working on fishing boats to decide it was impossible for any being, or god, to control the mighty power of the oceans.

Confident now, they caught the streetcar back toward the center of town and rode through Central Park in a hansom cab, marveling at the size of this greatest of American cities. Around noon, they purchased food from a vendor near the pond, ate lunch on the grass with other New Yorkers, and threw the remains of their sandwiches to the ducks.

By the time they returned to their hotel in the late afternoon, Rannei's feet ached from walking on the cobblestones and hard sidewalks, and her mind was filled to overflowing with all the sights they had seen. They enjoyed an early supper in the small cafe where they had started that morning. It was still light outside when they retired to their hotel for another hot bath and a long, languorous evening of lovemaking.

Early the next morning, Arne and Rannei rose and went to the train station, making sure to allow enough time to collect all their luggage and get it loaded on the train to Chicago. Even after that wonderful extra day, Rannei was sorry to leave New York. She felt there was so much more to see, but also knew there were no opportunities in this part of the country to buy land. Everyone they talked to said just about everything between the East coast and Chicago was already taken up. So, she boarded the train without demur, not guessing their fate would be decided so soon for them.

Chapter Two

*C*al Willard noticed the young immigrant couple right after he had seated himself in the train car. He watched the man and woman come down the aisle, the man carrying two small cases, the woman with a basket on her arm. They were a striking couple, dressed well enough they ought to have been able to afford to ride in second-class rather than this train car set aside for the poorest of immigrants.

Maybe, Cal decided, they chose to ride here to be with their community. He was a misfit in this car, too, but on his journeys west he sometimes chose to ride in the immigrant cars to sketch immigrants for the Dakota People book he was planning. He was thankful that he had chosen to do so this time, he was to think later. Otherwise, he would never have met the two people who would change his life so completely.

Some of the people in the car seemed to know the young couple and smiled and murmured greetings as the couple walked down the aisle. The two were obviously newly married, beautiful and much in love. The woman wore a blue, fitted suit, which Cal knew from his recent trip home was cut in cloth of the latest style. Except for the original and lovely touch of embroidery at the midriff, his sisters could have been wearing similar dresses.

The ocean-blue color of the dress made the young immigrant's eyes intensely blue, a shade almost purple under the black wings of her brows. The woman — or girl, really, she was so young — had skin so white it was almost translucent, yet it possessed an active, healthy glow. Her very black hair, which she wore in a shining crown of braids atop her head framed pale, youthful cheeks. With that black hair she did not look very Norwegian, but yet she was chattering away in that language to the others in the car.

The man beside her was equally striking, with sky-blue eyes, blond, almost curly hair, and a tall build as burly and broad as his wife's was slender. The husband had the casual stroll of a seafaring lad rather than the plodding gait of a farmer. What a handsome couple they made, Cal thought. His fingers itched for his artist's sketchpad. He would try to meet them as soon as possible, he decided.

The young couple seated themselves several rows ahead of him and across the aisle. The train had barely pulled out of the station when the conductor came down the aisle and paused to examine the young couples' tickets. Cal listened in unashamedly on the conversation. The conductor demanded to know why the date on the tickets were for two days prior. The blond giant was attempting to explain, in lilting half-English, half-Norwegian something about "New York and the sights to see," when Cal decided to take things in hand.

"Pardon me, sir and madam," he said with a bow to the woman and a nod to the frustrated husband. "Perhaps I can help explain your dilemma to Mr. Nelson here?"

"Oh, thank you, Mr. Willard, I can't make head nor tail of this man's garble," the conductor said, his face red with frustration.

"It's quite simple really, sir," the woman interrupted in perfect English before Cal could continue. "You see, we bought our tickets when we arrived, before we decided to stay over the extra day. We were assured by the ticket clerk it was permissible to travel with the day before yesterday's date on the tickets. We confirmed it again before we boarded this morning."

"But madam, why did you not explain the difficulty to Mr. Nelson if you understood him?" Cal asked, astounded.

"I was waiting until he and Arne stopped shouting at each other," the woman said demurely.

The conductor scowled, punched their tickets, and moved on, muttering angrily about "these immigrants keep coming... and how one is to understand their language, I do not know."

Cal bowed again. "Pardon me for the intrusion. My name is Cal Willard."

The woman's beautiful mouth was twitching, but she managed to say, "And we are Arne and Rannei Bergstrom. Very pleased to meet you, sir," before bursting into muffled laughter. "Oh, oh, that was so funny. You and that conductor looked like two angry fighting cocks, Arne."

"Also pleased to meet you, Mr. Willard," Arne said, rising from his padded bench to shake hands with Cal. Much to Cal's surprise, Rannei offered her hand too, but he recovered and took it in his own, bowing again as he did so.

"Now Rannei," Arne said sternly, "you must not carry on like this. What are people to think?"

But Cal had begun to chuckle, too, and by the time they had finished laughing over the incident, they were all well acquainted. When Rannei invited Cal to sit with them, he agreed at once and he crossed the aisle to settle in the vacant seat that faced the rear of the train car.

As Rannei looked out the train window, daydreaming or dozing, Cal and Arne fell into conversation. Cal learned he had guessed right. Arne was a sailor lad. Arne explained he was on the great adventure of his life to the United States and the West.

Their conversation unfolded in a halting mixture of English and Norwegian. Cal had learned Norwegian from his maternal grandmother, although he did not consider himself competent in it, as he was in several other languages. But he understood enough to realize Arne was no ordinary immigrant. He had a dream and a goal that impressed Cal.

They had boarded the train late in the morning, and by early afternoon Cal was wondering what vendors might be offering food at the next station, but Rannei, it seemed, had come prepared. She took out bread and cheese, cold sausage and apples and oranges from her basket. She cut chunks of cheese, laid them atop pieces of bread, and handed these to the men. Arne poured water from the water jug into pewter mugs and offered them to his wife and Cal. Cal set his mug down between his feet and pulled a flask from his pocket instead.

"Do you mind, Mrs. Bergstrom?" he asked Rannei. When she shook her head, he offered the flask to Arne, who poured the clear brown liquid into his half-cup of water. "Bourbon, America's national drink," Cal said, taking a long swallow from the flask. Politely, he did not offer any to Rannei. She did not look to him like a drinking woman.

"Ah! That washes down that awful bread," Arne said.

"Where are you heading for?" Cal asked them. It was almost the first thing one immigrant asked another. "Dakota country?"

"We head for the new state of South Dakota," said Arne. "My Uncle Jens spends five years in Minnesota and Dakota Territory. He says there are miles of land there, just to wait for someone to claim it. But he speaks most of all of South Dakota, and that is why we go there. We leave the train at Pierre."

"And that is where the train leaves us," Cal murmured. "That is the end of the line, as of course you know. I already have a ranch out in Dakota, northwest of Pierre on the Big Gumbo. That is all ranching country. I run sheep there. East of the river, the land is mostly taken, I believe, but there is still some good farming country along the Belle Fourche, south of Pierre, and some closer to the Black Hills. But you will be able to discover what land is available from the land office in Pierre. Were you interested in farming mostly, Mr. Bergstrom, or had you thought of ranching?"

"I know to farm; my father has a rocky little farm on a fjord in Norway. I know that and fishing, and I understand there is not many fish in this country! But mostly I want space, and land, and not many people close by."

"You sound more like a rancher than a farmer to me," Cal said. "If you want land and space around you, the Gumbo is the place for you. Why, it hasn't even been surveyed yet, so you can't file a regular claim. All you do is file preemption papers at the land office, then after six months, pay a certain amount. It isn't much."

"But how much, Mr. Willard? And will the land be ours legally then?" Rannei asked.

"Oh yes, it is perfectly legal. You would file a preemption claim, as I did, on a hundred and sixty acres. This will be paid in six months, and the fee is about a dollar twenty-five an acre. Then your claim is published in the paper, probably the Rapid City paper, since that is where the land office for that area is now. When it is legally surveyed, you will be able to file a proper homesteading claim. But you see, if you are just running stock, you won't plan on making improvements on it, which is what they call cultivating a certain acreage.

"Now, if you're talking the Gumbo, you wouldn't want to cultivate that. Can't, in fact. The soil is practically untillable. So, you do what the cattlemen do, file the preemption papers, and then use not just your own, but all the land to graze your cattle or sheep on. You can build a house and barns, as I did, and this also gives you squatter's rights." He laughed at the look on Arne's face. He looked like a man listening to a fairy tale.

"But that is wonderful! Do you hear what he says,

Rannei? We can use all the land we want, and we pay for only a hundred and sixty acres!"

"But what if other people have this same idea, and someone wants to graze on the same land you are grazing on," Rannei asked. "What would happen then?"

"That is why the Gumbo is so perfect," Cal assured her. "It is really good only for stock, and better, in my opinion, for sheep than cattle. No farmer in his right mind would settle there, and even ranchers stay off it. Some of them run their stock on it in the summer, but nobody uses it in the winter. It grows the best grass in the world, buffalo grass. It cures right on the stem so there is no need to cut it to make hay. The wind keeps it blown free of snow most winters, and the sheep can graze on their hay instead of having it fed to them." Cal paused for effect, amused to see Arne and Rannei leaning toward him intently to catch his every word.

"Once every ten years or so there will be a winter when the snow is so deep or crusted over the animals can't get to it," Cal continued. "That happened in 1886-87. Luckily, I had no sheep then, although I had filed my claim before that. I had my herd of horses, but they ran loose on the Gumbo. Cattle died by the thousands, but there again, sheep have an advantage over cattle. Sheep and horses will paw for their food through snow. Cattle won't. They must have it clear to browse. Of course, that winter the snow was too deep even to paw through, but hay can be put up, enough to tide one over the bad spots," Cal stopped and chuckled to himself, realizing he'd strayed from Rannei's question. "But about encountering other herders. Mrs. Bergstrom, I don't think there will ever be enough people on the Gumbo to worry about that. The Gumbo is an awfully long way from anywhere, and it is lonely. I'm certain that land will soon be up for sale too, and large tracts can be bought cheaply."

Rannei was looking more and more uneasy. She glanced often at Arne, who seemed to hang on Cal's every word. For her sake, Cal changed the subject. "But what about you, Mrs. Bergstrom? Are you from the same area of Norway as your husband?"

"Oh, please, you must call me Rannei, and I will call you Cal. I think we are friends already, are we not?"

"Indeed, I hope we are, Rannei, and may I call you Arne?" Cal looked at Arne for permission.

"Rannei sometimes speaks before it is polite, but yes, I am Arne and you are Cal," Arne said, offering his big hand again, as if sealing a bargain.

"Arne and I have known each other all our lives. We come from Bergstromfjord, in Norway," Rannei said, and began to describe the countryside there, the farms and herds and life she and Arne had left behind.

As she spoke, the train rushed on. Out the window, Cal saw they'd reached the outskirts of Binghamton, a tidy town of mostly brick buildings along the Susquehanna River. As Rannei went on in her melodious voice, Cal began developing a clearer picture of this young couple. Yet he also picked up from the young woman's pauses from time to time that there might be some parts of the story she was choosing, for whatever reason, not to share.

Chapter Three

*A*rne's family farm was not far from that of her family's, Rannei told Cal, so although Arne was five years her elder, they had attended the same village school. Arne had been friends with her brothers, and she tagged after them all. The three of them let her go everywhere with them; she was as good as any boy at fishing or swimming or sailing.

As the middle child of Lars and Kristin Andersen, and the only daughter in a loving family, her childhood was uncomplicated and perfectly happy. Lars Andersen was a well-to-do *bønde* in Bergstromfjord, with many cotters living in neighboring houses who worked for him. Lars' grandfather boasted that they were descended from the nobility; he claimed he could trace the line all the way back to that first king of Norway, Harald Fairhair.

Whether that was true or not, in the eighteenth century, the family had farmed vast estates. But then, instead of keeping to the usual custom of having the eldest son inherit the land and maintain his younger brothers and their families, their ancestor, who had many sons, parceled out some land to each of them. In this way, the land was gradually broken up into smaller and smaller tracts, and the one farm remaining was the sole inheritance of Rannei's father, Lars.

Lars considered himself lucky, however, for it was the original farm, and a large one, and he had managed to add to it large tracts of forest land, where he had built a very profitable sawmill. Her father had said he would not divide his land among his sons, but would leave the farm and his forest holdings to his eldest son, Hendrik. By the time Rannei married Arne and was leaving Norway, Hendrik was married to Aase, and they'd had a daughter. Hendrik had been assuming more and more of his father's duties, as Lars turned increasingly to the politics he loved.

The second son, Einar, was not interested in farming, although if he had been, room would have been found for him on the farm too, or in the lumber business. But he was a businessman, like his maternal grandfather, and after his marriage to the daughter of a rich merchant in Bergen, went into his grandfather's import business.

As for her two little brothers, Ole was seven, and Knut, five, when Rannei left home. Perhaps they would be the ones to follow her to America, she said. Bergstromfjord was changing rapidly, and the young men were less and less inclined to stay home on the family farms.

Like her father, Lars, Arne's father Johann was a *bønde* landowner, too. But Johann did not have such a large farm, and his land was not as good. Johann could have been a cotter and worked on Lars' estate to earn extra money, but instead he clung year after year to his rocky little farm perched high on the mountainside above the fjord.

Arne shook his head at this description, as if wondering how his family had survived at all. His mother was sickly and needed expensive medicine, Arne interrupted to explain, and it was only with the annual fishing trips made by his father and brothers to the Lofoten Islands that they had managed to eke out a living. When he'd turned twelve, Arne had gone off to the Lofotens with his father and brothers to work on the fishing boats. Every year after that, the money Arne made fishing went to help his family.

Back then, when Arne had been twelve years old, Rannei said, picking up her story, just after Arne returned from that first trip, he told her that someday he would marry her and take her off to America. They would have a big farm, he'd said, bigger than her own father's. Rannei had been seven years old at the time, and had not believed him.

But as each year passed, Arne's dream grew stronger. When he returned from the Lofotens, each time he'd tell Rannei that someday, he would have his luck; his luck would come in that season when the cod ran off the Lofoten Islands like molten silver, and he would be in a position to get his share. He would wait for his lucky year, marry Rannei, and they'd sail off for America. Year after year he dreamed his dream.

Rannei had seen the dream build inside Arne. Wasn't it she who first read Bjornson's story "Arne" to him, about the poet peasant so restless to leave his small farm and go into the world? She had witnessed a similar longing in her young friend's eyes as he'd talked of his dream, and he'd begged her to read "Arne" over and over until they both knew it by heart.

> *Ut, vil jeg! Ut!*
> *A så langt langt, langt*
> *Over de høje fjaelle!*
> *Her er så knugende tåerende trangt,*
> *Og mit mot er såungt og rankt,*
> *Lad det få stiginhen friste*
> *Ikke mot murkanten briste!*

In English it did not have the same ring to it, but Rannei made Arne learn it anyway, to improve his command of the language:

> *Out! I will out! So far, far from here*
> *Over the mountains so high!*
> *Below is so crushingly, consumingly near*
> *And my spirit is young, without fear.*
> *Let it to the heights aspire*
> *Not crushed on the crags to expire!*

Rannei had never felt this longing herself, she confided. To her, the mountains were beloved friends; to Arne they were guards to prevent his escape from a life he hated. She'd sympathized with him when he explained it to her; for herself, she would have been happy to have settled on a farm in Norway.

The fishing trips caused Arne to miss so much

schooling that instead of remaining in the class with her brothers, he had dropped back to being one year ahead of Rannei. By the time Rannei's brothers Hendrik and Einar were through with school and Hendrik had married, Arne was just finishing his last year. He could not think of going on to the secondary school, but continuing did not matter so much to him. He had his plan, and he knew how to wait. He must make a lot of money all in one season to have enough to go to America. There would be no saving it up, for his father had constant needs for money, for the mortgage, or medicine for his mother, or food for them all.

And it did happen as Arne had known all along it would. Last March, the cod had run as molten silver, and the bounty for the fishermen had been great indeed. Many fishermen had spent their money, but Arne hoarded every bit. Arne's brother Harald shared in the bounty too. Now in possession of a reasonable savings, Harald had proposed to Lisa, the girl waiting patiently for him for five years. His brother had chosen to pay the mortgage on the farm where he planned to work and raise a family with his new wife. Arne's older sister had already married, and their mother, who had been ill so long, had passed away the previous winter. That left the old widower Johann in the house with Harald, soon to be married, and Arne. For his part, Arne saw that if he married Rannei and stayed home as well, in a few years' time the farm would not be able to support two families. This was his chance to implement his plan, and he did not hesitate.

Arne went to Rannei's father, Lars Andersen, and politely asked him for his daughter's hand. They both knew this was only a formality. Rannei had long ago informed her parents that she and Arne would marry. However, since Rannei was not yet eighteen, her parents encouraged her to take more time before she married. Arne had informed her parents of his plan to emigrate. Naturally, they were unhappy to think a marriage to Arne meant she would go so far away from them.

Here Rannei paused in her story to Cal, not willing to divulge the other, unspoken reasons for her parents' hesitation. Although her parents both knew Arne well, and liked and admired him, they worried whether he was the right one for their daughter. Her mother Kristin had hoped Rannei would marry a cultured, educated city man, someone who could offer her beauty and talents the scope of opportunity they deserved. But there was no question of forbidding the marriage. Rannei had been brought up to make her own decisions, and her parents respected those choices as they always had. Rannei assured them she was marrying the man she loved. In the end, her parents had acquiesced and given their blessing.

Nor did Rannei speak of how generously her father had provided for his only daughter. Besides a wedding gift of household goods to start the couple in their American home, Lars had given Rannei a dowry gift of one thousand American dollars. He'd made a trip to the city of Bergen especially for the purpose, and the night before her wedding gave Rannei the thousand dollars in crisp new bank notes. He gave them to her in the presence of Arne, and told them both it belonged to his daughter, for her to keep for her own use, or to use for their joint good, as she saw fit.

Her father said other things to Arne, too, when they were alone. He told him that Rannei was not an ordinary girl, as Arne well knew, and that she would not be an ordinary wife. She had been brought up as independently as her brothers, and her views and opinions had been respected in the same way. He said he knew this would be trying to Arne at times, as it certainly was not the traditional way to raise daughters. Arne might find it hard sometimes, Lars said, to work out compromises when it might seem much easier to make the decisions himself. Rannei would certainly never be a meek wife, obeying her husband without question. She had been brought up to believe that marriage was a partnership.

Arne had to laugh at this, he told Rannei later. He described how he'd told Lars he could not imagine Rannei obeying anyone unless she wanted to.

Kristin also had a talk with Rannei. Rannei remembered fondly how calm and loving her mother had been to her. Kristin had told Rannei she must make allowances for the fact that Arne had not been raised as she had, with respect for the wife as an equal. Rannei must sometimes be the one to bend, to compromise; it would be harder for Arne than for her to remember always that they were partners. It was natural for a man to do as his father did, Kristin said, and reminded Rannei about Arne's mother, who never seemed to have a voice in affairs at Arne's home. In any case, a true partnership would be forged only after years of living together.

Rannei must remember also that here in her own country, her own fjord, where everyone knew her, no one minded what she believed. But in America, as a grown woman and wife, and perhaps soon, a mother, she could not always say what a young girl might. Rannei, who knew that her mother was the wisest woman in the world, listened carefully, and promised to heed every bit of her advice. Kristin smiled and kissed her daughter.

Rannei was sad at the thought of leaving her family, her beloved mountains and the sea and the farm, but when she was with Arne, she thought of little else but him, like any girl in love. The summer before Arne made his lucky strike of cod, they had made love for the first time, beside the waterfall above the *säeter* hut where the girls, and sometimes her mother, were making cheese, and where Rannei was also supposed to be.

It had been a rarely hot day, but Arne and Rannei swam in all but the coolest days of summer, at their secret swimming place. They had swum here since childhood days, sometimes with the brothers, sometimes by themselves. They always swam nude, each turning his back before disrobing, and Rannei going into the water first. Arne would always look away politely as she came out of the water, and she turned her back as she dressed. This time, however, when she had scrambled out over the slippery rocks and stood gasping on the bank, wringing out her cold wet braid, something made her look back over her shoulder. Arne was standing in the clear mountain stream, his head turned as if against his will, watching her. She ran to meet him as he came up the bank to her.

After that they were together more than ever. No one paid any attention, as they had always been together. Rannei did not become pregnant, a fact she attributed to Freya, her patroness goddess, and Arne to his luck. But if she had, they simply would have married sooner. The next season was Arne's lucky one.

The wedding happened fast, Rannei said aloud to Cal, and to other immigrant friends in seats nearby who had begun listening in. Rannei's father had already booked passage for their departure in mid-April, so they were married almost immediately on his return from the Lofoten Islands. The wedding took place in the district church on a rare cloudless day in late March, just one week after Rannei turned eighteen.

All the neighbors from up and down the fjord, and several fjords over, too, came to help Rannei and Arne celebrate their wedding. Einar and his new wife, Birthe, were there, and Hendrik and Aase, and little Siri, holding out her arms to be taken by her aunt in her wedding dress. All of Arne's relatives came too, his father Johann, brother Harald and his bride-to-be, Lisa, and his sister, Anna, who had married a cotter from the other side of the fjord.

Rannei's parents, handsome and smiling, brought her to the church, Kristin wearing her best blue skirt and white blouse and cap, with a silver brooch at her neck. It was a happy wedding, but Grandmother Engels could not keep from weeping. Rannei knew why. There was a strong possibility she might never see her grandmother again once she and Arne left Norway.

Grandfather Engels gave the couple a wedding journey, a week's trip to Bergen, where they stayed in the finest hotel in the city. Rannei visited all her favorite places with Arne, delighting in showing him the quays, the great cathedral of Bergen, rebuilt in the sixteenth century, and the Berganhus fort, with the adjoining Hakonshallen and Rosenkranz tower of the twelfth and thirteenth centuries. Arne was fascinated with the archaeological and natural history collections in the Bergen museum, while Rannei most enjoyed the art gallery and its collection of Norwegian paintings and furniture. They visited the parks by the Lungegaard Lakes, and even went to the theater, the first time Arne had seen a play. After the magical week together, they went home to prepare for the long voyage across the ocean to America.

Chapter Four

*B*y the time Rannei had finished her story, with Arne sometimes breaking in enthusiastically with his comments and asking her to sing "Arne's Song" so he could explain it to Cal, the afternoon shadows in the forest outside the train window had grown long. Rannei had repacked her basket and Cal had put away his flask. They had all been immersed in her story, Cal realized, the nearest immigrant passengers listening in as well, for they had all shared similar experiences.

Cal had pieced together a picture of Rannei's life in Norway, so different from Arne's and yet so entwined with his. He sensed her father and mother's apprehension at their daughter's marriage but also her long and abiding love for Arne. What a pair they were! How were the two of them to be happy in this land with such opposing ideas of what they wanted? For he sensed too, Rannei's strong pull back to the life on the fjord where she had been so happy. How was she to find that in the Gumbo, if he did indeed lead them there? He must be very careful indeed.

Cal settled back in his seat, to doze discreetly as the train rolled through fields and farms, tracts of woodland, over streams and through small settlements, making few stops along the way. At nightfall, a few of the immigrants in their train car begged Rannei and Arne for songs. Rannei picked up her guitar and, hearing the pleasant sound of Rannei's and Arne's mingled voices underlaid with the mellow tone of the guitar, Cal roused himself and gazed at the enchanting scene. Now there was a delightful image he wanted to be sure to render for his upcoming book, he thought, and reached for his sketchbook.

For the rest of the four day journey, Cal was with Rannei and Arne constantly. As hour after hour flew by, the train chugging through Ohio, then on through Indiana to Illinois, he helped Arne with his English, and pointed out interesting sights to them both; he talked about the Gumbo and his life there. Often he took out his sketchbook and made drawings of the immigrants in the car.

Rannei shared their food with Cal, and in return, Cal purchased meals for them all from the vendors on the station platforms during the stops. They never ate meals at the crowded eating-houses in the stations, instead preferring to picnic happily off by themselves.

In the evenings, Rannei and Arne moved to the back of the train car to sing for their audience. Cal listened with pleasure to Rannei with her guitar, her voice low and clear, yet rich, perfectly suited to the songs she sang. He watched her, fascinated. Who would expect to find such beauty and talent here, in this crowd of rather bedraggled immigrants?

Cal glanced around at the others listening rapt in the car. He was not the only one who thought her unusual. They all seemed to be staring at her, the women as well as the men and children. They urged her to sing tune after tune. But she refused to be the only one to receive the attention. She also played songs for Arne to sing in his rich baritone. Once she strummed a few lively chords and Arne began singing a sailor's chant in Norwegian. Several of the other men joined in boisterously. Cal knew the familiar folk song, which he'd learned at his beloved Norwegian grandmother's knee.

> *I'm ready now for my last trip,*
> *Sing, Sailor, oh!*
> *Away to heaven steers my ship*
> *Sing, Sailor, oh!*
> *The glass is running toward the end,*
> *See to your compass well, my friend!*

For the remaining days of the journey, Cal often found himself staring, but he could not help it; he was sure that a closer scrutiny would reveal Rannei as having some flaw. But he could discover nothing to mar her beauty. To his artist's eye, she was perfect.

Chapter Five

From the beginning, when Arne had first shared his dream with her in Norway, Rannei had seen in her mind's eye a cozy little cottage in a setting amid neat green fields, the tops of neighbors' chimneys visible from her kitchen window, the orchards, the flower garden, the stream meandering through it all. That was how she had always pictured their American farm. But the Gumbo sounded like another place entirely.

"There aren't any trees at all there," Cal was explaining to Arne in his pleasant, cultured voice. "Nothing except grass, and maybe a butte or two. I think you'd feel at home there, Arne, and really take to sheep ranching. You can see for miles, just like you can on the ocean. Yet it has a beauty of its own, like the open sea. The sunrises and sunsets are magnificent, and the thunderstorms! You can see them coming from miles away, sweeping across the land, trailing down fingers of rain, while all around is sunshine. I tell you, it is something to see, but it isn't safe to stand and watch. Lightning will strike the highest object, they say, and it may well be you."

Arne laughed admiringly, but Rannei was sure Cal was teasing. Nothing taller than a man for miles!

"I think I would like some trees around," she said to Arne. Arne squeezed her hand, his expression earnest.

"I'm begin to think Cal is right, Ran. We must go to the Gumbo if we want land, and if we want to ranch."

Rannei stared at him in consternation, but said nothing. She remembered how Arne had hated his father's rocky little farm, the soil so thin that, more years than not, the crops failed to mature no matter how hard the family labored. She had known Arne wanted land, but she had thought he meant farming land. Arne was not a rancher. What did he know about sheep? And now, it seemed, he did not want to be a farmer after all.

But Cal had said no farmer in his right mind would live on the Gumbo, and even the ranchers keep off it. How could they live without neighbors? A woman needed other women to borrow from, and gossip with, to sit with children when they were sick, to help each other in times of need. When a woman's time came, what good were men then? It was the women who came, as her mother had to care for the ill or a woman in labor. Countless times, Kristin had gone out in the dark of the night, bringing the soothing drink, the comforting words, the help that made it all bearable. Rannei thought of her soft leather midwife's case packed in her dowry chest. She had pictured herself going to help at births at neighboring farms, and the women coming to her in her time. It was not for men to do such things. Arne might be a good farmer, but a woman was not a cow or a ewe.

The men continued to talk, although now they'd gone on to other topics, perhaps sensing Rannei's unease. Cal always had a supply of whiskey or brandy, and he shared it generously with Arne, who drank a sip from time to time, but would not go beyond a certain self-prescribed limit.

Cal was telling Arne how his great-grandfather had been one of the early colonists in Pennsylvania, and his father still lived on that original farm. Cal had learned to speak Norwegian from his grandmother on his mother's side. His maternal grandfather, the younger son of an English lord, had married the daughter of Norwegian immigrants when he'd come to America. As a result, he'd been cut off without a penny. But, ambitious and clever, his grandfather had worked his small mercantile business into a prosperous chain of dry goods stores. Cal had been one of several grandchildren of these grandparents, and he'd inherited a fortune. He lived on the income from the trust. Cal's three older sisters were married, and his older brother would inherit their family farm.

Cal told them he had traveled to many parts of the world pursuing his avocation, art. He would not call himself an artist, he said, until he felt he could support himself on art alone. What he liked to do best were watercolors and charcoal sketches. He told them that he'd had a book of his sketches published through a New York publisher six years before. It was called African Journey, and was a pictorial account of his journey through Africa seven years ago, before he'd begun living on the Gumbo. At other times in his life, he had worked as a cowboy and horse trainer, and now, at the age of thirty-five, he was a sheep rancher in South Dakota, while completing sketches for a second book on Dakota pioneers.

He was returning now from a short visit to his parents. His mother had sent for him because of his father's illness, but he had recovered, and now Cal was on his way back to his ranch. He had left his sheep in the care of his herder, a young neighbor boy, but he was a little worried about them, as lambing was just barely over, and the increased herd might be hard for one person to manage.

Rannei and Arne both listened to this account in open-mouthed wonder. Cal Willard might be from another world, so foreign was he to their experience. It was hard to fathom a man like Cal Willard, not yet an old man, but free to do all the things Cal had done. A gentleman with money who chose to work at jobs only peasants would do in Norway. And an artist, too! Cal was so foreign to their experience, but he was also likable, so friendly and helpful with his advice that one could not help liking him.

Rannei was especially fascinated by his artistic talents. She had asked to see his sketches, and thought were very good, wonderful, even. All the same, Rannei did not like what he was telling Arne about the Gumbo.

"We must look carefully everywhere before we decide, Arne," she said over and over. Arne would agree absently, then plunge back into more discussion with Cal about the Gumbo, asking still more questions. Cal, seeing her reserve, did make an effort to tell them about what he knew of the other land available, but invariably, talk would return to the Gumbo. Seeing Arne so enthusiastic, so happy, Rannei doubted her own intuition. What was right for Arne must be right for her too, she told herself. She smiled and listened carefully, trying to ignore the uneasy feeling just under her heart.

Toward the end of the third day, they entered western Minnesota, and traveled on land so flat there seemed to be no horizon, just a merging of sky and land. Featureless as the landscape was, Rannei could not keep her eyes from the window. This was farming country, for she saw fields being worked, and here and there groves and clusters of trees, as well as distant glimpses of streams and ponds.

"This is not real prairie," Cal assured them, "this is just flat farming land. The soil is good here, but this is all taken. You won't see real prairie until you see the Gumbo."

"It sounds so different from everything we're used to. I'm not sure we can manage such a huge change," Rannei said.

Arne took her hand again. "Now Ran, didn't we come here to try something different?"

Rannei had to agree that they had, and nodded uncertainly. Ever since that warm July day by the waterfall, she'd known she was aligning her life with Arne's. In her mind, Rannei had always considered her wedding day to be the summer afternoon they made love for the first time under the benevolent gaze of her protective goddess Freya, there beside the stream with the mountain slope rising close behind them. She would have gone with Arne anywhere, of course, after that. Remembering, she flushed with desire, wishing it were night and they could be alone.

For as nights passed here on the crowded, noisy train,

they could only sleep sprawled out uncomfortably on the hard, if padded, seats, or lean their heads against the window or each other. The last time she and Arne had made love was in New York, in that dreadful hotel. Rannei put her hand caressingly on his, sliding her fingers along the calloused length of his palm, and curling her fingertips to rest there. It was their secret signal. He closed his hand over hers and squeezed back in reply. They did not look at each other, but looking up, she saw Cal Willard's eyes fixed on their clasped hands.

Chapter Six

*T*he train trundled in and out of towns, always west, to the river, the Missouri. West of the river — Rannei heard that phrase so often she was beginning to hate it, but there was no turning back. To the Missouri they came, arriving in the early afternoon in the busy, growing town of Pierre. The Chicago and North Western Railroad had put this town on the map just ten years earlier. It was also the end of the Railroad line, for there was as yet no bridge across the Missouri River. They must purchase wagons, supplies and horses here, for once they crossed the river on the ferry they would strike off across the Gumbo for Cal's ranch.

As Rannei waited on the platform for the men to make arrangements to store their baggage at the station, she decided she liked the town at once. However noisy and dirty it seemed, it was less noisy and dirty than either New York or Chicago had been. Here the bustle had purposefulness to it, and the great sky curling around the edges of the buildings was both majestic and serene. Shielding her eyes against the bright western sky, she looked toward the river, or where Cal had said the river was. All she could see was a few trees and the bright glint of the midday sun off flat water. A road led in that direction, disappearing at where the river was supposed to be, then crept out on the other side straight toward the western horizon. Tomorrow, or the day after, once she and Arne had purchased horses and wagons and whatever else they needed, they would take that road to the Missouri and cross to the other side on the ferry.

Taking it all in, Rannei tried to remember what Cal had told them about Pierre. It had grown to a population now of about six thousand, and was the trading place for the Sioux Indians, as was Fort Pierre, across the river. It was also the trading place for the cattlemen, ranchers and farmers both east and west of the Missouri.

Their train had arrived on a Saturday and Rannei could see many wagons and other wheeled vehicles crowding the street past the depot. People thronged the board sidewalks, as if the entire population of the area was in Pierre at once. At the center of it all was the train station, and it seemed the main event was the arrival of the train.

Rannei gazed around, wide-eyed. A wagon full of Indians, women and children filling the back with an old, old man and a youth sharing the one seat in front, was being pulled by a bony, weary-looking team of horses. The wagon creaked slowly up to the hitching rail by the edge of the platform. The old man had long gray braids dangling down the front of what looked like an army coat, its color long since lost under a coat of grime and the effects of the sun. His brown face was so finely creased it looked like a piece of crumpled parchment. The young boy beside him wore his black hair cut short, and his blue denim pants were as stiff and new as those of the boys on the depot platform. The Indians gazed impassively but attentively at the train and its discharged passengers like spectators at a circus. Just like I am staring at them, Rannei reminded herself, taking her eyes away from the Indians with an effort.

A young Indian girl came down the platform carrying a battered suitcase, threw it into the wagon and jumped lithely in after it. Rannei wondered where she and the Indians in the wagon lived. They must be from the reservation Cal had told them about. Perhaps the young girl had been to the Indian school in Kansas? Cal had also told them about the government's effort to take away the Indians' heritage and make them "Americans." Rannei wondered what the Indians thought about that.

Farther along the platform, past the passenger cars, Rannei saw men unloading and carting supplies to merchants' wagons. Rolls of coiled wire, wooden barrels that rattled and sloshed along, all propelled by eager hands. A trolley of crates, peeping with yellow chicks, went past. Rannei wondered in what town the chicks had been loaded. Surely the chicks could not go for too long without food?

More passengers were still getting off the train, looking about with wondering eyes and threading their way through the hubbub, calling goodbye to one another, grabbing hold of restless children.

As soon as Arne and Cal returned with hired men in

tow carrying all their baggage, they walked up the board sidewalks to the Pierre House. Cal said it was the best hotel in town, although there were several others also. The Pierre House boasted a narrow veranda, with benches placed along it facing the street. Several men sat smoking there in the cool May evening, watching the threesome as they came up the street, climbed the steps and entered the hotel. The silent scrutiny of the men embarrassed Rannei, but Cal and Arne nodded to them, and they raised their cigars in greeting.

The room the clerk assigned Arne and Rannei was not luxurious, but it was clean. It had a huge brass bed with a quilted coverlet, and on the wooden floor was a large rug made of braided cloth, much like the ones Rannei used to work with her mother. The clerk assured them there was fresh water in the pitcher on the stand, and they had only to ask for hot water and the boy would bring it up. Rannei immediately asked for two pails, one hot and one cold. She felt filthy from the four days on the train, and she saw what looked like some kind of tub behind a curtain in a corner of the room.

The clerk went away, shutting the door behind him, and as Arne moved about unpacking, Rannei began unpinning her hat and gazed out the window. The view looked east to the prairie, away from the river, back the way they had come. From the elevation of the second story, Rannei could see two or three streets meander off to the edge of town, surprisingly close. The streets merged into the edge of the prairie, a hill rising gently beyond, green and peaceful in the soft sunlight.

The streets were not like any streets she had ever seen;

they were merely rutted roads with houses and buildings placed rather haphazardly along them. Yet Rannei felt a kinship with this rough little town, a kinship she had not experienced anywhere else in America. I would like to live here, she thought, somewhere close to this town, where I can see people and get to know them, and learn more about the history of this country and the Indians. Now that they were finally alone, Rannei resolved to discuss their future with Arne. She would look for the right time to bring it up.

"I tell Cal I meet him soon, to go down to the land office before it closes," Arne said from behind her. "He says it always stays open late on Saturdays, and is closed on Sundays. I want to see what land is available around here so we can think about it over Sunday. Cal says, though, that for land west of the river, we will go to the land office in Rapid City."

Rannei took heart. Arne had seemed so enthralled with Cal that she had forgotten how cautious he was normally. She flung her arms around his neck and kissed him. "You won't just sign up for some piece of land without telling me?" she asked anxiously.

"Of course not! Aren't we in this together?" He held her back from him, looking tenderly into her face. "I want to do what is best for us, *yndling.*" Arne did not like the American equivalent word, "darling" and would not use it. "I will see what land there is, and you will have your say, as always."

Arne pulled her back against him and kissed her hard on the mouth. A knock on the door drew them apart. It was the boy with the bath water she had ordered. He set the pails down and Arne fumbled with the coins in his pocket as the boy stood there expectantly. Arne had learned about tipping in New York and thought it a most barbaric custom. But he had yielded to Rannei's entreaties that since he was now in America, he must act like an American.

"There," he said grudgingly, holding out a copper penny to the boy.

As the boy took it and departed, Rannei rushed over to close the door and threw the bolt.

"Alone at last," she said, whirling around on her toes and into Arne's arms. They kissed until they were both breathless.

"I can't let all that lovely hot water cool off," she told Arne, disentangling herself. "If you'd just pour the water for me, Arne, I'm going to have a real bath."

Arne poured the hot water into the round tin tub, tested it with his finger, and added cold water from the second pail. "Just right now, Ran."

"It would be lovely to wash my hair, too," Rannei said wistfully, unbuttoning the front of the dress she had worn for four nights and days. "But I guess I had better wait until I have more time to dry it. Maybe I can wash it tomorrow morning and open the window. This dress certainly needs a good brushing." She hung the blue traveling suit jacket and skirt over a chair back, adding "I don't suppose I'll need this dress for a while now."

Rannei brought along several skirts and waists woven out of homespun, which she knew would be more suited for work on a farm than her fancy town dresses.

"I will brush your skirt for you," Arne offered,

rummaging around in her carpetbag for the clothes brush. "Where is your corset?" he asked her suddenly as she stood in chemise and drawers.

"Haven't you noticed that I haven't been wearing it? I gave it to a lady on the boat. I'll never wear that monster again. Anyway, I don't need it, do I?"

Rannei stepped out of her drawers and pulled the chemise over her head and pirouetted naked in front of him. "I may not wear these either; it feels so good to take everything off! Don't look at me that way, Arne. I have to bathe first. Come here and wash my back. And I think you need a wash, too." She stepped into the tub. "Maybe we can fit in this together?"

"Together, Ran?" Arne looked so doubtful that Rannei burst out laughing. "I'm only teasing, Arne. You couldn't even get in here by yourself. Besides, if they thought we were in here having a bath together they would think we were immoral Norwegians and run us out of town. Maybe even feather us, like that woman Uncle Jens told us about."

"Tar and feather, Rannei," Arne laughed. "You mean the woman Uncle Jens says takes in clothes from the clothesline in her wrapper, which makes the good citizens think she is a loose woman and do that terrible punishment to her?"

"Yes, and wasn't that in Dakota, too? Scrub in the middle of my back, please, Arne."

"No, Montana, let me do your neck, now, and just behind the ear, that needs work."

It turned out he did more than the ear, and by the time the bath was over, Arne had stripped and been scrubbed too, and there was water all over the floor. Rannei wiped it up with the wet towel, then washed the towel out in the grimy water, hanging it over the washstand to dry. She looked at Arne, sitting damp and naked on the bed. "You'd better get dressed if you're going to meet Cal."

"I have no clean clothes," Arne said, but he made no move to look for any. Rannei smiled and jumped at him, tumbling him over onto the patchwork quilt.

"Um, you taste good," she said, and began to nibble his neck with soft lip kisses. Arne wrapped his long arms around her and rolled her over so he could look down into her eyes.

"Be careful," he warned her. "You see what that does."

"I know, but I can't wait until tonight, can you? It's been days and days."

She felt heat flooding her, rising from her toes, to the backs of her knees, and up into her belly, tingling in her breasts. Arne's face above hers glowed, as if in reflection. She lifted her arms to undo the braids wound around her head, and Arne put his mouth on her nipple. She gasped with the exquisite pain-pleasure of it and pulled the last of the hairpins out, tossing them onto the floor. Something wild and unstoppable was rising in her chest. "Arne," she said, "Arne."

Arne lifted his head and looked at her, their faces almost touching. His light blue eyes had darkened; the pupils expanding so they covered almost all of the blue, making his eyes look almost black. It was something that happened whenever he desired her or was greatly moved. She knew that she alone did this to him, and it was something he could not control. It always happened when they made love. It moved her even more deeply than his kisses.

She had never forgotten the first time she had seen this dark look of love and desire in his eyes, when she was just eight years old. She had fallen in a game, and Arne, chasing her, had stopped. As he reached down to help her up, she saw his pale blue eyes had become flooded by black, which both astonished and frightened her. Years later, Arne had told her he had fallen in love with her that day and decided to marry her. He had been twelve years old. It was the end of his childhood, but not yet of hers. It had taken her six more years to make the same discovery. She closed her eyes to shut out the memory and concentrate on that exquisite, almost unbearable physical sensation, for which she had not yet found a name.

When Arne replied to Cal's knock on the door a half hour later, his voice was so unmistakably languid that Rannei blushed, then giggled. What had Cal expected them to be doing, after all? Arne told Cal he would meet him downstairs in a few minutes, and Rannei found his clean clothes, then crawled under the coverlet for a nap before dinnertime.

Chapter Seven

*A*fter two days in Pierre, with wagons purchased and supplies, crates, chest and valises all loaded, Rannei, Arne and Cal met the ferry on a Tuesday morning in mid-May to cross the Missouri River. It would take them at least four long days to reach the Porter Stage Station. The station was the last sign of civilization for Cal and it was still fifty miles to his ranch.

After half a day's travel west on the stage road to Minnesela, they headed due north on another, less traveled road that Cal said would lead them to the Porter Stage Station. The Station sat at a crossroads, with traffic coming from the north intersecting with traffic from the abandoned Medora-to-Deadwood road to the west for people wanting to go to Pierre. Cal's trail from the northeast was the fourth spoke of the crossroads, but so far he was the only one who used that track.

It seemed incredible to Rannei that, once out of the river bottom with its scraggly cottonwood and willow trees, there were hardly any trees at all. Nothing but prairie as far as the eye could see. She especially missed the evergreen trees so beloved at home in Norway, although Cal assured her that in the hills along the western edge of the state they'd find pine trees and juniper bushes too. Only, of course, they wouldn't be going that far west. Sometimes, when crossing a small creek, Rannei would see the now familiar willow and serviceberry bushes, and occasionally a shrub with cream-colored, cone-shaped, fragrant blossoms.

Cal said these were chokecherry bushes. The berries were good for syrup and jelly, but too tart to eat fresh. The serviceberries were used to make a good sauce, as well as baked into pies. The Indians, he said, dried them and mixed them with tallow and dried meat, for use as a trail food and in wintertime.

Rannei took careful note of all these bushes so she could recognize them again once settled on their new land. There were even some on the Gumbo, hidden away along the creek banks, according to Cal. When Rannei pressed him, however, he had to admit that he didn't recall any near his ranch, but he was sure he had seen them somewhere along the creek. As for the willows, they looked similar to the willows at home. Rannei knew from working with her mother, the best herb woman in the whole fjord, that the thin inner bark made a medicinal tea, which was good for fever and headaches. At stops by the streams, she gathered some of it to take along in case there weren't any willow bushes on the Gumbo.

The Gumbo. Rannei still resisted the whole idea of settling there, but Arne had his heart set on it. When he'd returned from the land office in Pierre, he'd said he found no suitable land available. He'd told Rannei he wanted to follow Cal's advice and ranch on the Gumbo. Cal had told him there was a perfect spot for them near his place. It was perfect timing, because Cal knew a man named Hank Porter who wanted to get out of sheep ranching. Cal could introduce them and convince this man to sell his sheep to them at a fair price.

Rannei had insisted they knew nothing about sheep ranching. What if Arne hated it? What then? The Gumbo sounded like such a lonely place to her, she'd told him, but at least they'd have each other. And she did like and trust Cal, just like Arne. In the end, she'd agreed to try it, but only for one year.

On the second day out of Pierre, Cal and Arne had to pull their wagons off the track and let the stagecoach rumble past. Rannei thought the passengers did not look very comfortable, hanging on to the straps on the side of the coach and bouncing around like rubber balls. She was glad the necessity of buying wagons and horses in Pierre had spared them the stagecoach ride.

On the road, the nights were warm and dry. They all enjoyed sleeping under the brilliant starry sky, after cooking their dinner over a tiny fire using wood brought along in the wagons.

Five days later they arrived at the Porter Stage Station, the first time they would sleep in a house since leaving Pierre. They had not wanted to push the horses with their heavily loaded wagons too hard, so it had taken them a little longer than Cal thought it would. The Porters, it seemed, were good friends of Cal's, for besides being his closest neighbors and the place where he left the road to strike off across the prairie for his own ranch, the oldest Porter son, Tommy, had been herding sheep for him for the past three years. The Porters helped him in many neighborly ways, Cal said, just as he helped them.

They had reached the Porter place just after the noon meal, which they had eaten earlier, and Cal insisted on taking them straight in. The Porter family instantly surrounded them, so that at first, Rannei was sorry she had not insisted on one more night of camping by themselves. To her tired eyes, there seemed to be hundreds of them. Rannei found herself pressed to a fat woman's enormous bosoms, being hugged and kissed. Rannei's nostrils, sensitive after the days of outdoor living, were assailed by a complexity of smells, not all of them pleasant.

"Cal Willard! If you ain't the limit! Whereabouts did you find these two? You don't say! Oh, you pretty thing!" Sally Porter swept Rannei into another embrace, then let her go to call to her brood. "Mandy, fix those cold potatoes, and Poll, fetch that bacon from the cellar—Cal and his guests must be starved."

Rannei was overwhelmed. She could not seem to understand a word of the torrent of English that Sally poured on them all. Cal was laughing, proud of his surprise, as he found himself hugged in an embrace by Sally in his turn.

"No, Sally, thanks," Cal said, after extricating himself. "We ate hours ago. Some coffee would be nice, but no supper, please. Of course, you know I won't refuse a piece of that pie I see over there, but Arne and I must take care of the horses first. Now, my friends, I want you to meet your new neighbors, Arne and Rannei Bergstrom."

The two youngest children, a boy and a girl, who had both been hanging on to Cal's arms, stared wide-eyed at Rannei and Arne. The two oldest girls, who Cal informed her were twins, stood awkwardly against the wall. The two tall gangling boys, one a little taller and more gangling than the other, muttered shyly as Cal introduced them.

Rannei held out her hand, expecting the little bow and handshake with which even the youngest Norwegian child greeted visitors, but the little ones hid their faces in Cal's coat, and the older ones stared uncomprehendingly. Rannei faltered and almost dropped her hand, then remembered what Mother had so often told her. "Always be prepared to make the first move," Kristin had said to her over and over. "What might be called shyness in others will be called arrogance in you." Rannei knew her mother was right, but it was hard for her to always follow this advice, for sometimes she was, in fact, shy, and people were aloof with her.

Smiling, trying to hide her tiredness, Rannei went up to the smallest children, reached for their grimy little hands still clinging to Cal's arms, and shook them. The older ones, seeing that she was determined, shook her hand without bidding, giggling nervously at the strangeness of shaking hands with a beautiful, young and foreign woman. Rannei shook each hand warmly, murmuring each name.

"Amanda, and Polly, is that right?" She said to the twins.

"They call me Mandy," one of the girls said shyly.

"I'll call you Mandy, then, too," Rannei said. "But you both must help me tell you apart. And Jimmie, you are almost as tall as Henry. I know we will be glad to have you as neighbors."

As usual, Mother's advice worked. Once Rannei had made the first move, the Porter children could not have been friendlier. They all shook Arne's hand, too. Hank Porter came over and shook hands with them both, and Sally gave Rannei another hug and kiss into the bargain. The two little ones crowded around Rannei, trying to see who could get closest to the exotic guest, while the men and older boys went out to take care of the horses. Rannei, left alone in the warm, odorous kitchen with Sally and the children, answered their questions politely, and felt the tension gradually slip from her.

As Rannei took in the room, she saw that Sally was not at all like her mother. Sally Porter allowed the children to be dirty and sticky, and the meanness and messiness of the house was appalling. But it was really no worse, Rannei told herself, than many a cotter's cottage in the poorer districts of her own fjord. And the human warmth that stirred around this room was the same as the warm feelings that filled her mother's spotless kitchen.

Feeling weary, Rannei handed her shawl to Mandy — or Polly — and sat down in the rocking chair they pulled into the middle of the kitchen. When the little girl, Anna, leaned against Rannei's knee, Rannei lifted her onto her lap. The child stared with unabashed curiosity into her face. The child's soiled dress smelled of urine, but Rannei could tell that her hair, tangled in a reddish mass down her back, would be beautiful if washed and combed. Pieces of bed lint were tangled in the matted curls, a sign it had not been brushed for some time.

"I would have liked to have a sister," Rannei told the child. "I have only brothers, although I like them very much," with a smile for the little boy, Matthew, "but here, you have both brothers and sisters. That is lovely."

Enchanted, the children pressed closer. Rannei was soon answering their many questions about her family, telling them about her two older brothers, Hendrik and Einar, and the two little ones, Ole and Knut, and Father and Mother and the farm. "It's good you were raised on a farm," Sally said comfortably. "All this won't be so new to you then."

"I hope not," Rannei murmured doubtfully. She could not find the English words to express to Sally the difference between her father's farm, nestled between mountain and fjord, and the country they had just traveled through. It was a different world, and there seemed to be no way to compare them.

The men and boys came in, filling the room with their bulk and voices. The smaller children ranged themselves out of the way on the bench under the one window to make room for the older Porters and the guests to sit at the table. Sally and the twins hurried about, pouring coffee into heavy mugs, and setting down huge slices of pie before them all, and a pitcher of thick cream to pass around. Rannei, to her surprise, found she was ravenous. It had been a long time since she'd eaten pastry, and the dried apple pie was delicious. She was pleased to see Arne was winning Sally over with his extravagant praise of her cooking in his mixed English and Norwegian. Sally, delighted, insisted he have another piece of pie.

Then Cal had to tell them from the beginning where and how he had discovered the Bergstroms. He did so with great gusto, rolling his eyes and speaking in such an affected manner that they were soon all howling with laughter, Rannei as well.

"'Ra-lly, Mr. Willahd,'" Cal said in perfect imitation of the train conductor's accent, picking up the sugar tongs and clacking them as if he were punching train tickets to add to the effect. "'Whatevah ah we to do if these Norskies keep coming? I simply cahn't cope with that impossible language they will insist upon speaking. I sweah, they mix up their tickets on purpose to annoy one.'" Clack, clack went the sugar tongs. "And I'm about to explain it all to him when, out of nowhere, I hear this woman pipe up in precise, Norwegian-accented, English: 'If you will stop that dithering about, Mr. Conductor, and mind your manners, I will explain it to you. It is only a simple mix-up in dates. Any *stupenagel* could understand it!'"

"Oh, Cal," Rannei gasped through tears of laughter. "Oh, I did not call him a *stupenagel*! He wasn't stupid, he just wouldn't listen to me. Now you must tell the truth."

"Well, anyway," Cal said, "I saved poor Mr. Nelson from madam here, and that is how I met Mr. and Mrs. Bergstrom, and found new neighbors for us all."

"I see I shall have to tell the story, if you are to hear the truth," Rannei said, and explained about the confusion in tickets and why they had extended their stay in New York.

"A good explanation, but I like my story better," Cal said, and everyone laughed with him. Rannei saw how truly fond of him they all were.

"You say you will have neighbors, Cal," Hank said. "Does that mean these two plan on homesteading near you, on the Gumbo?"

"Yah," Arne answered for Cal eagerly, "right next to Cal it will be, on the Gumbo."

"The Gumbo," Hank said, turning to Cal. "You're taking the Bergstroms to homestead on the Big Gumbo?"

Again, Arne answered. "Yes, we go with Cal. He tells me how good the grass makes the lambs, and how you can have as much land as you want. And nobody lives there but him. Someday I will be a big sheep rancher, like Cal!"

Hank cleared his throat and looked at his wife. Rannei saw the look and felt again her strong doubts about homesteading in this unseen place.

"Cal, have you told them what the Gumbo is like?" Sally asked. To Rannei, her tone seemed accusing. "Did you tell them you are the only settler on it?" She turned to Arne and Rannei. "It does have good grass, but it is a hard country. Here, we live on the edge, so we can run our cattle and sheep on it during the summer. We can get to either Pierre or Rapid City, or even Minnesela on the road, but in the Gumbo, when it rains, you stay there, and in the winter, it is so far from anywhere you can't risk traveling."

"You know, there is land opening up along the Belle Fourche, and that valley has good farm land. In fact, I've been thinking of it myself," Hank broke in, "or even up along the North Dakota line, off the Gumbo. What about some of that?"

"But the Gumbo will never be thickly settled, Hank," Cal said. "That's the best part. We all could own the whole Gumbo before we're through. The rest of it may be better land for farming, but you've seen how the settlers are pouring in just the past few months. All you'd end up with is a hundred and sixty acres, maybe three hundred and twenty if you're lucky. That might be all right for farming, if it's good land, but for ranching you need more than that, lots more."

"If you can stand to live there," Hank said. He turned to Arne, who had been following the conversation intently, clearly struggling to understand the English, with Rannei whispering translations from time to time. "I hope you don't believe everything this crazy galoot tells you. He doesn't live on his land himself half the time. Here he's coming back from a trip back east, while my boy Tommy watches his sheep. But we ain't all Cal Willards. What're you going to do if you have to stay on that place day after day, eh, and never leave because it's so goddamn far… excuse me ma'am… to anywhere, and there always has to be someone watching the sheep?"

"Mr. Porter," Arne said politely, "we talk much on the train of this. My Uncle Jens, he spends years here in this country when it is a territory, and he tells me much about it. I want to be a rancher, not a farmer, and you say yourself it is good ranching country. I know how to live in rough country. I am a sailor in Norway, a fisherman, and nobody is crueler than Mother Sea. I fish the Lofoten Islands when I am twelve years old, with my father. We fish all day, sometimes, and catch nothing. Our boots and mittens are so frozen with the spray we must thaw away the ice at night before we take them off. I know how to be patient, but I want land, and Cal says that is where the land is."

"Well, and maybe you can do it, too," Sally broke in, "but what about this little wife here? No woman in her right mind wants to live out there, miles from anyone." Rannei saw all their faces turn to her, vague white blurs, but the expression on Arne's face was clear enough. She would not shame him in front of them all. All the same, she felt with sickening certainty that the Porters were right and Cal and Arne dreadfully wrong.

"We are agreed, Arne and I," she said faintly. It was the best she could do, and she saw that it did not satisfy anyone, including Arne.

"You see, they have made up their minds," Cal told them. "We're going to Rapid City tomorrow and file the preemption papers, so you can quit trying to scare off my neighbors, if you don't mind." He said it jokingly, but it ended the discussion.

Hank proceeded then to tell the story of how he had gotten into sheep ranching. A rancher near the Black Hills, passing through the Station one day, mentioned that he thought he would go out of the business, and Hank, always on the lookout for a good deal, agreed to buy his herd. After a year of it, he decided he was not a sheep rancher.

"The kids don't like herding and I don't have the time," he explained. "None of us do, with the stage business too, and Sally always busy cooking meals. Sheep take lots of time, let me tell you. Even if that's all you have to do, it'll keep you busy. They can't be turned loose like cattle. You have to watch them all the time. They're always getting over on their backs and dying if you don't find 'em and turn 'em right side up, or a coyote's after 'em — sometimes even a wolf. They can't protect themselves at all. Oh, maybe sometimes an old ewe will stomp her foot at the dog, but that's as far as it goes. It ain't such hard work, just tedious, and you do get two cash crops a year, the lambs and the wool, and then your meat too, if you like mutton. Most people don't."

It seemed a gloomy picture to Rannei, but Arne's enthusiasm did not abate. If anything, it increased. Rannei knew her husband well enough to know it would do no good to say anything at this point, when his interest was at a white heat. She had promised him in Pierre that she would try it for a year, and she meant to keep that promise.

When Arne proposed he take those sheep off Hank's hands, Hank agreed to sell Arne his sheep to get him started, as Cal had predicted he would. Rannei, listening as they discussed the terms, agreed they should go ahead. She knew Arne was sensible and would listen to advice when he thought he needed it. The only person he had disliked taking advice from was her father, but here in this raw country he understood he needed all the help he could get.

"Well," Hank said, "well, then, it's done, and we must celebrate. I think if anyone can do it, you can, young man. You look like a fighter to me, and you'll have your pretty missus and Cal to help you. I don't mind saying we'll be glad to have you as neighbors. Ma, fetch the brandy, and let's drink a toast to our new neighbors."

Sally brought brandy and glasses, and Rannei, sipping a little gingerly, for she did not really like the taste of it, saw the rest of the evening through a blur of exhaustion. Sally kindly sent her to bed when the younger children went, and at intervals, lying in the big bed—she thought it was the twins'—she heard them all laughing and shouting on the other side of the partition. Sally sat up with them, too, her loud comfortable laugh mingling with that of the men. Rannei wanted Arne. There was something they must talk about, but when he came to bed at last, all she could remember was how lonely she'd been without him. She curled herself into the solid comfort of his arms and legs. Nestled into each other's bodies, they slept as soundly as children.

Chapter Eight

*R*annei, Arne and Cal spent ten days at the Porter Stage Station, a time during which Hank explained to Arne that the herd of sheep included the lambs that had just been born, so a count would be necessary to determine the exact number. He and his sons helped Arne count them all. It turned out to be a little over one thousand, with a few extra for good measure. Hank agreed to sell them to Arne for two dollars a head, straight across.

As part of the bargain, that fall Hank would take half the lamb crop of wethers, and half of the older ewes Arne might want to sell. Hank explained to Arne that the wethers were the male lambs that were castrated when their tails were docked, and which were always sold as a money crop, with a few kept for food, "if you liked mutton." The ewe lambs Arne would naturally want to keep, increasing his flock. Hank also agreed to come with his boys in the fall and trail the wethers and ewes to Minnesela to be shipped to markets in the east.

After first consulting with Cal, Arne agreed to all the terms. Cal told him that a prime ewe was selling for four dollars, so he was actually coming out ahead on Hank's price. The fall drive would take about a week, and it would be a tremendous help to Arne if he didn't have to attempt that himself his first year.

"Hank likes you," Cal told Arne, "and he is determined to help you all he can, so don't be proud. It'll be your turn to help him one of these days. That is the way we do things in this country."

After the sheep had been counted, Arne and Cal took horses and rode to Rapid City, where Arne filed the preemption claim. Rannei stayed with the Porters, continuing to deepen her friendship with Sally and the children, doing what she could to help, and absorbing all the information she could about this new country.

Hank took her out to herd the sheep with him for two days so she would learn how, since he said she would be the one doing most of the herding while Arne was building the house and barns. Rannei listened to Hank's instructions and advice meekly enough, but privately she thought she'd rather help Arne build the house than chase the sheep, which were even more stupid than cows.

One day with Mandy's help, Rannei did the laundry for the first time since leaving home. There was also mending to do, and she and Sally and the girls spent an evening darning and chatting. That is, Sally chatted, Rannei mostly listened. Rannei was amused to learn how much Cal Willard puzzled them. Sally spoke of him with affection but seemed to think he was not quite of the same species as themselves. He had money, he was an artist, and he was from the East –all this was more than enough to set him apart. Sally said she regarded his habit of sketching people as an occupation not quite proper for a grown man, but he seemed otherwise harmless. Rannei remembered the drawings Cal had made on the train. She especially liked the one of her playing her guitar, with Arne at her side. Rannei assured Sally she thought he was a genuine artist. She asked Sally if she'd seen Cal's African Journey pictorial book by the New York publisher, but Sally said she had not seen it.

"Anyway," Sally said, "he can do wonders with a horse, almost talks to them, seems like." That seemed to redeem him, in her eyes.

Rannei also learned intimate details about all the people who lived within a hundred-mile radius of Porter Stage Station. Sally knew everyone, and had helped many of them in sickness and childbirth. Besides Cal, the Porters would be their closest neighbors, she said, but that still meant at least fifty miles away, an extremely long day's ride.

The more Rannei heard about the Gumbo, the less she liked it, and the more she felt in her very bones that she and Arne were making a terrible mistake. Out of loyalty to Arne, she hid her feelings from the Porters. On her part, Sally hadn't spoken her opinions aloud since that first night, and seemed to be doing her best to prepare Rannei for what was to come.

Life at the Porters was interesting, for there always people coming and going. The Porters operated a combination stage station and roadside inn, where the stage that traveled the Black Hills-Pierre Road changed horses, and travelers could sleep and get a good meal.

Besides the stage, there were the freighters passing through with their powerful six- and eight-horse teams pulling huge wagons loaded with supplies of all sorts. These goods were for the farmers, ranchers and merchants to the west. Cal was the only settler to the northeast.

The Station also saw a constant stream of men on horseback, businessmen, ranchers, farmers and adventurers traveling both east and west and occasionally a wagon load of settlers, usually heading west, or toward Pierre and the Black Hills. Indians passed along the road too, going to and from the reservation or, as Hank said, "God knows where," but they never stopped at the stage station.

Sally and the girls took care of the travelers who wanted to stay overnight, cooking their meals and housing them in the bunkhouse, which was divided into dormitories for men and women. Hank, with the help of his boys, had the horses ready when the stage pulled in, taking out the tired horses and caring for them, so they would be ready for the return trip, which might be several days or a week later, depending on the weather. Hank also mended broken axles, wagon trees, harness, or anything that needed fixing in his blacksmith shop.

The Porter Stage Station was a busy place, although Hank complained the freighting business had fallen off with the completion of the Great Northern Railroad from the northwest through to Rapid City in 1886. Business from Pierre was still good, and would be in the future, Hank said, as more settlers would come by that route, if they wanted to settle in the northwestern part of the state.

Rannei listened, fascinated, to the stories told around the Station as travelers came and went. Miners and ranchers from the Black Hills talked still of finding gold, although the heyday of the gold rush was long since over. Ranching now was more important than gold, since the Indians were safely on reservations.

She had heard stories of these gold rush days from Arne's Uncle Jens, who had been there himself in the midst of it in Deadwood in 1876-77. Uncle Jens had found enough gold to keep him comfortably back home in Norway the rest of his life, although Arne had always said he suspected his uncle's gold came from the gaming table, not the gold fields.

Another topic of interest was the weather. Everything depended on the weather, it seemed. The people spoke about famous storms of the past, made predictions of future weather, and worried over what it would mean if the coming summer was too hot or too dry. The amount of rainfall necessary for crops differed from one man to the next. It seemed there was no perfect amount of rain for anybody.

While Arne and Cal were away in Rapid City, Rannei frequented the Station yard amid all the comings and goings, trying to absorb everything she could. One thing she wanted to learn more about was the kind of clothes these Dakota pioneers wore. In her baggage, Rannei had packed many practical skirts and waists she and her mother had woven out of homespun at the weaving room at the farm, but the sight of homespun on a traveler marked him or her as immigrants. Rannei's grandmother had also made some divided skirts for her, a fashion so daring she said it hadn't started in Norway yet, but she had read in a newspaper from America that some modern young ladies wore them for riding. Rannei liked the idea of divided skirts, although she saw little evidence of any women wearing them who passed through Porter Stage Station.

Based on the working clothes of denim and leather these Dakotans wore, Rannei realized with chagrin she'd have little opportunity to wear her good town clothes here. The dressmaker in Bergstromfjord had made Rannei a winter dress out of dark red merino, which she especially loved and had been looking forward to wearing. But who would notice if she lived way out in the Gumbo, with no one but Arne and Cal around for fifty miles?

She also wanted to find out more about what was happening in this strange and rather terrifying country that was now her home. The talk, although not of politics or books or plays or indeed, any of the intellectual subjects Rannei had heard at home, fascinated her. Sometimes she even stepped forward to a group of men deep in discussion and, much to their surprise, asked them questions or offered an opinion of her own.

"Why do the men look so surprised when I speak my mind?" Rannei asked Sally one evening as they washed dishes after the evening meal.

Before Sally could answer, Mandy spoke up. "A woman isn't taken seriously, no matter what she says, don't you know that, Mrs. Bergstrom? A woman's place is to be seen and not heard. Keep your mouth shut, that's all we're good for, ain't it, Ma, that and...?"

"Amanda! That will be enough!" Sally said with unaccustomed severity. Mandy stopped in mid-sentence, flushing, and began vigorously to polish the tumbler she was drying.

Rannei looked at Mandy with new interest. Of the two twins, she was a shade the less attractive, but it was hard to say just how, since they were almost identical. Perhaps Mandy's face was a trifle broader and more square of jaw than her sister's, her skin a little sallower? It was strange the twins were so plain, since the rest of the Porters were quite good-looking. The girls had the strong jaws and long faces so attractive in the male side of the family, yet in the faces of the twins they looked overlarge, almost caricatured. Mandy's eyes, like her sister's, were an identical rather pretty shade of greenish-hazel set off with thick, short, dark eyelashes. The dark-brown hair was lustrous and long and needed only a good brushing to bring out the highlights. With care and the proper grooming, they both could be quite striking.

But it was Mandy's mind that interested Rannei most. The girl had a quick intelligence, evident in the questions she asked and the intentness with which she listened. And most importantly, she seemed to be the only one of the Porters who read books. Cal had brought her a book when he returned from the east, Rannei remembered, and recalled too the vivid look of joy on Mandy's face when he handed it to her.

For all the travelers through Porter Stage Station, the

Indians were a constant topic of interest. The Custer Battle on the Little Big Horn that occurred not so far away in Montana was still fresh on everyone's minds, although it had happened in 1876, fifteen years ago now. The subject of the "battle" at Wounded Knee, which happened just one year ago in this very state, was mostly avoided. Cal had not told her the terrible details. He just warned her it was a taboo subject here. The Indians were now all safely on reservations, and the less said about them the better.

She realized that the treatment of the Indians, which had seemed wrong from a distance, far away in Norway, was not that simple. Many people here had friends and relatives killed by those very Indians, and they were on the side of the argument that Rannei had never heard before.

What would Mother and Father make of all this?

One evening, the only guest at the Station was a freighter named John Jenkins, passing through with an empty wagon going back to Pierre. Sally and her daughters invited him to eat with the family rather than in the public room. Rannei helped Sally place the bowls and platters of food on the table when it was not yet six o'clock, for the Porters ate their "supper" as they called it, early, and it was June, with the long summer twilights just beginning.

As was the custom in America, dinner, the big meal of the day, was not served in the evening, but at noon. Still, supper was a huge meal too, it seemed to Rannei. Tonight, there were cold cuts of beef from an enormous roast Sally had cooked at noon, with the potatoes from that meal diced and fried in butter, as well as canned peas from last year's garden, thick slices of freshly baked bread, and, for dessert, applesauce made from dried apples. The pies had been polished off at noon.

Sunlight slanted across the table from the west window, outlining little Anna's hair in a red nimbus. The sun's rays gleamed on the blue enamelware plates and bowls, and caught the white whiskery stubble of John Jenkins in a halo of light.

For a moment Rannei was swept by the most vivid longing for the sun-filled, wood-beamed kitchen in her family's house above the fjord, with Mother and Father and her dear little brothers gathered around the old wooden table, with a fresh cloth laid each evening. How had she not realized how much she would miss them? Here on the other side of the world, she sat amidst a family, but alone. Without Arne here, she was not part of any family.

"It could happen again," Hank Porter said, picking up a conversation he'd been having with John Jenkins as the food was served. "The Indians ain't going to like the settlers coming into their reservation, even though they've ceded the lands." He glanced over at Rannei then, his look a little wary, as if she were an oddly bent wagon wheel that he might have to straighten on his anvil. Probably, Rannei thought, he was expecting to hear yet another one of her endless questions. She did not disappoint.

"Is the Gumbo part of the reservation?" Rannei asked.

The freighter laughed. "No, ma'am. You'll be safe enough there. Even the Indians don't want it. They think evil spirits live there, just like the good ones live in the Hills. Heathens!" he added contemptuously.

Rannei resisted a wicked impulse to tell him she thought that the Indian religion, what she knew of it anyway, seemed more practical to her than Christianity, and closer to her own beliefs in Norse gods. In her brief time here, she'd learned to keep quiet on that score. Religion was not a subject of great concern on the prairie, but it was obvious that heathens were not tolerated.

If the freighter knew of her beliefs, would he think her a heathen, she wondered? One would think it was safe to believe in whatever god, or gods, one wanted, but obviously that was not true, especially when it came to the Indians. And yet, America was supposed to be the land of the free, where one could worship as one pleased. What they might do to a white heathen woman Rannei had no idea, but she did not want to find out. Her refusal to believe in conventional religion had never seemed a problem at home to anyone but her mother.

Father had just laughed and said, "Oh, she'll outgrow it." That had also been the attitude of her older brothers and everyone else in the fjord. But she had never wavered in her convictions, not since she had seen the bloody Jesus on his cross in a Catholic church when she was ten. The disgust of the freighter for "heathens" made Rannei feel more alien than ever, but at least she was learning to think before she spoke. Mother would approve. But there was something menacing, untamed in these men, even in kindly Hank Porter, that frightened her. Rannei had never before been afraid to voice the most outlandish opinion or viewpoint, but she was afraid now. She wondered dismally if she would ever feel as free as she had at home.

During Rannei's reverie, talk at the table had turned again to the winter of 1886-7, when cattle by the thousands had died in Dakota Territory and in Montana, as well. That year marked the end of the big cattle drives from the east; in Hank's opinion, a good thing.

"It gave the small settlers a chance," he declared. "It showed those big companies back east and in Texas that they can't just come in here with thousands of cattle and eat off all our grass. Why, they'd run right over anyone's land, no matter who owned it."

John Jenkins murmured agreement.

Rannei wondered what these people thought of foreigners like herself and Arne coming in. Obviously, they had all been foreigners at one time or another, but if they were here a year or two, they seemed to regard themselves as natives, and only the newest newcomers as foreigners. And she had sensed a mostly unspoken reserve against sheep ranching, almost contempt. Clearly sheep were not regarded as highly as cattle. But when it came to the Gumbo, people saw it differently. It seemed nobody wanted to be on that land but Cal and Arne.

"But the sheep, they can live on the Gumbo?" she asked, a little timidly.

"Oh, yeah, that's a good place for them," the freighter said, with a sideways glance at Hank, obviously remembering that he was a sheep rancher. "It has the best grass for sheep, and there's lots of it. And sheep, you know, can live better on the prairie in the winter than cattle. They'll paw away the snow to get at the grass, where cattle won't.

That's what did in the cattle herds during the bad winters. They couldn't get at the grass."

"As long as sheep have shelter, they'll do fine in the winter," Hank said. "I haven't ever had to feed them hay in the winter, they just graze on the range. But then, I've only had them a year, and it was an open winter." He turned to the freighter. "Just sold my band to Mrs. Bergstrom here, and her husband who's off getting the papers at Rapid City. They're heading for the Gumbo, going to homestead next to Cal Willard. You know him?"

"I know Cal," John Jenkins said. "I hauled some supplies out to him the first year he was here." He turned to Rannei, his look frankly appraising. "So, you're going to live on the Gumbo. Well, you'd best tell your mister to put up some hay, just in case. I know Hank here didn't bother, but we're due for a good hard winter, in my opinion. These easy winters we've had ain't natural."

"Arne will want to have hay in, I know," Rannei said. "At home, the cattle and sheep must be fed all winter. It is hard to imagine they can actually eat grass then too."

"That's one good thing about the wind," the freighter said. "It does blow the snow away. Until there's too much snow, then it blows into drifts and covers everything up! Best not to take a chance on old Ma Nature!"

"I agree!" Rannei said emphatically. "We will most certainly not take chances!"

The adults chuckled at her determination, and Sally spoke up, urging everyone to eat before the food got cold. Rannei did her best to oblige, but her mind was teeming with ideas. So much to be done — a house and a sheep shelter to build, and now hay to put up. No telling what they were overlooking. And it was June already! Would it be possible to do it all before winter? They must leave at once, as soon as Arne and Cal came back from Rapid City.

But Arne and Cal could not possibly be back before Friday, at the earliest, and that was two days away. In the meantime, Rannei filled the hours with household tasks, learning all she could about the sheep and the land they were about to make their home. Mandy followed her about like a shadow. Rannei tried to draw out the shy girl, and Polly, too, but Polly was more unresponsive than her sister, and seemed to resent Mandy's absorption with their visitor.

Mandy was fascinated by Rannei's hair, and every night she begged Rannei to let her brush it. It became an evening ritual, as it had been at home. Rannei sat on the high stool like a princess on a throne while Mandy unpinned the braided crown, undid the plaits, and brushed the hair into a shining sable curtain. Next, Rannei showed them how to plait it into the soft loose braid she wore at night. The little ones, Anna and Matt, too, crowded around, each begging a turn with the brush.

Rannei put up with it patiently; she was used to it. It was almost as if her hair was not really a part of her, but something she owned and was responsible for, like her dress or her shoes, something almost public. While Rannei was growing up, the family used to gather in the big kitchen just before bedtime, perhaps with a snack or a warm drink, and her brothers would take turns brushing Rannei's hair. Then they would watch as their mother, Kristin, plaited it for the night. In the mornings, Kristin would unplait it, brush it smooth, and braid it again for the day.

In the Bergstrom family, there were two colors of hair. Like Kristin and Rannei, the two older brothers were "black" Norwegians, with black hair and blue eyes. Her father Lars and the two little boys were more typically fair, with light hair and eyes, like most Norwegians. All in the family shared the pale white skin. The boys had all inherited their father's athletic build, and Rannei too was taller than the average woman.

At home, Rannei was the envy of every young girl in the district for that hair, but to her it was a nuisance. When she was twelve, she told her mother something must be done to keep it out of her way, or she would cut it off herself. If she was allowed to do all the things her brothers did, she pointed out, she should not have to bother with long flowing hair that tangled with everything and picked up weed seeds and pieces of hay, and always needed washing. She should have just as much right as her brothers to wear her hair short.

In the Bergstromfjord, the custom was for young girls to wear their hair unbound, flowing down their backs, or plaited into two braids. Since Rannei's hair was so long, neither one was really practical, so her mother contrived a style that was charming and yet conformed to the standards. She pulled the masses of Rannei's hair up to the top of her head and plaited it into one long braid which hung down her back. A horse's tail, her brothers used to call it, to tease her. It was different from anything the other girls wore, but since it was not put up, it would not offend the married girls who wore their hair in coiled braids under their caps.

Soon many of Rannei's friends began to wear their hair the same way, and a new style evolved in Bergstromfjord. Rannei was relieved of the burden of her hair, and besides, she found she did not really want to cut it after all. Arne thought her hair beautiful, and by that time, it was very important to her what Arne thought.

All her life, Rannei remembered how her mother solved the quandary over her hair, for to her it illustrated exactly her mother's philosophy, that each person, however unique, had a duty to preserve their uniqueness, but nonetheless must try to stay within the accepted framework of custom and tradition in his or her society. Kristin had managed that with the new hairstyle. By not radically changing it, or allowing Rannei to cut her hair, she had still changed tradition, but in a way that was acceptable.

As Kristin pointed out to Rannei many times that because of her God-given beauty, she must think more carefully than other people about what she thought and did, lest what she considered freedom of thought, others might call arrogance. This was a hard lesson for Rannei to learn; that her very independent beliefs had a strong effect on others.

From the first it was evident that she would be beautiful—not ordinary prettiness, but rare and extraordinary beauty. In a handsome family, with a renowned beauty for a mother, Rannei was told she was the most beautiful of all. Rannei's eyes, like the parents and the brothers, were blue, but a deeper blue, a lapis lazuli blue, which turned almost purple when she was angry or upset.

These memories of her childhood and her family swam up in her mind on the evenings when the Porter children clamored to brush her hair and fawned over it. One night, Rannei said absently that perhaps she should cut it; it would be so much easier to manage when she was on the prairie. She was startled and amused to see that they all had the same reaction her family had had years ago, when she had become rebellious about her long hair.

"Oh, you can't do that," silent Mandy cried out.

"Count your blessings, girl," Sally chided her. "I've seen hair like yours but once in my life. My Grandma's hair was almost as long, but it wasn't as thick or this lovely black color, with those highlights, not blue, like the Indians', but silver, almost."

Even Hank, smoking his pipe, and watching her curiously, with what Sally called his "figuring out look," was moved to tell her that hair was "woman's crowning glory," or something like that. So Rannei gave up the notion of cutting her hair once again, but privately she resolved she would do as she liked once she was in her own home. There would only be Arne to convince then.

Chapter Nine

It would take the sheep a while to settle down, Hank Porter had told Rannei that morning, standing beside her under the still-red dawn sky, watching the sheep begin to stir and straggle off the bed ground.

"Wisht I still had the old dog to give you 'stead of this pup. That old dog, she's a good-un with the sheep, been 'specially trained for that, but Tommy has her now, out there at Cal's. My son'll help you train the pup, though. The pup's a bit scatter-brained, but he seems smart enough. Here, pup!"

The scraggly, long-haired, black and white dog — "some kind of shepherd-mix" — bounced joyfully up to Hank, then laid back his ears and whined reproachfully when he tied a rope around his neck. "Here, missus," he said, handing Rannei the other end of the rope. "He'll stay with you soon as he knows you, but you might have to watch him for a while. The sheep are afraid of him, one good thing, but, like I said, he's scatter-brained and it will take him a while to settle down."

The bandy-legged little man was much friendlier and more talkative now than he'd been at first with Rannei. Now he looked directly at her when he spoke, his pale blue eyes twinkling out of his thin tanned face. Rannei and Sally and the Porter children had already made their good-byes to one another back in the Porter kitchen.

Hank walked beside Rannei as they started off, the wagons leading, the cow Arne had bought in Pierre tied behind his wagon. Cal's black mare, Jubal, who had been left at the station while Cal was gone, pranced beside his wagon, no rope tied around her shining, arched neck. Rannei thought it wonderful how Cal had trained the horse to come at his call and to stay near him without any reins, obedient to his every command.

Rannei and the sheep brought up the rear of the procession, Rannei restraining the pup, Oskar, as she had already named him, with the rope she held. The wagons reached the end of the fence and turned northwest onto the track that Cal had worn into the prairie over the years.

"Keep them together now, the first hour or so. That way they won't panic. Sheep like to be in a bunch, but don't drive them too hard. The lambs will tire fast. Then they will need to spread out a little and graze."

Hank stopped and took off his dusty black felt hat. "Good luck, missus, you'll do fine."

She shook his outstretched hand. "Thank you for all your kindnesses, Mr. Porter. Please, please come visit us, all of you."

"We will, we will. Won't be long now until shearing

time at the end of June, and we'll all come give you a hand. Takes a while to get the hang of this sheep ranching. Take care, little lady," he called after her. He had stood there as long as she could see him, watching her out of sight.

Before very long their caravan of people, animals and wagons reached the Gumbo. The Gumbo — this land they had come so far to find. West of the River, people in Pierre called it, West of the River, that enormous land stretching away west of the Missouri in this new state of South Dakota. West of the River was also the Black Hills, and the Belle Fourche — Bell Foosh they said— river bottom, and all the land south of it to the Nebraska border, but their way led northeast.

And they'd made it here at last. Soon after their wagon train and herd spilled onto the track leading to Cal's and their new home, Rannei watched Arne and Cal and the wagons disappear out of sight, their windblown white canvas tops dropping below the next swell of the prairie just as dips in ocean waves engulf ships at sea. It did resemble the sea, Rannei thought, a petrified sea, with its long low swells cresting far into the distance. Cal had told her the wagons could travel faster than the sheep, as they would need to graze, so she should let them go at their own pace, as long as they were headed in the right direction.

In the sunlight, the short, white-gold buffalo grass danced and bowed over the swells, changing color and texture as the wind caressed it one way and then another. Cal said that the old grass was hay, cured on the stem, but from what she could tell, the sheep preferred the new grass, which was not quite as tall yet as the old grass.

The sheep, fanning out in front of Rannei, moved at a steady pace, nuzzling among the dead stalks for the tender new grass. The young lambs nibbled daintily at the short green stems, as if wondering what their dams found so inviting. Whenever the ewes made the slightest pause, the lambs knelt and butted at their mothers' teats for milk.

They would wait for her at the watering hole, Arne had assured her as they headed off. All she needed to do was keep the sheep heading along the wagon track.

There was no horizon. Far to Rannei's left, northwest it must be, two long narrow rocks, or buttes, as Cal called them, seemed to tower into the sky. This landmark was named the Mule's Ears, and as she'd stared at them throughout the morning, Rannei had decided they did indeed look like the ears of some giant animal, rising out of the earth, as if the head and body might appear at any moment. A butte to her right, not as high, with a flat top, must be Table Butte, the second one Cal had told her to look for. Her way, he'd said, lay between them.

The buttes should have been comforting to Rannei, something to relieve her eyes from the flatness and sameness of the prairie, but instead, she saw them almost as evil spirits, set to watch over trespassers of their domain. An unfriendly, cold feeling seemed to emanate from them, and she tried to avoid looking at them. She felt small, insect-like, exposed, under their malign stare.

Suddenly, Rannei's feet slipped and she landed on her rear. Daydreaming about the buttes, she had fallen down the side of a "burnout" onto bare dried Gumbo mud, so crinkled and crossed with fine-etched lines it reminded her instantly of the old Indian man she'd seen at the train station that first day in Pierre.

The dog Oskar, thinking she was playing, jumped about ecstatically, springing down on his front legs, his rump high, wagging his disproportionately long tail, licking at her face. Rannei looked about her. She had fallen over a slight bank less than a foot high, a depression on the prairie floor. Not a blade of grass or any other plant grew in an area perhaps the size of a tabletop, and the other edges leveled out to the prairie again, so the depression had but one high side.

Cal had warned her about these burnouts. Nothing ever grew in them, he told her, except later in the summer, a beautiful white lily called a Gumbo Lily. Rannei wondered what made these spots so infertile. The soil looked the same as where the grass grew, perhaps a bit grayer and dryer, that was all. She grabbed at Oskar's trailing rope, which she'd let fall, and set out after the sheep again.

By the time she caught up with the stragglers, the whole herd was across the track, bunched now, moving into the unmarked vastness to the west. She had to catch up with the leaders in a hurry, Rannei realized, and turn them north again, back onto the track. Trying to stay out of the path of the leaping pup, who jumped and cavorted beside her, she ran after the sheep until the pain in her side made her stop to catch her breath. Still, it seemed as if she was no nearer to them than before. What if she lost the sheep, or worse, herself and Oskar, in this strange and fearful Gumbo? The Indians feared to cross this place, inhabited, they believed, by evil spirits and little else. Would she become hopelessly lost, destined to wander forever in this terrifying sameness, where each swell looked like the one before and the one behind?

There was no way to mark the distance between herself and the herd, Rannei saw. Nothing to orient herself, or to use as a measure of height: no rocks, no trees, no bushes even, only the buttes, looming one on either side. The sheep with their sharp little hooves had obliterated the tracks of the wagon wheels, and except for ruts here and there, she couldn't even follow the wagon track. She had no way of telling where the trail lay. Then Rannei remembered Cal's instructions. As long as she kept the Mule's Ears on her left and Table Butte on her right, the wagon track had to be somewhere between.

Finally, she caught up with the old ewe that led the herd, but did not know how to get her to turn back north. Perhaps the ewe had decided she was going home to Porter Stage Station, for she stubbornly persisted in her chosen direction, with the rest of the sheep lining out behind her in that idiotic way they had of following the leader. By now Rannei had thought to tuck her skirts up over her white petticoat and tie her shawl about her shoulders so it wouldn't slip off, so she ran more easily. It was a bother, hanging on to Oskar's rope, but she did not dare to turn him loose. Without him she was entirely alone.

Rannei screamed with all her might at the lead ewe in Norwegian, and the old ewe stopped dead. She stared at Rannei with that stupid panicked expression that Rannei had already come to know. Then the ewe wheeled and ran at full speed straight north again, the rest of the sheep following her like beads on a string, all of them bleating madly.

Tears of rage and fatigue ran down Rannei's cheeks. *"Djevelen tar deg!"* she yelled after them. The devil take you. It was the worst curse she knew, one she had never said aloud until today. *"Faen! Faen! Til helvete med deg!* To hell with all of you!" Her cheeks burned with heat and her throat was so dry with dust and anger she could hardly breathe.

She sank down upon the grass, and Oskar, in an agony of whimpering abasement tried to lick her face, thinking, no doubt, that she was yelling at him. She patted his frantic head absently then pushed him away and stood. How shocked Kristin would be if she could hear her daughter now, swearing like Old John, the handyman back home. Whenever her mother heard Old John muttering his curses, she would say: "God hears him, and the devil too."

Rannei looked around fearfully. Far above, a bird wheeled in a slow arc, revolving as though it were tied by a string to the middle of the sky. It was a large black bird, perhaps a raven. Was it waiting for her to die so it could pick her bones? Loki, the old stories said, could change himself into a raven. This would be his country, if it were not the devil's, for it certainly didn't belong to her mother's God. The bird seemed to be the only thing alive out here. She could not see even a bee or an ant in the sparse grass. She felt so very alone. In sudden panic, Rannei rose and raced off again. She could not lose their sheep.

As she caught up with the herd at last, she saw with relief that they were beginning to slow down and spread out, idly snatching a mouthful of grass here and there, although still headed in the wrong direction. Having learned not to startle them, Rannei veered to one side and came up beside the leader again. Waving her shawl, and yelling at her, but more politely this time, she managed to turn the old ewe so she was headed east, between the two buttes. The rest followed, apparently accepting the truce.

Exhausted, Rannei allowed them to pass her by, falling in behind the stragglers. It seemed to her that hours must have passed since she had set out in the cool dawn, Hank Porter waving them off. But the sun was still only a little above the horizon. This sky oppressed her, weighing her down with its blue immensity. There was so much of it. She felt surrounded by sky, floating on an island of grass, from which any minute she might spin off into a blue void, driven by the omnipresent wind, adrift like a leaf in the sea.

Rannei longed for the haven of the canvas wagon top. She wanted her sunbonnet, which she had left in the wagon, not thinking she would need it. But her eyes and skin burned from the harsh light, which bounced off the pale grass. The light was like the sky and the wind; it flooded over her without cease. It was like being at sea in an open boat, and she felt as if she were drowning.

Chapter Ten

*C*al had not been immune to the difference of opinion between Arne and Rannei. He could tell by Rannei's anxious questions about neighbors and towns and the Gumbo, and her incredulous silences when he told her of the vast spaces of the Gumbo, that she did not share Arne's enthusiasm. And he well knew the loneliness of the place, how even the nearest neighbors were a day's ride away.

But by the end of their train journey Cal found himself pronged on the horns of his dilemma. He also could tell Arne had made up his mind and nothing would dissuade him. The Bergstrom couple would go to the Gumbo. Caught in a last-minute attack of conscience, Cal had tried to persuade Arne to settle elsewhere, anywhere. Then again, perhaps he'd only done so half-heartedly, because he had desperately wanted them to come to the Gumbo with him.

And then Rannei had seemed to agree, and Cal hoped for the best. He had almost forgotten his misgivings as they made their five-day journey from Pierre to Porter Stage Station. The prairie was at its best in the spring, and Rannei delighted in the spring wildflowers and the hidden nests of meadowlarks and prairie chickens she discovered. He found himself watching for things to point out to her.

Once, they had sat for an hour and a half over lunch watching a band of antelope with several enchanting young grazing, unafraid, not a quarter of a mile from them. Rannei also seemed to enjoy meeting the wagonloads of Indians and settlers, the cowboys on horseback, and the thundering freight wagons on the Pierre to Porter Stage Station stage trail. When they'd arrived at the Porters, she'd seemed happy there, too. Cal thought she'd hidden very well her natural fastidiousness regarding Sally's housekeeping, seeing quite rightly Sally's warm heart. Instead, Rannei had shown an interest in every aspect of the Porter's life.

On the trip across the Gumbo, they always stopped at noon, or whenever they'd reached the watering hole for the day, to let the sheep, horses and the cow water and rest for an hour or longer. Then Cal and Arne would go ahead with the wagons, the brindle milk cow tied behind his wagon and the crate with the two hens and a rooster that Sally had given Rannei riding in the wagon at the back, where the chickens could have some air. Rannei and the sheep trailed along behind the wagons, the sheep spreading out to graze, ambling along as they did so, snatching mouthfuls of the short green grass. After the first day and night, the sheep seemed as anxious as Rannei to keep the wagons in sight, as if they realized the wagons were the only home they had.

WATCHING Rannei as constantly as he did, Cal noticed her silence after they left the Porter ranch and struck off on the Gumbo. They still saw wildlife, deer, antelope, coyotes, and once, far in the distance, a lone buffalo, but the people were gone, the busy life of the trail and at the Porters behind them. They did not meet a single soul during the five days it took them to reach his ranch, nor had he expected to.

Cal usually made the trip to the Porters in one long day's ride, or maybe a day and a half if he had the wagon and didn't want to push the horses that hard. He had hired the Porter boys to trail his sheep starting three years before, not wanting to take the time himself. Because of the slowness of the past five days, or perhaps because for the first time he had company, Cal saw the Gumbo through new eyes, Rannei's eyes. He had never noticed before how barren it was of trees. There really weren't any, except for an occasional willow or chokecherry or serviceberry bush beside some water hole, and no mountains or even hills, except for the buttes.

He had always loved the vast sweep of the horizon; now he saw how ugly and featureless it might look to her. And he felt something of her horror, when, in the afternoon of the fifth day, they at last reached the spot on the little creek, upstream a half mile or so from his own house, which he had selected for Arne's house. Arne looked about him, took his bearings and said firmly, "This is perfect, Cal. Here is where we will build."

Rannei stared around her as if panic-stricken, Cal saw in dismay. "But there is nothing here, Arne," she said.

"And it's all for us," Arne cried exuberantly. "See that water, there, Rannei? That's the spring Cal told about, the best one in miles. We'll put the house here, close to it, so you won't have to carry water far."

Yes, Cal had seen then how it looked to Rannei, in a way he had never seen before, the series of water holes that made up this unnamed creek, sunken into the prairie, connected and rimmed by dark green slough grass; surely that wasn't what she had thought their creek would be. And that hill above it — perhaps it wasn't high enough to be called a bluff — seemed smaller than he remembered.

But wait, Rannei, he wanted to say, wait until you see a sunset, or the beautiful March days when you can look across the land and see three different seasons at once, watch it raining in the west and snowing to the north, while to the south the sun is shining on Table Butte. Wait, Rannei, for the lovely fresh July dawns, when the wind is miraculously stilled for an hour and the dew is cool and sweet on the grass. Or the wonderful October afternoons when the sun has warmed the frost from the ground and the grass blows golden in the wind—wait, wait, Rannei, this is not all there is. But, of course, he did not say any of this, and the next instant Rannei put away her panic, if that was what it had been, and was exclaiming with Arne over the spring.

Summer, 1891

THE BERGSTROMS and Cal arrived at the beginning of June, and got busy immediately setting up a second ranch. There was little time to spare. They asked the oldest Porter boy, Tommy, who had been minding Cal's sheep, if he could stay on the rest of the summer, and he agreed. This arrangement freed Cal to spend his time helping Arne. In two months, the men were able to accomplish the most pressing task of building a home for Rannei and Arne before the winter set in. Arne's capacity for work was astounding, and Cal, never having worked so hard in his life, set his teeth and tried to keep pace.

Henry and Jimmie Porter, younger brothers to Tommy, made several trips out to the Gumbo hauling wagonloads of squared logs from a mill near Minnesela. Then they stayed on to help build the Bergstrom house.

In the midst of it all, in early July, the shearing began. In addition to several itinerant sheep shearers, the entire Porter family came, all but the twins Mandy and Polly — someone had to run the Stage Station. In the midst of all the work, Cal enjoyed tasting Sally's cooking again. She had brought food and big pots to cook in for the shearing crew. He was glad to see Rannei grow animated as she followed Sally's directions and spoke of how it reminded her of the village festivals she loved. Maybe, Cal thought, she would adapt to the life of a sheep rancher's wife after all.

Then again, when Hank Porter had taken the wool clip

into Rapid City for them, Rannei had looked after the departing wagons with obvious longing, no doubt wondering when she'd ever have a chance to visit a town. Cal knew the feeling. A visit to civilization came as a welcome break after long, monotonous days on the Gumbo.

By the middle of August, when it came time to start the haying, the men had finished not only a house, but also a small horse and cow barn and a three-sided sheep shed.

These were more buildings than Cal had on his own homestead, and much better built, too. Arne had made sure Rannei would not have to live in a tarpaper shack. Her house was of squared cottonwood logs, beautifully notched and fitted together by Arne, chinked with Gumbo clay. The roof was made of saplings, also brought from Minnesela, laid against the ridgepole, covered with tarpaper, and, over those, six inches of tough prairie sod, the buffalo grass still growing out of it. Arne had thriftily cut the sod from the place he intended for the garden, next to the creek.

Under the covering sod of the prairie, the soil was almost solid clay, but at the Bergstrom's homestead location next to the creek, it was slightly better. Arne said with sheep manure mixed in it would grow garden produce. Eventually, with a great deal of watering, bucket by bucket, the patch did produce potatoes, beans and peas. The floor of the house was laid down with rough-cut planks, but Arne smoothed it with his carpenter's plane until its finish was like satin, with hardly a crack showing.

Cal's floor in his house, on the other hand, was still of packed clay.

Arne was ten years younger than Cal, but Cal learned things at thirty-five that Arne had apparently known all his life. Arne's long, square-tipped fingers could build anything and fix anything; he was a born homesteader. What he did not have he invented or made, and in those two months he was more at home on the prairie than Cal would ever be.

It was important to Arne that the open side of the sheep shed faced south, so as to provide protection from the north and east winds in the winter, for instance. Cal had no sheep shed at all; his sheep had to protect themselves as best they could under the lee of the creek bank. Cal's horse barn had been situated at one end of his shack, divided, of course, by a partition.

By the example of Arne's determination, Cal realized that he, Cal, would never be a rancher. It was something he had been suspecting for some time, anyway. Cal, by nature indolent, found the exercise of such energy tiring, although he knew it took nothing less to succeed. He marveled at Arne's ingenuity. Cal had been raised on a farm, too, but what different talents they had each gleaned from it.

While the men labored at building, Rannei and Tommy herded their respective flocks. This was not hard work, but Cal knew it was boring at times. Rannei had finished a sweater for Arne, and told Cal she was starting one for him. Sometimes, she asked to borrow from Cal's books to supplement those she had brought with her. Cal's were all written in English, of course, so she said they helped her build up her vocabulary. Cal would never forget the evening she was fixing the men dinner and said to her bewildered husband: "Get thee hence and fetch me some water, knave." It had taken all his self-possession not to guffaw loudly, as he knew Arne would not appreciate it.

Chapter Eleven

*A*rne, Cal, and Rannei had worked all day in the August heat, which smothered the land and puny humans like a rough woolen blanket thrown over them all. The heat was unrelieved by even a breath of the usually ever-constant wind. With determined malice, it seemed to Rannei, flying ants flew down her collar to release their acid agony on her sweating back, and salty sweat trickled down her forehead and stung her eyes.

In the early days of August, Arne had cut the grass where it grew tallest and raked it into piles in the meadows along the stream, using Cal's seldom-used five-foot Deering mower and rake, and Arne's own team. Now the hay had to be loaded into the wagon, hauled the rough mile or so to the hay yard next to the barn, and stacked. The three of them had already put up Cal's hay, or what he said he needed, enough for the horses and the sheep for a winter storm or two, as he had in previous years. He wasn't planning on a bad winter, Cal said. Another hard winter wasn't due for another five years, at the earliest. During the past three winters the sheep had had ample grazing. Cal couldn't convince Arne of his weather prediction, however.

"Hay will keep," Arne said. "We will be prepared."

Perhaps he had not realized, Rannei thought, how much more grass he had to cut here than at home in Norway. Here the grass was so short it took twice as much to make a stack. And here there was twice as much land, and, especially in the meadows along the stream, the grass grew much thicker.

Rannei caught a forkful of hay Arne threw up to her and with her hayfork pitched it into the corner of the rack, which Arne had made on the foundation of the wagon, first removing the canvas top, and adding boards for a rack on the sides.

From her perch on the hayrack she could see the sheep along the river begin to fan out of the groups where they had stood, heads in each other's shade, all the long, hot afternoon. Stupefied still with the heat, they moved slowly, nibbling lazily as they ambled along. She had been able to watch them from the hay field all day. She almost wished they would act in their usual maddening, erratic manner, so she could escape from the smothering hay for a while to chase them.

To the east she could see the stovepipe chimney of Cal's house. Then nothing, nothing at all until the flattened top of Table Butte to the south, which rose above the swells of the prairie. At a distance, it seemed less malignant and threatening than the day she had first seen it, looming over the entrance to the Gumbo, guarding it like an evil giant.

Now Rannei used Table Butte as her landmark to orient herself on that featureless land when alone with the sheep. By checking the sun's position in relation to it, she knew where she was and what time it was. Otherwise, she believed, she might disappear into the treacherous rollers of the Gumbo with the sheep and never find her way home, doomed to wander that sea of grass forever.

As she stared out over the prairie from her vantage point, she saw herself as she must have been that day in June, a tiny figure amidst the immensity of the prairie, following the sheep as they led her to their, and her, new home. Now — was it only two months ago? — she did not feel quite the terror she felt that first time she was alone on the prairie, alone with the sheep, the sky and the wind. Now she had her house to shelter her from the worst of the wind and relentless sun. But it was not yet home. Would it ever be?

Arne and Cal were walking to the next hay pile more briskly now, looking to the west, where a black cloud had suddenly boiled up against the sky. Almost a quarter of the hay piles remained in the meadow, but Rannei knew they would keep on until all of it was in, especially if Arne thought it would rain. She checked the horses, slumped dozing in the harness, left hooves cocked in the same identical way. Sighing, she jogged the reins. Raising their heads, the team plodded resignedly after the men. Arne turned and waved impatiently. Rannei gave the reins a harder slap on the horses' sweat-wet backs, but they did not break their sleepwalker's amble. Arne strode back and grabbed the near horse's rein near the bit, jerking it forward.

Rannei took off her sunbonnet and wiped her sweaty neck with it. She wore Arne's shirt with the sleeves tied at the wrist and waist, the tails hanging outside her skirt, almost to her knees. She had worn her divided skirt, tying them at the ankles. With the makeshift trousers and the huge shirt, she knew she looked laughable, but she didn't care. She itched all over from the hay dust, and her back stung from the ant bites. The hay had scratched her hands and ankles in the gap where her makeshift trousers had worked up over her boots.

Summers in Norway, Rannei had sometimes gone barefoot, but here she couldn't. The hard, hot earth stung her feet and the spiny little cactuses stung painfully, their spines almost impossible to remove, festering cruelly if left in the skin. Often a cactus pad came flying up with the hay and Rannei would carefully pick it out by one spine and hurl it as far as she could back out on the prairie.

The sun was unbelievably hot, so hot it felt to Rannei as if the god Odin was just then crossing the sky in his huge horse-drawn chariot, blazing his heat down on them all.

Rannei had always been fond of Odin, and respected this most powerful of the gods, but it seemed he did not belong here in the Gumbo any more than she did. Strange, when he had always seemed more real to her than her mother's God. Rannei pictured him in the clouds, hovering benevolently over the mountains and the fjords. She lost Odin the moment she entered the little white church on Sundays with her parents and brothers, demurely dressed in her lovely best blue skirt.

She could not find the Christian God inside her family's church, either. There was no picture of Him, or stories about Him, only about Jesus. These were interesting, and Rannei did love the tales of his miracles and how he healed people, and was kind to people. But then he was killed so cruelly. Every Easter she had heard the tale of his death and how he was supposed to have risen from the dead and gone to sit on God's right hand. But who, and what, was God? Rannei could not believe in Him, somehow, even though the pastor and Kristin had tried so hard to make her see it as truth. Finally, Rannei could not get past the horrifying spectacle of the Jesus she had glimpsed once in a Catholic church in Bergen, hanging on his cross and dripping blood. It seemed to Rannei that the Saga stories about the Norse Gods were better, for they were immortal and never died in the first place.

But she had loved summer Sundays out in nature, the fjord calm and blue under the sun, filled with the graceful boats that flew so lightly over the water, bringing the people across from the other side, and from up and down the fjord, to church services.

"Rannei! Look lively! There's a storm coming!"

They were waiting for her again. The horses began to move at the sound of Arne's voice, and Rannei clung to the shaking hay rack post in a trance of weariness. Listening, she heard thunder rumbling in the distance. She wanted it to rain, rain so hard it would stop the haying, so hard she wouldn't have to carry water to the garden ever again. She wanted to run naked in the rain, letting it wash the sweat and dust off her body, the soap from her hair. If only she could, by some magic, transport herself to the secret pool under the waterfall where she and Arne used to swim all summer long together. The thunderous force of the water, the almost unendurable cold of it, only made the moment when she could crawl out on the sun-warmed rocks beside Arne more exquisite. There by the waterfall they had first made love.

Suddenly, a blessed relief to her aching eyes, tears of longing were running out of the corners of her eyes, mingling with sweat on her cheeks, and tasting of salt and dust in her mouth. She had been dirty for days, it seemed. Her hair was dirty as soon as she stepped outside; the dust and wind seemed to cling to the film the water left on it. Her fingers left smudges on her white waists, and the collars of all their clothes were rimmed with a line of dirt that she could not soak out, no matter how hard she tried.

The hay came flying up at her now from both sides. The men did not look to see where she was, but pitched the hay up in a frenzy. She hardly had time to place the forkfuls before two more came up. Down below her, Arne and Cal worked in unconscious unison, like dancers in an endless dance, bending, scooping, turning, tossing, walking ahead to the next pile of hay without a pause in their rhythm. As Rannei stood on the rack, forking the hay into place, she, too, was a figure in that dance.

"Not much more now, Rannei," Cal called encouragingly.

Rannei managed a smile at him as he tossed up another forkful of hay. He was tanned to an oiled-leather color, and, with his white teeth and dark hair, he reminded her of her handsome dark-haired brothers. Somehow, he managed to look elegant, even in his sweat-stained blue shirt and dusty high boots.

The last possible pile of hay was tromped in, and they creaked back to the hay yard. The men walked beside the horses, but Rannei stood, sunk in the hay to her waist, breathless, holding to the post, too tired to climb down. With all her will she was attempting to force the black cloud overhead their way, hoping for rain to relieve this terrible heat. She did not care about the hay; they had enough already, and even if they didn't, they could cut some more tomorrow. She only wanted to lie down somewhere cool. Her head was beginning to ache, and her face felt tight and dry. She was not sweating any more, and she was so warm.

"Do we need Rannei this trip?" Cal asked after they had unloaded the hay. "There's only one load left."

Arne glanced at the cloud that was looming ever closer. "It goes faster with someone tromping. But what do you say, Ran?"

"I'm not so tired now," Rannei heard her words with dismay, and saw Arne grin proudly at Cal. Actually, she hardly cared anymore. She was beyond mere tiredness. Her body, like some machine, would go on forever until someone turned it off. She had always worked with the men at home, not because she had to, but because she liked being outside, and they all had boasted of her endurance.

But then there had been many hands to lighten the work, and always time for a swim on hot days. She had

wanted to suggest that to Arne in the middle of the afternoon. They had found a hole deep enough to swim in
farther up the creek earlier in the summer, and Rannei
managed a swim there most days, but she knew Arne was
not in the mood this day. He had work to do, and besides,
he didn't feel the heat like she did. It was the sun that
tired her so. It sucked every drop of moisture from her
body and gave none back.

"I would like a drink, Arne, please," she said. Her
throat felt full of hayseeds. Arne handed her the canvas-
covered canteen strapped to the front of the rack and
looked at her with concern.

"Are you all right, Rannei? Perhaps you had better stop
now."

"No, it's all right. There's only one more load."

She couldn't stop before they did. She took a swallow
of the lukewarm water and handed the canteen back to
Arne. He looked neither tired nor hot, but like some god
of the prairie, with his yellow hair sticking out from under
the dusty hat in ringlets and plastered with sweat to his
forehead. Hair glinted golden on his chin, for he had been
too busy for several days to shave. Hair curled too in a
dusty golden mat on his arms and out the open neck of
his shirt. Arne was never tired, it seemed to Rannei. He
had worked hard every day of his life, but the endless
work had only made him stronger.

He jumped into the open back end of the rack, holding
his pitchfork aloft like a battle-axe, and put down his hand
to Rannei to pull her in. The horses started off at once,
and Arne flung down his pitchfork and grabbed the reins.

"*Av vei*, Cal! *Yump!*"

Despite her fatigue, Rannei laughed as Cal scrambled hurriedly into the rack, just as the horses lunged forward. They didn't have much time. The thunder grumbled louder in the distance. She held onto Arne's arm to keep her balance, and he put his arm around her waist, his sweaty hand hot against her side. She felt all along her waist and thighs his vital force and energy pouring into her.

"*Rø, rø, krabbeskjaer*," Arne sang loudly, and Rannei sang too, pressing her aching head against his shoulder. "Row, row, row your boat," Cal joined in the chorus, in the halting Norwegian he had learned from his Norwegian grandmother. Rannei sang too, but she was thinking it was too much work for just the three of them. How much easier this haying would go with all the fun and companionship of the Porters and their crew, but Arne would not ask for any more help than he could repay with his own labor.

There had been more than Arne had estimated, but he was determined to bring it all in one load. As they headed for home at last with the hay piled top-heavy on the rack, Rannei walked beside Arne, who was leading Tor with a hand on the reins. A wind had sprung up, welcome relief to their sweating bodies. The enormous black cloud was almost directly overhead now, although the thunder still seemed muted and far off.

Suddenly, with terrifying rapidity, the sound was all around them, and the warm wind changed in mid-current to a gale so cold that goosebumps popped out on Rannei's arms. With a shiver, she pulled down the long sleeves of the shirt, which she had rolled above her elbows. The sky darkened swiftly from a hot August glare to an ominous blue-gray, as if they had been suddenly popped into the depths of the sea, yet Rannei could still see the sun shining far away on Table Butte.

A few raindrops fell, and then the rain was upon them like a wave deluging a boat. Arne pulled his felt hat down over his ears. Dirty rivulets of rain streamed down the horses' backs and along the hard-packed earth.

Rannei lifted her face to the chill rain and undid the braids around her head. If only she had some soap — but at least she could rinse the dust and sweat from it. She began to unplait her thick braids, holding the hair away from her head to let the rain through it. The rain fell with such force she could almost imagine herself under the waterfall.

The bleating of the sheep mingled with the drum of the rain on the hard earth. The sheep came streaming up from behind, heading in long swift lines for their bed ground. Did they think it was evening, or were they simply frightened of the storm? She had forgotten about them and wondered if Arne had too. Thank goodness they had followed their instinct to return to the bed ground instead of stampeding in the other direction.

The thunder had muted during the rain to a dull, almost constant rumble, but as the rain lessened, the crashing began again. It truly sounded like Thor's chariot wheels racing above in open sky. With no mountains to hinder him, he could sweep as close to earth as he dared.

Rannei considered Thor a kind god, a friend of settlers and farmers and fishermen, but easily angered. Perhaps he was battling the Jotuns, the evil frost giants, or Odin, even, for keeping the sky to himself for so long, unaware, in his anger, of the puny humans hurrying home with their toy animals and their play wagon. She had loved the thunderstorms at home, but here there were no comforting trees and tall mountains to protect them; they were in the storm itself.

The flash of lightning stopped them instantly in mid-motion. Rannei, jolted out of her fantasy, half-turning, saw Arne and Cal with open mouths, uplifted faces, the horses, eyes glaring white. Blue flame seemed to leap from the prairie, surrounding them, as if the pits of hell had opened at their feet. For a terrifying moment Rannei was sure they had been struck, all of them. She screamed wildly, and the horse Tor leaped forward violently, jerking his bridle from Arne's hand, dragging Tolander with him into a panic-driven gallop. Instinct plucked Rannei to one side as the horses sped past. The corner of the rack brushed her shoulder as it flew by, sending her reeling. When her vision cleared, she saw the wagon careening through the sheep and the rain, great gouts of hay flying, the men sprinting behind, Arne hanging onto his hat with one hand, yelling curses and commands. She could not move. Would the lightning strike again? A sharp acrid smell filled the air, but she saw no fire.

The wagon had caught up to the sheep. Like a maddened, headless monster, it plunged in among them. The herd parted before it like froth before the bow of a ship, the sheep determinedly reforming into their single line as soon as the wagon had passed.

Realizing that she was being left behind, Rannei ran after them. She did not want to be alone out here. The ruts in the wagon road were filling with water and she slipped and slid on the slippery gumbo clay. To keep her footing, she shifted off the road to the grass on the side and soon came upon the last knot of sheep. Rannei pushed in amongst them as if she were one of them. They paid no attention to her. Bleating anxiously, they plodded on, heads down, one behind the other.

The rain had settled to a steady drumming, and the flashes of lightning and the deep bass of the thunder were now muttering away over Table Butte. Every time the thunder sounded, the sheep would surge forward, baaing louder than ever, in a tone of almost human fear. Far ahead, Rannei saw dimly through the rain, the wagon flying off the curve in the track, where it ran around some burnouts, the horses pulling the wagon at full gallop on the straightest course for the barn. The wagon seemed to float in the thick air as it turned on its side, hay spilling slowly out. Moments later the horses reappeared, still running side by side, but without the wagon, the broken wagon tongue bumping along the ground behind them.

Rannei left the sheep as they filed to the bed ground and took the way the horses had gone. Soon she came upon a sheep lying on its side, kicking and bleating pitifully, a muddy track along its woolly back. At the bottom of the burnout, a foot below the level of the prairie, Arne and Cal were standing beside the wrecked rack and wagon, which lay on its side, the wheels more like round balls of clay, the rack still half full of hay. Arne picked up one of the pitchforks, which had fallen out of the hay, its tines pointing upward.

"The tongue broke," Cal said to nobody in particular,

pointing to the shattered end of the pole still attached to the wagon. "Well, that can be fixed."

"Oh, Arne! The wagon ran over a sheep back there," Rannei said. "It's still alive, I think. I–"

Arne looked up at Rannei on the bank above him. "*Dum!* Screaming at *tördonn!* We have no thunder in Norway?" He threw his hat on the wet grey mud and speared it through with his pitchfork.

They stared at each other through the rain. Arne's face was flushed with rage, his hair stuck to his head in wet snaky curls. Rannei pulled her own wet hair around, under her neck. She was shivering. It was not her fault. The horses had bolted as much with the thunder as with her scream, but she would not answer Arne.

She turned away, following the sheep to the bed ground, where the rest of the herd was gathering into a tight bunch, heads down. She did not look to see if Arne and Cal had followed her or not, or whether they were taking care of the injured sheep. She longed with a terrible intensity for her bed. After she saw the sheep safe, she went slowly up the muddy lane to the house, her boots heavy with big clumps of clay. She took them off on the step and left them there. All she wanted was sleep. To the west, she could see a faint line of blue.

The storm was almost over. She should wash her hair; now that it was wet, there would be water in the rain barrel at the corner of the house, but she was too tired, she had to sleep. She wrapped a towel around her wet head, dropped her soaked, muddy clothes, smelling of sweat and sheep, in a heap on the kitchen floor, and crawled naked into bed, pulling the quilt over her head.

❄

When Rannei awakened, sunset light from the open door lay in a pink beam across the bed, through the crack in the curtain, which partitioned off the corner that served as their bedroom. Arne must have pulled the curtain shut; she could not remember doing it. She lay a moment, listening for the rain, but all was quiet. The pillow was damp under her cheek from her hair; the towel had slipped off and the top of her head was cold. She could smell something sizzling, and, reluctantly, she sat up, fully awake now and remembering what had happened. What had possessed her to scream like that? It had seemed for an instant that Thor's hammer had been aimed at her, but that was silly. She had never felt that way before about storms, but never before had she had that feeling of being so completely surrounded by a storm, either. It had been terrifying.

She sat quietly on the side of the bed, listening to the sounds Arne was making. He must be frying something, and there was a clinking of dishes and the sound of water being poured into something — the coffee pot, she guessed. Was he still angry with her? It had not been a real berserker rage. Just temper, Mother would say. Probably he had been as hot and tired as she, only of course he wouldn't admit it, not Arne. He had been worried, too, about getting the hay in.

Or maybe he was angry because he realized the storm was Thor casting his thunderbolts, clearly telling them they were not welcome on the Gumbo. Rannei had always known that of course, but maybe Arne knew it now too.

They must move out of this malevolent land that he thought was the land of his dreams. It had all been too much for him. He'd had to strike out at someone, and she had happened to be in his way.

Poor Arne. He would be feeling ashamed now and sorry, and she would have to help him apologize.

It took a long time to get the knots out of her tangled, still damp hair, but she brushed it until it was smooth and shining, curling slightly at the ends, and left it loose, pulling some over her breasts and over the black curls on her pubis, until she was clothed in her hair. Arne loved it that way. She looked into the tiny hand mirror and saw her eyes floating huge and dark in the golden tan of her face. She gave herself a silent kiss. How could Arne resist her? Barefoot, she went out into the kitchen.

Arne was frying new potatoes in the black iron skillet on the top of the stove. He always fried potatoes when he had to cook something, although the little new potatoes were not good for frying. The room was very warm and the door was opened wide. Through it, Rannei could see the pink sky above the low bluff across the creek. The table, she saw, was haphazardly set for two.

Arne was standing at the stove, turning the potatoes. He glanced at her back over his shoulder as she came in, then down at the smoking pan, frowning. He had washed, for he had taken off his shirt and was nude to the waist, and the blond hair on his head and chest and arms curled silky and golden.

She stood still, overwhelmed by a rush of almost motherly love for him. He looked like a naughty little boy expecting a scolding, half sullen and half repentant. She waited until he looked at her again, letting the full force of her appearance penetrate to him, then she went to him and put her arms around his waist from behind, feeling the smooth hard flesh over his ribs tighten under her hands. He lifted a mass of potatoes and flopped them back into the grease, which splattered over the hot stove top, sending up little spirals of smoke. His arms were brown to just above the elbows, where he rolled his shirtsleeves. The whiteness of his upper arms made a sharp line between brown and white. The skin on his shoulders was white and smooth, the muscles satiny-firm beneath. Rannei rubbed her nose on his left bicep, and licked him with her tongue like a cat, tasting his unique taste, so different from hers.

"Arne..."

He put the fork back into the potatoes, and turned to her, running his fingers through her hair. The strands caught in the rough skin where calluses had grown thick on palm and fingertip. He pulled her hair off her breasts and pushed his chest against hers, running his hand under her hair into the curve of her waist, along her flank. She pressed against him, feeling him harden into her belly, and, against her whole body, the warmth of his. She felt the stubble on his chin against her neck and opened her eyes as they kissed. His stubby lashes, thick and straight, fringed his closed eyelids, but she knew that behind them, his eyes were black with desire. Out of the corner of her eye she saw smoke rising from the pan, and as Arne swung her up into his arms, still without speaking a word, she reached behind his back and shoved the pan to the back of the stove.

Chapter Twelve

*C*al stayed in Arne's barn until the worst of the storm had passed, helping Arne soothe the frightened horses and untangle the harness. Two of the reins had broken off in the wild dash to the barn; Cal thought they could probably be recovered by following the tracks tomorrow. The wagon tongue, they saw immediately, was a complete loss. Arne would have to make a new one. Arne was carefully drying the remaining leather harness with a burlap sack, hanging it up on the pegs, cursing in a steady stream of English. He has already discovered, thought Cal, that English is a more versatile language than Norwegian for swearing.

They did not mention Rannei. Arne, Cal sensed, was ashamed of his outburst at his wife. He had never heard Arne even raise his voice to her before. Cal knew it wasn't really Rannei as much as the wasted load of hay, the storm, and the horses that had upset Arne. Rannei had been there and the man had to yell at something. He was sure Arne had not seen the look of terror on her face when that first bolt of lightning had paralyzed them all.

Cal thought back to how Rannei had laughed at him in disbelief when he had first described the thunderstorms to them on the train. The experience today had come to her as a great shock. Then, too, she had been exhausted from working all day under that sun. It was enough to unnerve anybody. No wonder she had screamed. And, perhaps, she was not as strong as Arne thought. Nor was he, Cal thought wryly, standing up from where he had been crouched on the barn floor untangling harnesses. It was time to go home, or he would never get there, the way this rain was soaking in. It didn't take the Gumbo long to mud up.

As Cal rode out of the yard, he looked back and saw Arne standing in the doorway of the barn, his face raised to the rain like some great thirsty tree. The thunder muttered away to the south, and the sky was showing blue behind the black in the west. The ground sucked at his horse's hoofs; every burnout was a pool of water. Cal stayed on the grass, out of the trail that had been worn over the months between his house and the Bergstrom's. Even so he had to stop before he was halfway home and clean the balled clay from Jubal's hoofs. Cal felt no need to hurry out of the rain. He was already drenched to the skin. He had not been so clean in days. Jubal enjoyed it too. She tossed her head and pranced as best she could in the steadily thickening mud, snorting at the sucking sound her retracting feet made.

They would make up, of course, Arne and Rannei. It would take much more than a few unjust angry words to destroy that bond of erotic love between them, that even he, old clod of a bachelor that he was, could sense. Just as well for them both that Arne was not the sentimental fool that Cal was. Cal would be putty in Rannei's hands. All she would have to do would be to look at him as she did at Arne, and he would be her slave.

What a queen she would have made! Strange, or maybe it wasn't, he mused, that the great women of history were either beautiful or made others think they were. Helen of Troy, for instance, or Cleopatra, or Queen Elizabeth—and Shakespeare's heroines were all lovely ladies too. Rannei was a heroine if Cal ever saw one, and although she was Arne's wife, she seemed more beautiful to him every day.

Did that mean beauty in women equaled power? Probably. Beauty, especially sensuous beauty, controlled men, and it was men who wielded power. Yet Rannei was so unaware of her beauty, or at least she seemed to be. Cal would never forget how she'd looked, nor how he felt, when he saw her plodding home among the sheep, her absurd trousers dragging wet and muddy around her ankles, that black, black hair clinging to the curves of her breast that showed through the sodden shirt. By then, her first look of terror had been replaced by an expression of blind survival, the look of a child abandoned by its parents, driven, like the sheep, by animal instinct, to find cover. Cal had to turn his back so he would not go to her and shelter her in his arms. That fool of an Arne had not even looked at her. Remembering this, Cal felt angry with Arne. How could he be more worried about his horses and that damn load of hay than that precious girl?

Chapter Thirteen

*W*hen he had first beheld the Bergstroms on the train, Cal had figured Arne as less capable than determined, just another immigrant dreamer setting out on the great adventure of his life, hoping to find land and settle in the great American west. But as Cal got to know Arne, he had been impressed with the astuteness with which Arne listened and learned. Despite his enthusiasm, which might have seemed like impulsiveness in others, Arne had a clear, decisive mind, while Cal himself was inclined to vacillate.

Rannei was another matter. She was, Cal quickly realized, even more of a mystery than most women. She was not typical of the average woman immigrant with her fashionable clothes, her music, her educated and intelligent mind, and her imperious beauty. Yet sometimes she seemed a simple young girl, speaking eagerly and affectionately of her brothers, her parents, the farm she loved. Gradually Cal pieced out a picture of her life: the well-to-do parents who had given her every advantage, especially the perceptive, emancipated mother; the worldly grandparents who had exposed her to the cultural life of Bergen, as well as the cosmopolitan life of the wharves; the loving, close-knit family.

All of that had produced this chameleon, colored with the mood of the moment — but always charming, never vain, never exerting the power of her beauty, and obviously deeply in love with her husband. But now this, Arne's fit of temper at Rannei, was more upsetting to Cal than he liked to admit. He wondered if Rannei would stand up to him. Through all the time he'd spent with her, Cal caught glimpses of Rannei's strong will, which fascinated him. Even more fascinating was the subtle way she exerted that will on Arne, never opposing him directly, never arguing, but with a word, a glance, the very force of her presence, conveying to him what she felt. Maybe in the end, she would win.

Lately, he thought, troubled, slogging home in the diminishing rain, he seemed to be losing his objectivity where his young neighbors were concerned. It was really most unlike him to feel an almost savage anger at Arne this afternoon, and as for Rannei, better not to explore that further — perhaps he had merely felt sorry for her, as he would have for any woman in her circumstances. Perhaps he would leave in the spring, anyway. There was that expedition to the Yukon he had heard about while he was back east, and although he hadn't mentioned it to anyone, he had taken the precaution of writing down the leader's name, a Lieutenant Frederick Schwatka. Even before he made the journey to New York, he had known what his gathering restlessness of the past year meant. It was getting time to move on, and, if having neighbors wasn't helping, then what could?

Jubal tossed her head impatiently. Cal realized he had been holding her up at the banks of the creek, staring at the rising water for some time. It rushed gray and muddy over the tops of the slough grass, which bent and streamed in the current like green eels. It always amazed him how quickly the creek could rise after a rain, then just as quickly subside. The rain had come on the verge of drought, as it usually did. There would be enough water now until the fall rains. Lifting his hand, he flicked the rein ends lightly, and, snorting, Jubal stepped into the swift waters to cross.

The rain finished the haying. Even Arne, after rescuing the hay that had fallen out of the overturned wagon during the storm, said he'd decided he had enough hay for all but the most severe winter, and maybe enough for that, too. Now, at summer's end, in the sunny September weather, the tempo of life slowed. Cal sent Tommy home for a vacation. While Cal much preferred working with his horses, rather than herding sheep, he knew Tommy would like to see his family. So for a time, Cal herded his own sheep, following them all day across the prairie. He glimpsed Rannei and Arne from time to time, sometimes together with the sheep, and at other times Rannei was alone, but he kept at a distance.

Cal found himself enjoying the quiet days. He had been so busy all summer helping Arne that he had not read as much as he usually did, and he turned eagerly to his books and his sketchpad. He had brought a packet of new books back with him, and he interspersed these with re-reading books from his trunk, where he kept them to protect them from the leaky roof. He lent many of his books to Rannei over the summer, as she had ample time for reading as she herded sheep.

Cal was delighted to find that Rannei loved books as much as he did, and that she read well in English. They spent pleasant hours during the summer discussing what they had read, or what she was reading by Norwegian authors. She promised to lend him her precious copy of the Edda and to help him with the Norwegian translation, as soon as he had the time. She loved to explain the gods to him. She spoke of them as reverently as most people spoke of their Christian God. He thought this embarrassed Arne at first, for he caught Arne watching Cal out of the corner of his eye as if to see how he was taking it, but gradually, Arne seemed to relax. Perhaps he realized Rannei's theories intrigued Cal, and that Cal was no Christian zealot when it came to the subject of religion.

Part of Cal's fascination stemmed from watching Rannei's face as she talked about her beloved Thor, or Odin, and, especially, Freya. Her face, sometimes almost haughty in repose, would kindle and sparkle. Her eyes would glow deep blue and her cheeks would flush. Cal, glancing at Arne, caught him watching Rannei with the same mesmerized look he knew was on his own face. Cal had to laugh inwardly at how idiotic the two of them must look, sitting there with glazed eyes and open mouths, fools before a pagan queen.

Cal was not bothered by the fact that Rannei was not a Christian. He was not religious himself. He had met people of many different faiths during his travels, and thought religion was whatever one believed. It was part of Rannei's charm for him that she had taken for her personal religion one so different from the society in which she had been raised. Yet, as he came to know her better, he decided it was yet another expression of her imaginative, original mindset. Perhaps in another society she might have become one of the great women in history in whatever role she chose. Who knew what would become of her in the Gumbo, where the main requirements for success were a pragmatic heart and a strong body.

ONE DAY THAT SEPTEMBER, Cal wandered after his sheep reading Electra. He was enthralled by this play, one of his favorites. He found himself reading aloud to Tippie, the dog, savoring the timeless, tragic words, the speech where Electra mourns her murdered sire, unaware that her brother Crestes is about to avenge his father:

"Nay, the best part of life hath passed away from me in hopelessness, and I have no strength left; I, who am pining away without children, whom no loving champion shields, but, like some despised alien, I serve in the halls of my father, clad in this mean garb, and standing at a meager board."

For some reason, this passage conjured a picture in his mind of Rannei wandering in the midst of the sheep after the storm. She had stood there among them, if not as a "despised alien," at least having no "loving champion" to shield her. He closed the book with a determined snap.

"My God, Cal Willard," he said aloud, "you are a senti-mental fool! Now where are those damned sheep?" Had he lost the sheep, mooning about? They were hard to see now against the dun-colored prairie grass, and he scanned it anxiously. Ah, the last of them, disappearing in the direction of the Bergstrom homestead, probably heading for water. Only they weren't supposed to water there; that was where Arne watered his sheep. Cal always took his farther down the creek, to keep the two bands separate. He swore aloud, and Tippie looked up at him apprehen-sively. She was more used to Tommy than to him, and did not work as well for him.

"Come on, Tip," he said to the dog. "I'm not scolding you, good old Tip." Tippie wagged her tail, but she kept a wary distance from him. He would have to pay more attention to her, he decided. Tommy, who let her sleep on his bed at night, something that Cal found offensive, spoiled her. The first night the boy had been gone, the dog had lain on the floor all night, whining and looking at Cal with reproachful eyes, but she had not ventured to jump in with him.

Cal caught up with the stragglers as the leaders of his herd grazed their way down the gentle slope to the watering holes. He could see the Bergstrom's sheep well to the south, holed up for the afternoon upstream. He sent Tippie to turn the leaders downstream toward their usual watering place, and the ewes obeyed reluctantly.

Now that his herd was safely turned around, Cal decided to stay at this pleasant spot to eat his lunch and finish Electra. He walked back up the slope and found a burnout with a conveniently high bank to rest his back against while he ate and read. The bare gray clay felt soft and cool under his outstretched legs. He accompanied his bread and dried mutton with the water from his canteen, mixed with bourbon. After he had cleaned up every scrap, with a few thrown to Tippie, he opened his eyes and read awhile, but the sun glared off the white pages, and he closed his book with a yawn.

His sheep had disappeared over the slope, but he knew they were already at their usual watering place. It would be safe to leave them and go home for a while. He would come back later on Jubal and round them up.

He started to get to his feet, then sank back down again. On the west side of the creek, upstream, Rannei and Arne had just risen naked from the grass and were strolling hand in hand toward the largest ring of green slough grass, which concealed, he knew, Rannei's favorite swimming hole. It was larger and deeper than most of the others and had the distinction of having the only chokecherry trees, or indeed any trees, in the area.

It was evident they had not seen him. Cal was so close he could see the little yellow flowers tumbling from Rannei's unbound hair. He could not take his eyes from that hair, falling down her back to her knees, and over her breasts, so that she was clothed in shining, living black, her arm and shoulder startlingly white in contrast. By her side, Arne stretched and yawned, the sun glinting on the golden hair on his chest and thighs and belly, like Thor in the flesh. I must be dreaming, Cal thought incredulously. I can't be seeing what I'm seeing, a man and woman, naked as the day they were born, strolling in the bright sunlight in the middle of a Dakota prairie.

The open unconcern of Arne and Rannei shocked him. Cal had been taught nakedness was a matter for indoors, in darkness, behind drawn curtains. Even then it was considered shocking. He'd encountered nakedness in broad daylight in Africa, of course. His father thought his sketches of African women with their proud, upright carriages and pendulous breasts were scandalous, pictures not fit for mixed company. His publishers too had seen fit to ban those sketches from his book. Cal supposed his father had probably never even seen his mother naked during all their married life. Yet here were these white immigrants from Norway cavorting about in the middle of this god-forsaken prairie, without one bit of shame. Cal felt a bubble of laughter rise in his throat. It was wonderful, that was what it was. Marvelous!

Automatically, he hunkered down to the floor of the burnout so as not to be seen, his first thought being not to embarrass Rannei. Yet behind the protective screen of buffalo grass, Cal's eyes never left her, that slim white figure framed by a curtain of black hair poised above the fringe of green slough grass. Without dropping his gaze, his fingers searched his pockets for his charcoal stump. Damn, he had forgotten his sketchpad. He remembered the blank pages at the back of Electra. They would have to do. He began sketching, hardly ever looking away from his subject.

Rannei's hair — how often had he longed to see it that way? Completely undone, it hung shining and rippled from braiding, filled with that lustrous warm white light, even in the bright sunlight. They had reached the edge of the swimming hole, Cal knew, although he couldn't see the actual water. Peripherally, Cal saw Arne flash through the air in a flat dive and heard the splash as his body hit water, but his gaze remained riveted on Rannei. He could not have looked away even if she had looked up and seen him. She was trying to catch all that mass of hair on top of her head, but it would not stay. Like a live thing, it kept slipping down, alternately revealing and concealing parts of her white body as she caught it up again.

Cal had never seen anything so beautiful. That gorgeous mass of hair against that whiteness, the luscious curves tantalizingly revealed and then concealed — his chest ached, and he gasped. He had been holding his breath. He let it out slowly, glanced down at his sketch, then up again at Rannei. She had succeeded in twisting her hair into a knot at the top of her head, wound round itself. A few strands hung down her neck. For an instant longer, she stood there, revealed in all her perfection, and he stared unashamedly. Her body was perfectly proportioned, as he had known it would be, the breasts full and firm, the nipples pink against the white flesh, her waist curving in under the rib cage, the lovely swell of her hips accented by the bush of curly, black pubic hair between them, the long, but not too long, slender legs — Cal's charcoal flew over the paper.

But he shouldn't be spying on them like this. They surely imagined themselves alone. What innocents! Adam and Eve before the fall, only of course they weren't innocent in that sense, if Cal had correctly surmised what they had just been doing there in the grass. He had read Milton not long ago. The Gumbo as the Garden of Eden might have looked after the fall — yes, he liked that. God was punishing Adam and Eve by killing all the plants and trees with the hot blaze of his wrath, planting cactuses to tear their feet, sun to burn their tender bodies, harsh wind to sear them. Driven weeping from their lost paradise, Adam and Eve would soon learn to protect themselves in this harsh land.

Cal could hear Arne and Rannei laughing and shouting now, the sound of water splashing. Arne rose suddenly out of the hidden water, out of the rough slough grass like some golden god of the Gumbo, his body a startling white against the brown of his face and forearms, laughing, splashing. It was the first time he had seen Arne at play. Then Rannei popped up under the chokecherry bushes, a sea nymph seducing a god, strands of hair which had slipped down coiled around her breasts like eels. She splashed Arne back, and Oskar, the pup that the Porters had given them, and who never left Rannei's side if he could help it, leaped barking and springing foolishly on his long back legs along the edge, uncertain whether this was really play or not.

Arne began to coax the dog into the water, and when Rannei clapped her hands and called him, he backed off. In the end, the dog made a desperate rush forward into the water, disappearing between Arne and Rannei. Cal could hear him splashing furiously, and the tall grass on the bank waved wildly.

Cal quickly sketched Arne and Rannei from the waist up, which was all he could see of them. Rannei's black head under the bushy tree, her body half-turned so only the curve of her breast and waist was visible; a front view of Arne's impressively muscled torso. "After the Fall," he would call it, and all around he would frame them with the rough slough grass and flat bleak prairie and harsh light — no romantic mountains or limpid streams here — just a suggestion of the sheep in the background and the dog watching from the bank.

At last they emerged from the water to dry in the sun. Rannei, standing, wrung the water from her hair, twisting it like a rope. She brought a brush out of the basket beside her, and sitting on her skirt, began to dry her hair. It covered her like a black shawl as she sat cross-legged on the blue skirt, completely absorbed in untangling her hair.

The charcoal was becoming blunt. Cal rubbed the end of it against his thumbnail to sharpen it. Maybe he should use watercolors for this scene. He could accent the hair in that symphony of pale colors, the bluff of the prairie grass behind her, the pale blue sky accented by the deeper blue of her skirt. He'd include fleeting glimpses of her white body. A mermaid, or Odin's daughter, doing her toilette — but no, this picture belonged in his series of the pioneers of Dakota. What a sensation it would cause! He wondered if he dared.

Sitting beside her, Arne took the brush and began to run it down her hair. Better and better. The two of them, all lines and angles, the innocent sensuousness of it all! By God, Cal had more than enough for a book, pictures of scenes collected through the years on the Gumbo. Some of these of Rannei would make wonderful paintings, too. He could do a whole series of her alone. An exhibition, maybe... why not? He would ask her to pose for him, it would be more respectable than showing these clandestine images.

Arne put down the brush and began to plait one side, Rannei, the other. After she'd fastened the shining coils of hair around her head, Arne rose and dressed. Rannei pulled on drawers and a chemise, slipped her waist on, and her skirt. Now more than anything, Cal feared being caught. He lay flat on the floor of the burnout scarcely breathing, keeping his head below the level of the bank.

When he peeked again, Rannei was packing her towel and brush and remnants of lunch into her basket. Arne held out his hand for it. Cal's nose itched violently. He was afraid he would sneeze. Would they never leave? He heard sheep beginning to bleat in the distance, a sure sign that they were leaving the water. Arne must have heard it too, for he gave his hand to Rannei, and together they wandered off in the direction of their band.

Cal waited until they were safely on their way, then he rose and started off to find Jubal. The experience left him depressed and lonely, and more than vaguely lustful. He knew the sketches were good, and the prospect of the paintings he could make from them exciting, but that was not enough. He wanted what Arne had. He envied Rannei and Arne their freedom with each other.

Who in the world did he know who would do what those two just had? His sisters thought it daring to "bathe" covered from neck to ankles in a bathing costume. And Rannei was every bit as much a lady as they were. Rannei needed and deserved other people, as Arne needed land. In the end, she would not be the wife Arne needed, that was the tragedy of it. Beauty and talent and sensitivity were superfluous in the Gumbo; what were needed were strength, single-mindedness, and a stoical will to endure. Rannei hated the prairie as much as Arne loved it. She had seemed happy enough today, it was true, but he could not forget her face in the storm, lost and blind with terror.

Cal reached his corral fence and leaned on it. It was made of poles he had cut from young pines in the Cave Hills. The bark had peeled off long ago and the wood was cracked and dried. The sun, sinking lower in the west, starkly illuminated his little shack. Cal hadn't really looked at it for a long time. It was ugly. Holes gaped here and there where the tar paper had torn and the roof sagged at one end. He would have to bank it up around the bottom with hay and clay before winter, and another layer of tar paper wouldn't hurt. If he rode off now and left it the way it was, the Gumbo would soon reclaim it. Arne's house would probably stand forever. It was solid the way it was built, out of real logs. The chimney was made of clay and small stones instead of just a stovepipe sticking through the roof.

All the vague discontent that had simmered within Cal over the past year suddenly crystallized. Yes, he would leave. If it weren't for the Bergstroms, he would take his sheep to Rapid City or Pierre tomorrow, and catch the next train east. He couldn't do that of course, at least not for a while. He had brought Rannei and Arne here out of his loneliness, and so he was responsible for them until they were safely established, but not here, not on the Gumbo. For Rannei's sake, he must try to undo the harm he had done and persuade Arne to homestead somewhere else. It was not too late. He hadn't paid for the land yet and didn't have to for a while. The hardest part would be persuading Arne to leave. Perhaps the best approach would be the most straightforward.

Cal must admit to him that he had been wrong in urging them to come to the Gumbo. He would point out that Rannei hated the country and could never be happy here, and that for her sake if no other, Arne must relocate somewhere else. If only Arne could be made to understand the possible consequences of keeping Rannei isolated here year after year — he'd even heard of women going mad. He didn't fear for Rannei that way, as much as he feared her losing all she possessed so abundantly, her beauty, her bright vitality, her love of life and people. All that must not be dribbled away, by days and months and years of toil in which she had lost faith. She would endure, he had no doubt of that... but as she was now?

Then again, Cal didn't have to convince them tomorrow. One winter on the Gumbo might well change even Arne's mind. The man had no idea how bleak and lonely and boring winters could be. In the spring he might be more willing to find some friendlier spot.

Cal spotted Yellow Bird and Red Wing, his team horses, hobbled not far from the barn. Jubal had seen Cal by now and was approaching at a trot, tossing her head and whinnying. Cal never hobbled Jubal; she wouldn't leave the other horses, or him, either. Swinging himself up onto Jubal's bare back, he shook his head to clear it of the conflicted emotions he felt inside. It was time to get to work, to go bring in his sheep. He clicked his tongue and Jubal started off at a canter.

Chapter Fourteen

*T*he next evening on the way over to the Bergstrom's, Cal heard Arne's baritone and Rannei's alto, supported by the soft liquid sound of her guitar, well before their homestead came into view. Jubal pricked her ears and stepped softly, so they did not see him at first. Arne and Rannei were the perfect picture of contented pioneer man and woman, sitting on the doorstep in the warm evening light, Rannei strumming her guitar. They were singing something in Norwegian, and did not see him until he was at the hitching post. Rannei strummed the last chord and smiled up at him.

"Don't stop," Cal said. "Sing me a song, please."

Rannei never needed to be coaxed. She loved to sing and play as much as her audience loved listening to her, and now she swung gaily into a song they had sung on the train:

They give you land for nothing in Jolly Oleanna,

And grain comes leaping from the ground in floods
of golden manna,
And ale as strong and sweet as the best you've ever
tasted,
Is running in the foamy creek, where most of it is
wasted.
And little roasted piggies, with manners quite
demure, Sir,
They ask you, will you have some ham? And then
you say, 'Why, sure, Sir.'

Rannei beamed up at Cal as she made up a new line to the song. "Well, sir, how about some coffee, sir, seeing as we're out of ale, sir?"

Cal sang back, "Why sure, Mrs. Bergstrom." throwing off the rhythm, and they all laughed at the way he failed to fit the words to the melody. Rannei finished on her guitar with a splendid run of chords.

"The pot is on the back of the stove," Rannei said, handing her guitar to Arne.

"No, I'll get it." Cal said. "Sit still, Rannei, and sing some more."

But Rannei was already on her feet and going through the door. She pretended his gallantry amused her, but he knew she liked it too, although as she often told him, mockingly, it was women's work to wait on men. She brought out the coffee pot and a mug for Cal. The mug was her "company" one, drained from the boiler pot always kept on the stove, Norwegian fashion, to which new grounds were added to the old daily, until it became too full and too black to drink. It was still hot from the supper fire, and she poured out a cup for Cal and refilled Arne's and her own, and then seated herself on the lower step between and below the two men.

A silver sheen lay on her black hair, wound tonight into a heavy chignon at the nape of her neck. A tendril curled against her sunburned ear. She wore a white cotton waist with a homespun skirt of the deep blue color, bordered with a geometric design in bright yarns. Her neck was tanned despite the sunbonnet she wore most of the time, and inside the collar he could see a thin red line of sunburn. He forced his mind away from his memory of her nakedness and took a sip of his coffee.

"We haven't seen you for a long time, Cal," Rannei said. "What have you been doing?"

"Being a sheepherder again," Cal answered, "until tonight when Tommy came back, thank goodness. Those sheep just don't have the proper respect for me, and Tippie doesn't either."

"You aren't firm enough with either the sheep or the dog, Cal," Arne said, only half-teasing. "You must show them who is boss, you know."

"I suppose so," Cal said. "Tommy can have them. I much prefer working with horses. But I was thinking, Arne, that it is time we made our winter supply trip to Minnesela. It's almost the tenth of September, and we don't want to get caught in the rain. The weather won't be dependable much longer."

"Yah, we were just now talking of it," Arne said in his slow careful English, which he always used with Cal in order to improve it. Cal, on the other hand, often spoke Norwegian to Arne for the same reason.

"We need so many things," Arne went on. "More potatoes... ours didn't grow too well, and the flour is almost
gone. I think we will need four wagons to bring it all back,
Cal."

"I will have lots of room in mine. But first, and maybe
tomorrow, we'd better start hauling some coal for winter.
We'll be able to find some wood for kindling, too, by the
butte."

"I think I already have enough for us both." Arne
nodded toward the side of the house, where rough chunks
of coal were stacked almost halfway up the log wall. "After
I got the hay in, I had some time, and it didn't take all
that long."

"The devil you did!" Cal exclaimed. "But how did you
know where to find it?"

"Don't you remember, you pointed it out to me when
we came this spring," Arne said. "It was right where you
said, the first high bank of the creek you come to, going
west."

Of course; Arne's sense of direction was unerring.
"But I was going to help you, Arne."

"You help us too much already," Arne said firmly. "I
think to repay you a little. There is a load on the wagon,
there, to bring to you tomorrow, and more here if you
need it."

Cal saw the look of pride on Rannei's face, and realized
how important it was to them both that he accept, so he
did so as graciously as he could. Arne must have hauled
coal for a week, by the size of the stack. The trip to the
coal mine, an open pit dug into the side of a steep bank on

the creek, took almost a day, including the return and the digging. He should have known Arne was not idling his time away herding sheep when there was work to be done.

Jimmie and Henry had arrived the week before, as promised by Hank in the spring, and helped Arne and Cal separate the wethers and older ewes they wished to sell and trail them to Minnesela stock yards to markets in the east. It would be the second money crop for the Bergstroms.

As they sent the young men off with provisions for the seventy-mile trip, Cal thought how much they depended on the young Porter boys. When he was that age, he and all his friends were still in school, and not treated as grown men with responsibilities. Arne, of course, having worked as a man from the age of twelve, thought nothing of it, he was sure.

"So now we go to town, eh, Cal?" Arne said and Cal agreed. They were scheduled to meet the boys in Minnesela and put their money in the bank, or what was left of it after buying supplies. "How long do you think it will take to trail that bunch seventy miles?"

Cal thought a minute before answering. "Last year it took about a week. I think if they make an average twelve to fifteen miles a day that is good."

"We can always wait for them if we have to," Arne replied. "I just don't want to leave Rannei alone any longer than necessary."

"You'll get a good look at the Belle Fourche River on this trip," Cal said to Arne. "It's mighty pretty country, and with a railroad track finished, and talk of a dam for irrigation, land there would be ideal for farming. Lands to the north are still open too for ranching."

"What with the railroad and the dam, I think it is pretty well settled soon," Arne said.

"Are there trees there?" Rannei asked.

"Yes, along the river, and it's close to the Black Hills too, which are very pretty, small mountains really, lots of rock, and lakes."

"I'd love to see that country, wouldn't you, Arne?" Rannei looked at Arne pleadingly.

"Sometime we will, Rannei. We'll take a trip all through the Hills to Deadwood, and all around. Uncle Jens told us much about that town. But when do you think we should start for town, Cal?"

"Maybe we'd best plan on leaving the day after tomorrow. Can you be ready then?"

"Yah, sure I can."

"Arne, will you see what land is left along the Belle Fourche? It wouldn't hurt to look," Rannei persisted.

"We're not even settled in one place yet, and you're talking of looking for another one! For sure there will be more people there, and more people means less land. If that's farming country it isn't sheep country. We're going to own all this Gumbo one day, Ran, wait and see."

"It will be six months in December, Arne," Rannei said quietly. "I think I would like to know what else is available, just in case."

"Oh, just in case, eh!" Arne sounded almost jovial. Cal wondered what Rannei meant by six months. Six months' pregnant was the first thing that came to mind, but he dismissed that idea. Surely he would have had a hint from Arne if that were so.

Rannei said no more. Instead, she picked up her guitar and began to sing softly to herself in Norwegian. Cal promised her silently that he would do his best to drag Arne along as much of the Belle Fourche country as he could, and they could probably find out, too, in Minnesela, about the land around there. He would find out himself, if Arne wouldn't.

In springtime the eider cleaves its way, sang Rannei, now in English,

> *North where the fjord looms leaden-grey,*
> *It plucks the tender down from its breast*
> *To fashion a warm and cozy nest*
> *But the fjord-side fisherman—heartless clown!*
> *Plunders the nest of its precious down.*

Cal, listening to the mournful tune, knew he had been right about her. She would never be happy here.

> *The faithful eider, thus bereft,*
> *Plucks more down to replace the theft.*
> *Robbed yet again, in some nook of the shore*
> *It feathers its dwelling yet once more.*

The notes throbbed sadly in her voice.

"Rannei and I have been making a list," Arne said as Rannei continued her song. He pulled a paper from his shirt pocket and a stumpy lead. "You must tell us the English weights, for Rannei is not sure of all of them." He poised the lead over the list on his knee, but Cal did not look his way, instead listening as Rannei finished the song.

> *But with the third time, outraged quite,*
> *It spreads its wings in the cold May night,*
> *And turns to the south its bleeding breast,*
> *South to the sun lands for warmth and rest.*

"Oh, those songs of Rannei's! They are so sad, all of them," Arne said. "But perhaps we should go in and light the lamp, Ran?"

Cal saw Rannei shiver. She looked tired now, and sad. "Yes, let's go inside. The darkness comes so much earlier now."

She picked up her guitar. Arne gathered the mugs, and they all went inside. Cal and Arne sat at the table as Rannei lit the lamp. Together, all three of them went over the list, Rannei contributing only when Arne or Cal asked her a question. She had listed the food she thought they would need for the winter, and the amounts in English measures when she knew them, and in Norwegian when she did not. Now, with Cal's help, they translated the amount into pounds, measures, barrels and boxes. It did not seem possible to them that they would need at least three hundred pounds of flour for instance, or one hundred pounds of sugar, but Cal assured them they would use that much and more. There would be no renewing of supplies until the following spring.

Finally, Cal stood up. "That should be enough," he

said. "We'll have two days to add to the list, if you can think of anything else, Rannei."

"Rannei should be able to manage here fine," Arne said. "There is only the cow to milk, the chickens to feed, and the sheep to watch."

Cal glanced at Rannei and saw the sudden look of disappointment on her face. She must have known it wouldn't be possible for her to go, but perhaps she hoped there'd be a possible way to arrange it. Cal didn't see how. They needed both wagons, and two men for it, and Tommy could not manage both bands of sheep.

"What can we bring you, Rannei?" Cal asked gently.

"Oh," she said, and he heard the little catch in her voice, "just a tree to plant by the door."

"You shall have it," Cal promised, and he meant it. She would have her tree if he had to throw out half the wagonload for it. Was Rannei beginning to realize this was the way her life would be, year after year, minding the sheep while Arne went to town without her? It made Cal sad to think of it. Some years, if the two of them were lucky or prosperous enough, they might hire a herder to help out, but most of the time she would be living her life out on the prairie. He cast about for something to cheer her.

"There may be mail for you in Minnesela," he told her. "And we can take any letters you want to write to your family."

When he left, promising Arne to be back just after dawn tomorrow, Rannei was sitting at the table beside the lamp, writing a letter to her family.

My Dear parents and brothers:

I hope you have received our letters and even now some are awaiting us in Minnesela. I long for them daily, and hope that when Arne returns from his supply trip there he will have some for me. We never have visitors, so there is no hope of receiving any before then.

I reported on the sheep clipping in my last letter, and must tell you how much we have done since. Our wool clip brought a good price, our neighbor, Cal Willard, says, yet it does not seem much for all that we must have for the winter. Arne and Cal have already separated the ewes and lambs that they wish to sell from the other sheep, and two of the Porter boys will drive them to Minnesela, the nearest railroad head, to sell. It is where we sold the wool.

Cal and Arne will meet them there to make the sale and to purchase our winter supplies. They will be gone for ten days, at least, and I will stay here with the sheep. Tommy, Cal's herder, will be at Cal's place too, so it is not as if I were entirely alone. And of course, I have Oskar! He seems to grow more foolish daily, but he is good company, although not always a lot of help.

Our garden did not do well. Vegetables do not grow as they do at home, but perhaps when the soil is worked more it will be better. The potatoes were small and few but very good tasting. They do not get enough water, but the soil is so hard and dry it is hard to carry enough water to it.

Arne has finished the sheep shelter. It is open on the south, and the long north wall is of small logs. The two ends are double rows of logs, the space between filled with gumbo clay mixed with hay. It is a new method Arne has devised, since there is so little wood hereabouts. He hopes the hay will keep the clay from melting in the rains.

I help Arne with the sheep herding whenever he is busy with other things, which is most of the time. Now, when he returns from the supply trip, he will begin a pasture for the horses and cow. In this country they use something called barbed wire for the fencing. It is wire strung between posts, and the wire has little barbs, quite sharp, on it. It sounds cruel, I know, but it is the most practical to use, Cal says. Arne will have time for the pasture this fall, for there are no crops to get in.

It seems strange, Father, but no one farms this gumbo soil. Now I can understand why. It is fit only for grazing. The rich land of which we have heard so much about in Dakota certainly isn't here! There is some still left along the Belle Fourche River, which I feel Arne must look at on his supply trip.

Arne is quite content with his ranching life, as they call it, and does not care to farm, but as for me, I would like a nice plot of ground for a garden, and another thing I would wish for is a tree. You cannot imagine how desolate this land looks without trees. There is not a single tree in sight of our house. I think it must be the lack of trees which makes the summers seem so much warmer than at home.

I cannot yet feel at home here. It is all so strange and barren and no people! I hope soon we will have nearer neighbors, but now the closest are the Porters, more than fifty English miles away. That is not as far as it may sound, Ole and Knut, for you must remember that one of our American miles is equal to not quite six English ones. How far is that in Landmil? That is something for you to puzzle over. You must give me the answer in your next letter, Ole, now that you are old enough for school.

Arne will bring back our entire winter's supply of food when he returns from Minnesela. Think of that! We will not be able to go anywhere all winter, and surely will not see anyone but Cal

Willard and Tommy Porter the whole season. We are lucky to have them near, at least. But I do wish Cal and Tommy had wives, so I could have women to sit with. It seems strange to have no women near. I miss you, my dear Mother, and long to see all of you and talk with you. Please do not believe that I have grown melancholy. I am in good spirits, and keep myself busy, as I promised, but I do so long for you all.

Greet Einar and Birthe for me, and Hendrik and Aase. Has Aase had her baby yet? And how is little Siri? You must tell her sometimes of her Tante Rannei, so she will not forget me.

Ole and Knut, I hope you are good boys, and study hard, especially English with Mother, for when you are bigger you must come and visit your sister, and it is well to know English here. Even Arne speaks English now.

My love to you all, from Rannei.

Chapter Fifteen

*R*annei watched Arne and Cal and the wagons disappear out of sight in the southwest before she turned, and towing Oskar with her, headed back toward the remaining herd. She had her lunch in her pocket and a book to read. She settled down on a small rise above the creek to watch the herd peacefully grazing on the grassy slope.

The silence was absolute, not even the twittering of birds, many of which had flown south for the winter. How wonderful it would be to be a bird, Rannei thought, and just fly away when winter came. At home there had been birds in all seasons, even in Bergen when she had gone to live with her grandparents to attend secondary school. And always people, people to talk with and attend concerts and plays with.

The most alone Rannei had ever been, she realized now, had been in the summer months in Norway spent on the mountainside helping to tend the cows and goats and making cheeses with the village girls who helped her mother. The animals had come when she called them by name, and offered a certain kind of companionship. Rannei used to know each tall pine there, and loved how the mountains rose all around to shelter her.

In Bergstromfjord, the mountain stream was a comforter and friend, and could be endlessly interesting, dropping down into a waterfall or meandering through a meadow into deep quiet pools where she could watch the fish, or jump in for a refreshing swim.

At night when Rannei returned to the *säeter* hut, the house girls were making butter or cheese, or some of the family was sure to stop by, and Arne would often join the Andersen family for supper.

Whenever Rannei thought of her childhood, it was in terms of light. Cool green sunlight, filtered through the sea and the trees, in summer; blinding snow light and fire-light in the winter; dancing glare of sun off the sea in all seasons. It was not this harsh glare of light off the yellow, previous year's grass, unbroken by any hint of green that was this prairie country.

Here on the Gumbo, Rannei knew utter loneliness. Here, with only Oskar and the sheep, and the great bowl of the sky upended over her head, and the wind blowing against her all day across the empty prairie. Each night Rannei felt great relief as she crept into the house, after the sheep were on the bed ground, pulling the door shut behind her. But each morning she had to go out again.

The third night Arne and Cal were gone it happened. She was safely in bed, the blankets snug around her neck, dreaming that she was sailing in the fjord with her father.

But then her father's boat changed into a rowboat, and she was pulling on the oars as hard as she could, for high on each wave she could see the cod cresting, uttering strange cries as they bore down on her. Then the cries became the terrified bleating of sheep, and Rannei finally came awake enough to realize the bleating was coming from the bed ground, wilder and more frenzied each minute, interspersed with Oskar's wild barking.

Rannei lay rigid a moment, not wanting to believe it, wanting only to snuggle back under the comforting blankets, but the sound crested past the house and broke, scattering away to the west. The sheep must be running. What could be chasing them? Oskar? His manic barking was growing fainter and fainter. *"Dum dog! Faen Yaevel!"* she swore at Oskar. But the devil may as well take her, for it was her fault for not putting the sheep in the corral, although Arne had told her they would be all right on the bed ground.

She fumbled hastily for stockings and boots in the dark, fastened her skirt over her nightgown, and ran into the kitchen. Her warm cloak was on the hook by the door, the sheep crook leaning in the corner. She grabbed them both in one hand, fumbled the door open with the other, and stepped out onto the back step. It was dark, and she hesitated a moment, shutting the door, dragging the cloak over her shoulders. Where was that dog? As if in answer, another wave of baaing and barking surged out of the west, but fainter.

Oskar!" she called angrily and began to run in the direction of the sounds, putting her feet down cautiously on the dark ground. She would give him a beating he would never forget, that *helveteshund*! The next instant she felt sorry she had called him a hellhound. Maybe it wasn't his fault at all. Maybe he was in danger. She began to run faster. She could see a little better, her eyes adjusting to the dark.

"Oskar!"

She could hear the shrill barking louder now. Suddenly it changed to shrill howls, louder and louder, coming straight at her. She stopped, uncertain. Something, some black shape, was rushing directly at her. Rannei screamed from the very bottom of her stomach and flung up the sheep crook defensively. The demon flung itself upon her, slavering and howling and whimpering as she struck at it blindly. Moments later she recognized the familiar black and white head and the wildly flailing tail.

"Oskar, you idiot!" she croaked in relief. The young dog lay across her feet as if in terror. She looked around, wild-eyed, but she could see nothing. She pulled her feet out from under him and knelt down beside him and him and touched his head. It was oddly sticky, warm and wet. In the dim light she could tell one ear was dangling down against his head, strangely out of place. She felt his blood pulse through her fingers. He was hurt. Something out there had torn at him, something out there in the darkness. For a fearful second, she thought she had done it with the crook, and she sobbed in sympathy. But, surely, she had not hit him that hard.

Oskar was whining and trying to lick her hand. She laid down the crook and tore a strip of cloth off the bottom of her nightgown and tied it around the dog's neck, to hold his ear against his head and stop the bleeding. Oskar was soaking wet and trembling against her knees. The chill wet from the heavy cold dew of night was seeping through her gown. She got up, pushing the dog off her knees gently. She had to find the sheep and whatever awful thing waited for her out there in the darkness.

"Come, Oskar," she said firmly, holding him by the knot on the bandage. He must come with her no matter how badly he was hurt, for she couldn't face the demons out there alone. There was no need to hold Oskar, however; he wouldn't leave her. He pressed so tightly against her legs she could scarcely walk. They preceded cautiously, the sheep crook ready in Rannei's right hand, her left lightly touching Oskar's head.

Oskar stopped and made a whimpering sound. She stopped too, peering into the shifting levels of darkness. There was an object darker than the ground in front of her, and Oskar was looking at it, growling. Whatever it was, it didn't seem to be moving. Rannei went toward it bravely, the crook at the ready, and poked at it. It did not move. Oskar stopped growling and pushed at it with his nose, so she went up to it too, and knelt down beside it. It was one of the spring lambs, its eyes wide open, its neck ripped from the ear down to the shoulder, a great gaping hole torn in its stomach. In the darkness, she could make out a glistening loop of intestine protruding from the gash. The lamb was still alive, just barely.

Rannei's stomach heaved. A bitter bile burned through her nose and fingers, which she tried to hold back by pressing her hand against her mouth. Oskar—no, Oskar hadn't done this. It was Loki's son, the evil Fenris wolf, who was having his cruel sport. Her head felt faint with terror. Rannei swung her head around frantically, searching for the wolfish shape, expecting to see it materialize out of the mist, which seemed to coalesce wherever she looked. Rannei could not stop heaving, although there was nothing left in her stomach to heave. Her legs felt heavy, as if filled with water. No, she would never be able to run from this evil thing. Oskar whined again and nudged the lamb. Its hind leg jerked, and the pup leaped back against Rannei.

"Oh, you poor thing," Rannei said to the lamb. What real evil could have caused this dreadful damage? And how could she help this poor mutilated creature? It was obviously dying, and suffering too. She wiped the vomit off her fingers on a clump of grass and looked around. She would have to kill it, but saw no stones, nothing to hit it with. Still, she couldn't leave it there dying in agony.

There was only the crook. Resolutely, Rannei stood up, stepped back, and with all her strength brought down the back of the heavy crook on the lamb's head, just behind its ear the way she had seen her father kill fish. The lamb gave a gurgling gasp, its legs shot out straight, and it lay still. Gasping in shock at what she'd just done, Rannei tugged at Oskar's bandage and pulled him away.

No time to mourn; there were still sheep to find. Rannei moved ahead shakily, the night evolving slowly into a ghostly gray dawn. Gradually, she came upon groups of sheep, one or two by themselves, heads to the ground panting. What if they were all scattered about like this? Rannei thought with despair. A tired panic began to seep into her stomach, and she had to force her legs to move ahead, one after the other, in search of the main herd.

Coming over a small rise, Rannei happened on the wolves suddenly. There were four of them — surely, they were wolves — three of them were smaller, but the fourth one was bigger than the coyotes she'd occasionally seen loping across the prairie. Cal had told them about the timber wolves, but said they usually stayed closer to the badlands and the rivers.

The three smaller ones were growling and tearing at a whitish mess on the ground. The larger one stood guard, ears pricked, teeth bared at Rannei in a kind of horrible grin. For an instant she and the wolf stood transfixed, the wolf as surprised as Rannei.

Then Rannei heard a sobbing, growling noise, and realized it was her own. The wolves were tearing at another one of her lambs. A hot, black wave of rage and hate almost lifted her off the ground. Shrieking like a Valkyrie, she lifted her crook in both hands above her head and brought it down, hitting about her as fast and hard as she could. She stepped forward so quickly that she hit one of the three smaller wolves across its back. The animal turned and ran, as did the others, scattering, making little doglike yips in their throats. Oskar ran barking after them, stopping after a short distance, careful not to get too far from Rannei. A short distance away, the four wolves stopped, their heads turned back over their shoulders, staring at Rannei with an almost human look of surprise and curiosity on their faces.

Rannei ran and shouted at them again. They moved farther off, but when she stopped, so did they, staring, watchful. If only she had some rocks, anything, to throw at them, Rannei thought. But she had only the crook, and she could not let go of that. The wolves seemed to be aware that she was harmless, but retreated anyway. Doggedly she kept after them, until they gave up and moved off in a steady trot, one behind the other, the biggest one in the lead. Rannei stopped then too, a hot pain jagging in her side, watching and waiting to be sure they'd gone for good.

The dawn had come without her noticing it, but it was a dark and gloomy sky. Guided by the bleating of the sheep, coming from a different direction than the one the wolves had gone, she walked to the west, gathering up stragglers as she went. She found the main band of them a bit farther on. The ewes bleated plaintively to their lambs, which, almost old enough to be independent of their mothers now, still dropped to their knees and gave a token tug or two on their dams' udders, as if seeking solace from their mothers after their ordeal. But the danger had passed. Stopping now and then to graze, the sheep began heading as a band back to more familiar grazing grounds. At least, Rannei hoped they were. She could see what she thought was Table Butte in the right place, to the south, the direction the wolves had gone.

As it grew lighter, Rannei tried to count the sheep, but it proved almost impossible. She did find six of the ten leader ewes, which Arne had marked with painted numbers on their backs, but that meant four others and their followers were still missing. As the band drifted slowly along, she ranged back and forth behind them, looking for more injured. Along the way, she encountered two more lambs, slashed and dead. Without the ritualistic dividing of the day, the sheep drifted aimlessly, seemingly as dazed and bewildered as Rannei felt. Oskar pressed constantly against her legs, still unwilling to leave her side. As the morning progressed, the foggy mist did not lift. Without the sun, Rannei had no idea what time it was. She was thankful she had snatched the heavy, homespun wool cloak from the door hook. The cloth was damp, but the hood covered her head warmly and kept the chill from her body. Her feet were soaked through, however, and so numb she no longer felt them.

By midday, it felt to Rannei as if her whole life had dwindled to following the sheep, but she dared not leave them to look for the missing leaders. She did not think of going home for dry boots and food. She and the sheep and Oskar were inextricably welded together. Where they went she would follow, and she would fight the wolves to the death. They would not take any more helpless lambs.

Sometime during those endless hours, the wind began to make tentative passes through the fog, at last blowing the thick mist away. Rannei had never seen anything as wonderful as the blue sky and sunshine that finally broke through, illuminating the fog that still drifted along the ground in patches. As the last of it cleared, she saw Tommy's familiar thin shape on his roan horse materialize out of the prairie.

At the sight of him, Rannei sat down hard on the damp clay on the edge of a burnout and stayed there. Tommy reined in above her, and she looked up. He was watching her anxiously.

"You all right, Mrs. Bergstrom?" He nodded delicately in the direction from which she had come.

Rannei understood that he had found the lambs and knew what had happened. She plucked at the edge of her gown that showed beneath the skirt and cloak. She must look terrible. The hem was torn and muddied, and sometime during the day the thick braid she wore at night had come undone. She pushed her hood back so she could see Tommy better, and smoothed at her hair with her muddy, stained hands. Tommy dismounted, letting the reins drop to the ground. The horse stood obediently while Tommy fumbled in his saddlebag, producing a piece of her own cheese and a hunk of her bread, which she had given Cal. He handed them to her, and she ate ravenously, suddenly aware she had not had anything to eat all day. She was giddy with hunger, but she chewed slowly, savoring the tastes in her mouth. Tommy gazed politely away while she ate, out over the sheep. They had stopped their aimless drifting, and finally spread out to graze.

She finished eating and wiped her hands on a tuft of wet grass, then tucked them inside her cloak, under her breasts, to warm them. "Did you see the wolves?" she said at last, when she could trust her voice.

He nodded, bringing his eyes to her face. He was thin, almost to the point of emaciation, but his face had a clean, bony look and his eyes were a deep soft brown beneath the stained felt hat.

"I found four of yours they'd killed," he said. "I would have butchered them but then it was too late. Ain't good unless you catch them right away. They weren't chewed up much. Reckon it was just a female, teaching her pups to kill. They do that sometimes."

She'd never thought of the poor dead lambs as meat, but of course she should have. Arne would be so angry, with at least four of his precious ewe lambs dead, and all that meat wasted. But she didn't know how to butcher, and how could she, with no knife?

"Don't worry, missus," Tommy said. "Ain't nothing you could have done. Most important thing was to round up the sheep."

Tears began to pour down her cheeks at his kind words. She bent her head, hiding her face from him within the shelter of the cloak hood.

"I suppose I should have done something about them, but it was so awful," she sobbed out. "They came in the night, and I ran out after them just as I was. I thought it was Oskar who chased them, but the wolves almost killed him. They weren't even afraid of me, the evil things. And I had to kill one of the lambs, it was still alive." Her voice was trembling, out of control.

"There, there, Rannei, missus, don't cry," Tommy said, patting her clumsily on the back. He sounded horrified, and even through her tears Rannei sensed his embarrassment. She willed herself to stop, wiping the tears off her cheeks with the back of her cold hand.

"Did they kill any of your bunch, Tommy?"

"No, just by luck I put them in the corral last night, and most times wolves won't bother them there." He didn't ask her if she had penned hers; he knew she hadn't. "I caught a glimpse of the wolves heading for the Cave Hills, reckon that's where they came from."

He bent to examine Oskar, who was curled into a whimpering ball. Tommy pulled up the edge of the cloth and looked at the torn ear. "We'd best get Oskar home and that ear sewed up. Do you have any creosote at home? It looks bad."

"The poor dog, he was so brave, and I hit him because I thought he was a devil. Yes, I'm sure Arne has some left from the sheep shearing."

"Well, it's almost five, and the sheep are heading in, so why don't I take you home, missus, and on the way, we'll see if you have any sheep over in that direction. I can fix Oskar up for you, and Jake here will ride double, I think."

Tommy mounted Jake, and gave Rannei a hand up. Jake did not like Rannei's flapping skirts, and he danced and skittered about, but Tommy handled him masterfully. Rannei held the boy around his thin middle. He didn't seem quite so embarrassed with his back to her. The simple human contact comforted her. She felt real again, her sense of time and self, restored.

"I've never seen fog like this here," she said to Tommy's back. "Does that mean it will start raining soon, do you think? I hope it doesn't before Cal and Arne get back." She remembered the tales she had heard about the impossibility of travel on the Gumbo when it rained, and the way the mud had balled up on the wagon wheels in the August storm.

Tommy seemed to think about that a while, maybe rehearsing his answer so he wouldn't alarm her. Goodness, she thought, I must have scared him, poor boy, running about in the rain in my nightgown, killing lambs and chasing wolves like some demented witch. He probably thinks he has to handle me carefully, or I'll become violent and then what would he do? She stifled the unseemly giggle that quivered in her still empty belly.

"I don't think the rainy season will start yet, missus. Besides, we don't usually have a rainy season. It just rains once in a while. This is only fog from the dew. Clearing off like this, now, usually means it will be nice tomorrow, just like the weather we've been having."

"*Hostfred*, that's what we call it at home," Rannei said. "Autumn peace."

"That's nice," Tommy said, and Rannei gave him a little squeeze. She couldn't help it, he was sweet and reminded her of Hendrik. She missed her brothers even more than she thought she would, especially around the Porter boys. Or perhaps, she thought, she missed being a sister; a wife was not the same.

They caught up with the sheep that were grazing purposefully toward the creek and home, and Tommy made a wide detour behind them, swinging south. To Rannei's delight, they soon came upon two more small groups of sheep, also heading for the bed ground. And here were the missing four leaders, with at least fifty sheep besides.

"I think that's probably most of them," Tommy said to her, maneuvering Jake so as to gather them up and send them in the direction of the others. Next Tommy guided the horse across the creek and up the rise that separated the two homesteads, to check on his own herd. The sheep were scattered out to the east of Cal's house, grazing in a settled way toward the corral. Apparently convinced all was well, Tommy turned Jake back across the creek and they rode up to Rannei's back doorstep. Rannei jumped off. Tommy tied Jake to the rail and came into the house with her.

The fire was cold ash, so Tommy started one while Rannei brought Oskar inside and washed his wound with water. The sight of the wound did not bother her; she had helped her mother many times at births and was used to the sight of blood. She knew what she was dealing with here. The unseen terror that had destroyed the lamb was what had frightened her more than its blood. She found the needle and waxed thread Arne used to sew up the gashes sometimes inadvertently made in the sheep at shearing time. At Tommy's instruction, while she held the skin in place, he sewed the torn flesh together.

Oskar whimpered and squirmed under her hands, but he did not protest too much. He seemed to know they were trying to help him. When the wound was stitched together, Tommy poured a mixture of creosote and water over it to keep it from becoming infected. Cal and Arne used the mixture on every possible kind of injury, from the gashes and nicks left in the sheep at shearing time, to the stumps of the tails which had to be docked off the lambs in the spring. Arne had even poured the mixture over a deep cut on his own hand, despite Rannei's protests. The cut, to her surprise, had healed.

"You'd better keep him in the house for a while," Tommy said. "He'll try to scratch out those stitches if we don't watch him."

Rannei pulled up a rug beside the stove and coaxed Oskar over to it. She found some crusts of bread, soaked them with milk, and fed them to the dog one by one. He ate them from her hand, but refused to eat unless she fed him, just like her little brother, Knut, when he was ill, she told Tommy. Tommy poked up the fire and put the coffee pot over the burner to warm. With a little water added, he said, there was enough in it from yesterday. Rannei thanked him. She had only a precious handful of coffee beans left until Arne returned, and she did not want to use those until the coffee in the pot was too weak to drink. As Rannei knelt by the stove beside the dog, the warmth began to penetrate her cold feet, and she shivered. How cold and hungry she was! Tommy's lunch had only whetted her appetite.

"Listen, Tommy," she said. "I will make some *melja* for us, only of course, I don't have the fish liver that goes with it. But there is some bacon left, and you put that over pieces of *flatbrød*, grate cheese over that, then pour treacle — molasses — over all. Oh, it is delicious! Will you stay and eat with me? It won't be long, and your sheep will be all right, won't they? It will be ready in fifteen minutes."

Tommy hesitated. She watched him vacillate between duty, shyness, and an obvious desire to stay with her. He was lonesome too, she realized, and probably always hungry, from the looks of him.

"Tell you what might be better, missus. I'll go milk your cow, then go home and pen my sheep and yours too, then come back and eat with you."

"Oh Tommy, you are a dear boy! But you must stop this missus business and call me Rannei, since I call you Tommy. If you're sure it wouldn't be too much trouble, I do need a bath and some clean clothes. I'll put the water on right now."

"Better let me fetch you some before I go." He poured what was left in the bucket on the washstand into the pot Rannei gave him and started out the door.

"There's an empty bucket on the porch," Rannei called after him. "Take that too, as long as you're going."

She took the flat round package of flatbrød down from the shelf and began to break it into pieces in the iron skillet, humming under her breath. What a comfort to have a man around! He would remember to see if the chickens had gone to roost in their little house at the end of the barn and shut the cow in for the night. She wondered what would have happened to her if Tommy hadn't come when he had. Perhaps she might have curled up out there with Oskar in one of the cold wet burnouts, wrapped in her cloak, and stayed forever. She shuddered at the thought. No, she would have found her way home somehow. At night, the wolves might return.

Chapter Sixteen

$\mathcal{A}$rne was not as blind to Rannei's dislike of the Gumbo as Cal thought, it seemed. The first day out, they stopped at a water hole to rest the horses and Arne, between mouthfuls of bread and cheese, said he wished with all his heart that Rannei could have come with them.

"I know how lonesome it is for her," he said. "There is no help for it, this time. But not always she stays home. Next year I hire one of the Porter boys too, at least during the busy season. It is hard at first, but if only she will be patient, she has all she wants."

He paused, but Cal said nothing. He wondered if Arne knew what his wife wanted, what his picture of her longing was, and how it differed from his own.

"You see for yourself, Cal," Arne went on. "Rannei is not like other women. She is so *skjønn*, so, so beautiful, of course, and the only girl among brothers. It is not that they spoil her, but they indulge her too much, perhaps. It makes her too tender, too fanciful. She likes not harshness, or ugliness of any kind, and she knows not how to bear true hardships."

Cal handed his whiskey flask to Arne, who handed it back to Cal, untasted. Arne almost never drank in the middle of the day, especially when he was working, but Cal continually forgot this, as he drank at any time of the day himself.

"As for me, life is always hard," Arne said without the least trace of self-pity in his voice. "I know it. Nothing is easy for me, as it is for Rannei. My father fishes all his life, yet never owns his own boat, or even shares in a boat. Always he is a member of a crew, only. And his luck is poor. But mine isn't. Luck is mine and I have luck here."

Cal listened to this unusually long speech from Arne and searched his mind for how to reply.

"I know you will, Arne," Cal said. "You would have luck anywhere, though. I've been thinking, perhaps it was a mistake to bring Rannei out here. My mistake, mostly, to urge you to come. I did not realize at first how differently she would see the Gumbo. I think Rannei is courageous enough to live anywhere, but as you say, she is a special person, who needs beauty, and perhaps people, like most women. The question is whether she will ever find beauty here, and will she be happy if she does not? And if you want to own most of the Gumbo, as you told me you do eventually, she'll never have any close neighbors."

"Rannei must learn to see the beauty of it," Arne said.

"It is beautiful; at times, very beautiful. If I see it, surely she can. I try to leave some of the Gumbo for others, so we have neighbors, too!"

"You know, Arne, there is still much good land to settle here in Dakota, besides the Gumbo. Don't you feel it would be worthwhile to look around at least? It does not seem to me that Rannei will change her opinion of the Gumbo any time soon."

"But Cal," Arne said, reasonably, "the Gumbo is the only place I want. Oh, don't think I not look around me when we are at Rapid City! I see the land and it is good land, but farming land, cattle land. I want space to run thousands of sheep, space I only have on the Gumbo. Someday I am the biggest sheep rancher in the Dakota. Rannei must to change her mind. I tell her we try the Gumbo for a year, but now I see it is exactly right for me. Somehow I make Rannei see that too."

"But if you agreed to a year, Arne, what about your side of the agreement? Surely, to be fair..."

"Now you are like Rannei's father," Arne said. "That is the trouble. They raise Rannei with the notion that the wife has as much say as the husband in everything. It works for Lars and Kristin because Kristin manages everything, and Lars minds not that. But I do. Rannei has her say always, and I try to please her in most ways. But sometimes, I think, the husband has the final say. I am older than Rannei. I know what is good for the two of us. This is important to me, and she must learn to trust me, and try to like it."

"And after a year, if she still absolutely does not like it, what then?" Cal knew he was invading the privacy that Arne valued so, but he felt he had to know. This, he sensed, would be his last chance to help Rannei, and he must take it. Surprisingly, Arne did not seem to resent it.

"I cannot leave, Cal." His voice held both finality, and sadness. "She has to stay. I give anything, anything, to make Rannei happy, anything but leave the Gumbo. She has to stay."

It was useless. Arne was immovable as the Mule's Ears. Cal could see the justice of Arne's logic. In the opinion of almost any man he knew, Arne was acting reasonably. The husband had the final say. The only trouble was, Cal understood that such conventional justice did not apply to Rannei. She was not a typical wife, and if Arne forced his wife to stay on the Gumbo, he would be the loser in the end. Rannei's resentment would be too strong.

Arne laughed suddenly. "Now stop the worry, Cal, about Rannei. She makes one believe whatever she says, because she is who she is. I know how it is! But she is very strong, too, and she will accept it, wait and see. And you know we end up here anyway, with or without you. I feel this Gumbo land is my destiny."

Arne began to pack up the lunch, and Cal, knowing the subject was dismissed once and for all, went to hitch the horses to the wagon. Cal looked forward to getting to the Belle Fourche river valley. It lived up to its name as "Beautiful Fork," as it was the confluence of the Belle Fourche and Redwater Rivers and Hay Creek as well, so it was fertile, and well-watered.

Since their route took them west and south of the

Porters, Cal did not expect to see them this time, nor did they see their sheep and the Porter boys along the way.

Cal knew more people in Minnesela than he did in Pierre, and the acquaintances he encountered, after they'd stabled their horses, unhitching and leaving their wagons in the stable yard, were all full of talk about the railroad bypassing Minnesela and establishing the new town of Belle Fourche. The townspeople were to a man indignant about the railroad's treachery, the knell of doom for Minnesela. Since Belle Fourche was only three miles to the west, it would undoubtedly merge in time anyway, thought Cal. He was careful not to say so, however.

At their hotel, Cal and Arne learned at the front desk that Jimmie and Henry Porter had not yet checked in, so after settling in and washing up, they brushed the dust from their felt hats, and walked to the general store, Peterson's Trading Center. They were tired from the long day's trek and it was getting late in the day.

Cal could not help marveling that, despite his still limited English, Arne was completely at ease with everyone he met. Set against other men, Arne looked startlingly handsome with his sun-bleached, golden hair and mustache against his tanned skin, and his pale blue eyes. Now free from the pressures of work, he was charming to all he met. Cal was amused to watch the women of Minnesela appraise the tall Norwegian from under their hat brims, and how eagerly they urged him to bring his wife and come for a visit. Cal thought he would never truly know the man, surprised that at first he had thought Arne uncomplicated.

When they entered Peterson's Trading Center, the tall,

lanky storekeeper, Ole Peterson, was perched on a stool behind the counter adding up his accounts in his ledger. He looked up with a smile of welcome for Cal, and Cal introduced his companion.

At the sound of Arne's name, Ole Peterson gave an exclamation of delight. Leaping from his stool, he stretched out his hand, first to Cal, then to Arne.

"Could you be the Arne Bergstrom my brother Lars has met on the boat this spring? Lars has told me of you, and your beautiful singing wife too! Welcome to Minnesela!"

Ole and Arne immediately rattled off a long conversation in Norwegian that Cal could not follow. Occasionally one of them remembered to include him, speaking a bit more slowly, but then off they would go again.

When Ole went to wait on a customer, Arne explained to Cal that Ole's brother Lars had taken up a homestead on the Belle Fourche and had already harvested his first crop. Ole himself, he said, was planning on moving his store to Belle Fourche in the spring, as were many of the other merchants and townspeople.

"Well, hello, Cal Willard." A big voice boomed behind them. Turning, they saw two men, one barrel-chested and short, the other lean and tall, walking toward them. "I didn't recognize you at first," the barrel-chested man said, "all duded up like you are in your town clothes. This is my range boss, Slim, my nephew, come out west for his health."

The four men shook hands and Cal introduced Arne to his friends. Joe Jimson had a body to match his voice, a head shorter than Cal and Arne and enormously wide. The man wasn't fat, but broad in the shoulders with a body that continued in a solid line all the way to his boots. Joe Jimson wore his dress-up clothes — nankeen trousers stuffed into high boots, a greatcoat, and a flat felt hat. The coat hung open, revealing the straps of two holsters, filled with ivory-handled guns.

Slim, the nephew, was as slender as Jimson was wide. His long yellow face featured deep-shadowed eyes, and a generally unhealthy look. The lad — he could not have been over twenty years old — appeared to Cal to be mortally ill, so that Cal averted his eyes, hoping the horror he felt at this prospect didn't show on his face.

"I trained horses for Jimson for a few months," Cal told Arne, "when I first came to Dakota. He runs cattle up north, near the Cave Hills."

"The cattle business sure ain't what it used to be, though," Jimson boomed. "Winter of '86-'87 damned near wiped us out. We're still going, but now the damn homesteaders are moving in on us. Yep, the big times are over for the cattleman. Where you from?" he asked Arne.

"Ya, well, I am a damn homesteader. I run sheep over on the Gumbo by Cal," Arne replied in his slow, deliberate English.

"A Norskie, eh? That's a good place for sheep and honyockers and Cal, there, out on the Big Gumbo."

Cal hoped Arne realized the man was joking in his ponderous way. Arne did not look amused. "I am from Norway, ya," Arne said slower than before.

"And a damn big Norskie too," Jimson said and

laughed. Cal laughed too, to show Arne it was a joke. But Arne didn't laugh. Cal felt a thickening in Arne, as if his body had suddenly become denser.

"You're looking at a man who can work circles around any of those so-called hands of yours," Cal said to Jimson. "Just about did me in this summer, keeping up with him. You watch him; he'll own half the state someday."

"The hell you say," Jimson said, but Cal heard the respect in his voice, and could sense Arne relax, the dangerous darkening growing lighter. "Well, I better stock up on bullets, boy," Jimson said, and turned toward the ammunition shelf behind the counter. "I don't trust those honyockers as far as I can see them. First one tries to settle on my land is getting himself shot, right, Slim?"

"Right, Unk," the boy grinned, showing teeth as yellow as his face. His fetid breath made Cal hold his own. Slim, Cal decided, was as unpleasant as he looked.

"Oh ya, ve ville," Arne said, his tone just barely civil. Cal knew it was meant as a measure of his contempt for Jimson and Slim, and saw that Jimson was wondering whether to take offense. Cal hurriedly held out his hand to Jimson.

"Nice to see you again, Jimson, Slim. We'd better go see about the horses, Arne."

Arne had already turned away, without offering his hand, to look for more items on his list. Cal watched Jimson decide not to make an issue of it, on the basis, Cal was sure, that a damn Norskie and a honyocker, to boot, didn't know any better.

When the men had gone, Cal went over to Arne and

shook his head at him. "Take it easy, will you? Those two had guns, or didn't you notice? If they had decided to be insulted, we'd be in trouble."

"Aah, don't worry, Cal. I'm an old sailor, remember? I take men like that apart with my bare hands." He almost spat on the floor, and then seemed to think better of it.

As they were about to leave, Peterson's wife, Alma, a tiny round woman with sparse brown hair worn in a skinny knot, came in from the living quarters at the back. She greeted Cal warmly, and when he introduced Arne, she took his hand, smiling up at him.

"Ole has told us of you and your beautiful wife, Ronnie."

"Rahn-nay," broke in Peterson. "My wife is not Norwegian, you see," he said to Arne.

"Next time you must bring Ronnie and her guitar," Mrs. Peterson said, ignoring him. "We have so little music here or beauty either, and she must be lonesome out there on the prairie."

"Thank you, Fru Peterson," Arne bowed gallantly over the little woman's hand. "She will be most glad of a friend to visit."

"And Cal, how good it is to see you," Alma said, turning to him. "I think it was last spring that we saw you last. Have you been back east again? Now you must both come and eat with us. The children will be eager to see you."

Cal and Arne agreed to her invitation. A pleasant evening ensued, Cal talking to Alma and the two Peterson sons, eight and ten years old, and Arne chatting in

Norwegian with Ole. Cal and Arne retired early, and the next morning, the second day they had been in Minnesela, Jimmie Porter awakened them at their lodgings. They had arrived in Minnesela late the night before, and deposited their herd in the stockyard holding pens before finding their rooms in the hotel and tumbling into bed.

After a hearty breakfast in the hotel dining room with the hungry boys, the four went down to the stockyard to see about their sheep, selling them to the stockyard buyer at what Cal deemed a good price. With this transaction accomplished, Cal went with Arne to the bank to deposit the money. Arne opened a new account, keeping enough money on hand to be able to pay the Porter boys for their work, and also entrusting them with the money owing to Hank Porter for their father's share of the sale. Cal also gave a generous tip to Jimmie and Henry for their good work. Then, with the Porter boys' help, Cal and Arne hitched up the wagons and drove to the Peterson Trading Center to load and pay for their goods. Having purchased all the supplies they needed, Cal and Arne wanted to set out at once. The Porter boys decided a little fun was in order and planned to stay in town overnight.

It was almost eleven o'clock before Cal and Arne got underway, and once out on the Medora Stage Road, which they would follow for a short distance, they saw that the weather had changed. Rain began to drizzle from an overcast sky, and a cold wind blew. Cal pulled up the collar of his coat and hunched himself down on the wagon seat for the long day's drive ahead. No lingering about by water holes today, he thought. The horses, too, settled down at once, pulling steadily into their collars. The road underneath was firm and hard. Cal foresaw no trouble, at least for the first part of the journey. A muddy Gumbo, however, could make things difficult.

Once out of the Belle Fourche river valley, Cal and Arne left behind the line of trees by the river, heading northeast on the rough wagon road they had come in on, gradually entering the Gumbo region. It began to rain harder, not a drizzle any longer, but a fine, steady rain.

Apprehensively, Cal watched as the wheels sank deeper and deeper into the ruts of the road, the mud beginning to cling. The horses pulled harder and harder. Finally, Cal, whose wagon was in the lead, pulled up. He found his shovel in the toolbox built on the outside of the wagon and began to clean the mud off the wheels. Arne, seeing what he was doing, did the same. The horses were only too glad to stop. They rested with their heads down against the fine driving rain. Cal saw they would not be able to go much farther this day and went back to consult with Arne.

"Well, Cal," Arne said calmly. He wore his sailor's oilskins and he looked an odd sight in the midst of the prairie. The horses rolled their eyes at him warily whenever he moved, although by now they were too weary to snort. "A few more miles are all the horses can take with this load, what do you think?"

"You're right," Cal said, feeling vaguely irritated at the delay. "We can probably make it to Rabbit Butte. There's wood and water there, and shelter for the horses. We can camp there. And hope this damn rain lets up," he couldn't resist adding.

The day had thickened into twilight by the time they

reached Rabbit Butte, not yet their turnoff point for the homestead. The butte looked desolate and lonely, sticking up out of the Gumbo. Small twisted clumps of juniper grew about the base, and in pockets here and there on the gray clay sides. Cal had stopped here before. He knew about a small spring on the south side, with good grass for the horses and protection from the wind.

After the horses had been watered and picketed, Arne and Cal scrambled about on the wet slippery slopes until they had enough dead wood for a small fire. It was as dismal a camp, thought Cal, as any he'd ever seen, but Arne seemed philosophical about it. They had drawn the two wagons up parallel to each other and had stretched a tarpaulin from the canvas tops of the wagons to cover the space between, forming a crude shelter. Another tarpaulin served as a groundcover.

There was plenty of food at least, and they cooked some fresh beefsteak they had bought in Minnesela in a skillet over the fire and mopped up the grease with fresh bread. They had oranges for dessert. Cal thought he had never tasted anything as good as the fresh, sweet fruit. He was thoroughly tired of the dried and canned fruit they ate most of the time. Cal brought out a packet of hard candies he had bought and gave some to Arne. By the time they reached the brandy and coffee, he was feeling better. He'd been nipping at the brandy bottle all day; it had been the only thing that made the day bearable. The road had softened faster than Cal thought it would, and he couldn't help recognizing it was going to be a long drag home. It occurred to Cal that he had been drinking a good deal since he came to the Gumbo, although he seldom was drunk. God, he thought, I'm not cut out for this sort of life. The fire warmed the front of him, and the brandy the inside, but his back was freezing. What am I doing out here anyway, he mused, a man who likes his luxury and comfort?

He passed the bottle to Arne, who took a good long pull. Now that his day's work was done, it seemed, Arne would drink. Once he'd told Cal that any amount of liquor affected him strongly, and so he was careful how much he drank. It was a sort of family failing, Cal gathered. Arne told of his father flying into wild "berserker" rages, and he himself had been in this state on several frightening occasions.

"It's something we Norse cannot help," he'd told Cal almost proudly. "It is how the Vikings nerved themselves up when they were raiding a village, you know. Only I think they have some kind of secret drink that is stronger than what we have. One forgets everything and does anything. But me, I like to know what I'm about."

So now he drank sparingly, as always, and when he reached the stage where he deemed it dangerous to go on, he refused the bottle, wrapped himself in his bedroll, appearing to listen as Cal drank and talked.

"Alaska," Cal told Arne, "it's truly the last frontier, Arne, but no ranching, I believe, in that country, and not much farming. In fact, I don't know what they do, except fish, I suppose. There are rumors of gold, though. I've been thinking I might join this expedition that is forming to go up there. Wouldn't be until next spring, anyway."

"You mean, give up your ranch here?" Arne sounded

incredulous. "What would you do with your sheep and land?"

"Sell it all, probably. Or just leave the land. I don't have much more than rent money in it, if you want to think of it that way. And sheep are bringing in good prices now." He paused, the obvious answer occurring to him, and, no doubt, to Arne at the same time. What a fool he was! Here he was trying to persuade Arne to leave on one hand and offering him every enticement to stay on the other. Waving land and sheep in front of Arne's nose was like putting water in the way of thirsty sheep. There was no turning either of them once they had a whiff of it. Cal took another swallow of brandy, the last in the bottle, and searched frantically for a way to divert Arne from what he'd just confessed. God help him, he'd meant to keep his plans to himself until he'd done all he could for Rannei. "That's just an idea, of course, nothing will come of it, I'm sure," he added lamely, and too late, for Arne had sat up in his bedroll, his sleepiness banished in an instant.

"Will you sell the land and the sheep to me, Cal? It is a wonderful chance for me to increase my herd and land, too. That is, if you really feel you must leave." He mistook Cal's hesitation. "I have the money. I've just about used up all my cash, but there is some extra we save, and the money in the bank now."

"Oh, hell–" Cal said helplessly. "It's not the money, Arne, you know that, but are you sure you want to stay? You know we found out about that land along the Belle, and in the Hills. You don't want to saddle yourself with more land and sheep, if there's a chance of–"

"We stay," Arne said decisively and held out his hand to seal the bargain.

God knew he hadn't meant to do this. God knew, but would Rannei? Where had he gone wrong? This was what he got for meddling in other people's lives. There was nothing he could do. Cal shook Arne's hand.

Chapter Seventeen

*R*annei became more certain with each day that passed that she would never see Arne again. If she thought of Cal, it was only that if Arne were lost, so would Cal be. How could Cal resist that malignant force out there, if Arne could not? She was sure that force had sucked them both down into the Gumbo mud, like the maelstroms that Grandfather Tryvason had told her about, that suddenly sucked down even large fishing boats during some great storm or upheaval of the sea, never to be seen again. Even Arne's great strength and powerful will would not save him. She had known all along that this would happen. They were not meant to live in this place, forsaken by all but the wolves and the wind.

All that remained for her now was to find her way out of this *Muspelheim*, this hell-place, and back to Norway. While the days passed and the men did not return, she went mechanically about the daily business with the sheep, the chickens and the cow, planning her escape, the details relentlessly working themselves out in an upper level of her mind. She and Tommy, her mind-plan went, would take the sheep, Cal's and theirs, in one large bunch to the Porters. The Porters would know where to reach Cal's parents to deliver the sad news, and she would send a telegram to her family, and Arne's, in Bergstromfjord. She would leave the sheep with Hank, who could sell them to another unwary homesteader. She'd ask Tommy to accompany her to Pierre.

Once she was in Pierre, she could find her way home to Norway. It was only here that she was lost. She had enough money, the dowry money her father had given her. She saw clearly now that this was what he had intended it for. He had not wanted her to be entirely dependent on her husband.

Her mother, too, had been concerned about her marriage to Arne, how they would manage as husband and wife. Rannei knew doubts had plagued both her parents.

Rannei had thought then, listening to them both with affection, that they did not know Arne as she did. He loved her so, he would do anything for her; together they could work out any problem. She could not explain to her parents how subtly, at times, she made him see her point of view. In Pierre, it was true, it was she who had bent, not he, but at least he had agreed to reconsider life on the Gumbo in six months, or a year at most, but she was beginning to doubt that promise now.

As the summer went on, she had grown increasingly uneasy. Arne seemed as set on staying here as he had been on her. He had set his mind on her when he was twelve and had never changed it, and now his obsession with the land showed the same degree of obstinacy. The Gumbo had become her rival for his attention, and it was true she resented Arne's fascination with a place that she hated.

But now, with her husband's disappearance, she had to face another reality entirely. Arne was gone, lost out there forever, and she would never see him again. She had thought once, not so long ago, that she could not live without Arne, that if he died, her heart would naturally stop beating. Yet here she was, sanely planning the rest of her life without him. Yes, she felt sane, and also heavy with a cold, dead numbness, which saw her through each day to its end. Somehow, she went on, replying calmly to Tommy's clumsy reassurances, penning the sheep at night, doing the chores, cooking her supper, brushing her hair. She thought of how happy her family would be to see her; her father had wept as she left. She did not think any further into the future than that.

The tenth day was a bright, windy day. The rain had ceased the day before and already the Gumbo was beginning to dry. As Rannei went about her chores, she looked up and saw the white canvas tops of the wagons bloom above the horizon. Instantly, her legs gave way and she sank to the ground, her arms crossed over her spinning heart. The white tops were slow-moving specks at first. As she sat watching, her blood roaring loudly in her ears, a sick feeling spread like melting pudding in her stomach. The imaginary life she had built for herself in the past days was scattered to the prairie wind, smashed like the overripe puffballs the children used to throw at each other in schoolyard battles. She felt a sharp stab of regret; she could not go home after all.

The wagon tops billowed suddenly larger, so close she could see the horses and the men on the wagon seats. Swallowing her disappointment, Rannei's heart steadied, her ears cleared, and a purging tide of joy lifted her to her feet. Arne! Arne was home! *Takk*, Freya, oh thank you! A troubling thought chased through her mind. Had she prayed to Freya to bring Arne safely home, or just numbly accepted the fact that he was lost? Surely, she had prayed.

Rannei ran across the prairie toward the oncoming wagons, letting the thought go, running to cleanse herself from head to toe of her evil thoughts. Joyfully, Oskar bounced ahead and around her.

She kept her eyes on the wagon, so when she ran over a burnout bank, her feet momentarily skimming through air, she felt weightless with joy, then landed gently on the flat wrinkled surface. Sometimes at home Rannei had felt this way. Running down the mountainside she would suddenly leave the ground and run on air, returning gently to the earth again much farther down the mountain. Or had she only dreamed it? The sensation, and the memory it conjured, was so vivid. Everything would be all right now. Arne was home, he loved her, she loved him, what couldn't they do together?

Rannei reached the track ahead of the wagons and, so as not to frighten the horses, put her hand on Oskar's head to quiet him as they waited for them to arrive. But the horses, she saw, were past frightening. They plodded along with their heads down, pulling wearily in a way she had never seen before, in a shambling gait. Tolander, if indeed it was Tolander, was gray instead of black, and same for Tor, the bay's once glossy coat flecked and splotched with gray mud, as were the wagon covers. Arne peered at her, red-eyed, out of a muddy mask. His shirt-sleeves were covered with mud from shoulder to wrist, and great murky streaks were smeared down the front.

When he saw her he stopped the horses, the mask of his face cracking into a smile. He held down his hand to help her up. She seized it and sprang up on the seat beside him, throwing her arms around his neck. He hugged her awkwardly with his free arm, kissing her on the mouth. His lips tasted gritty and little gobs of mud speckled the stubble on his chin. Even the stubble looked gray instead of golden. He looked, incredibly, like his father.

"Oh Arne," was all she could say.

"Hello, Rannei. Well, you see, we finally made it."

"Oh Arne, I thought you were lost in the Gumbo. I thought I would never see you again!"

"Now, *yndling*, it wasn't as bad as all that. We were stuck in the mud a few times, as you can see, and had to keep stopping to rid the wheels of mud. I tell you, it is hard to believe," he said with a note of respect in his voice. "The mud stopped the wagons, just stopped them; the horses could pull no more. Look at how tired they are. We must get them fed. It was too far for them to come today. I shouldn't have taxed them so much, except I worried about you, Rannei. Are things well here?"

Cal had pulled his wagon up beside them now, looking equally grizzled and mud-coated, and was listening in. She nodded at him in greeting.

"Oh–" she said. This was not the time to tell Arne about the wolves, Rannei knew, but she hesitated too long.

"The sheep?" Arne said anxiously, looking to the north from the direction she had come. "The sheep, they are well?"

Rannei looked to the north too. The sheep were grazing homeward; she could see them easily. But the sheep! Always the sheep first! Was Arne now more worried about the sheep than her? The happy weightless feeling evaporated. Rannei sat heavily on the wagon seat and, in English for the benefit of Cal, told them about the wolves. Arne was incredulous, and before she was through with her recital, he was swearing softly in English. He did not ask Rannei why she had not put the sheep in the corral and she did not bring it up.

"Six lambs dead! Such waste! We talk about wolves only yesterday, Cal and I. We see coyotes and Cal said the wolves do not bother much. Are you sure it was wolves, Rannei?"

"Yes, the biggest one, I think it was the mother, was much bigger and hairier than the coyotes we saw last spring. And Tommy saw them too."

"I get my hands on that old bitch she-wolf and her pups, she won't last long, I promise you that. I hope you think to butcher the lambs, Rannei?"

It was the question Rannei had been dreading. "One was too torn to butcher, even if I had thought of it, which I didn't. I was too worried about finding all the sheep and getting them together again. They were scattered all over, and I was afraid the wolves would kill some more."

Arne ignored her explanation. "By God! I know better than to leave a woman in charge! All that meat to waste! Just cut its throat with a knife to let it bleed and gut it out was all you had to do."

The injustice of it was like a blow in the face. The hot flush of anger washed away her sense of guilt over the unbutchered lambs.

"Damn yourself! You would have something to yell about if I had let the sheep scatter so we never found them! And besides, I don't know how to butcher, and I didn't even have a knife! It was hard enough keeping those bleating idiots together, not knowing whether you were coming back or not!"

Rannei knew, even in her anger, that in a minute or two he would be sorry and apologize, but she was so angry she could not wait for his apology. She stood up, gathered her full skirts in one hand, and leaped over the slowly turning wagon wheel, hearing in mid-leap Arne shout her name — "Rannei!" — in shock and outrage. She landed nimbly on the grass and was off up the trail, running for the house. She had seen, as she landed, Cal's horses shy tiredly, and had heard Cal speak to them, but she did not even look his way. When she reached the house, she slammed the door decisively behind her.

Rannei had seldom been so angry. Of course, Arne was tired and stunned with the loss of his precious lambs, but he shouldn't have accused her of ineptness. Just because she was a woman! She had done the best she could; if only he knew how she had suffered, and how lonely she had been!

She slammed kindling into the stove and threw in

chunks of coal on top of it. Of course, he expected her to fix his supper the same as usual and wait on him as she always did! Her hands went about the familiar tasks while anger blazed in her unwilling heart. She went to the root cellar for potatoes and cheese, noting automatically as she did so that the first sheep were appearing over the bluff above the creek, heading in for the night.

The next time she looked out, the wagons were pulled up next to the back step and Arne was leading his team to the barn. Cal was unloading some odd-looking gray coils from the back of his wagon and stacking them on the ground. That must be the barbed wire for the pasture. His team still stood in harness, looking as if they were asleep.

Rannei went into the house and busied herself peeling and cutting potatoes into the smoking skillet. She added onion and covered the pan. Later she would put in chunks of her own cheese. Arne loved potatoes prepared that way. She put slices of salt pork into another skillet. She was sick of the stuff. Her mouth watered for the fresh food she knew Arne must have in the wagon; an apple, or even an orange.

She went to the door and looked out. Arne was not visible, but Cal was. He looked up and smiled at Rannei. She greeted him a bit sheepishly and came out onto the step. She wondered if she should tell him about how his sheep were all right; Tommy had looked after them well.

Cal took a long burlap wrapped bundle from under the seat. A few withered leaves stuck out of one end.

"Here's your tree, Rannei," he said, handing it to her. "I did the best I could. It's a lilac bush; if you plant it by the corner there, it should grow."

"Oh Cal, a lilac bush! That's better than a tree! It'll have blossoms on it in the spring!" She flung her arms around him, bundle and all, and hugged him. His tired eyes lit up and he smiled a wide pleased grin.

"Had to look all over Minnesela for it. It came all the way from Iowa a few years ago, or its mother did. But it should be planted right away before the roots dry out. I'll just go dig a hole right now. My shovel's handy."

"No, you're too tired," Rannei protested. "It'll wait until tomorrow."

Despite her protests, Cal dug the hole anyway, and they planted the lilac shoot. As they worked, Cal said casually, "Sorry about the wolves, Rannei. I hope they didn't frighten you."

Rannei shot him a grateful look. At least Cal cared about how she felt. "A little, except at first I thought it was poor Oskar who was chasing the sheep, and then it looked like the Fenris wolf?"

Cal looked at her blankly.

"You know, Loki's pet?" she added. "Tommy saw them too, but they didn't kill any of your sheep. But I forgot to put the sheep in the corral that night, as I should have. Only don't tell Arne that," she whispered hurriedly as she saw Arne approaching from the barn.

"Of course not, and anyway, it's not your fault. There haven't been wolves in this part of the country for several years, although occasionally they do drift down from the Cave Hills. Sometimes they kill a lot more lambs than that, too."

Rannei's eyes stung with tears. Dear Cal, always so kind and understanding.

"I'd better check those potatoes," she said and escaped to the house, blotting her tears with her apron. She turned the potatoes, and went out again, ignoring Arne who was talking to Cal, and invited Cal to supper.

Arne gave a slight frown at the invitation, then quickly smoothed his expression into a welcoming smile. "Ya, you do that, Cal," he said cordially.

"Thank you, Rannei. Although it smells delicious, some other time," Cal said. "I must get these horses home, and Tommy probably is watching for me. The poor boy is probably out of food by now."

Arne urged Cal no further.

Once Cal departed, the sense of strangeness between Rannei and Arne grew. Arne went to carry water and put it on the stove for his bath while Rannei went out to the barn to milk the cow. When she came back, he was sitting in the laundry tub in front of the stove, his muddy clothes and boots in a heap on the step. To fit his enormous frame in the tub at all, he had to sit doubled up, his knees drawn to his chin.

Rannei turned away to hide her smile. Arne looked ludicrous with his head perched on his knees, bumbling about for the soap. He sat silently at first, but gradually the warm water began to have its effect, and, no doubt, Rannei thought wryly, he could only sit that way just so long without becoming uncomfortable. He sighed, stretched as best he could, and splashed loudly. He wanted her to begin, but she would not. This once he would be the first to say he was sorry. And it was his fault, too.

"Would you wash my back, please, Rannei?" he asked at last, humbly.

She turned to him triumphantly. "Of course," she said sweetly, and soaped his back and hair, then rinsed him with clean warm water from the stove. His ears had little clots of mud in them, and his neck was rimmed with sweat and mud. She washed as much of him as she could reach, and all the time she was doing this, he talked, telling her of the trip from beginning to end, and of Minnesela, a friendly little town.

"Next time we go," Arne said, "it will be to Belle Fourche. It is three miles farther than Minnesela, and already some of the stores are moving there. The store-keeper in Minnesela where we bought most of our supplies, Rannei, is brother to Lars Peterson. We met him on the voyage over, remember? We ate supper there one night, with the Petersons. Lars has a homestead on the Belle Fourche, and Ole is planning on moving his store to the new town."

He told her how the coming of the railroad to Belle Fourche meant they would be able to sell the lambs and wool there instead of making the much longer trip to Rapid City. Next time, Rannei would go along for sure. They would have Jimmie or Henry stay with the sheep. Mrs. Peterson, the storekeeper's wife, had urged him to bring her. She sent her greetings, and also a bundle of Ole's Norwegian newspapers.

Rannei listened to this flood of words, her heart softening by degrees. She thought how distressed he would be if she told him the plans she had been making when she imagined she'd lost him. She must have been a little out of her mind with loneliness, she decided. Rannei put water on for coffee and wiped Arne's back with the rough towel.

In the end, when he had talked himself out and they sat at the table after supper with their coffee, Arne turned to her. He asked her how affairs had gone at home in his absence, and she decided to say nothing at all about her fearful days. She told him about the wolves again, how strange and fearsome they had looked with their long teeth and the blood on their fur, and how unafraid of her they had been. He said nothing more about her failure to butcher the lambs, and made a muttered apology for yelling at her, which she accepted.

When she told him she had noticed something had been at the dead lambs, Arne nodded.

"Probably a coyote, but maybe the wolves are still about. I'll take the gun out tomorrow. Maybe I can kill them, or at least scare them away. If not, they may hang about all winter."

All through supper one or the other of them had gone automatically to the door to see if the sheep were heading toward the bed ground in a satisfactory manner. The sheep would gather on the bed ground of their own accord, and, once all were assembled, could be driven into the corral. Rannei corralled them every night now, ever since the wolves came. It was already growing dark.

Arne stood and went to put the sheep in. Rannei went out to shut up the chickens, which had already gone to roost. In the corner of the barn, penned off from the horses, was the surprise Arne told her to look for — two half-grown pigs, snuggled together in a mound of hay

Arne had thrown down for them. What a treat! Now they could raise their own bacon and ham. Rannei didn't know much about pigs, but Arne surely would. His father always kept pigs.

Darkness had already fallen when at last they began to unload the wagon. Arne was as eager to show Rannei all he had bought as she was to see it. The hundred-pound sacks of flour and sugar he stored in their bedroom corner behind the bed. Rannei marveled at the tight white weave of the flour sacks and the pretty floral pattern. There were a hundred uses for such fine material, but maybe first, once the sacks were empty, she would make curtains for the kitchen window.

He'd brought cases of canned tomatoes and vegetables which were taken down to the root cellar, as were the sacks of dried peaches and apples and prunes, rice and macaroni, and tins of Arbuckle coffee beans. There were tins of kerosene for the lamps, and wonder of wonders, a barrel of salted herring. Rannei squealed in delight when she saw it and flung her arms around Arne's neck.

"How did you guess I wanted fish more than anything?"

"Because I am a Norskie, too, *yndling*," Arne said, laughing. "Thank God there are Norskies in Minnesela too, and in the right place – our friend Peterson! He hauled these all the way from Minnesota for his special Norwegian patrons, and he had but one barrel left. He said he will order us another barrel with his next order. They are delivered to Minnesela all the way from home."

"Shipping prices must make them terribly expensive,"

Rannei said, watching Arne pry off the wooden lid, her mouth moist with longing for the salty, oily taste.

"These must last us until spring," Arne said. "They will keep well in the cellar, but let's have some now to celebrate."

Rannei poured them each a cup of coffee and they ate the little fish slowly, even the bony, paper-thin tails, crunching the tiny fragile bones thoroughly and licking the delicious salty taste off their fingers. Arne carried the barrel down to the root cellar then, so as not to tempt them, and they resumed the unpacking of the wagon. In one big wooden box, into which he had packed a number of small articles, Arne found the roll of Norwegian newspapers Mrs. Peterson had sent for Rannei.

"It is The Scandinavian, the Chicago newspaper, the one Uncle Jens sends when he is here. She says you must come stay with her next time we come to town. She is a good woman, Rannei, you will like her."

Rannei was sure she would too. To think that a stranger had known of her loneliness out here, and sent her something to read, the very thing, outside of a letter from home, that she needed most. She had written her parents when they had arrived there in June and told them to send letters in care of Porter Stage Station. Her mother, she knew, would write as soon as she received it. A letter from home was even now on its way across the ocean to her, she felt sure. When one did arrive, the Porters would find a way to bring it to her.

Arne was still rummaging around in the big box, which would make a wonderful cupboard, he said, with some shelves added. He took out a large pail of molasses, a box of cube sugar, which Rannei hid immediately behind a pitcher on the highest shelf so as not to tempt them. Such treasures had to be rationed out with the after-dinner coffee and for guests, if they ever had any. He also produced the thread and needles she had asked for, and some lovely warm red flannel Mrs. Peterson had picked out for her to make underclothing for herself and Arne for the winter.

As they unpacked and stored the items, Arne told her all the news he could remember that he had gathered from the Petersons.

It was getting late and Arne was asleep on his feet with weariness. "Come, Rannei, we go to bed. The rest waits until morning."

"But all this mess…" Rannei put down her cup on the wooden box and waved her hand at the heap of boxes, crates, and still unsorted supplies cluttering the room.

"It will keep." He reached over a sack of potatoes and pulled off her apron with one tug. Tossing it over the crate, he pulled her to him by the waist.

"I miss you, Ran," Arne said, fumbling with the buttons on her dress. One popped off and landed on the floor with a tiny ping. "Why always so many buttons? Never mind, I find it for you in the morning." He pulled her unbuttoned waist off her arms and her skirt over her head. "You are much nicer to sleep with than Cal. He snores." He tossed both waist and skirt over the bag of potatoes. "Now your hair, Ran…" The fine strands caught on his calloused fingers as he undid the thick plaits.

After Arne drifted off to sleep, Rannei crept out of bed quietly, brushed her tangled hair, plaited it quickly into her night braid, and blew out the still-burning lamp on the table. Sometimes Arne left it on when they made love, a treat as delicious to her as the pickled herring, but usually he was not so wasteful of the coal oil. Through the one window above the table she could see the late September moon shining brightly outside, transforming the frosty world to silver. The stars, dimmed by the moon's brilliant light, glittered faintly. Arne was sound asleep, breathing heavily through his mouth, or she would have woken him to share it with him.

She pulled the quilt up snugly around his shoulders and lay back down beside him without putting on her nightgown, feeling his human warmth all along her chilled naked body. On the brink of sleep, she remembered how the day had begun, her conviction Arne had been dead or lost. Now Arne was safely home, the peace restored between them. Still, the plans to leave the ranch if Arne did not come back that she had woven during those terrible days lay over her spirit like a residue of Gumbo dust.

Where had those thoughts come from? Closing her ears to them, she lay still, willing the music to dance in her mind instead, and there, finally, she heard it, that faint distant tune that had haunted her all her life — a tune played on no instrument she had ever heard, a tune without notes, or words, but so infinitely sweet and thrilling that she lay straining to hear, and so, listening, fell asleep.

Chapter Eighteen

he days had begun to shorten, drawing in upon themselves at either end. In the middle of October, the mornings were white with frost, the days warm and clear. It did not rain, and the wind blew day after day, bleaching the color from the grass until it stood almost white against the sky. Despite the cold weather at night, it was sometimes almost hot in the middle of the afternoon, so it was not quite cold enough for the butchering. Cal longed for fresh meat. He marked the yearling wether in his band of sheep that he would butcher, and noted how Arne each day tethered his wether in a choice plot of grass to fatten it, even feeding it a few oats intended for the horses.

Much to Cal's relief, Arne told him he had decided to defer the digging of a well until the following year. Cal would have helped with the well, of course. It was a job for two men. But Arne said he needed instead to fence in a horse and cow pasture. The pasture would be large enough to provide forage for the Bergstroms' horses and cow most of the year, even in winter, until the snow covered the sun-cured prairie grass. They had bought barbed wire in Minnesela and the Porters had brought in posts for fence when they came for the sheep shearing. Although Cal went over to the Bergstrom homestead almost every day to help Arne dig fence post holes, he spent most of his time at home. There was only one post-hole digger, anyway. Cal would be of more use when Arne was ready to set the posts and string the wire.

Besides, Cal was working on a secret project of his own. While Tommy herded the sheep and did most of the cooking, Cal spent most of his time out in the corral with the sorrel mare he had brought in from his herd of horses.

When he'd first came to the Dakotas, Cal had planned to be a horse rancher, and after leaving his position as horse trainer for Jimson, he'd bought fifteen horses from another would-be rancher who was selling out. Cal soon discovered that the reason the man was selling: the market for horses was no longer as profitable. Most ranchers and riders had their own strings now and were settled enough, so they no longer had a desperate need for horses. Realizing this, Cal decided sheep would be a better venture, so Cal reluctantly turned his horses loose on the open range and took to sheep ranching instead. He kept track of his horse band, though, and from time to time caught and trained a horse or two to sell to someone who needed a saddle horse or a team. Now, he knew, with the opening up of new lands for homesteading, horses would again be in demand.

He had wanted to train the sorrel mare the moment

he'd seen her running with the herd that spring. She'd be ideal for Rannei. The horse was one of the fillies he had paid little attention to at first, a scrawny yearling. Now she'd grown into a sleek two-year-old and he couldn't take his eyes away from how she floated across the prairie with a beautifully liquid gait.

Cal was too busy during the summer to take the time to train her, but in early September, just before the trip to Minnesela, he'd brought her in and began to work with her. She probably had some Arabian blood in her, he realized, with that height and head. She was tall for a mare, almost sixteen hands, with a deep sorrel coat, cream-colored mane and tail, and four white stockings. Cal's experienced eye saw that she was perfect for Rannei, gentle and affectionate, yet spirited, too. On his return from Minnesela, he spent another week or so with her, making sure she was ready. Cal grew so fond of her, in fact, he hated to give her up. He would have kept her for his own if she had been intended for anyone but Rannei.

One afternoon about coffee time, when Cal knew Rannei would be in from the day's herding, Cal rode over on sleek, black Jubal, leading the sorrel mare by the reins. She wore an extra saddle he had acquired in payment for a horse at one time and never used. The saddle was a little smaller than he liked, and too elegant, but it was perfect on the mare, and she lifted her feet daintily, as if aware of the pretty picture she made.

He found Arne and Rannei sitting on a pile of the posts intended for the pasture. Arne was on the second leg of the pasture perimeter now, at the west end. Another two weeks, Cal thought, surprised, and Arne will

be setting posts. He swung off Jubal before their astonished eyes.

"*Gledelig jul, Fru Bergstrom*," he said, with as courtly a
bow as he could manage. "Your Christmas present,
madam."

Rannei stared at him, then rose and reached for the
reins he held out to her as if in a trance. The mare pricked
her ears forward, and watched Rannei alertly.

"But it's not Christmas," she said.

"Christmas is a little early this year," Cal said, smiling.
"I just happened to find my errant horses close at hand,
several months ago now, and this little mare looked
lonely. Besides, she is too beautiful to be allowed to run
loose. Someone will surely steal her, and I have enough
horses anyway. You have to take her, Rannei. She has
nowhere else to go."

"But you can't do that, Cal," Rannei murmured,
looking at Arne.

Arne was scowling. Cal had foreseen that Arne would
not like him giving Rannei such a valuable gift, but he had
planned it all carefully.

"No, you can't do this, Cal," Arne said, echoing
Rannei. "This is a good horse, too good to give away. And
you've helped us enough. I say no."

"I'm not giving her to you, Arne," Cal pointed out.
"I'm giving her to Rannei for a Christmas present. I can't
let the horse run wild any longer, as I said, and I want
someone to have her who will love her and treat her
kindly. She isn't worth anything to me. I have enough
horses out there. And see, she likes Rannei."

Cal had kept the mare in check, as she had been

trained, but now she extended her nose and was gently snuffling Rannei's neck, taking in the scent of this strange new human. Rannei put her hand out slowly and laid it on the sleek neck, resting her cheek against the velvety nose. She looked at Cal, a look so deeply, humbly grateful that Cal felt his throat constrict.

"Thank you, Cal," she said softly.

They both looked at Arne, who took a sip from his coffee and ate a piece of rolled-up lefse. Cal and Rannei waited in silence, Rannei stroking the mare's neck.

"Well, all right," he said gruffly at last. "Since Rannei accepts, what can I say? It is too much, though, Cal."

Rannei's face blazed with joy. She wanted her husband's approval, Cal saw, and with that look she erased all resentment from Arne's face. What did it matter as long as Rannei looked like that, Cal thought, and he knew that Arne was thinking the same thing.

"Well, let's see you ride her," Arne said, all gruffness gone. Putting down his coffee cup, he rose from the posts and approached the mare, stroking her on the neck as she looked at him nervously. He slid the reins around her neck and held her as Rannei mounted in a graceful flash of skirts.

"The stirrups need adjusting," Cal said. The mare stood quietly while Cal shortened the leathers to fit Rannei's legs. "This isn't a sidesaddle," he said apologetically. "But I didn't think you would use one, anyway."

"Heavens, no," Rannei said, laughing down at him. "At home I always ride astride. The skirts are full enough, you see. Grandmother had the dressmaker make some divided skirts for me, and I will wear them to ride, later."

Her short full skirt was tucked neatly under her thighs and knees, almost like full trousers, so that only the top of her high boot showed. Even so, Cal could imagine what a sensation the sight would cause on a country road at home in Pennsylvania. All the ladies he knew rode sidesaddle.

"Don't go too fast at first," he warned as Rannei reined the horse about and started her off. "She is not used to you yet, and the skirt might frighten her."

"Rannei can ride anything," Arne boasted, as they stood watching her trot off on the mare. "Her father has good riding horses, not only *fjordhest*, the fjord horse, but fine saddle stock, and she rides them all and gentles the colts too, see?"

Cal watched as the mare broke from her disciplined trot into a floating gallop and Rannei floated with her. She had a good seat and knew what to do with her hands, Cal saw with appreciation.

"Her father is a great rider, and he teaches them all to ride well," Arne said.

They watched until Rannei and the mare grew small in the distance. "One poor old horse to pull the plow, we have on my father's farm," Arne went on. "Only the rich have horses in Norway, like Rannei's father. And here already we have three, and that horse you give Rannei is as good or better than anything Lars Andersen has. It's why everyone in Norway wants to come to America!"

It was a long speech in English for Arne. Cal thought how often he mentioned Rannei's father, and how it seemed to rankle, this difference that he imagined in their family status in Norway. Perhaps Rannei's parents had not thought Arne good enough for their daughter? Or perhaps Arne imagined they did not, and he was determined to prove it wasn't so?

"Here, I already have more land, more sheep, and horses, too, than I ever dream to own in Norway," Arne went on, bitterness apparent in his voice. "Me, the son of a poor *bønde*! Soon I have more land than Lars' family ever owns, and sheep to put on it. And I share my land with no one, as he must, with his sons. I own it all myself."

That certainly explained Arne's desire for land all right, Cal thought. But did Lars Andersen really felt this way about Arne, or had Arne only imagined it? Somehow, from what Rannei had told him of her father, Cal had not pictured him as a vain man. Did Arne see Cal's gift of the horse as another example of a rich *bønde* patronizing a poor one? Cal felt vaguely ashamed of himself. He thought he had known how Arne would react, but he saw now he hadn't gone deep enough. Perhaps all along Cal had been insulting this immigrant's stubborn pride, when all he'd wanted was to selfishly enjoy their companionship.

"I don't understand the class structure in Norway," Cal said. "But from what you have told me, it seems to be that way somewhat in the East, where I come from. Even out here, you know, the ranchers look down on the farmers, and the farmers on the homesteaders, and everybody hates the Indians. But perhaps here more than anywhere, a man is free to make his own class. People do respect a man who works hard and acquires land by his own efforts, no matter what his background.

"You remember Jimson, and his remark about

Norskies and sheep men? Even for all that, Jimson would be the first to be your friend if you are successful here, because Jimson respects hard work and 'hoss sense' more than anything. And you will make it, Arne, not because of the help I or anyone else gives you, but because of your horse sense and your ability to work harder than anyone I know. If I've helped you, you've repaid me a thousand times by simply being my neighbor and saving me from my lonely life. In the end, I think what counts here is what kind of man you are, not money or who your father was."

Arne was still gazing after the vanished horse and rider, but Cal could tell he'd been listening. Cal waited silently, afraid to spoil the moment of intimacy, so rare with Arne, by saying anything more. Arne glanced at him out of the corner of his eye. He did not seem embarrassed, as Cal thought he might. Perhaps he was glad to talk about it, Cal thought.

"I understand that you help us. You are a good man, and I know, too, you are lonely. Do not think I resent your gift to Rannei. I wish only that I could give her gifts like that. I know I do this, someday. Now, I thank you for the horse, Cal. You make Rannei happy."

It was simply said, but Cal sensed the emotion behind the words. Arne would do anything to make Rannei happy, except for the one gift she wanted more than any other. He could not leave the Gumbo. It reminded Cal of what he wanted to ask Arne, and he began, a little hesitantly.

"I really came about something else, too, Arne. Tommy wants to go home for a while, and I don't relish the thought of herding sheep. I would like to spend the winter working up a few horses into saddle mounts. Ole Peterson said his brother Lars wanted two good saddle horses and I think I know where I can sell a couple more. The rest I'll round up in the spring and sell in Pierre on my way east, or to someone in the Hills, maybe, who'll buy them on the range. You said you wanted the sheep and the land, and if you still want them, you can have them now. My band added to yours won't be any harder to herd than yours alone. You can have all my hay too, except what I need for my horses."

Arne went back to digging a hole without replying. Cal watched him draw the digger out, release the clod of clay, shining where the iron had smoothed it, and plunge it in again for the last digger-full. When he finished, he stuck the tool into the pile of dirt beside the hole.

"Of course I want the sheep, Cal. We agree on that. But I worry about the hay for all those sheep. You know I think you put up more. But then, it will be the same if they are yours. Ya, I take them now, and pay you for them too."

"There's no need for that right now," Cal said. "Wait until spring, if you like, or shearing time. I'm in no hurry."

"No, I take them now, I pay for them now."

Damn stubborn Norskie, Cal thought, looking at Arne's determined face. Where would he get the money? Probably, in his prudent fashion, he had some stuck away somewhere for emergencies. Cal thought fleetingly of the careful way Arne had spent his money in Minnesela, scrutinizing every item, deliberating before he bought the smallest thing. He'd assumed that Arne had to watch every penny, but he had enough saved, of course. He wouldn't have made the deal if he hadn't, not Arne. Yet Cal hoped it wouldn't leave them short.

"Good, then," Cal said, forcing a heartiness into his voice he did not feel. He held out his hand, and they shook to close the deal. "Now, let me spell you for a bit. Why don't you take Jubal and see if Rannei is having trouble with the mare?"

Cal watched Arne ride off, noting he was not the natural rider Rannei was. Then again, he rode as competently as he did everything else, and Jubal, Cal noted wryly, tried none of the tricks she sometimes did with him. Cal put his mind to the hole he was digging and tried not to think about the consequences for Rannei of the deal he'd just struck. Ah, hell, he worried too much. He would be out of the whole mess in a few months. He had made a mistake, this time, letting himself get involved. It was something he would avoid in the future.

A half hour later, his underarms running sweat, Cal looked up to see Rannei and Arne, atop the horses, loping back across the prairie. Rannei's coil of braids had come undone and her long plaits of hair floated out behind her. As they pulled up, he could see that her face was flushed and her eyes vividly blue. She looked again like the girl who had run ahead of the wagons in the springtime, picking the yellow buttercups and laughing with delight when she discovered a meadowlark's nest. She dismounted in a flash of blue skirts and white petticoats, still holding the mare firmly by the reins.

"Oh, Cal, she is perfect, and so lovely. I will name her

Freya, for the goddess of beauty. Unless you've already named her?"

"No, I left that up to you. Yes, Freya suits her, for she is a very vain lady, and requires much attention." He rubbed the soft nose that was nibbling his pocket for sugar. He had taken more pains than he usually did with this horse, but she had to be perfect for Rannei. In the process, he had grown too fond of her. He would miss the horse.

"Now, Rannei," Arne said with his old authority, "you must take her to the barn and rub her down and give her some water after she is cooled. She can be tied to the stanchion beside the cow tonight. I make her a stall tomorrow."

"Yes, Arne," Rannei said meekly, giving Cal a laughing smile over her shoulder. "Thank you, thank you," she said as she went by, brushing his cheek with her lips. "I love her."

Arne was watching, smiling. He waited until Rannei was out of earshot, then he said to Cal, "And I pay you for the saddle and bridle. They are not cheap." Cal started to protest, but Arne silenced him firmly:

"Ya, I will. Now I milk the cow. Come with me and visit."

The sun, Cal saw, was nearing the western horizon, and from the near distance he heard the bleating of sheep. "No, it is late, Arne, and I had better cook supper tonight, or Tommy will fire me."

He swung up on Jubal, waved goodbye to Arne, and to Rannei, who came to the door of the barn to wave to him, and headed for home. Everything was settled as he wished, but he felt none of the eagerness he usually did at the conclusion of an old business, the beginning of a new adventure. In any case, it was too late now to undo whatever it was he had done. Shrugging off his worries, Cal nudged Jubal into a gallop.

Chapter Nineteen

*R*annei was happy almost in the old way. It was
exhilarating to fly over the prairie on the back
of the fleet mare. She felt in control of Freya, and of the
sheep, and the prairie. From her new vantage point on
Freya's back, the Gumbo looked less threatening, merely
land and grass. There was something between her and it
now, some other force to be reckoned with, but this force
felt friendlier. Rannei could pretend, no, believe, that the
mare was really Freya in disguise. For the first time, she
was enjoying the tedious job of sheep herding.

Meanwhile, with Cal's help, Arne set about putting the
posts in the holes they'd dug, then strung the barbed wire
for his horse pasture. Now the horses and cow could be
turned out in the pasture daily, one less chore to do since
the animals' picket lines did not have to be changed
several times a day.

One evening about a week after Rannei received the
gift of Freya, she sat in her rocking chair after supper knit-

ting a mitten for Arne, humming a little as she rocked gently back and forth, her mind on whether to make the star point of the pattern begin on the cuff or start it below the ribbing. Arne, when he began to speak, took her entirely by surprise. He spoke long and eloquently, much as he used to when sharing his dreams, and Rannei listened without interrupting him, her hands idle on the knitting, her eyes fixed on his face.

"We will be rich one day, Rannei," Arne finished. "Rich! Who would believe we would have this much land already, and sixteen hundred sheep! We will save our money, and when the land around us is put up for sale, we will be able to buy it all. And all those lambs to sell next fall, and the wool from all those sheep. Next spring we will hire Tommy as herder. I'll need help with the lambing anyway, and you won't have to herd sheep like you did this summer."

The words, and their ominous meaning, were coming at Rannei too fast. The salient facts stuck in her mind and she went back over them, trying to absorb what Arne was saying. Cal was leaving. That was shocking enough. She had known he was thinking about it, but apparently, his plans were already made. Now they would have no neighbors at all. Besides, she would miss him. And he was selling Arne his sheep and land. She could not seem to grasp it.

"Cal is leaving?" she asked incredulously.

"Yes, but not until spring."

"And he is selling you his land and sheep?"

"Ya, as I told you, Ran."

"You have told him we will buy them?"

"Ya. We talked about it in Minnesela, and when he brought you Freya he asked if I would take the sheep now, so he won't have to keep Tommy here all winter. It is as easy to herd a big bunch as a small one, so it won't matter to us. Cal will stay here until spring to work with his horses, and he will let me have his hay if I need it, too."

Rannei could not believe it. Arne, the sensible one, seemed to have lost his wits. It was so unlike him to agree to take the sheep and land without paying for them, presuming on Cal's friendship. "But Arne, the money. How will you pay him?"

"We have your dowry money, Rannei."

The blood of anger and betrayal rushed to her head with such force she thought it would burst. The words tumbled about in her throat but she could not sort them out in any coherent fashion. Arne was looking at her anxiously.

"You did all this, it is settled?" Her voice was so thick and choked it felt like it was not her own.

"We shook hands on it. I did not have time to discuss it with you, Ran." His tone was almost conciliatory. "But you know the money was for some great need, your father said, some emergency, and this is a wonderful chance, Rannei. He is selling them to me very cheaply. We would never have such a chance again. We must have that land, and those sheep, Rannei, we must!"

"But that is my money!"

"It is our money, Rannei. I know I should have consulted you, but there was no time, and–"

"And you knew I would not agree. That money is mine,

mine alone. Father told you that, in front of me, I heard him. I was to use it for what I wished."

"Ya, but it isn't your money alone, now, Rannei. It's yours, yes, but what is yours is supposed to be mine, isn't that true? Just as what is mine is yours."

"And not only that," Rannei went on as if she had not heard him, "but to buy those sheep as if you intended to stay here forever! I have not agreed to stay here yet. We were to talk about it in six months, and it is almost that now, and I tell you, I don't want to stay here at all. And I certainly don't want more sheep!"

"Now listen, Rannei. What do you mean, not stay here? I thought there was no question of that. You surely don't expect me to walk off and abandon this place after all the hard work I've put into it!"

"But you agreed we would decide for sure in six months! Why did you say that when you had no intention of leaving? You lied to me!"

"No, I did not lie. I did not know I would want to stay here myself. But I can't leave here, Rannei. It's all I've ever wanted. It's perfect."

"But what about me, Arne? I hate it! I'll never be happy here. I won't live here the rest of my life!"

"Not live here," Arne repeated. "But where would you go, Rannei?"

In one swift motion, Rannei dropped to the floor, and threw her arms around his knees. She felt him flinch as the knitting needle, still in her hand, pressed against his leg.

"Oh Arne, not where would I go. Where would we go? Us. Anywhere. I'll go anywhere you want, anywhere but here. We could go to the Belle Fourche, or the Black Hills, or up into Montana somewhere along a river. Oh Arne, Arne, I beg of you, please, if you love me, take me from here. I cannot — cannot — live here. Something terrible will happen if you make me stay here."

She felt Arne's hands on her shoulders, trying to raise her. She resisted with all her strength, clinging to his knees. He must promise, he must. She heard his voice from above her, heard the pity, love, exasperation, and underneath it all, the inexorable will.

"Rannei, you are not yourself. You will think differently tomorrow, after you have thought it over some more. Think of me, Ran, and how we planned in Norway for this. Don't you see we can't leave now? It is the one chance I've waited for all my life. I have here everything I have always wanted. In time, you will like it too. I know it is not quite what you thought it would be, but you must try, Rannei, for my sake."

Rannei sat back on her heels and looked up at him. "I have tried, Arne. I have tried for nearly six months, and I hate it more all the time. I have done what I promised. Now, you must keep your promise."

Arne looked perplexed. "But what did I promise? Come on, Rannei, get up off the floor. I said only we'd try it for six months or a year, and see how we liked it."

It was true. He had not promised more than that. She had assumed that if she didn't like it, they would go somewhere else, and if Arne balked, she could talk him into it. She hadn't counted on Arne becoming so obsessed with the Gumbo.

"Well, then, if you won't leave, I will. I will take my

dowry money and go back to Norway for a while, until you come to your senses."

Arne looked stricken. "Are you crazy, Ran? You'd go home and leave me? What a fool they would think you to come running home without your husband six months after you left!"

"Oh, no, they wouldn't. Mother and Father would understand. That is exactly why Father gave me the money. He knew I might need it someday, and he was right."

"Bah! Your father and his fine ideas! He certainly made good use of his wife's dowry money! I don't care what he says, when a man marries, his wife's dowry is his too, by rights. Who ever heard of giving it to the wife alone?"

"He gave us all that other money, too, that was your part of the dowry. This money was mine for a wedding gift, and you can't have it, not for those sheep or land or anything else, unless I agree."

"You damn stubborn woman," Arne roared, his face flushing bright red, his eyes bulging. "That money is mine too, I say. And we're not leaving here, and neither are you."

Rannei rose to her feet and gathered up her tangled yarn. Some of the stitches had slipped off the needle. She began to put them back on carefully, one by one. Her tears had stopped. She looked at Arne coldly.

"You love this damn land better than you love me. You never acted this way in Norway."

"Well, neither did you!" Arne said, practically spitting with anger. As his control slipped, Rannei felt hers harden. She would never give him the money, never.

"I told Cal I will buy those sheep, and I will. You will have to do as I say. A wife has to obey her husband!"

"So that is what you truly think, is it," Rannei said icily. "All that talk about respecting me as a person was just to impress my father, I suppose. Well, whether you know it or not, I am a person, with just as much right as you to make decisions, and if I decide to go home for a while, I will use my money for it."

"*Faen Yaevel,*" Arne bellowed, completely out of control. He started toward her, his fist raised. Rannei's blood rose hotly in her face, and she felt an insane urge to leap at him like a cat and sink her claws into him. She thrust the knitting needle at him like a knife. Her voice was chilling, and it stopped Arne short, his fist inches from her face.

"Touch me and I stab you!"

For a second, they stared at each other, Arne with his clenched fist upraised, Rannei with her knitting needle pointed as his gut. Gradually, the red faded from Arne's face and he backed away, his eyes bewildered.

"Rannei..."

Without a word, Rannei dropped her knitting and its needles into the rocking chair and walked across the room to the water pail. She took the dipper from its nail on the wall, filled it from the pail, and sipped the cool water slowly. She felt sick. Had she and Arne really been on the verge of hurting each other?

She stood there with her back to her husband, hearing him open the door and go outside, to the privy, probably. She waited until the door shut, then darted into the bedroom corner, and unpinned the soft leather bag filled with her dowry money from her chemise where she'd carried it on her travels. Taking the key from the niche in the log where she kept it, she unlocked the dowry chest, and thrust the bag deep into the corner, locked the chest, and hid the key in a new place, a space where the roof met the top log.

Trembling, she pulled off her clothes and put her nightgown on. By the time Arne returned to the house, she was in bed, far over on her side, the covers over her head, her hair still in its day plaits. She could not remember ever going to bed before without brushing her hair. When he came in, she lay very still, trying to quell the nausea that rose in her throat. Arne — Arne had been going to hit her! And she had wanted to hit him back.

The thought of the terrible scene would not leave her. It felt wrong to be so angry at Arne. But if she submitted to him now, she would never have any money of her own, and be trapped here forever. In back of it all was a tiny new awareness that grew and grew until it blotted out all else. Her husband thought of her like that. He had treated her like his property, his sheep, as if she had no mind of her own. How dare he! Love had nothing to do with this. This was a battle for possession of her very soul.

She had tried to live on the Gumbo as she had promised. But he didn't care how much she hated it here. It was what he wanted, so they must stay. Only she wouldn't. She refused. He had lied to her. He had never meant to leave. As Arne climbed into his side of the bed, she felt his lumpish anger gradually soften into the heavy breath of sleep. Rannei still lay rigid and unmoving until, in the early predawn, she heard the rooster crow.

IN THE LAST week in October, it turned cold, although it did not snow. The wind whistled and shrieked out of a sullen grey sky finding the minutest cracks between the thick cottonwood logs. Arne hunted down the cracks methodically, carrying his bucket of mixed gumbo clay and green cow manure, chinking the outside, while Rannei ran her hands over the inside to feel the draft, then stuck a straw through to show him where the cracks were. His hands grew rough and red from the contact with the cold, wet clay and colder wind, but Arne persisted until everything was well chinked, then put another coat over the first layer.

This was all done with the greatest politeness from them both. Since that dreadful night, neither of them had mentioned the dowry money again, although Rannei moved the key to a new hiding place, in a butter crock where Arne never looked. She suspected he was as miserable as she, but she would not speak of it, and neither would he.

When it came to the herding, she did not have to take the sheep so far out on the prairie now to graze, and Freya could carry her swiftly back and forth to the house, so she could sometimes leave them for several hours if the weather was not too cold. As it grew colder each day, the sheep kept on the move and did not hang about the watering hole in midday, as they had in the summer. There was no further sign of the wolves.

Once Arne had successfully chinked the house for the winter, he took over the greater part of the herding, so

Rannei was free to make the inside of the house as snug and cheery as she could for the winter. She spread her treasured braided rugs on the floor, and hung the wall tapestry she'd finished weaving when she had been seventeen and already planning on marrying Arne. The scene was of Freya, the beautiful one, bearing with her a fallen warrior who she had chosen to take back with her to Asgard, home of the gods. Against a bright blue background, Freya was driving her cat-drawn chariot across the *Birvrost*, the Rainbow Bridge. Until now the tapestry had lain carefully rolled in the bottom of the dowry chest. Rannei had been afraid the dust and heat might harm it in the summer, but now she needed the bright colors in the dreary fall weather. Hung on the log wall, it glowed with a light of its own, like a fine oil painting.

With the colder weather, it was time for the butchering. The wether Arne had tethered out all summer was sacrificed first. Rannei knew how this was done, and she did not watch, glad to be riding Freya that day, out with the sheep. Once when Rannei was a small girl, she'd watched her father butcher a lamb, and she never forgot the strange, almost passionate look on her father's usually gentle face as he drew a deep cut with the knife across the woolly throat. The blood had spurted out right into her face, and for days Rannei could not get rid of the taste and smell of it from her mouth. When she came in that afternoon, the sight of the liver and heart soaking in a pan of cold water on the porch made her gag slightly. But she washed the organs several times in cold water, and that night as she fried them up and some mutton chops too, the delicious aroma overcame her squeamishness. Cal and

Tommy stayed for supper, all of them hungering for fresh meat. They all ate until they could hold no more.

The meat was hung in the cool wind to age for a few days. More could be butchered as needed, through the winter. Next year, Arne said, if they were lucky there would be a pig to butcher. Before warm weather came in the spring, they would butcher more wethers, and smoke and dry the meat for a summer supply.

The sheep were intoxicated with the cool weather and their own devilishness, it seemed to Rannei. They were on the move constantly, galloping about, eating on the run, snatching mouthfuls of grass as they half-walked, half-ran in that queer, loping gait that kept a person on foot moving at a fast walk to keep up.

Now that she had Freya to ride, Rannei did not mind. Rushing along over the prairie, she handled the sheep with an ease that secretly delighted her. The sheep, too, seemed to respect her more, and paid attention when she yelled at them, turning back and heading meekly in the right direction. Oskar loved to frisk along at Freya's heels, although sometimes he dropped behind when she went too fast. When he caught up to her, he'd hang his tail down and look at her reproachfully.

The horse gave Rannei power, she knew, power which she as a woman lacked. Is this how Arne feels, she wondered, this sense of control, of being in charge of life? From the mare's back, she could see the two tracks leading out of the Gumbo, one toward the Porters and Pierre, and the other to Minnesela. Either way led to civilization. Freya could take her there, she mused, considering. It was not so impossible now.

Then another thought began to intrude on every daylight hour, and much of the nighttime ones too. Rannei was two weeks overdue for her monthly period. It had been two weeks since the quarrel with Arne, and perhaps that had upset her schedule, as she knew could happen. Deep inside, however, the sickening certainty grew that she was pregnant. It was surprising it hadn't happened earlier, but now, after what had happened between her and Arne, Rannei realized what a complication a baby would be.

Privately, she grew terribly angry with herself. She knew she should be happy to have a child, but she just couldn't feel that way. So she ignored her queasy stomach as best she could. Then one morning, as she fried lamb chops for breakfast, she had to rush out in the yard to be sick. When she turned to go back into the house, she saw Arne standing in the door watching her.

She pushed by him without a word, but the smell of the meat made her feel shaky. Arne pushed her gently onto the bench at the table, and finished cooking breakfast himself. He looked pleased all through the meal, while she quivered with hatred, unable to force a bite between her lips. As Arne went out to the sheep, he laid his hand for a moment on her hair, the first time he had touched her since the night of their quarrel.

"Take care, Ran," he said as he left.

When the door closed behind him, Rannei burst into a passion of tears. She cried and sobbed for an hour, but that night she and Arne resumed making love. The tension had eased outwardly for Arne, anyway. Now that he thought she was pregnant, he seemed to consider that reason enough for all her past actions, and he began to humor her with a solicitude that Rannei found comical at times and at other times maddening.

She herself felt calmer now, drained of all emotion, and without consciously admitting it to herself, she went about the business of trying to abort the fetus growing within her. She lifted impossible weights, heavy scuttles of coal, and pails of water to try to press it out of her. She rode Freya until she was exhausted, hoping the jarring might do the same. She took long, hot baths, sitting cramped in the little tub, so as to loosen it from her womb.

Nothing worked; she was too strong. Rannei remembered her mother saying it was a sin to abort a pregnancy. "We have no business playing God," she once overheard her mother telling someone. Rannei did not believe this, because she did not believe in her mother's conception of God. Stronger, more powerful gods dwelt here, in any case, and only from them would she find help. Alone on the prairie, face down on the cold ground, she prayed to Frigg and Var, and especially Freya, her own special goddess. It was useless to beg any favor of Odin or Thor. They were men and did not concern themselves with such matters.

Day followed day, and gradually the morning sickness lessened. As Rannei's appetite returned, in despair, she realized there was nothing she could do about the pregnancy. Instead, she must plan, and think out what she was going to do. Surely Arne loved her still. He seemed happy about the child, and although he had not mentioned the money again, she still waited for him to do so. They must talk about it like civilized people. Surely, they could work it out. She must be patient with him, love him, talk to him. There had to be a way.

As she waited for the right time to talk to Arne, slowly, Rannei's feelings began to change toward the alien being growing within her. She no longer wanted to purge it from her body. Stubbornly, it clung to life, was a part of her, after all, and a part of Arne, too. One day, she thought she felt a strange fluttering in her womb, like a butterfly held in the hand, and a wonder and fierce protectiveness filled her toward that minute bit of life. Rannei would survive, she decided then, and so would her child.

Arne seemed to think she'd resigned herself to remaining on the Gumbo. The intentness left his gaze, and he ceased watching her so closely. Rannei was glad for the respite. She had to conserve her will and energy until she needed them. She went about her daily tasks efficiently, without thinking about what she was doing. She drew into herself. At one point, Arne told her that the look in her eyes reminded him of cows and ewes and mares about to give birth, that veiled and inward, waiting look.

He did not mention the dowry money, and Rannei could not. They had to talk about it, but neither of them could begin. Rannei became increasingly uneasy, for she knew Arne too well to suppose that he would give up his plans so easily. She felt sure she could convince him, especially with the child coming. The Gumbo was no place to raise a child. Surely, even he could see that. A queer, stubborn pride held her back from saying anything. Arne knew how she felt; she had made her position clear.

Maybe, she decided, in his methodical way, he was thinking things through. With the pasture done, Arne was more often about the house. Either he or Rannei would ride Freya to take them swiftly to check on the sheep. Freya needed and enjoyed the daily exercise while Tor and Tolander were quite content to stay in the corral or barn. They were not saddle horses and knew their place, Arne joked. The two of them were together more, and in the lengthening evenings they sat together, Arne's hands always busy, braiding a new hackamore, or mending a harness, Rannei with her knitting or a book. Neither mentioned the dowry money.

Chapter Twenty

One cold, grey afternoon, the very last day of October, Rannei sat alone, playing softly on her guitar, singing her favorite songs to herself. She had stayed in the house all day, feeling tired and lazy. The nausea, which she thought was finished, had returned. Arne had come in for lunch, but rode away on Freya right afterward. Rannei was glad to be alone. She made herself a pot of tea and sipped it all afternoon, doing nothing but enjoying herself.

As twilight came on, she rose several times to look out the door, to see if either Arne or the sheep were coming. If he did not come soon, she would have go out and milk the cow, which would spoil her rare day of luxury. Moving slowly about, she washed potatoes and coated them with grease, putting them into the oven beside the roast that Arne had cut from the lamb that morning. As she did so, she sang to herself one of her favorite songs, "Synnove's

Song." She had sung it many a time to Arne in the days of their courtship.

> *Oh, thanks for all since the days long past,*
> *When we played about on the purple heather!*
> *I thought that the merry times would last*
> *Til we should grow old together.*
> *I thought we should run on hand in hand*
> *From the birches – how we used to love them!*
> *To where the Solbakke houses stand,*
> *And on to the church above them.*

The smell of the roasting mutton made her queasy. She had hoped that was behind her, but she supposed it was better than eating too much and growing fat. Her mother said there was no excuse for a woman losing her slimness. Even after five babies, Kristin remained slender and straight. "A little willpower is all one needs," her mother used to say, about that and so many other things, "a little willpower…"

The thought of her mother brought tears to Rannei's eyes. On afternoons like this in Norway, they often sat together in the big, wood-timbered room, in front of the fireplace, drinking coffee and talking together. Almost every day there would be visitors, some woman from the village bringing news, or one of Father's friends, down from Bergen.

After school and play in the late afternoon, the noisy little brothers would troop in, chattering and laughing, each eager to tell Mother and Rannei the latest happening in their world of village and farm. They would throw their jackets and books down on the table until Rannei made them hang their jackets up where they belonged and put their books away. Then they would all settle down before the fire for coffee with hot milk in it, and fresh-baked cookies, until it was time to help with the chores. After the animals were fed and the chores done, the lamplight glowing through the window beckoned them from the cold air in to supper.

Rannei wiped her cheeks with her apron and went to the door again to see if Arne was coming. It was almost twilight now, later than usual for the sheep to be coming home. She could not see Arne, but spotted the first of the sheep streaming down the hill toward the creek on their way to the bed ground. She stood watching them in the open door, the cold, chill air damp and smelling of snow. She loved to watch the sheep come home like this, trailing down the hill, one behind the other, treading the same path they walked the night before and the night before that, long thin grey lines winding down the hill like beads spilling from a pan.

There were always three lines, and the same leaders always led them. Only the lambs disdained the assigned order and cavorted, rushing in a mob to the steepest part of the hill, the clay bank overhanging the creek. They ran along the rim playing follow the leader, defying gravity, hanging, it seemed, by their sharp little hooves, carried across by their momentum, then turning and rushing back faster than before. As always, Rannei held her breath, expecting to see one of them fall, but then they were all safely across. In another month or two, Rannei knew, the lambs would lose their playfulness and turn into stodgy sheep, like their dams.

The leaders reached the creek crossing, and Rannei began to swing shut the door. Since all the sheep were on the hill, Arne would not be far behind. But then she paused, for over the edge of the hill came not Arne, but a fresh surge of sheep bunched together as if being driven. Her first thought was that Cal's band had mixed with theirs somehow. Turning, she snatched her cloak off the hook beside the door, and spun around to go out, then stopped, staring. Behind the sheep, two horsemen now appeared. Arne, on Freya, and Cal, on Yellow Bird. Driving the sheep in one band!

In that first blinding moment of realization, Rannei felt a wrench of dismay, for both herself and Arne. How could he dare to do it? How could he so wantonly destroy what could never be restored between them?

"No," she screamed, "No, Arne!"

She whirled around and ran across the kitchen to the shelf where she had hidden the key to her dowry chest inside the butter crock. It was still there. She snatched it and flung herself across the room to the chest at the end of the bed. Trembling, she knelt on the floor and turned the key. Lifting the lid, she saw at once that the blanket on top of the contents was rumpled and not replaced exactly the way she had folded it, and the skein of yarn on top was out of place. Even as her fingers dove frantically into the corner where she had hidden the money, she had lost hope. In despair, she pulled the contents of the chest across her lap—lengths of homespun, embroidered pillowslips, skeins of yarn, tablecloths. The money was gone. Arne had taken it and bought Cal's sheep.

Bubbles of anger, desolation, terror, and panic erupted inside her, rising in her throat. She retched, and her eyes clouded with a red-black mist. Almost all her life to this moment had been firmly based on Arne; he was her other self, the one person she knew better than anyone, the very bedrock of her life. That he had done this to her struck her at her deepest concept of selfhood. If Arne did not listen to her, if she had no control over him, she had none over anyone and she was not the person she thought she was.

Rannei remained on the floor, kneeling before the chest, holding tightly to the carved wooden handle on the front. The blood roared in her ears and her heart pounded sickeningly. She heard someone panting, and realized it was herself. She was like a person dying and being reborn, and in a way, she knew she was. The old Rannei, the child she had once been, no longer existed. Her love for her husband was dead. Rannei sank back upon her heels and let go of the handle. Her palm was marked with red lines where she had held on.

Men's voices sounded outside. She heard Arne say in a loud, cheerful voice, "*Faen Yavel!* What's the door open for, Rannei? Rannei, you there? Hey, Ran!"

She looked up. Arne had entered the house and was standing in the middle of the kitchen, looking through the pulled-aside curtain to where she sat amidst the treasures of her dowry chest. For a second, they stared at each other, then Cal appeared behind him, looking puzzled, saying cheerfully, "Hello, Rannei!" He glanced at Arne uncertainly when she neither moved nor spoke.

The smile faded from Arne's face, and his red face flushed redder. He crossed the floor in two quick strides and jerked the curtain across. "Rannei's not feeling well today," he said, and in answer to Cal's embarrassed murmurings, insisting, "No, hell, man, have some coffee first."

Soon the door closed behind Cal, and his footsteps faded down the path. Then Arne was back at the curtain again, looking in at her, as she stared back.

"Are you all right, Rannei?" His voice came from a great way off. "Listen to me, Ran! I had to take it; I had to. It was the only way we could buy those sheep and now they're ours, and we have Cal's land too. We're rich, the biggest and richest ranchers in the Gumbo. Rannei, listen!"

He slipped to his knees beside her, his arm around her rigid back. "Come on, now, Rannei. It isn't that bad. Rise up, and let's have supper and celebrate. I'm hungry as a wolf!"

She could smell the whiskey on his breath. He and Cal must have been drinking all afternoon to celebrate their bargain. She turned her head and looked him full in the face. His eyes had that glassy blue-white hue from too much drink, and his face was flushed with liquor and the cold wind. Against the vivid coloring of his face, his golden eyebrows and mustache shone, each hair vibrantly alive. His face seemed distorted somehow, each feature slightly askew so he almost had the appearance of a stranger. She felt as if she had never seen him before.

Arne, mistaking the flicker in her eyes for interest, pulled her to him and kissed her on the mouth. She did not move nor turn her head, but her lips felt numb and dead. Arne felt it too. "Well!" he said uncertainly, getting to his feet and trying to draw her up with him. "Well! Can you say anything, Rannei?"

Rannei began mechanically to smooth and fold the contents of the chest as she put them back in. Arne sat down on the bed.

"You stole my dowry money." Her voice crept out of her rusty throat.

Arne's smile dimmed, but did not vanish, instead subtly shading into a grimace. He looked down at his big hands, which rested on his knees.

"I did not steal it, Ran. I took what is ours and bought that land and sheep for both of us. I ask your pardon, but you forced me to do it. You know you wouldn't let me have it."

"It was mine. You stole it."

"Stop that! I tell you, I did not steal it. It was ours, not yours."

"Then if you will admit it is mine, too, I'll take the half the sheep back to Cal and get half of the money back."

"It is yours, but mine, too. We are man and wife and I acted for both of us, for your good, as well as mine."

"Only I'm to have no say in my own good, is that it? If the money was ours, as you say, then I had as much right to use it as you did. But it wasn't ours. It was mine. Father gave it to me. You heard him say it was mine, and that we had to agree, at least, on what to use it for, but we didn't even talk about it. How dare you!" she screamed suddenly, jumping to her feet, tossing the last blanket into the chest and slamming down the lid. "How dare you snoop around in my chest, steal my money, and treat me like this? You had no right!"

"Now, Ran," Arne, said retreating as she advanced toward him. "We talked about this the other night. I don't like to treat you this way; I want to talk things over with you always, but sometimes a man has to have the final say. A wife cannot make all the important decisions when it's the husband who knows more about it. I'll always take care of you and protect you, but I have to do what I think is right."

"Then use your own money and allow me the same right. It's not even the money that's the most important, but that you did it without talking to me about it, as if I wasn't a person, but a piece of property like that cow out there!"

"Rannei, you must not carry on this way. It's bad for you, and the baby, too. What's done is done. I'll admit it was wrong to take the money without your consent, but I will not let you order me around like some old fishwife."

Rannei heard the rising temper in his voice. Arne had bent all he was going to, but she could not give in to him. It wasn't the money, really; it was a question of her very survival as a person, independent and free.

"Now listen to me, Rannei," Arne was saying. "That is enough of this nonsense. Let's settle this for once and for all. I am staying here on the Gumbo, and so are you, and so are our children. When we go home, we'll all go together, when I can afford it. You are my wife, and the sooner you realize it the better for both of us."

Rannei knew Arne believed he was being just. She also knew she must accept his decision if they were to continue as man and wife. But if she did, it meant she would always live on his terms, and that the Rannei Andersen she had known would simply cease to exist. She could not give in. Her feelings were strong on this matter; they were out of her control. She wished then with all her heart it could be different, that she could love the Gumbo and be the wife to Arne he wanted. But it wasn't possible. She shook her head slowly.

"Arne, don't force me. I will hate you, and I don't want to hate you. Don't force me to live here like this. I simply cannot. Do you want me to pretend the rest of my life? There is an evil here that will drive me out. I cannot bear it. It is ugly. I can bear the loneliness but not this ugliness, never to have anything beautiful around me again, to touch or look or feel... to hate the wind the rest of my life. To watch my children grow up knowing nothing but this prairie. I can't, Arne, don't make me."

"*Yndling*," Arne said tenderly, putting his arms around her and pressing her head against his chest. "You must rid yourself of these notions, don't you see, it is all in your head? You make yourself believe these things. Do you try to find the beauty, I ask you? It is here all around you, but you refuse to see it. Do you think any of this would be any good without you, my *yndling*? I beg of you, if you love me, try for my sake. Come, now, forgive me for taking your money. Yes, I admit I was wrong if it will make you happy. You can have your money back at shearing time, and I will never touch it again, I promise. We must be together, Rannei."

He stroked her rigid back, patting her clumsily as if she were a stubborn child. She stood upright within his encircling arms, neither responding nor drawing way, filled with such grief she could hardly endure it. Words crashed and tumbled and slid into one another in her head like huge unwieldy blocks of ice, words it would do no good to say.

It is not all in my head, not at all. And I will never, never forgive you, Arne.

Chapter Twenty-One

*C*al could not rid his memory of the sight of Rannei kneeling among the scattered treasures of her dowry chest, the look on her face akin to that which he'd seen only one other time, on the day of the storm — a human being driven to the limits of endurance. Arne had told Cal frankly it was Rannei's dowry money, but what he had not told him was that Rannei had not agreed to Arne buying Cal's sheep with it. If he had known, he lamented to himself over and over, he would have found some way to insist that Arne pay him in installments, or would have refused to sell to him at all. Anything not to be the cause of that broken look on Rannei's face.

Cal galloped home, and as he sat down to the supper Tommy had prepared, he was so upset he could not eat. Cal sat up half the night finishing the second bottle of whiskey he and Arne had opened. After a polite drink or two, Tommy went to bed early, saying he wanted to be on his way home early the next morning. In the course of that night, Cal laid a dozen plans for rescuing Rannei, or thinking of ways to make the situation more bearable for her.

He could give her back her dowry money, in secret, of course. But Arne would find out eventually, for Cal was sure she meant to use the money to get away from the Gumbo, perhaps even back to Norway. To give the money back would mean the end of his friendship with Arne, of course. Cal had no doubt about that.

All fall Cal had watched Rannei's unhappiness increase, and he sympathized with her feelings more than he wished he did. After all, wasn't he about to leave this prairie, and for reasons similar to Rannei's? He didn't hate the Gumbo, as she did, but he could see why she didn't wish to stay.

It had to be the loneliness — hadn't Cal himself enticed, yes, that was the word, enticed the Bergstroms out here because he was lonely? It followed, therefore, that part of the responsibility for Rannei's unhappiness lay on Cal's shoulders. He knew that they wouldn't have come to the Gumbo if he hadn't been there, like the devil, whispering in Arne's ears. Rannei would have persuaded Arne to settle somewhere else, on the Belle Fourche, or near Pierre, or even Rapid City. Feeling responsible, Cal felt he had to find a solution they both would accept.

Here was where Cal became confused. Thinking as hard as he could — and whiskey always improved his thinking, Cal told himself — he could find no answer that would satisfy both Rannei and Arne. Cal had seen clearly on the trip to Minnesela that Arne was quite simply determined to stay where he was. No power on earth, Cal felt, could move that man from what Arne seemed to think was his destiny on this earth.

His destiny in the shape of Cal Willard, not Almighty God. That was the part Arne missed. And now Rannei was paying for what Cal had brought on them, and Cal must pay too, by watching her suffer, knowing full well he was the cause of it.

Yes, Cal admired and liked that damn Arne, and wanted to help him out. But he loved Rannei. That was the crux of the matter, as clearly as Cal could make out in his whiskey haze. He loved her and wanted her for his own, and, if he had to take sides between the two, it would have to be Rannei over Arne. Not that Cal had a chance of being loved in return. He had no illusions about that. Rannei loved Arne, he'd seen that plainly enough. She just couldn't live with him on his God-forsaken prairie, that was all. Either way, Cal would lose, no matter what. If he helped Rannei, he lost Arne's friendship, but if he simply left for Alaska, he lost them both.

Sighing, Cal got up, put another piece of coal on the fire, opened another bottle, picked up a piece of the cold mutton Tommy had left for him, and sat down with his feet by the tiny oven. It did no good to wish that he had never seen the Bergstroms on that train. He had headed for them like a thirsty sheep for water on a hot day. Rannei was too pretty. He had never seen such a beautiful woman, and the Lord knew he was drawn to her. What in God's name possessed him to talk to them as if he intended to spend the rest of his days in the Gumbo? Hadn't he even then been thinking of selling the ranch?

Cal groaned aloud. A weak, meddling fool, that was what he was!

Yes, he was guilty as hell, but the thing was done. It was too late now to cry over what was done, and hindsight — everyone knew about that. But how to get Rannei out of this mess? Rannei was just as unalterably opposed to living on the Gumbo as Arne was to leaving it. It had shaken Cal when Arne mentioned Rannei was expecting a baby. That certainly complicated matters. What a tangle! If only he could, Cal would marry Arne's wife and raise their child without a moment's hesitation.

Only Rannei had never given Cal any indication she thought of him in that way. She didn't flirt with him as almost every other beautiful woman he had ever known did. Certainly, she and Arne had a strong sexual bond, and Arne obviously adored her. And for Cal to get tied down to a woman, even Rannei — That would be the end of your roving days, then, Cal Willard, me lad, Cal thought to himself.

Or maybe not? Rannei might be excited about the gold-hunting adventure in Alaska. Then again, what did he need with gold? He hadn't really touched the principle of Granny's money. The interest had been sufficient to keep him going so far. He could dip into that money and settle down in some more agreeable spot. He'd use some of it for beautiful things to buy for Rannei and for trips. It would be exciting to share the sights with her and see those beautiful blue eyes widen in delight at the wonders of the world.

Or they could have a little horse ranch where he could train and sell Arabians. A place beside a river or lake, with lots of trees. Rannei could swim naked all day and he could paint her. He could spend the rest of his life painting her.

Maybe she'd agree to go off with him. He must talk to her. Maybe it was not as serious as it looked. Maybe being pregnant was making her fanciful. He had known it to happen to women before. Pregnancy made them moody, unpredictable. He must be fair to Arne. Maybe she just needed a change of scene, some people other than him and Arne and Tommy to talk to, a trip to the Porter's, for instance. He mustn't leap to conclusions just because he was drunk. He mustn't make another mistake.

The hour was late when Cal found paper and pen and wrote a note to Rannei. He'd send it with Tommy, who was stopping by to say goodbye to the Bergstroms on his way home the next morning. The note suggested casually that Rannei might like to ride along with Tommy for a visit to the Porters, and later he or Arne could fetch her back. Even Arne would have to admit she could use the visit. If she made it to the Porters, she'd have the option of leaving for good, or returning. She'd have her chance to decide, and Cal wouldn't be involved. But she'd need money, if she truly wanted to get away.

The dowry money. Cal took the bank notes out of his notecase and slipped them into an envelope.

Next, he wrote the note.

Dear Rannei,

I am returning your dowry money. Forgive me, I didn't know it was yours. Please, do not tell Arne, but take the money if you go with Tommy. You may need it.

Cal

That was discreet enough, as long as Arne didn't see it. When the ink had dried, Cal folded the note and put it between the bank notes in the envelope. He fell asleep in the chair in front of the stove planning how he could suggest enough to Tommy, without making him suspect him of wrongdoing, or compromise Rannei.

In the morning, he woke cold and stiff to find Tommy building the fire. Cal's head ached, and all he wanted was to go to bed and sleep eight hours, which he planned on doing as soon as Tommy was out of sight. As they said goodbye, Cal handed Tommy the envelope with the money and note, explaining to the boy that he thought Rannei might like to visit his family, and perhaps ride along with him.

"And Tommy, give her this when Arne's not around," he finished. It sounded terrible, but Cal couldn't think what to say without making it sound worse. He wished his head wasn't so fuzzy. He couldn't think clearly. He added lamely, seeing the puzzled look on Tommy's face, "It's some money I owe Arne that I want Rannei to have. She needs some money of her own to spend if she goes with you. I'll explain it all to Arne later."

"That's nice of you, Cal." Tommy's honest face shone.

He believes everything I tell him, thought Cal, a little ashamed. But then, he knows I like to give presents.

Tommy put the envelope carefully into the inside pocket of his sheepskin coat. Then Cal handed him another envelope, this one with Tommy's name on it.

"Here's your pay, Tommy, and a little bonus for the

work you've done around here, and all the extra things you didn't have to do. And if you ever need a recommendation anywhere, I will be happy to write you one."

Thanks, Cal," Tommy gulped. "I hate to leave, you know that. Maybe Arne will hire me in the spring. He'll need help then. Tell him I will work cheap."

"I will, Tommy. He couldn't find better help anywhere, and I'll tell him that too. Greet the family for me and tell them I'll be out in the spring."

He watched Tommy down the trail and waved as the boy paused on the rise between his place and the Bergstroms'. Then he turned to go back inside and crawled into his bed, holding his aching head gently.

A few days later, Cal could wait no longer to learn if his scheme had worked. Hopeful, he rode Jubal over to the Bergstrom homestead, ostensibly to see how the sheep were adjusting. As he rode down the trail above the creek, he saw the enlarged band spread out to the south, and on one side, Freya grazing on a picket. Cal swore at the sight of the mare. If Rannei had gone with Tommy, she would have ridden Freya. Depressed, he rode on to the house and dismounted at the barn, tying Jubal in an empty stall and loosening the saddle girth.

Rannei opened the door to his knock.

"*Takk for sidst*," Cal said as he usually did when greeting her. "Thanks for last time."

His Norwegian was a joke between them, for the same words in his mouth never sounded the same as it did in Rannei's or Arne's. Rannei liked to tease him about it, but she did not smile today, and he saw that it was not a good time for jokes.

"Well, Rannei, I came to see if you were at home. I thought perhaps you would be making a visit."

"No, I did not want to go," Rannei said softly, but Cal saw the red-rimmed eyes, and the violet shadows beneath them. His stomach felt queasy, unsettled at the sight.

"It is just like spring out today," he said inanely. She did not answer. "Any coffee in that pot, Rannei?" he asked desperately. Was she angry with him?

"There is always coffee." She took cups from the curtained shelf and poured them both some. "And some cookies." She put a plate of butter cookies on the table and they sat down.

Rannei sat facing the window, and Cal looked at her intently. Her face seemed different, thinner, the hollows under her cheekbones more accentuated. The summer's tan had faded into the pearly white complexion he remembered so well, but the underlying color that once gave her that unique look of vitality was gone. The lovely, vibrant young girl was gone. She looked still beautiful, but beautiful in a more mature way. Here was a woman who had suffered.

Cal noticed with a sense of shock that the high collar of her waist had a spot on it, and a slight tinge of grey showed around the collar edge. He would not even have noticed it on anyone else, but on Rannei, who had always been so fastidious, it seemed to be magnified out of all proportion. Wherever he looked, his eyes ended up returning to that spot. Not wanting to think about how much she suffered and why, he reached for a cookie and kept his eyes on his coffee.

Rannei, who had been staring blankly out the window,

looked at him and smiled ruefully. With one hand she tucked a stray wisp of hair behind her ear. Her shining wealth of hair was twisted into a loose knot on the top of her head instead of the usual smooth braids. "I look a sight, I know. I haven't had time to braid my hair yet."

Involuntarily, they both looked at the wooden clock on the wall. It was almost eleven. Cal searched his empty mind for something to say. He had never found it difficult to talk to Rannei before. Something had gone wrong. She seemed reluctant to talk to him, almost sullen. The miserable feeling in Cal's stomach deepened. Cal thought uneasily, *she is angry about the money.* He put down his cup, now empty, and watched Rannei stand and go to the stove for the pot to refill it.

Before he could think about it and lose his nerve, he said quickly, "Rannei, I am sorry about your money. I knew it was your dowry, but I did not know Arne had taken it without your knowledge. Believe me, I would never have accepted it if I had known. Forgive me."

Holding the pot poised over her own cup, Rannei's hand began to shake. Cal could see the flush spread out of her neck, up to her cheekbones. She filled her cup and replaced the pot upon the stove, but kept her back to him.

"Rannei?" Cal said at last, hearing his voice low and guttural with emotion. "I'm truly sorry. I felt the only way I could make amends was to return the money to you. It is yours, by right. If I had known how you felt about it, I would never" he stopped. He had said that before. He was handling this badly. He didn't want to offend her further.

Finally, she turned and faced him, her chin up, her eyes moist. "You know I can't accept that money back,

Cal. It is a debt we owe you, and since Arne saw fit to take the money to pay you, I can't take it back, even if it is mine. But he had no right to it, even so." Her voice thickened with passionate anger. "The money was mine. My father gave it to me in Arne's presence. He told us both it was mine to do what I wished. I thought Arne understood. My father wanted me to be independent, — he thought women should be — and Arne had always agreed. Then he took the money, stole it from my dowry chest. We had talked about buying your land and sheep, Cal, and I told him I would never agree to him using my money for that. He had no right, no right–"

Cal sat helplessly, wishing he could undo it all. "I blame myself, Rannei, for mentioning I was leaving. I never meant to do it, truly, but when I told him I was giving up sheep ranching, he jumped at the chance and asked if he could buy my property. What could I say?"

"Oh, I'm not blaming you, Cal," Rannei said. "I know how Arne is. He has probably been planning on that ever since you first said you might leave someday. I guess I did blame you, at first, for bringing us here. But if it had not been you, it would have been someone else. I think the gods mean for Arne to settle here. And you've helped us so. If it hadn't been for you, I couldn't have stood it this long. Although I suppose, if you hadn't helped Arne so much, it might have been harder for him, and maybe he wouldn't have wanted to stay. I don't know. But I do know that you meant well. And Arne loves this dreadful place as much as I hate it. I know you think I am not a proper pioneer woman, but it's not that. I am not a coward; truly I'm not. I could have been happy almost anywhere, any place, that is, with trees, and neighbors and hills. I'm not afraid of hard work, but I have to believe in it, and I can't, not here." She put her apron to her eyes and turned away.

"I understand, Rannei," Cal said gently. "Because we are alike, you and I. I'm leaving for the same reasons, and I'm not a coward either. Some people can live here and some can't. But I do blame myself for bringing you and Arne here, and I want to do all I can to help you. You must accept the dowry money. There is no need to tell Arne now. Tell him at shearing time when he has the money. He can pay me back then, or when the lambs are sold, or over several years. I don't need the money. I told him at first to do it that way, but he wouldn't listen."

"No, he wouldn't," Rannei said bitterly. "It was more honorable to steal my money than to owe it to you, and you know why, Cal? Because I'm only a woman, and his wife besides! But having the money back won't help. Arne has refused to let me go anywhere, and now with the baby coming, he won't hear of it. He is so stubborn. Once he is set on a course, it is useless to try to change him. He used to listen to me before, and respect my opinion, but now he is like a man possessed."

Cal was overcome then by a strange mixture of relief and disappointment. There is nothing more I can do, he thought. No one expects any more of me, even Rannei.

He drained the last of his coffee and was about to rise when Rannei said, in a voice so desolate it hit him like a blow, "See, it's snowing. I felt it this morning, when I threw out the dishwater. I could smell the snow in the air. We will be trapped here until spring, now. There will be no way out, and the baby — to have my baby here — I can't bear it." Her hands at her sides clenched into fists, then she put them to her face.

Cal pushed back his chair and went to her. Standing behind her, not touching her, he could see the snow clouds sweeping toward them on the wind, trailing long white fingers across the prairie to the north, leaving white streaks wherever they touched the earth. And with incredible speed, like some ghostly, enormous cat, the storm pounced on them, flinging snow at the window, rattling the glass, plucking at the roof, shrieking insanely around the corners of the house. Its icy breath knifed through a crack Arne had missed under the window. Rannei shrank back as if from a mortal enemy, and Cal instinctively put his arms around her, and hugged her against him.

"It's all right, Rannei," he soothed, as if she were one of his skittish horses. "We're safe and snug here. You'll get used to these storms. They're so awe inspiring partly because you can see them coming like that, often long before they strike."

He could feel the smooth heaviness of her breast on his wrist through her loose dress, the softness of her hair under his chin. He lowered his lips to the soft knot of hair. It was warm, as he had known it would be; the lustrous white light made his lips burn with desire. Her hair smelled of her, and he inhaled deeply. She leaned back against him. He tightened his arms about her, yet he knew she was not being seductive. She craved human warmth. He could have been any comforting body at all.

"I can't stand it, Cal, I can't. Arne can't make me stay here. I'm not his cow or sheep, I'm a person and I have a right to decide my own life just as much as he does. And there's the baby to think of now. How can we raise a child out here? Oh Cal, year after year, it will be the same–"

"I know, I know," he crooned, cradling her in his arms, rocking her gently. "I know, Rannei, but Arne loves you. He needs you." *And so do I. Come with me Rannei, let's run away together and I promise I'll take you anywhere.* Only those words, he could not say.

Rannei turned impulsively into his arms and laid her head against his chest, her arms desperately tight around his waist. He felt a sensation of intense pleasure and tenderness as her body came against his, her breasts full and firm, her figure taut under his hand. He patted her on the back and tried to remember she was distraught and needed comforting, not another complication, which she would be aware of in another second if he did not control himself.

"Yes, he loves me, I suppose," Rannei said, her voice muffled against his chest, her ear pressed to his thundering heart. Did she think it always beat like that? "But he loves this place better than he does me now. He even loves the sheep more than me. How can I win out against a bunch of stupid sheep and empty land?"

No, he could not leave her. There had never been any question of it, he realized, not from that first moment on the train. Ever since he'd laid eyes on her, his fate was tangled with hers, inextricably. He had always stood outside it all, playing the observer, the artist, sketching lives but not involving himself, seeing people as lines and angles, two-dimensional. For the first time in his life, he realized, he was going to do something his better judgment told him was absolutely, insanely foolish, and he would do it simply because he couldn't help himself.

He would do it because it was right, the honorable thing to do. He would not kiss her and tell her he loved her, as every nerve in his body was begging him to do. He knew that she would respond, but only because she was lonely and heartsick and terrified. It would be easy, even. She would be grateful and might think it was love, at least for a little while, but he would know better. He could wait.

He held her away from him with his hands on her shoulders. The cold air where the warmth of her body had been hit him like a blow, and he forced his hands to keep from cupping the face she held up to him.

"Listen, Rannei. I'll help you. I can't leave you here when you hate it so. But we must plan. You're to keep the money. We'll tell Arne nothing for now. In a month, I plan on being ready to leave; the horses should be all right by then. You can leave with me. We'll go to the Porters, then to Pierre, and from there you can go home to Norway, or come to my parents' home with me, in Pennsylvania. My mother and sisters would love you dearly, and take care of you until your baby is born. Whatever you decide is the way it shall be."

"Oh, Cal," Rannei's mouth trembled. "You are so good, too good-hearted. You'd do that for me? But Arne will never let me."

"Yes, I know." Cal could not help himself. He pulled her close for one last moment, then kissed her chastely on the forehead, a kiss a brother might have given her. "We'll have to leave without him knowing, then."

Rannei pulled back and searched his face with intent blue eyes. "Arne will never forgive us, either of us. You know that, Cal."

"Yes, he will. He'll forgive you, and it won't matter about me, because I'll be someplace else by then," Cal lied, forcing down the hard lump stuck in his throat. It would matter more than she would ever know.

As if the words had conjured him up, he heard Arne's step on the porch outside. Rannei heard it too, and they stepped away from each other as Arne entered the kitchen, shaking snow from himself like some hairy, golden pony. Snow sculpted his mustache, and the ends of his hair sticking out of his stocking cap. His cheeks were brilliantly red. His pale blue eyes swept over them. For a second, no one spoke. Cal was not sure if Arne had seen them in each other's arms, but at the moment it did not seem so, for he greeted Cal then with his usual ease, and Rannei turned immediately to the cupboard to fetch a cup and poured Arne's coffee, then refilled Cal's cup as well.

We were watching the storm come," Cal said. "It really blew in fast, didn't it? Only this morning I was thinking it was spring again." His voice sounded tinny in his own ears, the words coming too fast. He was almost blathering, for God's sake. He forced himself to stop. "Need any help with the sheep?"

"Tak, Cal, but I headed them toward the bluff a while ago and I think they will stay there out of the wind. I've never seen the weather change that fast."

"Typical Dakota weather," Cal said, and gave himself a mental kick. Rannei did not need to be reminded of that.

Rannei urged the men to come and sit, adding more

cookies to the plate on the table. Cal marveled at her. Not a sign on her calm lovely face revealed that a moment before she had been in tears, near hysteria.

Cal followed her lead, finding it hard to believe the desperate things they had just been speaking of. Rannei's health and sanity depended on Cal now. He felt a new purpose well up within him.

As they sat over their coffee, the wind outside grew louder and louder, increasing from gusts that rattled the window to a steady howl that leaned relentlessly against the house. Catching one of Rannei's apprehensive glances at the window, Arne laughed. "Never fear, Rannei. That wind can't blow this house down. An old sailor builds for the wind."

"But Arne, it's snowing much harder now than it was at first."

"You're right, Rannei." Cal got up to peer out the window. It was almost impossible to see anything out there now. "I'm afraid we're in for a good old Dakota blizzard. It was too warm this morning, I should have known. We'd better see to the sheep, Arne."

Arne was already pulling on his coat, Rannei running to find scarves for them both. "We leave the horses in the barn," Arne said decisively. "They are no use in a storm like this. The sheep aren't far, if we can get them to the corral."

If we can get them, Cal thought, following Arne out the door. Arne was coolness itself. No doubt he was used to storms, as any sailor must be. A storm on the sea might seem the same to him as a blizzard on the prairie. Maybe it was, for all he knew.

"Stay in the house, Rannei, and do not worry, now," Arne said, his voice muffled through the folds of the scarf she was winding over his cap and around his face and neck. Cal did the same with the grey woolen scarf he had been given, and Rannei came over to knot it in back for him.

"It might take us a little while, Rannei, so keep the coffee hot," Cal said as reassuringly as he could.

"Arne, Cal, be careful."

Rannei shut the door behind them as they slipped outside. The last glimpse Cal had of her was her white agonized face between the edge of the door and the jamb.

"God, look at that!" Arne shouted exultantly, and then they were out in the swirling whiteness, all sounds lost save that of the wind. Cal lurched toward Arne, grabbed him by the arm, and pointed toward the barn.

"Rope," he shouted close to Arne's face, to be heard over the wind. "Tie us together."

Arne nodded. Together they plunged for the barn. Arne pulled the door open, straining against the wind, and they tumbled into the warm dimness. The dogs, Oskar and Tippie, whom Cal had given to Arne, came over with tails wagging to greet them.

"Whew!" Arne shook himself like a dog coming out of water. "Good idea, Cal. The rope is right here."

Arne took a coiled length from a hook on the wall. Even behind the thick log walls, they could hear the wind roaring like a freight train. "Better tie that scarf tighter," Arne said critically, and Cal obediently did so. Arne had been in control since they stepped out the door, and Cal, half-resenting his air of authority, nevertheless was glad to relinquish command.

Cal unsaddled Freya and Jubal while Arne shook down some hay for them from the half-loft above the stalls. The cow and the horses stood contentedly munching, watching the men with mild curiosity, but even Jubal, who never liked Cal to go anywhere without her, showed not the slightest interest in going outside with him.

"They're smarter than we are," Cal said, pointing to the horses.

"Yah, well, they have us to do the dirty work," Arne answered. He tied one end of the rope around his waist and handed the other end to Cal, who did the same. "We can follow the fence down to the corner, then it is straight ahead to the bluff, if we can keep a straight course." He whistled to the dogs to follow and together they pushed the barn door open and went out into the blizzard.

Cal had never been out in an actual blizzard before. The winters since he had come to live on the Gumbo had been mild, and Tommy was always there to watch the sheep. The saving grace to their efforts now, Cal realized, might be that the ground was still brown enough to give them some sense of perspective. With no snow on the ground, they didn't run the danger of being caught up by ground and air and sky blurring to the same whiteness, making it impossible to tell direction, or what was up or down. And if it did not snow harder than this, it might be all right. He was no martyr, willing to die with a bunch of sheep. He pushed away memories of old-timers' scare stories about men going out in blizzards found frozen to death only yards from warmth and safety.

Yet here he and Arne were, blundering through a genuine Dakota blizzard to an uncertain fate. My God, thought Cal, what would happen to Rannei if we both died out here? Forcing himself to concentrate on the task at hand, Cal stumbled along after Arne's confident back, shielding his face from the wind with one upraised arm.

Soon they left the fence on the east side of Arne's horse pasture and struck out into the swirling white blankness. The wind was blowing now from what must be east, directly into their faces. Cal hoped it would stay that way. If the wind held steady, it would be at their backs while bringing the sheep in. They would never get the sheep to face into that wind. It would be impossible.

Even with Arne taking the brunt of the wind's icy blast, the cold clawed under Cal's cap until his scalp ached with pain. He was thankful for the scarf Rannei had given him. Without it, he knew, his cheeks and nose would be white with frostbite. He breathed through it, trying to catch the scent of her on the wool.

Cal slogged along blindly behind Arne, until the force of the wind suddenly diminished and he could dimly discern, from his wind-burned eyes, the gray mass of sheep huddled against the bluff. Arne had reached it right on course. They did not stop until they were among the herd. Between the bluff and the curve of the creek was a natural little pasture, one that Arne had used all summer for a bed ground, sheltered from the wind on the east and south. The sheep stood packed together, their heads tucked under each other's bellies against the fine crystals of drifting snow.

Arne stopped at last, panting, and turned to face Cal.

Only his eyes showed in the slit between his cap and scarf, his shaggy golden eyebrows frosted with snow. His voice came muffled through the icy white circle on his scarf where his mouth was. "Now we take them home."

Cal grunted. Absurdly, he wished for a pencil to draw a sketch of this scene. Thor, the god of storm, stood before him in the swirling snow. "Hope that wind holds steady."

"It will," Arne said confidently. "Where are the dogs? Good girl, Tip," he said, spying Tippie behind Cal's legs, where she was sensibly staying out of the wind. "Where's Oskar?"

"He might have gone back to the house," Cal said guiltily. He had in truth seen the dog turn tail and run toward Rannei and the warm kitchen after they left the barn, but he had not called him back. The dog was too young and inexperienced to be of much help in a situation like this.

"Damnit, we need him," Arne said in disgust. "Well, we will do the job without him. We take the sheep out of here, though? They're out of the wind here."

Cal heard the note of indecision in Arne's voice. "This might last for days," he said. "If we can get them to the corral we can feed them, and the shed will give them protection. If the wind changes, the snow will pile up here for sure."

"You're right, Cal. Well, if you're ready, I am." Arne removed the rope from his waist, while Cal did the same, coiled it, and put the coil over his shoulder. "Wind's still due east." Cal glanced at the top of the bluff and saw, indeed, the snow was blowing off the top of the bluff not too far above their heads.

"You take this side, Cal, I'll take the other, and Tip can bring up the rear. We aim for the fence, then it's a straight shot in with the wind at our backs. They won't like to move, but I try to keep them headed." Arne disappeared into the elusive whiteness, his voice blending with the keening wind, urging the sheep to move.

It was hard work. The sheep stubbornly stayed put at first, burrowing into the collective mass with their heads, ignoring the shouts and blows the men directed at them. Cal began to sweat under his heavy sheepskin coat. Drops of sweat ran down his armpits and along his ribs. Better keep moving, he thought. We'd catch pneumonia in this wind.

Was there anything more stubborn than a damn sheep, he wondered? Or more stupid?! Getting nowhere, Cal kicked at a fat ewe in frustration, which only sent her deeper into the huddle. Cal pounded on her back with fists in a frenzy, yelling all the obscenities he could think of.

In the end, it was Tippie who rescued them. Veteran sheep dog that she was, Tippie leaped onto the solidly packed backs of the sheep, working her way to the middle of the pack, where they stood with their heads down, packed into their circle. Finding the exact spot where the heads all came together, she leaped down into the small space and began to bark wildly, nipping at noses with her sharp teeth. The sheep gave way before her and the knot loosened and began to untangle. As they began to scatter, Cal saw Arne on the other side, patiently pulling the sheep out one by one and pointing them west.

Following Arne's lead, Cal worked his way along his

side, doing the same, pulling them out one by one and sending them after the others. Urged on by Tippie, more and more began heading west at a fast walk. Cal walked alongside, keeping pace, afraid to let them out of his sight, lest he get lost himself. On the south side, Arne had the harder job. The sheep were inclined to head due west, the wind at their tails, but in order to reach the fence, they had to go northwest for a while, with the wind at their sides. Cal wondered if he should help Arne, but someone had to push the stragglers along, and Arne seemed to be keeping them on course.

With Tippie barking and rounding up the rear stragglers, they tacked across the prairie and hit the fence right at the corner. Arne stayed to the west of the band, then, so the sheep wouldn't pile up against the fence, and Cal and Tippie pushed them along from the rear. Now the wind blew directly into their sides, so the leaders kept trying to turn tail into the fence. Time and again the entire herd stopped and began to huddle until the leaders were chased out of the circle and headed north again. Cal thanked God for Tippie. It seemed she was the only one the sheep would obey.

The snow was falling more heavily now. The light had darkened — whether from the hour or from the thickening snow, Cal could not tell. He wondered what time it was. It must have been almost noon when they started, because he remembered it had been eleven o'clock when he and Rannei were talking, but he had lost all sense of time. Well, it didn't matter; he wouldn't be able to go home until the storm lifted, and that might be three days or more. And in that length of time, there was no telling what might happen in that little house with all three of them locked up together.

Finally, after what must have been an hour or more, the snow-riddled sheep reached the corner, and poured around it, almost running, the wind chasing them west up the lane. It wasn't long then before the band funneled through the corral gate, bleating in a steady chorus, Tippie's joyful barking telling men and animals that they were home and safe at last.

Cal gave a tremendous sigh of relief. Surely this first blizzard wasn't an indication of what the winter would be like? But of course he hadn't yet spent a full winter on the Gumbo. And after all he'd told Arne about not putting up any more hay! It would be just like Arne to turn out to be right after all. Wearily, Cal followed Arne's snow-blurred bulk through the deepening snow to the house.

Chapter Twenty-Two

*C*al was so cold that he could not, at first, feel the warmth of the air inside the Bergstrom home, but the strong, rich smell of mutton boiling on the stove assailed him, and his stomach tightened with hunger and growled demandingly. He had eaten that morning, early, but he was terribly hungry. He pulled off his frozen mittens and held his numb fingers over the stove to soften, checking the clock on the wall. The hands stood at three. Rannei was unwinding Arne's scarf. The knot was frozen and crusted with snow and would not come undone. So was Cal's. He pulled his scarf off over the top of his head and stood it, frozen into a white fuzzy ring, on top of the coal box.

The heat made his fingers sting and he shook them hard. The gesture sent snow from his coat sizzling onto the stove lids, and he realized that his face was beginning to melt, too. His mustache and eyebrows were caked with snow and ice. He started pulling it off, his eyes watering with pain, but he kept at it, for the melting water was running down his face. He took off his coat and saw that snow was pounded into the suede leather like flour into meat. It, too, was frozen stiff into the shape of his body. He hung it on the wall peg where it could dry.

Oskar, looking not at all repentant, was licking the snow from Tippie, who had come in the warm house on their heels, while Rannei undid Arne's scarf, pulled the mittens from his hands, and undid his coat, all the time making little pitying noises. Arne bore it with an air of indulgent patience. He did not seem cold, or even tired, but merely hungry, sniffing from time to time at the steam that rose from the pot on the stove.

"Don't carry on so, Ran," he said. "Nothing happens, the sheep are all right and so are we. All part of a rancher's life, eh, Cal? I'm starved, Rannei. You know a little exercise whets the appetite. Let's have some of that mutton stew I smell over there. The devil! It's three o'clock, no surprise that we're so hungry then."

Cal's ill humor vanished. He had to laugh at Arne's English, which sometimes had a peculiar rightness about it that charmed him. Arne laughed too, although he did not understand the reason, and poured himself and Cal each an inch of aquavit from the bottle.

"Here, this will warm you, Cal. It is what we fishermen drink after a long day hauling the cod. We are frozen stiffer than this, I tell you."

Cal took a cautious sip of the fiery liquid, while Arne tossed his down in one gulp. Cal liked brandy better, but his flask was in his saddlebag out in the barn. It would have to stay there, for the present at least.

"I made dumplings," Rannei was explaining to Arne. "You said not to leave the house, and there were no potatoes up here."

"Oh, good," Arne exclaimed. *"Innbak frukt,"* he explained to Cal, and carried the heavy iron kettle to the table, where Rannei had a trivet waiting.

When they sat down to eat, the dumplings were delicious, fluffy and even textured, piled on top of the steaming mutton, a stew cooked with carrots and onions Rannei had brought up from the root cellar the previous day. Cal thought he had never tasted anything so good. He filled his plate twice. This is what makes it all bearable, he thought as he sat back at last with a sigh of contentment, food and warmth and a drink to come home to out of the storm, and most important of all, a woman.

Arne was still eating. He ate twice as much as Cal. "You sound happy now, Cal," he said.

"We bachelors don't get many meals like this, I can tell you. I told Tommy to take some cooking lessons before he comes back." He waited for Rannei to fill the coffee cups before he lit his pipe, first thanking her for the meal, as he always did, in Norwegian, and asking her permission to smoke. It was the only time he liked to smoke, after a meal such as this.

"Takk for maten, Rannei," Arne said, and shoved his plate away. Cal offered him some of his tobacco, which he as politely declined.

Anyone watching us, Cal thought, *would think life was perfect for all of us right now.* It was all an illusion. Who would guess the turmoil in Rannei, for instance, so young and beautiful, calmly sipping her coffee as if all she was thinking about was how thankful she was to have her man back? And all the time Cal and she were plotting to disrupt, if not ruin, all their lives. Perhaps, of the three of them, Arne was the closest to being one piece inside and out, but then maybe not. Maybe Cal just didn't know what Arne was thinking. He may well have some dark plot of his own hatching.

"Do you realize how important you women are, Rannei?" Cal said in a deliberately teasing voice. "Where would we be, without you women to civilize us? Not eating *innbakt frukt!*"

"I don't know why not," Rannei said tartly. "You men could make it as well as any woman, if you tried. You and Tommy are just too lazy, that's all."

That had not been his intention.Why had he brought the subject up, anyway?

"I suppose we could, if we had to, Rannei," Cal said, realizing that it must sound as if he had been needling her. "But I mean, to be truly civilized, it takes a woman. At my place, Tommy and I have to come home to a cold house, start the stove going before we can warm ourselves, then wait while the meat cooks. Often, we don't have the patience to wait. We just open a can of tomatoes and warm up the beans, and eat it all with a hunk of bread. That would satisfy our need for food, partly at least, but civilization, it seems to me, is more than that. Man needs more than mere substance. He needs the inner comfort that satisfies his soul as well as his body. That comes from finding the house warm, a delicious dinner of dumplings and stew waiting, and a beautiful woman to look at while he eats it."

Cal had been carried away with his theme, and now regretted his speech. Rannei was looking down at her plate, pushing a piece of the mutton around with her fork. He was making it worse, he realized. He'd chosen the worst possible subject, when what he actually wanted to do was express his appreciation for her presence. He hoped Rannei didn't think he was reproaching her for leaving Arne.

Rannei turned her head to stare out the window, and all he could see was her profile. A wisp of hair curled against her ear, and he looked away before he was tempted to reach over and tuck it back. Her hair had been brushed and braided in its usual smooth coils. A trembling started in his stomach. He wished he hadn't held her in his arms and felt her against him. It had been done so innocently on her part, but remembering, he wanted her.

Arne seemed not to be paying attention to either of them. He was dipping a sugar cube, his special treat, into his coffee, then sucking it abstractedly. Cal thought he was probably thinking about the sheep, until suddenly Arne looked directly at Cal, his pale eyes almost silver in the light of the lamp.

"Ya, you are right, Cal, we need the women, but don't make her conceited. She already knows her own worth, as all women do. Why, in Norway, the women run everything. In our little village, when the men go fishing, the women manage very nicely by themselves; until they run out of food, then they're glad enough to see their men come home. Only then it is hard for them to give up the reins, you see. But they let us think we are the bosses, at least until we go to sea again."

"Well, in Norway, the men listen to their wives," Rannei said in an ominously quiet voice. "They grant they have some sense, at least."

"Nobody says they don't," Arne said. A stubborn note had entered his voice.

Well, thanks to me, thought Cal, *we are about to have a quarrel.* He had never heard them speak that way to each other before. He should have known they were in no mood for a philosophical discussion. He had touched too directly on the source of their trouble.

Pretending not to notice the hostile silence, he said, "What I really mean, I guess, is that neither a man nor woman can get along without the other very long. Men do their part by providing food and shelter, and the women provide the comfort, as well as a few other things, of course."

Rannei was listening, her chin in her hands, the lamp-light slanting across her hair, gathering all the silvery lights into a gleaming bar across the crown of her braids.

"That does for a man's physical comforts, and his spiritual necessities, too, which you must agree are usually one and the same! But what about women? What about their soul, their inner well-being?"

"We are only men, Cal and I. That is something only you can answer, Rannei!"

"What satisfies my soul?" Rannei asked. "Who knows? It is different for different women, of course. My mother always said women need something apart from the house and children and husband to keep them thinking, and it usually involves other people: helping them in some way, or perhaps they draw some inspiration or comfort for themselves from their care for others. I'm sure there are few women hermits."

"Your mother is certainly not a typical Fru," Arne said slipping back into Norwegian, which he always did in stressful moments. "She likes to help people, and work outside her home, but my mother hardly set foot outside the house."

"Was your mother truly happy, Arne? I remember visiting her with my mother, many times. She, too, wanted something else, she did not know what. She could not express it, and so she simply endured her life. Her solace was religion, but even that wasn't enough in the end, when she was so ill. It seemed to me she was a very unhappy woman."

"My father is not a happy man either, if it comes to that. But they are not worse off than most people. Your parents are the exception, not the rule. Most marriages aren't like theirs. It's not realistic to expect it."

"But they worked at it, Arne. It didn't just happen. They had many arguments, but they always worked it out in the end. It was very hard for them both sometimes, but they loved each other, and they tried always to see the other person's viewpoint."

They had forgotten him. Cal wished he could somehow fade away or become invisible so they would keep on talking to each other. Both voices had lost the bitter, querulous tone with which they had started, and perhaps for the first time in many weeks they were really listening to each other.

"Don't expect me to ever be like your father, Ran," Arne said, resentment edging into his voice. "He may be a saint, but I'm an entirely different person."

Rannei stiffened in her chair. "I don't expect you to be like him, Arne; no one could be. But you could certainly learn a few lessons from him!"

They were back to where they had started. Cal sighed, and Arne turned to him. "You see what it is like to be married, Cal? I think maybe you were pretty smart after all."

"You should have married that cow, Minnie Upsala, then," Rannei said, standing. "She wouldn't have said one word back to you, and besides that, she doesn't have a brain in her head." Rannei gathered up the plates and turned her back on them both.

"She has no father, either. She may be grateful for a good man," Arne retorted.

Saddened and a bit embarrassed to see Rannei and Arne reduced to common bickering, Cal stood too, gathered up the remaining dishes and carried them over to Rannei at the counter. She poured heated water from the kettle into the dishpan and began washing. The blizzard had sucked all the light from the sky, although the clock on the wall said barely five o'clock. The wind howled unceasingly around the sturdy log corners of the house and plucked viciously at the edges of the roof.

For the moment, talk had ceased. Cal picked up a towel and dried the dishes Rannei put into the rinse water. None of them had said what they wanted to say. Perhaps it was impossible for Arne to understand Rannei's feelings about the Gumbo. To him, the Gumbo was everything he desired, all that his soul required. He had such a sturdy soul it would survive anything, Cal was sure. He remembered again the day they arrived at the ranch site, and Rannei, exclaiming, unbelievingly, "But there's nothing here!" and Arne replying, "Ya, and it's all for us."

It was impossible, the whole business, and for a moment Cal wished that he was free to leave and let them work it out the best they could. Only they probably never would, both being what they were. He couldn't stand to think of Rannei's spirit or soul or whatever she wanted to call it being twisted and eroded by her hatred of the Gumbo and bitterness toward Arne. He was committed, anyway, to helping her now, but he owed Arne something too, one last try to convince him to leave the Gumbo or lose Rannei.

Cal spent the night in front of the stove on the buffalo rug he had given Rannei, wrapped in one of Rannei's mother's handmade quilts. The second day of the blizzard, during an infinitesimal lessening of the storm in the early afternoon, Cal and Arne tried to feed the sheep hay from the stacks in the hay corral adjacent to the sheep shelter and corral. They had managed to get some of it over the fence to the hungry sheep before the wind resumed, stronger than ever, blowing the hay from their forks back into their faces.

There was no chance to get the sheep to the spring-fed watering hole in the river, so they resorted to eating the snow that had blown into the corral. The sheep could get by on the snow, but the horses and cow were a different matter. They were safe and snug in the barn, but they needed water every day. Arne and Cal carried buckets full of icy water in to them, rather than bring the animals out into the storm.

By the time they were through with their chores and the cow had been milked, the storm was in full force again. The men retreated to the house and drank coffee and brandy, Cal having retrieved his flask from his saddlebag. During talk of Cal's plans for Alaska, seeing his chance, Cal said he might leave earlier than he had planned, maybe right after Christmas. Generally, around that time, they could count on at least a few days of good weather.

"That might be your last chance to visit the Porters until spring," Cal said, turning casually to Rannei. "You could ride along with me, and then one of the boys could ride back with you."

It sounded absurd the moment he said it. Of course Arne wouldn't agree to let her go in the middle of winter when he hadn't earlier. It was Arne's last chance, if he but knew it, to show his wife he understood what she needed. Rannei planned on leaving anyway, but Cal wanted Arne to agree, to give Cal his permission to take Rannei away. If Rannei thought she was free to go, she might really go no further than the Porters.

Rannei's face brightened. She turned to Arne. "I'd like to do that, now that I'm feeling better. It would be a change, and I could ride Freya."

Arne's look at Rannei was so incredulous that Cal felt instantly the impossibility of the whole scheme. *Now,* he thought, *Arne sees the whole plot. I've fumbled it.* Awkward with embarrassment, he packed tobacco into his pipe, spilling half of it on the table.

"Really, Rannei," Arne was saying with forced patience. "How you can think of such a ride in your condition, and in such weather too? You might not get back before spring. I think we settle that when Tommy goes. You just forget about it now until after the baby comes. You know yourself, Cal," he said reproachfully, "how fast the weather changes. I can't think how you suggest such a trip. It is certainly foolhardy. I can't allow it."

"You can't allow it!" Rannei pushed herself back from the table so abruptly her chair crashed to the floor. "What makes you think you are the one to decide? I'll make up my own mind, do you hear?" She rushed into the bedroom corner and jerked the curtain closed. They heard the thud as she flung herself on the bed. The sound of her sobbing, muffled in the pillow, carried clearly through thin barrier.

Arne looked at Cal, his face guilty, embarrassed, exasperated, bewildered, but not accusing, thank God, Cal thought.

"Pardon, Cal," he said in a low voice. "Rannei is not herself. She has never been so moody like this. It must be the pregnancy that makes her act this way."

Cal leaned forward and fixed Arne's eyes with his own. "Arne, listen!" he said with all the force he could compel into his voice. "Listen to me! Rannei should be home with her mother, her family. She needs them right now, more than she needs you. Let her go, she will come back. I will lend you the money, take her to New York. I promise you, you'll be sorry if you don't, you'll regret it all your life. Let her go. Her health will crack, her mind—already, you see how she is showing the strain."

Arne stared at Cal as if he could not believe what he heard. "Go home?"

"Yes, go home," Cal whispered urgently. "Rannei is very unhappy, I can see for myself. It is wrong of you to make her stay, and she will end up hating you. If you let her go now, have her baby at home with her mother, she will come back to you, but if you force her to stay... Arne, if you love her, let her go!"

Arne dropped his fixed gaze to his coffee cup. His big hands, clasped around it, slowly tightened until Cal saw the knuckles whiten and the veins pop out blue under red chapped skin. At last he raised his eyes and looked Cal straight in the face. The pale eyes dimmed, a strange dark light flooding them, turning them almost black. Cal remembered seeing that unusual effect once before on the train, when Rannei had taken his hand.

"Cal, we are friends. You help me so much I can never repay you. But I cannot accept this from you."

Cal knew he meant both the money and the advice, and he bowed his head before that look. Arne went on coldly, "Rannei is my wife. I know her better than you do. She is stronger than you know. She is not losing her mind; she is only angry with me. She will get over it. If she leaves now, she will never return unless I leave also, and that I never will. I need her too much, and I love her besides. No matter what she thinks at the moment, she must stay with me. Don't think I'm being cruel. She will come to her senses once the baby is born. I know Rannei."

Cal knew he had said enough, even if he thought that

Arne, of all men, might know her least. "Beg pardon, Arne. I only wanted to help you both. I did not mean to intrude."

Arne's eyes, when Cal looked up again, were their usual pale blue.

"You are too goodhearted Cal, that is your trouble," he said, the old affectionate tone returning to his voice. "Any woman can talk you around. Lucky for you that you aren't married."

Cal knew by the bantering tone of his voice that the subject was irrevocably closed. He had been pardoned for his bluntness this once, but he wouldn't be again. He felt more sympathy for Rannei than ever, yet he could also see the justice of Arne's position. They were both as right as they were both wrong, but he had chosen his course and he would stick to it. To drown out the sound of the convulsive sobs behind the curtain, he got noisily to his feet and poured himself and Arne another cup of coffee.

Chapter Twenty-Three

*D*uring the next few weeks, Cal avoided the Bergstrom homestead. He was possessed of an almost insane urge to be gone. He could not bear the sight of Arne, so unaware of what his friend and his wife were plotting behind his back. Cal kept busy, telling himself, and half-believing it, that he couldn't spare the time. He worked with the horses most of the day, and at night he worked at sorting out the accumulations of almost four years.

The useless things he had acquired living on the Gumbo appalled him. The little he wanted to take with him was mostly what he had brought with him. He left all the dishes, utensils and provisions on the shelves for Arne. It was a goodly amount, since he had stocked up on provisions in Minnesela, planning to stay most of the winter. He would leave a note saying he included the shack and its meager furnishings in the price of the land

and sheep. Arne was too practical, he knew, not to make use of them, whatever his feelings toward Cal might be by then.

Cal packed provisions for several days, and his tin plate, cup, fork and spoon, in the leather fold-over case he had carried into the rain forests and the savannahs of Africa, into Australia's outback and into the steaming wonders of Yellowstone Park. As he put them into his trunk, his memories of those days crowded upon him. That dent in the plate, he recalled, had been put there by a mad bull elephant one night who had torn up his camp in a demonic rage. Fortunately, Cal and his bearer managed to escape by climbing into a tree.

That night in Africa, Cal had witnessed what it was like to be in the grip of an out-of-control fury. As Cal clung, swaying in the branches of the swollen-trunked baobab tree, he had envied the beast. He'd felt an almost irresistible urge to yell with all his might, to urge the elephant on, to leap down and join in trampling his things into the dust. Cal thought of that night whenever he ate from the plate; the exhilarating fear he felt, perched in the giant tree, watching the elephant's mighty foot tromp on his various belongings.

Cal laughed to himself in wonder. He knew what Arne meant when he talked about the berserker rages. *Men and animals, we're all the same,* Cal thought.

He always made it a point never to carry more than would go into his large, ironbound leather steamer trunk. But as Cal looked over his piles of clothing and books, sketch pads, paints and canvases, he realized would have to make an exception to the rule. He couldn't leave any of his precious canvases and sketchbooks behind. So many of them were of Rannei and the Dakota pioneers he had drawn and painted.

As Cal emptied out his steamer trunk in order to repack it, he was in a queer mood of dividedness. One side of him pretended this was only another move of many he had made throughout his life, that he would be able to simply ride away and leave the little shack and this life as easily as he left all the others. This idea made him happy and peaceful. Sorting out his trunk, Cal experienced both nostalgia for his past life and a vague feeling of excitement for the new. Then his thoughts would jolt back to the unhappy present.

For instance, when picking over his books, trying to decide which to take and which to leave behind, he experienced a dilemma. Rannei loved the Milton and the Browning books of poems, but Cal could not imagine Arne reading them. He agonized too over Shakespeare's Complete Works and Spencer's Fairie Queene and his books by Arnold: The Poems of Matthew Arnold, Culture and Anarchy and Other Writings, Literature and Dogma and Mixed Essays. Arne might conceivably be more interested in those, once he'd learned to read English better. In the end Cal left behind Arnold's Mixed Essays, the book of Greek plays and the Shakespeare. The slim leather volume of Dante Cal wrapped carefully in its oilskin and added it to his trunk. It had been around the world with him, after all.

Cal must plan. The painful thought pricked him back to the present. He was running off, yes, it amounted to that, and that was how it would look in the eyes of the

Porters, Jimson, and all the other people he knew in Dakota, running off with another man's wife. How could he prevent their discovery before they'd made it safely away from here?

Since he took along the steamer trunk, Cal would have to take the buckboard, and Rannei would naturally have her baggage. Jubal and Yellow Bird were trained to the buckboard, although they didn't like it much. The two horses Cal was training for the Petersons would follow behind, tied to the buckboard. It would be a slower way to travel, perhaps, but it was the best he could do. He had promised Peterson the horses, and in this country, running off with a woman was condoned sooner than going back on a bargain.

They would arrive at the Porters and stay overnight. The next day, weather permitting, he would leave the two horses with the Porters and he and Rannei would leave for Pierre in the buckboard. It was a bad time to travel, but he would have to hope that the weather held.

At times, the magnitude of what Cal was planning overwhelmed him. Could he really be going through with it? He'd always thought of himself as a multi-faceted man: artist, drifter, dreamer, adventurer, lover and horseman. But never, until now, had he seen himself as Cal Willard: bounder, cad and a damn fool. That was what they would call him once he left with Rannei, in Dakota at least. "That damn fool Cal Willard." He could never come back to the Gumbo again.

Even at the thought, he could see Jimson spitting through his teeth at the mention of his name, although

Jimson was the last person whose opinion Cal cared about.

Arne would be the one they felt sorry for. *I don't want to come back anyway,* Cal told himself bravely. There were lots of places to go, places where they had never heard of Cal Willard. Once they were free of the Gumbo and Arne, Cal and Rannei could go anywhere and live happily ever after. That was, if only he could convince Rannei to remain with him. *Maybe in time she could learn to love me,* Cal thought.

But what if she couldn't? Cal couldn't help wondering from time to time if it wouldn't be better to just leave without her, to slip away at night without saying goodbye to either of them. Arne would think it was just good old sentimental Cal, hating to say goodbye, and Rannei, what would she think? Would she get over it in time? Would she accept the life she had, or would she do something desperate, like trying to run off on her own? Yes, she probably would, and she would never make it. And once the baby was born, who knew how it might change things? She needed his help, and of course he knew he never intended to leave without her.

But still, he felt tempted one moonlit night, as time edged closer to the day when Cal would help Rannei leave the Gumbo. The moon shone bright enough on the snow to light the way, and travel would be swift, with only two inches of snow on the hard, frozen ground. The trail would be perfect, and he could be at the Porters by morning. But no, he wouldn't abandon her here. He'd given his word.

Cal shook his head ruefully, as he scraped bits of food into Tippie's dish. He had meant to leave the dog for Arne

273

after the blizzard, but the dog had followed him home anyway. The Norwegian would need two dogs now with the larger herd, and Oskar wasn't much good. Cal patted the dog's head affectionately and she thumped her tail, then got up lazily to eat. She always slept in the house, although Arne said it spoiled a dog to let them do that.

"Poor old Tip," Cal said, "you'll have to sleep in the barn with Oskar now."

Cal pulled the coffeepot to the hottest part of the stove to warm it and thought of Christmas Eve, the next time he would see Rannei. His eyes fell on the blanket-wrapped bundle leaning against the wall. It was his Christmas present to her, which he had bought in Minnesela on the fall trip. He had imagined it would give her pleasure, but now that notion was useless. She couldn't cart along a gilt-framed mirror when they left here. He would think of an excuse for giving her another present besides Freya.

Still, he would give it to her anyway; had to, in fact, since Arne knew Cal had bought it, and if he didn't, would wonder why. Cal had carried it carefully all the way from Minnesela wrapped in an old quilt Mrs. Peterson had given him. Arne had laughed at him, saying that the blue beads, which were his present, were much easier to carry. So they were, but Cal wanted Rannei to have the mirror to remind her how beautiful she was. It had seemed important at the time.

It seemed a long time since Cal had seen Rannei; not since the blizzard in early November. Arne had dropped by several times to drink a little brandy and visit in between making his rounds to check on the sheep. Arne was working on a surprise gift for Rannei as he sat in

The Big Gumbo

Cal's shack. He said he planned to give it to her the day before Christmas Eve as a special present. Arne told Cal he was to spend Christmas with them, and that Rannei wanted him to come early on Christmas Eve.

"It's when we celebrate our Christmas, you know," Arne said, and made him promise.

Chapter Twenty-Four

*E*arly on the twenty-fourth of December, Cal packed his saddlebags with gifts and bottles and lastly, while Jubal stood patiently waiting, he carried out the large, blanket-wrapped mirror. Cal had known it was going to be a nuisance to carry, but now he discovered he couldn't even mount his horse while holding it. Finally, he leaned the wrapped gift against the cabin wall, mounted, and bent down to pick it up from where he sat in the saddle. Holding the awkward parcel balanced carefully before him, Cal started Jubal slowly off over the frozen trail to the Bergstrom's. The horse did not like the strange burden he was carrying and snorted and rolled her eyes as they went, expressing her objections.

The day was clear and cold, the sparse snow on the ground blown into sculpted ridges and rows, the prairie grass exposed between them. The contrast of the smooth white drifts, the dark blue shadows, and the golden, dried hay was startling. The snow and the grass rolled away to the horizon, to the pale blue of the sky. The wind had not yet started its daily harassment and the entire world was quiet, still and cold. Held to a walk, Jubal picked her way daintily, keeping to the side of the trail.

When he reached the Bergstrom homestead, Cal found he couldn't dismount, encumbered with the mirror as he was, so he shouted until Arne heard him and came out, calling boisterously, *"Gledelig Jul!"*

Arne was in high spirits and his huge vitality spilled into the cold air with the heat from the open door.

"Merry Christmas," Cal said, returning the greeting as cheerfully as he could. Arne came over and took the cumbersome package from Arne so he could dismount and remove the saddlebags. Then Arne took Jubal to the barn to unsaddle and feed her, while Cal stumbled into the house laden with his gifts.

Rannei looked up as he entered, a long wooden spoon in her hand, the Christmas greeting on her lips.

"Gledelig Jul, Cal!"

Cal sucked in his breath. The wan pathetic girl who had wept in his arms the month before was gone. The Viking queen from the immigrant train stood before him. She wore a dress of dark red merino that he had never seen before, with a high waist and full skirt, a creamy froth of lace edging the low round neck. Her hair was wound in a shining coronet high on her head, and her face was flushed with the heat from the stove, so her eyes appeared even bluer. For an instant, they looked soberly into each other's eyes. Then Cal put his bundles down on the floor, leaned the mirror against the wall, shut the door firmly against the cold, and bowed to kiss the hand she held out to him.

"*Gledelig Jul, Fru* Bergstrom," he said softly.

"Cal, we've missed you. I was afraid–"

Afraid he was going to leave without her. "I was busy with the horses, Rannei, and getting ready to leave. We will go after Christmas, the first clear day."

"Oh, Cal," she turned away to hang up his coat and hat and started to say more, but just then they heard Arne's step so she turned back to the stove, stirring something simmering in a large black pot. Arne came in, still full of cheer.

And with good reason. The room looked festive enough to raise even the gloomiest spirits. Cal was especially drawn by the Christmas tree, a juniper bush set up and decorated in one corner of the room. Arne had brought it back from a recent coal expedition, he explained, as Cal went over to examine it. Arne had dug the bush up, roots and all, from the clay bank above the open coal pit and brought it home wrapped in burlap. Without telling Rannei, he had planted it in a blue enameled pot, one she'd discarded due to a hole in the bottom, and hidden it behind one of the haystacks. Yesterday, he'd brought it inside for Rannei as a surprise.

Cal was impressed by the decorations. Arne explained how he had carved little figures of cows and trolls and a lamb from pieces of wood, but Cal already knew about that part. Arne had done this in Cal's shack over the past several months, painting the ornaments bright colors using Cal's oil paints. To add to the decorations, Rannei had attached bright bows of yarn on the branches.

"Now we have a little aquavit," Arne said, and poured the liquor into the tiny glasses. The aquavit bottle was more than a third of the way empty now, Cal noted as he walked over to the table. Only he and Arne were drinking. Rannei did not like the potent liquor.

"*Skål!*" Arne saluted him, and they clinked glasses.

"*Skål!*" Cal repeated.

Arne tossed his drink back in one gulp, and Cal manfully did the same. *Thank God I brought plenty of brandy along,* Cal thought, trying not to shudder at the burning taste of it.

In the middle of the afternoon, Rannei made coffee and they ate *fattigmans* and *lefse* warm from the iron griddle, buttered and sugared, and rolled into a cylinder. The *fattigmans*, which Rannei translated as "Poor Man's Cookies," were Cal's favorite. He loved the crisp, delicious cookie, made with butter and cream and cardamom seed and fried in deep fat. He remembered his little Norwegian grandmother making them every year as a special treat for Christmas; remembered watching as she carefully rolled the dough out to almost paper thickness, cutting them into diamond shapes and then cutting a slit in the middle of the diamond and pulling one end through.

When he reached a responsible age, Cal had been given the job of carefully putting each one on a wooden paddle and placing it in the kettle of simmering oil. He had to watch until the dough became the proper shade of light yellow and bubbles appeared on the surface. Then he lifted the cookie out of its bath onto the prepared flour sack towel. As the air filled with the scents of cardamom, he waited impatiently for the cookie to cool. As fryer cook, his was the task of tasting the first one to see if it was properly done, and if the oil had been just the right temperature. The smell of cardamom brought it all back to him, and as he related the memory of his grandmother, Rannei and Arne both smiled.

"I remember it the same way," Rannei said. Then her face grew unaccountably sad.

Perhaps, Cal thought, *she was recalling her warm and cozy farmhouse kitchen where she grew up in Bergstromfjord.*

Arne, seeing her expression, got up hastily and pulled on his coat.

"Time for the chores now, before it gets dark," he said cheerily.

Cal offered to help, but Arne refused. With milk bucket in hand, he went out the door. Cal watched out the window for a moment, noting that the sheep were already trailing home from the top of the bluff. No doubt they had been grazing up there all day on the cured prairie grass between the snow ridges. When the daylight began to wane, the sheep sought out drinking water with blind instinct, heading toward the spring at the base of the bluff. The ice along the edge had to be chopped through every day, one of the chores Arne had set out to accomplish. From inside the house, Cal could hear the blows from Arne's axe alternating with the loud bleating of the sheep. Luckily, as the spring's flow lessened with winter, the sheep wouldn't need as much water, as they took in snow along with the grass as they grazed.

Rannei spread the table with an embroidered white linen cloth she had obviously taken out of her chest for the occasion. It had been ironed smooth and glistened with starch. She spread it out on the table with an abstracted frown, rubbing the creases with the palm of her hand. The center had a design of a flower in a stylized, geometric form, worked in blue and yellow yarn. The same colors were used in a blanket stitch around the edge.

Cal went over to sit in Arne's chair, which had been pushed back against the wall. The westering sunlight slanting in the window behind Rannei caught the edges of her skirt in ruby light. Above the gleaming white tablecloth, the white oval of her face glimmered beneath the black crown of hair. She had paused in her work, standing transfixed, caught in some dream or memory of her own, her hands holding the knives and forks she'd been about to set down. He would sketch this image in black and white, Cal thought, adding a touch of red to the dress, and maybe a hint of yellow to the tablecloth.

Cal patted his inside pocket in search of the charcoal and sketchpad he usually carried there. He located the charcoal, but not the paper, which he'd forgotten to transfer from his other coat. Without moving a muscle, so as not to distract Rannei, Cal's eyes searched the room for a drawing surface. He saw a piece of weathered wood standing up behind the coal bucket. Arne must have been saving it for kindling, but it would do. Cal rose quietly, picked up the board and quickly sat down again. Having stirred from her trance, Rannei set three plates on the table and arranged the knives and forks around them exactly so. She put blue linen napkins beside the plates.

Cal sketched the pose quickly, that was the important part; just a suggestion of the log-framed window in the background and a hint of the log wall. Her face, half bent, absorbed in what she was doing, but conveying a suggestion of what? Reflection, grief, memories? Now the table, with hasty lines to indicate the pattern on the cloth, then the figure again, the light along the crown of hair and the edges of her dress—

He realized Rannei was watching him, had even said something, perhaps. "Just a minute, Rannei," he said distractedly. "If you don't mind."

"It's pretty, isn't it?" she said absently, smoothing the cloth, laying down the last napkin. "I made it years ago, when I was fifteen, I think, the first one for my chest. Even then I was planning for my own house in America."

Cal looked up, setting the piece of wood down in his lap. Rannei had not even noticed what he was doing, he realized. This picture would make a good painting in oils. It would be good to get back to his brushes again. With all the sketches he'd made, he had enough material to last him for years.

"Cal," Rannei's voice broke through his trance.

Glancing instinctively at the door, he rose and went to her, keeping the table between them. They faced each other across the brilliant cloth, and for an instant Cal saw himself, an intruder in his own painting. Rannei's eyes were dark and secretive, the light catching the outer tips of her lashes and glossing the sides of her hair. The light was not bright, but Cal felt himself exposed before her. Heaven knew what she saw in his face. She glanced down at the table, rearranging the napkin and fork, then past his shoulder at the door.

"He won't be back for a while. It will be the last chance we have to talk."

Cal felt a small but positive leap of joy and excitement flame beneath the heavy feeling of impending doom. He could not help it; she was so lovely, despite the misery on her face.

"You're sure you want to do this," he said, in as neutral a tone as he could manage.

"Yes, I have thought about it constantly. You see how Arne is. He'll never let me go, even to the Porters, and I must go now before it is too late for the baby. Once we could have talked of it, he and I, and he would have let me decide what is best for myself. He would let me go if I thought I should. But now he is a different man; he has changed since he came here, or perhaps he has revealed his true self to me. Now he owns this land, he thinks he owns me too."

"He loves you very much, Rannei," Cal murmured, looking at the shape of her eyes. They were both long and wide; odd how he had never noticed that they were wider at the top of the eye. It made them look larger than most women's eyes. And then her eyelashes set them off, curving up like that, so thick and black.

"I know he does, Cal," Rannei said. Cal flinched from the anguish in her voice. "And I love him, truly I do, but how much longer can I care for him if he keeps me here against my will? I know he will hate me in the end because I am not what I was. He is stronger than I am. He will survive, you know that. I will leave, hoping perhaps he will change his mind, for I cannot. He'll have to decide whether he wants the Gumbo or whether he wants me and our child."

"Well then, Rannei," Cal said as calmly as he could.

"We will leave the first fairly warm, clear day. If it is too cold and windy, it is too hard on the horses, and us too. We will take the buckboard. There is no top on that, but we need it to bring the luggage. My extra horses can trail behind, but you will have to leave Freya, I'm afraid. Arne will have her out with the sheep, although it would be better–" Cal stopped mid-sentence. He had been going to say it would be better to take the mare with them, just to stop Arne from following. But he could not say it. Surely Arne would have more pride than that.

"I will leave a letter explaining everything to Arne," Rannei said, as if she had read his mind. "After what I will say, he will know it is useless to come after us. He will see I am in earnest, and besides, I will promise to come back to Dakota, just not the Gumbo."

"Remember to dress warmly, take what you need for clothing, and bring along some food. We will need provisions for the journey. We will go straight to the Porters, stay there overnight, and leave for Pierre the next day."

"Must we stay at the Porters? I would rather not."

"I would rather not either, but it is the only possible place, and we can't risk camping out in this weather. We'll just tell them you are going home for a visit, which is the truth. They won't think anything of it."

"I hope not." Rannei sounded doubtful. "I will be ready, Cal, at a moment's notice. There won't be much to take. I will leave almost everything for Arne."

"Good," Cal said, almost briskly. "Then it is all settled." He sat down in his chair again and took up his unfinished sketch. That was the proper attitude, friendly and concerned, but without getting too close. His heart pounding, he forced his concentration to his drawing.

When Arne came in from his chores, the table was set, Cal was smoking his pipe, and Rannei was busy at the stove. Arne removed his outdoor clothes and stuck his frosty mustache into Rannei's ear. The little scream she gave sounded so forced, so near to tears, that Cal looked away in alarm. Oblivious, Arne only laughed.

Cal stood and walked across the room to set the piece of board with his sketch on it against the wall. Then he went to the pan of dishwater to wash away the charcoal that had dirtied his fingers. As he dried his hands on the towel hanging on its peg, his fingers left behind dirty smudges. He looked at the towel ruefully. Rannei, catching his look, smiled and shook her head, then lifted one shoulder in the smallest of shrugs. What did it matter? the shrug seemed to say. They would be gone before she'd have time to wash the smudges out.

For Cal, it was a Christmas Eve unlike any other. In previous years on the Gumbo, he had largely ignored it. Tommy usually went home for a few days to be with his family. Alone, Cal would cook an especially good meal, perhaps, and open a bottle of brandy to drink after dinner. As a treat for the horses, he'd feed them a ration of his precious oats. This year, he had looked forward to having Christmas with the Bergstroms, picturing a happy pioneer celebration with a warm fire, good food and company, and the look on Rannei's face when she opened her gift from him.

Outwardly at least, his dream had come true. Even Cal had trouble, at times, remembering the conversation he'd had with Rannei only that afternoon. She seemed determined to let nothing mar the celebration she had planned. He guessed that this was not just because she wanted to appear as normal as possible to conceal their plans from Arne, but because in a way, it was her last gift to her husband. Whatever the effort cost her, she was giving him the old Rannei for a little while, as nearly as she could.

When he saw Arne's obvious delight and relief at her performance, it seemed almost cruel to Cal, but he knew she did it out of love. He admired her complexity, but all the same, it made him uneasy. Was he rescuing Rannei, or betraying his friend? But with drink after drink of aquavit plied on him by Arne, Cal pushed the thought away. He could think about it tomorrow.

For the Christmas feast, Rannei had prepared lutefisk as her mother had always done, soaking the precious dried codfish Arne had purchased in a lye solution until it was soft and almost gelatinous. Of course, her mother used fresh cod, but cod would not have been fresh by the time it arrived in Dakota, Rannei said with a laugh. She had wrapped the almost translucent mass in cheesecloth and boiled it briefly. This delicacy was served with melted butter, boiled potatoes, applesauce, canned tomatoes cooked with bread, and for dessert *"Rullepolse,"* rice pudding with raisins and cream. Cal's contribution was a good white wine, along with the brandy, which was served with the coffee. It was all delicious, and the men's lavish praise made Rannei glow with pride.

Afterwards, Cal and Arne washed and dried the dishes while Rannei cleared away the dinner table. She was as excited as a child, or pretended to be, about opening her

presents, which were arranged under the juniper
Christmas tree wrapped in lengths of homespun and old
newspapers. Cal thought he had never seen anything so
brave.

"In Norway," Rannei said, "we use pine boughs and fir
to decorate the whole house. Oh, it smells so good! We
would all help find the fir for the Christmas tree and the
children would decorate it with little wooden ornaments
they made themselves, like these, all painted so prettily.
And Father would look all fall for a yule log grand enough
to burn for several days in the fireplace. You must not
think this humble celebration is how we Norwegians celebrate Christmas!"

"This is not Norway, and we make our own celebration
in our new home," Arne said firmly. "The animals have
had their feast, and I tied suet on the lilac bush for the
birds, even though I think they all go away here in the
winter. And there is a light in every room, as we always
did, even if there is only one room. Every year we will dig
up another tree or bush and plant it by the house in the
spring. We make our own tradition. Now we pour the
wine Cal brought, and sing around the tree."

"And the feasting and the dancing," Rannei went on
dreamily, as if Arne had not spoken. "For two weeks we
celebrate, Cal, and on Christmas day, after it gets dark,
the young men go from farm to farm in sleighs, greeting
their neighbors while the girls stay home to welcome
them. Sometimes the men wear masks, animal faces or
funny faces with strange noses, and we pretend we don't
know who they are. Then of course they expect a treat
before they leave for the next house."

"What Rannei likes best about Christmas is the pagan part of it," Arne said teasingly.

"It always did seem a shame to me that the Christians had to spoil the lovely old sun worship," Rannei said. "After all, they might have picked another time of year just as well, and left that part of it alone. Imagine how much closer people felt to nature when they thought they had a part in controlling it, the feeling of power when they thought their dancing was bringing back the sun!"

"How you can be such a pagan? Coming from your family, I do not know," Arne said.

"Mother is religious, it is true, but she has always respected my beliefs," Rannei said indignantly. "And Father, too. We were never made to feel we even had to go to church if we didn't want to."

Cal listened with fascination to the conversation. What a sensation Rannei would make in his mother's parlor if he brought her home with him, he thought, smiling to himself.

"Now you're laughing at me too, Cal."

"No, I've just never known any pagans before, especially women pagans. It's not the usual thing in America!"

"I think America needs us then," Rannei said. "Maybe I'll start a new cult out here on the prairie!"

"You can be as pagan as you like tonight," Arne said. "Now sing us some songs, Ran."

Arne lifted her guitar from where it hung on the wall in the corner and handed it to Rannei. Cal refilled the wine glasses and lifted his to Rannei and Arne.

"*Skål!*" they said in unison and clicked their glasses

together. Rannei sipped her wine, and, putting her glass down, began to tune her guitar and strum it softly.

"*Det kimer nu til Jule-fest,*" Arne sang out in his fine loud baritone.

"The happy Christmas comes once more," Rannei sang, putting the words into English for Cal's benefit. Cal had not heard Rannei sing for weeks. He listened hungrily as her rich vibrant alto came up and under and through Arne's deep voice, until both were laced together in lovely warm strands of sound. They finished the song together in Norwegian, then taught Cal some of the words and they all sang it together, "*Jeg er så glad hver julekveld*" — "I am so glad each Christmas Eve."

"That's enough for now," Rannei said after another song, laying aside the guitar. "I want a present, please."

"Here is Cal's first." Arne handed the blanket-wrapped package to Rannei. She exclaimed at the size of it, and the weight, and when she unwound the blanket from it, her delight in the ornate, gilt-framed mirror was abundant and unfeigned. She propped it against the wall to better view them all in it. Arne said he would put a peg up for it in the morning. Rannei even exclaimed over the worn quilt it had been wrapped in, marveling at the tiny stitches in the design.

Cal opened his presents next — a tin of choice Norwegian pipe tobacco that Arne evidently had been hoarding, and a blue knitted scarf and cap and mittens from Rannei.

For Arne, Cal had wrapped up a pair of fur-lined deer-skin gloves he'd found in his trunk, and a harmonica he had never learned to play. Arne, with genuine delight, tried the harmonica out at once. Rannei's present to Arne was a shirt made from blue homespun, sewn with meticulous stitches, and laced up the front like a sailor's blouse.

Arne gave Rannei his gift the last of all. When he fastened the string of blue beads around her white throat, the necklace lay just above the creamy lace of her neckline. Arne asked Cal to hold the mirror, and Cal, looking down from above as they gazed into it side by side, saw their two faces in startling contrast, Arne's blond head pressed so close to Rannei's dark lustrous one. The blue of the beads reflected the blue of Rannei's eyes and shone against her white skin. The whole effect made a perfect portrait framed by gold. He must remember to paint them that way. He wished again he had brought his paints along.

Rannei stared at their reflection for an intent moment, fingering the blue beads, and Arne gave a startled look at himself. "By damn," he said. "I've forgotten what I look like after all this time."

Cal never quite remembered afterwards exactly what happened the rest of that Christmas Eve. He knew the three of them sang more songs, and he hazily remembered Arne playing his new harmonica, quite credibly, too. Rannei sang a few of her mournful folk songs and Cal recalled singing with her. The emotional details, mercifully, were lost forever under a haze of brandy. He woke up the next morning in front of the cold stove wrapped in the buffalo hide, as he had awakened many other such mornings when it had been too cold or too late to go home.

God, it was cold! Cal pulled his stiff boots on quickly lest he be tempted to crawl back again into his warm nest.

He yanked his coat off the peg on the wall, and struggled into it. He saw the fire had gone out completely during the night, so began the process of making it. Arne had apparently forgotten to bank it as he normally would have. He had remembered, however, to split some kindling in preparation for the morning fire. A neat pile of it lay on top of the coal in the box. Cal saw ruefully that sometime during the previous day, Arne had burned the piece of board on which Cal had made the drawing of Rannei. Arne probably never noticed it at all. Well, never mind. Cal would draw it again in his sketchbook. He remembered every line and color.

The kindling caught with a satisfying little crackle. Carefully Cal began laying tiny pieces of coal on top, waiting until they began to catch before adding more. This, he thought, this was life as he'd known it for some time—the cold room, the fire beginning to click, his feet cramped in the cold boots. This reality, this part of his life was now over. It had ended for him at the table yesterday with Rannei's pleading words. He would never again lay a fire in Arne's stove on a cold winter morning.

For a while after Cal met Arne and Rannei, he had thought it might be possible for him to settle down, to commit himself to something, but it had all been fantasy. *It's just like you, Cal's father would say. You never could stick with anything, could you, son? What could he tell his family but more lies?* He loved Rannei, but it was absurd to think Rannei would ever love him. Life was not that simple; when looked at closely what seemed perfect was not, and paradise did not exist anywhere.

Chapter Twenty-Five

*T*he day of departure for Rannei and Cal arrived in mid-January, when early sunshine and a clear sky promised a warmer day. Arne left early with the herd, as usual. As soon as he disappeared on Freya, herding the sheep over the rise, Rannei took the carpetbag from under the bed, keeping an eye out the window for any sign of Cal. Sure enough, he appeared driving the buckboard not long after Arne was out of sight.

Hurriedly, Rannei layered on sweaters and her warmest woolen dress, the woolen scarf and the mittens. Picking up her carpetbag which held her few remaining clothes, she strode to the door, pausing only once to gaze about the room. She was leaving everything else for Arne. The wall hanging, the dowry chest, and all that was in it. All except her copy of the Edda, now tucked away in the carpetbag, and the doeskin bag containing her dowry money, pinned under her chemise between her breasts.

"Is that all you're taking?" Cal asked as she stepped

outside, shutting the door behind her. "What about the chest?"

"I have left it," Rannei said simply. "It is a sign to Arne that we might still have a life together, if only he will come with me to someplace else. Anywhere else but the Gumbo."

Cal looked surprised.

"I have explained it all in a note," she added. He nodded uncertainly.

Despite the sunshine, as Rannei climbed up beside Cal on the exposed seat of the buckboard, the cold wind dug into her. Cal snapped the reins and they moved off at a swift pace. After several hours, though, he stopped the buckboard when she told him she could no longer feel her fingers and toes, and she walked alongside for a while to restore the circulation. When she climbed back on the seat, he arranged the canvas tarpaulin around them so the wind could no longer reach to their bones.

Cal did this all hastily, glancing continually over his shoulder, his nervousness apparent. Rannei herself felt indifferent as to whether Arne discovered their absence and followed them. The Norns who decided one's fate had already decreed what would happen. She had given her life into their hands. There was no use trying to change the order of events. She wanted to tell Cal this, but it was too hard to shout against the wind and the noise of the wagon wheels crunching over the frozen earth.

As they rode along, Rannei looked to the sky and spotted a wheeling hawk above them. How must they look to the bird, she wondered, two huddled human forms on a tiny wagon pulled by toy horses inching their way across this frozen land. The glare of the sun on the snow made her eyes ache. Rannei wondered idly if she might become blind, as she had heard men sometimes did here in the winter, where there were no trees to break the whiteness, nothing to relieve the starkness except the occasional brown edges of burnout banks showing through thin snow, the golden tops of the clumpy grass, and the two thin tracks of frozen mud stretching straight ahead. She pulled her scarf over her eyes and listened to the squeak of the harness, the blowing breath of the horses, and the crackling of iron wheels against frozen earth.

It was a long, freezing day with next to no conversation between the two of them. It was dark when Cal and Rannei arrived at the Porters, the dogs barking to announce their presence, Rannei feeling faint with hunger and cold.

A voice boomed at them out of the darkness. "Stand and identify yourself!"

Rannei almost fainted with terror. Had they come to the wrong place? Or had Arne somehow gotten here ahead of them?

"What in tarnation?" Cal exclaimed, pulling away the tarpaulin, but not in time. A gunshot whistled over their heads, and Jubal and Yellow Bird started, lunging and straining at their harness. The two horses tied behind the buckboard squealed and kicked too, so all around them was a whirling mass of horseflesh. The buckboard lifted off the ground and tilted dangerously. Rannei had to grip the sides with her numb fingers to hang on.

"What in hell is going on here?" Cal bellowed. "It's Cal, damnit, Cal Willard!"

All at once men's voices were all around them, explaining with apologetic voices.

Rannei heard "late" and "young men causing trouble" and felt herself lifted down and carried inside, into the familiar smells and sounds of the Porter kitchen. As soon as she was brought into the lamp-lit room, she recognized in the man who was carrying her the face of Hank Porter. He set her down gently in a chair before the stove. Sally and the girls surrounded her, fussing and exclaiming and asking questions. Rannei felt so overwhelmed she couldn't say a word.

When Cal entered, a sudden silence fell.

"Arne? Where's Arne? Is he hurt? What's happened?" Several voices asked at once.

"Why in tarnation did someone shoot at us, I'd like to know," Cal asked irritably. "We might have been killed!"

"It's only that there's been trouble with some young fools trying to jump claims down along the river," Hank said sheepishly. "And when the dogs raised such an uproar, and it was so late, I thought...."

Rannei glanced at the big homemade clock framed in an oxbow yoke on the wall. The hands were at eight o'clock, late by prairie standards. Most people were in bed shortly after sunset, especially in winter.

"But what are you two doing out here in the middle of the night" Sally asked.

"I brought Rannei out to take her to Pierre," Cal answered before Rannei could reply. "She wants to go home to have her baby."

Everyone exclaimed over this news and pressed forward again, urging tea and fresh baked cookies on the two travelers.

"But where is Arne? Why didn't he bring her?"

"She's tired out, poor thing," Sally scolded Hank. "In her condition, and all the excitement."

Sally told Mandy to take Rannei to her bed. Mandy tucked Rannei in, placing a flannel-wrapped flatiron against her frozen feet, then crawled into bed beside Rannei to warm her. Rannei was just drifting off to sleep when she heard Arne's voice in the next room all too clearly.

"My wife... run off...," he was saying, and other words too, Norwegian words she hoped nobody else understood.

Rannei rose and went back into the lamp-lit kitchen, where Sally's shadow danced like a witch's on the wall as she poked the fire in the stove, her nightcap bobbing on her head.

"Hurry and dress!" Arne yelled at Rannei in his loud voice, stamping his feet and banging his hands together. "We must start back at once."

Rannei felt as if she'd woken to a living nightmare, a needle sticking into her at the point of ultimate pain, piercing to the very core of her being. Go back? After all she'd been through, after all she'd told him about how she felt, could Arne understand none of it? Had he really come to force her back to the Gumbo?

All the Porter children had crowded into the room by now, the girls from the room behind Rannei, the boys from the bunkhouse. Rannei stared helplessly at them all, and at Arne and Cal, everyone stunned to stillness like actors in a play who were unsure of their lines. She could not move or speak, but stood frozen at the threshold to the kitchen, a quilt from the bed draped around her. Little Anna had crept over to huddle under the quilt with her, shaking with cold and fright.

"Are the bad men come?" the child kept repeating, over and over.

Arne stood in the middle of the room, his face still bright red with cold, his eyes blazing with anger. Then Hank entered, wearing his long grey union suit, his sparse sandy hair standing straight up.

Sally moved from the stove then, walking over to murmur soothing words at Arne as if he were a child having a tantrum. He couldn't possibly think of forcing Rannei to start back out on such a long journey tonight. When she mentioned the claim jumpers, Cal lifted his hand tentatively toward Arne's shoulder, his mouth open, but Arne whirled on him.

"*Falsk venn!*" Arne spat out, flinging the words at Cal. "False friend."

Without warning, Arne swung wildly at Cal, his face contorted into a devil's mask of hatred. Cal pushed him off and ducked just in time to escape the blow. The Porter boys and Hank leaped into action then, grabbing both Cal and Arne by the arms. Arne flung them off like puppets. He stepped forward and seized Cal by the front of his shirt, pushing him out the still open door and into the yard. As the Porter men raced to follow, Rannei heard thuds and grunts and sobbing curses. The girls and Sally also ran to the door, while Rannei stood speechless, pressing frightened little

Anna to her side. Soon the men were rushing in again behind Arne. His mouth hung open, and his nose was streaming blood.

"Now?" he demanded. "Now will you come?"

Behind him, Cal was carried back in, one arm thrown across Hank's shoulder, the other across Tommy's, his leg oddly and horribly twisted. Cal's eyes were closed in his white face.

"I think his leg is broken," someone said.

Rannei looked from Cal to Arne, then back to Cal again in horror at the harm she'd brought upon him. She wanted to speak, to tell them the truth, that she was leaving the Gumbo for good, but she could not. What Arne had done to Cal, the nightmare of it all, made her escape impossible. She would have to stay so they would not know the truth.

"Get your things!" Arne ordered.

Rannei glanced at Hank, who looked sorry, but firm. "I will not interfere," he said. "Not between a man and his wife."

Sally stepped forward, her eyes full of tears, and murmured softly, "You must go with him, Rannei, he is your husband." Then she turned to Arne. "But why not wait until morning? It's so late tonight, and possibly dangerous, and Rannei is in no condition to travel."

Arne ignored her, continuing to stare at Rannei. At last, gathering her dignity and the quilt around her, she went into the bedroom to dress. Sally came in and bundled her up well, telling her all the while not to worry, that she would be there to help her with the birth. Soon Sally was leading Rannei through the kitchen and out the door, where someone lifted her onto Cal's buckboard and tucked a warm flatiron under her feet.

Rannei noticed a fresh team harnessed to the buck-board, and then she saw Freya standing in the yard with head down, spent. Rannei called Freya's name, and the mare looked up. Rannei began to sob, and struggled to climb back down and go to her horse, but Arne's hand gripped hold of her arm and prevented her. Rannei heard Tommy's voice then among the men gathered in the dark yard, saying gruffly he would take care of the horse, if it wasn't too late already.

Arne snapped the reins and the horses set off down the starlit trail. All that long ride home, Rannei said nothing and Arne said nothing. Stunned and spent, as dawn came Rannei watched the red eye of Odin lift inch by inch above the horizon, rising above the great empty prairie as he watched their little wagon move over the frozen snowy earth.

Chapter Twenty-Six

*A*fter the first weeks, Arne's rage subsided and he was patient with Rannei, abnormally so. But she felt indifferent, one way or the other. Her body felt totally nerveless, unable to experience any emotion whatsoever. She did not even experience panic at the thought she might have to live this way for the rest of her life. She did not harbor anger at Arne for the way he had humiliated her before the Porters. The Rannei who had laughed and wept and grew angry had fled that night at the Porter's house, leaving this shell of her old self behind.

But despite everything, she survived; her body lived on with a will of its own, pulling her each day into a smaller and smaller space, until it seemed she existed only in the very center of her being, in her womb where that tiny kernel of life flickered. Rannei may have died inside, yet her shell lived on, a turtle's house, protection for the baby that sprouted within it. Perhaps, she imagined, when the baby was born, Rannei would no longer be needed and cease to exist entirely.

Nothing touched her, physically or emotionally. One day she burned her hand badly on the stove and did not even notice it until Arne's horrified cry when he came home in the evening and saw the burn. It festered for days, but she paid no attention to it. Somehow, it healed on its own.

Sometimes Rannei knew Arne was speaking to her, but she could not understand the words. What he said made no difference to her now. He pleaded and raged at her in turns, sometimes begging her to forgive him, other times saying he would never forgive her. He coaxed her to play her guitar, and sang to her or played the harmonica when she could not. Once in the night, she woke to hear his labored weeping. She listened, unmoving, until at last he slept again.

There were cold days when it snowed all day and the wind blew, sending the snow horizontally against the house, causing Rannei to wonder how any human being could exist in such isolation and loneliness day after day and keep their sanity. On those mornings, Rannei could not stir herself and lay in her bed all day, her head covered with the blue quilt she had made long ago, listening for the music that used to exist in her soul, but she no longer heard it, had not heard it since the days on shipboard. Arne left her alone, cooking his own meals without complaint.

On finer days, Rannei walked outside for fresh air, and did her chores with the chickens and pigs obediently enough. The female pig had piglets too early, months before she was expected to. Two of the eight were killed when the sow lay on them, leaving six piglets in all. When Rannei ventured outside to do the evening chores, she would look in on them. The mother pig, grunting contentedly, was usually lying on her side in her deep bed of hay, her huge swollen teats splayed out, a tiny pink piglet attached to each one. Rannei's throat constricted at the sight and, unexpectedly, her eyes filled with tears. She wondered if the mother pig felt affection for the piglets tugging at her teats, or was it just instinct?

Arne talked endlessly of names for their baby, discussing with himself his favorite ones when Rannei never replied. He didn't care if it was a boy or girl, he said. A boy could help him when he was old enough, but a girl would be more company for Rannei. She knew Arne thought everything would be all right once the baby was born and Rannei could occupy herself with it. She knew better. As she rocked in her chair, her hands always busy knitting clothes for the child or stitching soft red flannel into tiny garments, she pretended sometimes that maybe it could be that way. Maybe they could all live happily ever after. But most of the time she knew it wasn't possible. Her love for Arne had broken inside.

The pregnancy was all that she had left, and her one remaining task was to protect it. Her hands continued to knit the little sweaters and bonnets, and to hem the flannel sheets and diapers, but she could not think beyond that. She did not want to discuss names with Arne, or whether it would be a boy or girl. Although Rannei read and re-read her Edda, this time the stories failed to comfort her.

One evening toward the end of February, Rannei sat reading as usual beside the murky light from the coal oil lamp. She practically knew the story by heart. It was one of the sagas. She sat with her eyes closed, the words running through her head like a litany. She felt Arne's eyes upon her like a heavy hand on her head, but she would not open her eyes.

Finally, he cleared his throat, so Rannei knew he was about to speak and meant to be heard. Reluctantly, she closed the book, keeping one finger in it to mark her place, and lifted her head, opening her eyes to acknowledge him. Arne was sitting in his chair in the shadows, braiding a rope halter, his nimble sailor's fingers working of their own accord. He cleared his throat again.

"You feel better now, don't you, Rannei?" he asked. "You're never sick in the mornings, now." He spoke to her in a soothing tone, the same tone he used to calm a frightened or balky animal. "After the baby comes, you'll be so busy. And only last winter, remember how we would sit in front of the fire in the evenings and plan for just such a time as this? Our child is coming, Ran."

Arne's eyes pleaded with her. Better an angry Arne, against whom she could defend herself, Rannei thought, then an Arne who was begging and pleading.

"It can all be that way again. We can forget what happened and forgive each other. I have forgiven you. We will love each other again as we used to, and more, because of the little one. We will do well on this ranch, I feel it, and in a few years, you shall have whatever you want, even a trip home. But you must forgive me, Ran."

Rannei felt something tremble dangerously in her

breast. Despite herself, she could not ignore the entreaty in his voice. Somehow, she must reassure him, not only for his sake, but also for her own. And for her child.

"Please, be patient with me," she said, the words coming out rusty and low.

He leaned forward to hear her, watching her in supplication. It struck her painfully, like a blow beneath her heart that his eyes had changed from sky blue to storm cloud gray. How could that be?

"I cannot forgive you," she went on, "until you understand why I left." She wanted to explain about Cal again, how she had left with Cal only because she could not go alone, but the more she tried to exonerate him, the less Arne believed her. "I can't feel anything now, Arne. It will take time. Perhaps, in the spring, after the baby is born..."

That was not honest, blaming it on her pregnancy. But Arne seemed to see this as opening enough. He flung the halter rope he'd been braiding off his knee and knelt beside her, placing his head on her lap. Of its own volition, her hand crept to that thick golden mat and she stroked his hair. Why could she not weep too and forgive him and love him as before? She stared at their shadows, enlarged and distorted, against the wall. There must be something lacking in her that she had not the grace to forgive him, but she was so empty.

They sat for a long time, Arne's face in her lap, his shoulders shaking with sobs. After a while he rose, his face wet with tears, but between his reddened lids his eyes shone their familiar blue again. Without a word, he gathered her up in his arms and carried her to bed, undressing as her tenderly as in the old days, undoing her braid and brushing her hair so it fell around her like a shining cloak. Gently, he made love to her.

It was the first time since Christmas, and Rannei discovered with uneasiness that although she could feel nothing emotionally, her body responded as it always had to his, as if it truly had nothing to do with her spirit. Always before she felt such love and tenderness toward Arne that she'd assumed it was a necessary part of the sex act. Now, she found it was perfectly possible to experience the same physical sensation without feeling any emotion at all.

Afterward, as Arne snored beside her, Rannei lay awake a long time trying to make sense of her feelings, and how they contrasted to the way her body had responded. Did she still love Arne after all, and just not realize it? Or was the sex act entirely independent of love? The only way to find out, she finally decided, was to wait and see, as she told Arne.

The winter that had started so ominously with the November blizzard failed to live up to its threat. January, which they'd been told was usually the coldest month, had been bright and sunny, with only a few days of snow. The same weather continued into February. The wind blew constantly, of course, but not at gale force. The snowstorms came mostly at night or in short squalls during the day. The wind kept the light snow off the grass, piling it in little drifts in the dry holes of the creek and against the burnout banks. The long, rolling breakers of the Gumbo were kept bare by the wind, and the sheep had good grazing. Arne never tired of telling Rannei stories he had heard about the infamous winter of 1886-87, and rejoicing in his own good fortune.

Sometimes the sun, shining so intensely out of a deep blue February sky, made Rannei think it was spring. Until she stepped out into the cold wind, that is. The dogs welcomed the sun as well, sleeping curled up on the step to the house. The sow and her new little ones lay in the sun that shone through the lee side of their pen, the piglets grunting with pleasure as they fed. The hens, too, clucked about in front of their coop, their white feathers ruffled about their necks like white petticoats blown up, pecking at the precious grain mixed with table scraps Rannei threw to them.

The eleven white Leghorns managed to produce enough eggs for Arne's breakfast, with some left over. To make them keep, Rannei put them into a crock filled with a mica solution mixed with water. That way, they would still have eggs during the time the hens began to brood. They needed more chickens; it was why they had the rooster, after all.

As for the rooster, he marched about in the midst of his harem, his red crest held high, turning his neck stiffly this way and that, alert for danger. Rannei did not like him. He had flown at her once, and she had knocked him down with the handle of the pitchfork. Since then they had avoided each other, existing on a truce, the terms of which were that neither trusted the other.

One night, Rannei woke to hear water dripping off the roof. She thought she was dreaming and went back to sleep, but the next morning Arne told her a thaw had set in.

"I think it must be a Chinook, the wind that is blowing in from the west," he said. "I have heard of it; it is strong and fresh and melts the snow, but it is temporary only." Both of them knew it was Cal who had told him that, but Cal's name was never mentioned by either of them.

Rannei went to the door to see for herself and stood, smelling the air.

"It's a sea wind, Arne!" she cried out involuntarily, surprised that Arne had not noticed it. She stood, drawing in deep breaths of salt brine and fish and the open sea until she was dizzy.

Arne came to stand beside her. "You are right," he said, looking puzzled. "How could that be here?"

They were miles from an ocean, how far she had no idea, in the very midst of a continent. But the fact remained — it smelled of the sea and held the promise of spring. It heartened Rannei as nothing else could have done.

The thaw lasted four days, with a warm sun and the wind blowing steadily, cold and dry, out of the southwest. Arne took the sheep out farther than they had been all winter, keeping a wary eye on the sky. Rannei walked outside in the slush and mud, visiting the barnyard, walking along the creek and up to the top of the bluff.

The thaw melted most of the snow, and when it turned cold again on the fourth day, the ground lay bare all around. It did not snow again for a week, but the weather was grey and sullen, with little sun.

Arne was usually busy with the sheep all day, so Rannei had gradually resumed her daily chores, feeding the chickens and pigs, milking the cow.

When the cow went dry in early March, Rannei worried whether her baby would be affected by her not having milk to drink. Then she remembered her mother saying cheese was almost as good for a pregnant woman. Rannei had stored up neat rows of cheeses throughout the summer and fall, kept on the shelf in the root cellar covered with damp cloths as they aged, so she began to add more cheese to their meals.

Almost against her will, Rannei felt herself drawn into the stream of her life together with Arne, but it was not as it had been before. Her body responded to Arne's as it always had, but there was no joy in it. But at least they had real conversations, their minds understanding each other in that quicksilver way that had always seemed like magic to her.

She told Arne about the claim jumpers she'd heard about at Porter Stage Station. They never mentioned anything else that had happened that night. Arne could not seem to remember anything about the claim jumpers. Rannei did not remind him that Sally had tried to make him stay because of the trouble. Arne speculated endlessly on how that trouble had been resolved, but they did not find out. Not a soul came near them all winter.

One day she saw herself in the gilt-framed mirror that Cal had given her, where Arne had hung it up for her on Christmas morning. She passed it many times a day, but this time she really looked and stopped, shocked by the stranger's face she did not recognize, that of a different woman. She was ugly. This woman had shadows under her eyes, which had never been there before, and deep hollows under her cheekbones — had she lost weight?

Her face and neck and body seemed thinner. How could that be, with the baby's bulge so huge? The hair was as black as ever, the skin as smooth and white, but something subtle had changed in the blue of her eyes, an intensity of shade; a light had gone out. "I have suffered," she said aloud to the face that was hers, and yet not hers. "That's why I have changed. I will look this way the rest of my life." After that she avoided the mirror.

Arne did not comment on her appearance. He seemed to have come to terms with himself about their relationship. They made love regularly, which seemed to convince Arne that all was well, or at least, better than it had been.

March began with a snowstorm, and it snowed every day for a week, with the wind howling continuously. Arne worried about the young pigs, so unseasonably born, and spent an afternoon hauling logs and posts from Cal's ramshackle barn, which he was dismantling, to make them a better shelter, and filled it lavishly with hay. The small pigs seemed so defenseless with their pink skin showing nakedly through the sparse white hairs on their bodies, but all the same seemed to thrive.

By the end of March, the worst of the winter appeared to be over, so Arne began to concentrate his efforts on planning for the lambing, which would begin about the middle of May.

Cal had left a number of lambing pens at his ranch, and Arne hauled these to his sheep shed and made more. These were made from saplings wired together, two on each side, to form a triangular-shaped pen when stood upright. These he planned on putting up along one side of the sheep shed, and in the corral, ready to receive the ewes and their lambs who were born during the night.

At all times, at least three separate bands of sheep would have to be kept apart, Arne explained to Rannei. Arne would take the main herd, or "drop" herd out to graze each day and take care of any new lambs that were "dropped" that day. Rannei saw that managing the two smaller groups of lambs and ewes would be up to her, but how the two of them could do it all, she had no idea.

Rannei wished she could suggest to Arne that he ride to the Porters and hire Tommy to help. She knew he would refuse, of course, but she did not see how they could do it all alone. The baby was due in the latter part of June, as near as she could tell, and she wouldn't be able to do as much as she would normally. Then what about a doctor or midwife for her when her time came? Arne had promised the doctor would be there when she needed him, but how? Her only hope was that Cal or Sally had not forgotten her, or that Arne would swallow his pride and go himself. But surely the Porters would come to help with the shearing in mid-June, as they had last year.

Rannei waited to see if Arne would suggest it, but he seemed so absorbed in details of the lambing that he thought of nothing else. There was a little time left; she would wait a while before she said anything — it was his place to think of it, after all. She longed with all her heart for her mare Freya. She worried about her and missed her as she might have missed another human being, and even if she couldn't heave herself into the saddle, the horse would have been an immeasurable help to Arne.

Chapter Twenty-Seven

*O*ne day in early April, Arne came home with a bouquet of pussy willows. "The *puspil* are out, Ran," he shouted jubilantly, handing them to her. "I found these by the swimming hole. Spring is here."

As Rannei took the branches from him and rubbed the gray velvet of the catkins against her face, she felt a stirring of panic. How vigorously the baby kicked within her at that very moment. Not long now, and it would be forcing itself out as ruthlessly as the piglets. She felt suddenly faint. The protective shell she had built around herself the past months was cracking. No, it was too soon. She wasn't ready yet for any of it.

Perhaps sensing her panic, Arne grabbed Rannei by the arms and lowered her to the bench, his face losing its ruddy healthy color.

"What is it, Ran?" he asked, his voice rough with fright. "Are you — it's not time?"

"No, no, not yet," Rannei gasped out. "But Arne, it is

only two months before the baby comes. What if it comes early, and no one is here to help me?"

"Don't worry about that, leave it up to me," Arne said. "I told you I would have a doctor when your time comes, and Sally will come, too."

Rannei bit her tongue to keep from asking how he was going to manage that.

"Anyway," Arne went on, "I'll be better than the doctor myself by that time, with all those lambs to practice on, and the cow is soon to give birth."

"I'm not a cow or ewe," Rannei said, and almost laughed. She felt a shift, a lightening of the hard knot under her heart, a longing so intense tears started to her eyes. Would it ever be the same between them? Just to love him in the old uncritical way, and be happy? Too soon, there would be the baby, a living, actual creature to be concerned about, making it all the harder to convince Arne they must leave the Gumbo. But somehow he must be convinced and they must leave, or he must let her leave.

The rain fell often that month, turning the Gumbo into sticky clay and raising the level of the creek. All the snow was washed away or melted, and here and there in sheltered places, a tinge of green began to show. The ewes rushed about after it regardless of their pregnant condition, mad for the taste of the new grass.

One day as Rannei stood on the step, breathing in the smell of rain and wet earth, the smell of spring, she saw the buds on the lilac bush were swelling. After that she looked every day and was rewarded at last with a pair of new-born green leaves at the top of the spindly stem.

Tears, the first she had shed since her flight with Cal, flooded her eyes as she brushed the tender green leaves with her lips. "Dear Cal, I am so sorry for all the pain I have caused you and Arne too. Please forgive me," she said to the leaves. She vowed she would soon find the courage to say it to Arne and make it right between him and Cal. She would see Cal again somehow.

Arne herded the sheep to the east, where the land had not been grazed for months, and bedded them down at night on Cal's old bed ground. Arne slept in Cal's shack on those nights, telling Rannei he had decided to use it as a camp from which to graze the sheep in summer to the east and north. Rannei stayed at home alone.

Arne made no mention of the things he had found in Cal's house, although Rannei knew Cal must have left most of his possessions. One evening Arne brought home two of Cal's books and laid them on the table without comment. One of the books was The Complete Works of William Shakespeare. Rannei started at the beginning and read it through. Gradually, Arne brought others, but he and she never discussed them.

During this time, as they waited for the lambing to begin and as her pregnancy ripened, they both prepared for the arrival of the baby. Rannei finished the last of the baby's tiny garments, the little flannel shirts and dresses, knitted booties and little caps, and folded them carefully on the shelf in the bedroom, ready for use. Arne began weaving a cradle out of willow withes. He cut them from along the creek, stripped them of the leaves and stems, and cleverly wove them into a cradle-shaped basket. He made a high hoop handle for it and fastened its ends to either side so Rannei could lift the basket and carry it from place to place. The rockers he fashioned out of several willow branches, fastened together and dried into a proper rocker shape. For the inside of the basket, Rannei sewed a mattress sack out of the flannel and filled it with washed and carded wool she had saved from the shearing. The result was a warm and snug portable baby bed. When Rannei put the mattress into the cradle, she added a small quilt she had pieced together. For the first time, it felt as if the baby was really coming.

With the arrival of May, the buttercups sprinkled like bits of sunlight along the creek side, and small white heather-like flowers appeared above banks of snow on the north side of the river bluff. Rannei walked up the trail above the creek, puffing with the exertion, to gather a bouquet for the table. Along the top of the bluff she found the purple pasque flowers she remembered from the year before, which reminded her of the anemones at home. With cries of delight, she bent laboriously to pick a few. The first flowers of spring! At home in Bergstromfjord, she used to walk in the woods when the birches were showing their first tender, brilliant green leaves to pick the blue anemones and yellow coltsfoot. Ah, if only she had those birches here! Even one would help ease the emptiness.

Reveling in the sunlight, Rannei gazed out toward the south, toward the Porters and freedom, toward home. The homesickness she thought she had successfully buried in the snows of winter overwhelmed her, the tears running down her cheeks like rain. Turning to the vastness in the east, she spotted Arne and the sheep and felt torn from all she had ever dreamed. Slowly, she started for home, hoping once she put her flowers in the pewter vase she had brought from Norway, it might revive her spirits.

That night Rannei broached the subject again of the doctor. Wasn't this a good time for Arne to go to the Porters or to Minnesela to let the doctor know when to come? And wouldn't they need supplies soon? The last flour sack was only half-full. To wait until after lambing was too close for comfort, even if the baby wasn't due until the end of June. She was so large already, it might come early.

Arne smiled at her indulgently and told her it was impossible to leave at this time. He couldn't leave her alone with the sheep. He had noticed one ewe that looked as if she might be ready to birth, and once one started, others were sure to follow.

"It is hard to be patient, Rannei, I know," he told her. "But you must see it is impossible now. There is time for it all, and it all comes about as planned."

Rannei gave up in despair, and that night prayed to Freya, which she had not done in a long time, and consigned herself to the goddess' care. There was nothing more she could do.

ON THE FIFTH day of May, Rannei was hanging the weekly laundry on the clothes line, the south wind blowing her skirts against her legs and flapping the sheets and clothing briskly. She had washed all morning amid the spring smells of sun and damp earth. The exertion of scrubbing the clothes on the washboard, of lifting the heavy pails of hot water, of wringing out the clothes and carrying the heavy basket to the clothes line, made her back ache and her feet tight and swollen within her boots. The flapping laundry made so much noise that she didn't hear Tommy ride into the yard on his little roan mare.

"Howdy, missus," he greeted her.

Startled, Rannei whirled and gaped at him in astonishment.

"Oh, Tommy, I am so happy to see you!" she cried out. "And you brought Freya!" She would have hugged him if he hadn't been on his horse. Instead, Rannei ran over and flung her arms around Freya's satiny neck. "Freya, you darling!" she said, hiding her face against the horse's neck to hide her tears. Freya nickered throatily and pushed her nose into Rannei's apron pocket, looking for a treat. Rannei laughed, delighted, and smiled through her tears at Tommy. "See, she remembers me. Oh, I missed her so. I worried about her all the time."

"She was right sick for a spell," the boy said, glancing around, probably to see if Arne was nearby. "But she's alright now, and Pa thought you'd like to have her back, and Ma wanted to know how you were, and the baby, and, and all," he finished lamely. "There's letters from your folks too, came last week. I knew you'd want those."

"Bless your dear mother and father," Rannei said fervently. "And bless you too, Tommy." Tommy's face turned bright red with embarrassment at this last. It meant a lot to Rannei that the Porters still cared after all the trouble she'd caused. Then the mention of the letters sunk in. "Letters from home! At last!" she said eagerly.

"And they don't even know what is happening here with me." She hadn't had a chance to send them word about the baby. Overcome, she buried her face in her apron, and sobbed convulsively.

Tommy cleared his throat. "Here they are, missus," he said hesitantly, holding them out. "I put them in my coat pocket. I knew you'd want them right away."

Rannei wiped her face with her apron and gave Freya, who had been snuffling sympathetically into her neck, another hug. "Well, come on in, Tommy," she said, clutching the packet of letters to her breast. "I know you're hungry after that long ride, and I need a cup of coffee myself."

She left him in the yard to tend to the horses and escaped to the kitchen. Tommy gave her a good long time to compose herself and to read her letters before he came in. His manner was still stiff, and he stood with his hat in his hands, not sitting down until he said what he had to say.

"I mean, ma'am, if Mr., er, Arne, wants help with the lambing, Pa says I can stay."

Rannei smiled at him radiantly, stood up from the table where the letters were spread out before her, and removed Tommy's hat from his hands. She hung it carefully on the hook on the wall, then gave him a hug. "Oh, Tommy, of course we need help! I was just desperate, wondering how we were going to manage by ourselves, and me in my condition. I'm sure, now that you're here, he'll be happy to see you. At least I think so. He just didn't want to ask for help, you know."

They looked at each other doubtfully. Surely Arne

wouldn't be so proud and foolish as to send Tommy away when they needed him so. She wouldn't let that happen, that was all, Rannei thought with a surge of her old confidence.

"Now, Tommy," she said briskly, "we're just going to forget what has happened in the past and start from right now. We're still friends, I hope; at least, I feel we are. Of course, we will pay you for your help."

"Whatever you say, missus."

"And Tommy, stop that missus business." She imitated his drawl and he laughed, their old camaraderie suddenly re-established. "Don't worry about Arne. He'll be glad to have someone to help him besides a pregnant woman and two rather irresponsible dogs, or one at least."

"That Oskar still as foolish as ever?"

"Every bit. I don't think he'll ever be a sheep dog."

Tommy sat at the table, and Rannei placed coffee and cake before him. Then she sat down across from him and he began to talk, telling her all the news. There had been no more trouble with the claim jumpers, and nobody had been hurt.

"Just some young fools," Tommy said, sounding so like his father that Rannei smiled.

"Wait until Arne comes," Rannei interrupted. "He'll want to hear. He was worried about his friend on the Belle Fourche River." Rannei paused. Before Arne came in, she needed to find out about Cal. "And how is your family, Tommy?" She asked, twisting her fingers nervously in her lap.

"Ma sends her love and says to tell you she remembers when the baby is due, and she will come in good time for it. She'll send the doctor out from Minnesela, too. Ma's helped birth lots of young'uns," Tommy added, trying to look anywhere but at her bulging belly.

Poor boy, thought Rannei. *He hadn't expected me to look quite this way, I suppose. I must look a fright in other ways, too.*

Rannei felt for her braids, only to realize they were slipping down her neck. Her skirt was bedraggled and stained from doing the laundry. She must clean up before dinner.

"And Cal," she asked, trying to keep her voice casual. "How is he? Was his leg–?"

"Wasn't his leg, it was his hip," Tommy said. "We had to send for the doc. Doc said he would probably always limp, but it's pretty well healed by now, only he can't use it much yet. He said to tell you all hello, and that he was sorry he couldn't come see you, but that you would know how it was, with Arne misunderstanding it and all."

Rannei heard Cal's words in Tommy's voice and felt faint with relief. Dear Cal, she should have known he would smooth it over somehow. The good opinion of the Porters meant so much to her. She was grateful she still had it.

"I'm so sorry about his hip," she said. "I do hope it will be all right in the end. You must tell him when you see him that Arne understands what happened now but he is still a little angry with him." Cal would understand that.

Tommy nodded and took another bite of cake. In chatting with Tommy, Rannei's English seemed miraculously to have returned, but she noticed the much stronger accent she had now, and she saw Tommy give her a confused look a time or two when she pronounced words wrong. Once, she had known them perfectly well. It wouldn't take her long to remember it now that she had someone other than Arne to talk to.

Tommy offered to go out and milk the cow, and while he was gone and supper was cooking, Rannei washed her face, brushed and braided her hair and put on a clean skirt and a smock she had made for her pregnancy, a shirt loomed of natural-colored homespun, embroidered around the square yoke with a pattern of little blue wind-flowers, the kind of bloom that grew everywhere in the woods of Norway. When Arne came in looking confused and a little belligerent, as he had seen Tommy milking in the barn, she was ready for him.

"What is this, now?" he asked.

She repeated what Tommy had said to her, letting Arne make up his own mind. He thought about it, rubbing his hand over his face tiredly.

"Ya, we do need help," he said at last slowly. "And Tommy, he is a good boy. What do you think, Rannei?"

"I think we need help too, Arne," Rannei said, and gave him a pleased smile. It had been easier than she had thought. "I think it is very kind of our neighbors to help us. And Arne, I will feel so much better, knowing that the doctor and Sally will be here when I need them."

Arne capitulated at this. "Ya, ya, that is good that they know. I was worried also, you know, Rannei, but I did not see how I could leave you here alone right now."

Rannei put her arms around his solid bulk and gave him a hug. "You were doing all you could, Arne, that I know," she said, and for a moment longer, they stood embraced. She felt his lips in her hair, and his grief at all that had passed between them trembled in his big body. After a moment he pulled away, turning so she could not see his face as he took off his coat.

"Well, since he is here, we work it out, but he must wait for the money until shearing time."

"I'm sure he won't mind waiting. I think he was even going to do it for nothing, only of course, I told him we'd pay wages," she added hastily, seeing Arne's frown. "And look, we have letters from home." Rannei's mother and father had both written, Kristin sharing all the latest doings of everyone in the family and neighborhood, including Arne's family. Her father had written about the latest work on the farm and Norwegian politics.

There were no letters from Arne's family, but then, he hadn't written to any of them. Both Rannei's parents expressed their certainty that Rannei and Arne were the most successful of homesteaders. At the time they had written, of course, they had only the first letters sent from the Porters a year ago. Now they would have received the letter Rannei had written in the fall and would know that she and Arne were on the Gumbo. Although Arne said little, Rannei knew he was as happy as she, almost, to hear from home at last.

When Tommy came in with the milk pail, Arne greeted him almost as usual. Clearly, the matter had settled in Arne's mind. Rannei poured the milk into the crock to cool and put supper on the table while the two men talked. Arne was as starved for news as she, Rannei realized. Tommy, who was hungry and anxious to dig into his food as always, had to tell about the claim jumper scare all over again, from beginning to end, between bites of mutton stew and dumplings.

As Rannei washed and dried the dishes and tidied the kitchen, she listened to the men speak of recent news, noticing how Tommy carefully never mentioned Cal. She must not dwell on that dreadful night in January any longer, she told herself. There was nothing she could do about what had happened, and now she had her own child to think about. Drying her hands, she returned to the table, where the men sat in the comfortable gloom, still talking animatedly.

EVEN WITH TOMMY'S HELP, the lambing kept them so busy Rannei wondered how they had dared think they could manage alone. Her pregnancy hindered her more and more, for, besides helping with the sheep, she had to cook and clean for two men. She did her best and worked without complaining, but at night she was so tired she could hardly wait until the dishes were washed and she could go to bed.

It was Rannei's task to head her band of ewes on their grazing course, following along after them, watching, always watching, for coyotes and wolves, for lambs that strayed off by themselves, or ewes that got over on their backs and couldn't get up again, a danger now with the heavy fleeces they all had. If they weren't found right away and rolled over, they would bloat up and die. Meanwhile, Tommy spent his days moving the day's drop, as he called it, to the corrals, stationing the newborn lambs and their mothers close by outside of the corrals. That evening, they would be added to the small corral with the "new" bunch. Then Tommy had to check constantly on that bunch and be ready to assist Arne with the drop herd at any moment.

All this time she hardly saw Arne, for he was with the drop herd all day and half the night, since he hated to wake Tommy to take his rounds at night. They should have an extra man for night duty, Rannei realized, for someone had to check on the drop herd at least hourly during the busiest time. Some of the younger ewes had trouble birthing their lambs and, always, the man on duty had to make sure the lambs suckled at once, to secure their identification with their mothers as well as provide the necessary nourishment.

There were those mothers who simply refused, despite all measures, to claim their lambs, or, as happened in a few cases, the ewe died, leaving an orphan. These lambs, "bum lambs," created more work for Rannei, for they had to be fed by hand and she was the only one who was close enough to the house and had any time at all. Tommy told Arne that bum lambs traditionally belonged to the children and wife of the rancher, and Arne told Rannei she could have all the lambs and proceeds from them. Rannei rather liked this idea but thought it hardly worth the time she had to spend with them.

She was so tired during this period that she had little time to think about the birth of her baby. Her burden grew heavier and heavier, until she was forced to walk cradling her belly in her arms as though the baby had already been born. It was so active — it kicked and squirmed and punched her from within as though demanding to be let out at once.

Sometimes, as she walked about after her sheep, Rannei would sing the Norwegian lullabies she remembered her mother singing to her little brothers, one hand resting on top of her belly, the other against her side, where she imagined its little head to be. Amazingly, this seemed to calm the baby, who grew still and heavy against her hand. Perhaps it really could hear, Rannei thought, amazed.

The weather remained fair, with occasional cool, cloudy days, until they were more than halfway through the lambing.

Friday of the third week in May, their routine began as on every other day. The previous day had been bright and clear, and morning dawned without a cloud. At the midmorning feeding, Rannei was carrying the milk bottles out to the barn, trying to ignore her aching back, when she noticed a low gray cloud on the horizon to the southeast. The wind had picked up and was blowing harder, with a cold edge to it.

Rannei was feeling cross, tired, and out of sorts. She hated the whole lambing process and all the hard work it entailed. Besides, she couldn't remember her back ever aching this badly before. After she fed each lamb, Rannei shoved it away from her crossly. Finished at last, she hurried back to the house. She was making *flatbrød*, and it had to be done by noon because right after she fed the lambs again, she had to go back to help Tommy with the sheep.

At noon, as she headed out to the barn, she was

alarmed to see the clouds covering half the eastern sky. The wind now screamed instead of gusting. She smelled rain and snow on it, and, filled with unease, hurried through the feedings. She wasn't quite through when the barn door flew open and Tommy ran in.

"Rannei, hurry, get your bunch to the bluff bed ground right away. We're in for a storm. I started them that way, but I have to go help Arne with the drop bunch. The other bunch is alright; they're already heading into the corral." He was out the door without waiting for an answer, and she soon heard his horse's hooves thudding away to the south.

Rannei pushed the lambs back into their pen, and hurried to the house and snatched her warm cloak and scarf from the hook. She tucked a piece of bread into her pocket, threw some coal on the fire, and shut the drafts down so there would be fire when they returned. Even in the short time she was in the house, the weather had grown markedly cooler. Outside, the wind felt strangely layered, the top still warm and mild, the middle bitter with snow. A few drops stung her face; she couldn't tell if it was rain or snow, or both.

A half-mile from the bed ground she met her bunch of ewes and lambs. They were grazing at a rapid walk toward it, as if they too felt the urgency yet could not quite forego another nip at the tender young grass entirely. Sometimes they did seem to have a little sense, Rannei thought. She bunched them up and drove them along faster, wrapping her arms around her bulging belly to somehow ease the strange clenching pain in it. The sheep seemed glad to reach the familiar safety of the bed ground, and she left them there out of the wind, contentedly suckling their lambs.

Heading back toward the house, she went in a northerly direction toward Tommy's drop herd, for she knew he probably needed help with his new arrivals. Soon she met him herding in three new lambs and their mothers at a slow pace. One lamb, newly born, was straddled across the saddle in front of him, the mother bleating anxiously at his horse's heels. Rannei told him she would take them into the shed while he went back to help Arne with the rest of the drop herd. She wrapped the newborn lamb, still wet but licked clean by its mother, inside her cloak, and headed toward the sheep shed, the lamb's mother at her heels, occasionally butting Rannei with her head to remind her just whose baby she held.

But progress was slow. Every so often, when the ewe heard no response from her lamb, she'd run foolishly off in the direction from which they had come, bleating frantically. Then Rannei had to take the lamb, now warm and drowsy, from under her cloak and lay it down in the wet snowy grass and prod it to call to its mother. The mother would run back, butting at Rannei and standing over her baby protectively. When Rannei tried to reach for it, the ewe would stamp her front foot. All efforts to prod the lamb to its feet were useless; it was still too weak to walk. Eventually, Rannei managed to get to the lamb, pick it up and carry it as before, until, within a short distance, the whole thing happened over again.

Increasingly exasperated, after the third time the ewe broke away, Rannei came up a new way of carrying the newborn, tucking it under one arm, its legs dangling down so the mother could smell her lamb. In this way, feeling more ill by the minute with the strange cramps in her stomach, Rannei drove the little group toward the shed. Snowflakes had begun to fall and obscure her vision. It was wet, and her boots were soon soaked through.

All the lambs were very new and would only go a short distance before they would lie down and rest. One in particular, besides the one she carried, was very frail. He would go a few yards, then lie down, while his mother, a young ewe with a surprisingly maternal cast of mind, stood over him, licking him and cajoling him in the low throaty bleat that ewes used only to their lambs.

Finally, he lay down and refused to get up. The snow clung to his long eyelashes, and he was soaked to the tender pink skin that showed through his thin, crinkly wool coat. He was shivering. Rannei picked him up and tucked him under her other arm, and proceeded onward, its mother also trotting behind. The lambs were not heavy, but they seemed to increase in weight as she staggered forward, her cramps now coming at intervals, almost sickening in their intensity. Maybe the exertion has made me have false labor pains, Rannei told herself. It was far too early for the real ones, of course, but if they were like these, they wouldn't be very pleasant.

She focused her whole being on reaching the shelter of the sheep shed, getting the lambs to safety, and herself back in the haven of her own house. By the time she finally maneuvered the sheep to the shed, the snowfall was heavier, but still with rain mixed in. Soaked through to the skin, Rannei was so cold, and the cramps were coming closer together, and more painful each time.

I must get inside, she thought. First, however, she struggled to pen each ewe with what she hoped was its own lamb. She put the second lamb she had carried and its mother into a pen with plenty of hay, nestling the lamb into it. If the mother couldn't keep it warm, perhaps the hay would. As she closed the pen gate, she looked back and saw the lamb still shivering in the hay, the mother backed off into a corner, stamping her feet. Rannei wondered if, in the confusion, the newborn lamb had suckled. The poor thing certainly looked as if he needed some nourishment. She looked at the ewe doubtfully. She was a large ewe and not friendly; it would be impossible to set her up on her rump, as the men did, and suckle the lamb that way.

Carefully, Rannei opened the gate again and stepped inside. Perhaps she could back the ewe into a corner and approach her from the side. It might work. Rannei picked up the shivering little bundle again, and holding it with her right arm, she crowded the ewe into the corner. She saw a full teat protruding from back of the hind leg. Now if she could just hold the ewe there and let the lamb suck a little — she knew lambs usually suckled from the side, but this particular ewe's udder was so swollen with milk it stuck out behind. It was not actually milk, Rannei knew, but a thick yellow fluid that was extremely nourishing and provided the lamb with energy enough to enable him to survive the important first hours.

She leaned her hip against the ewe's flank, reached down clumsily over her belly, and seized the teat from behind. At the touch of Rannei's hand, the ewe reacted in outrage. She leaped forward and sideways, striking Rannei hard with her rump in the side of her belly. Rannei dropped the lamb and fell sideways, hitting the other side of her belly against the lower rail of the pen. She grabbed the top bar and hung there, unbalanced, the wind knocked out of her. Somehow, she controlled her trembling knees enough to sink onto the hay instead of falling.

Rannei knelt there, her cheek against the rough bark of the rail; in her nostrils the smell of the wood mingled with the wet wool odor of the sheep. She felt nauseous and beads of sweat popped out on her forehead and ran down onto her nose. Another of the terrible cramps stabbed through her. Still holding to the rail with one hand, she leaned over and heaved dryly. Bile burned her throat and ran out her nose and her mouth onto the hay. Her womb spasmed and knotted painfully. Behind her the ewe stamped and called to the unresponsive lamb.

Arne will be so angry, was her first coherent thought. She remembered suddenly the summer storm, the lightning, and the horses careening over the prairie, Arne yelling at her although it had not been her fault. Why didn't I tell him that? she thought. It wasn't my fault. This wasn't her fault, either. She shouldn't have tried to handle the big ewe by herself, but Arne got so angry when a lamb died. A strange moaning sound filled her ears, and she looked around at the ewe, now standing in the opposite corner, over the curled, still body of the lamb, which, somehow, she must have dropped. The ewe stared hostilely back at her and stamped her foot. Rannei realized the sound was issuing from her own throat.

An unbelievable pain knotted her womb, and she dropped her head onto her knees and curled her body into the hay. Her back was a red-hot poker of pain, her whole being one huge ache. The knowledge that she was going into labor flooded into Rannei's brain. It can't be, she thought frantically. I'm not due for another month. In her mind, she heard her mother telling a mother-to-be that a backache was often the first sign of labor. Rannei's had been aching all day, and then the exertion of moving the sheep and carrying the lambs — oh no, it simply could not happen now. It was too soon, and she was all alone.

The contraction eased, and she tried to stand, clinging to the side of the pen. She must get to the house, to her bed. It must not happen here. A warm wet liquid streamed down the inside of her thigh and leg, filling her boot. There was no doubt about what that meant, she knew. Her water had broken and the birth was beginning. Blind panic filled Rannei. Moaning, she sank, to her knees again. Was she to die here alone, giving birth in this pen like an animal on the ground? Oh, no, it was too cruel.

"My God my God my God," she said aloud, hearing her own words incredulously. She never prayed to God, no, it was Freya who must help her now. "Freya, beautiful one, help me," she choked out, but another contraction, worse than any before, forced her down to the hay. She curled up as best she could, her knees drawn up, her hands curled around her belly under the cloak. Her back eased a little as she breathed deeply and slowly, willing herself to surmount the pain.

With each ebbing pain, disconnected thoughts flashed through her brain. Her mother always said first babies took longer in coming. How long did Rannei have? Everything was ready at the house, if only she could get to it, the nightgown and the clean sheet, so neatly folded inside the wooden chest, on the very top where she could reach it easily. The little case of herbs and instructions beside it, written in both English and Norwegian, which she knew by heart.

First, be sure the hands of the deliverer are clean, well washed with soap and water. She saw her own hands, filthy, smelling of oil from the sheep's wool, covered with pungent orange birth coating from the newborn lambs. Would her baby look like that, all orangey? No, she remembered. Human babies had a waxy, yellowish substance all over them. Helping her mother, she had washed it away from one more than once. What else must she have? Clean linen for the bed, and for the mother, a clean gown. She looked down at her crouched form, her skirt pulled up and around her belly, stained and wet. Even her petticoat was sodden.

BIRTH IS A NATURAL PROCESS, she heard her mother Kristin saying, *there is nothing to worry about if all goes well.* Mother had to call the doctor in to assist her only a few times, but one time, the mother had died, with the doctor right beside her and Mother holding her hand. Rannei had been a small girl then, watching wide-eyed from the doorway. But better not to think of that.

Somehow, she must get to the house. Rannei pulled herself up again and tried to stand, but another contraction forced her down. This was pain, real pain, such pain as she had never felt before. She screamed in agony and saw the ewe lower her head and back as far into the corner as she could.

The pain ebbed again, and Rannei lay panting in the hay. It was impossible, she could not do it by herself. Through the open side of the shed opposite her, she could see the snowflakes whirling, big, blobby pieces of white. Her forehead felt icy cold, but the sweat poured down it. There was no time, no time at all. She would never make it; better to stay here out of the wind than have the baby out in the yard. Her worst nightmare was being realized: the baby would come and no one was beside her to help.

Arne!" she screamed with all her might. "Arne! Arne! Help me! Tommy! *Hjelpe meg! Hjelpe!*" There was no sound except for the bleating of the sheep and the shrieking of the wind. She screamed and screamed. It eased the pain a little. Where was Arne? The ewe kept to her corner. The lamb must have been dead; it wasn't moving.

The poker of fire in Rannei's back had now become a band of fire that ran all the way across it. As she reclined back in the hay, her knees came up automatically, the position for birthing. She could feel the ewe's breath on her face, but she had stopped snorting and stamping and had moved closer, staring down with her white, foolish face into Rannei's with a look of almost human interest. *She knows what is happening,* Rannei thought wildly. *Was it the same for her?*

The hay jabbed against her skin, made tender with pain. She mustn't wait any longer, Rannei realized. The last contraction had a bearing down quality that was different from the others. She must make ready. She lifted her soaked skirt to her waist, no time to take it off, and pulled at her petticoat, fumbling at the fastenings until they pulled loose. She did her best to spread it out on the hay on either side of her. She wore nothing beneath her petticoat — she had given up wearing drawers when her waist expanded. Her boots she left on — that didn't matter now.

Suddenly Mother was there, and a great peace filled Rannei. *You are not alone,* Mother's voice said, *I am with you. We can do this together. It is a task that must be done, and then you can sleep forever.*

"Push, push," Rannei chanted with Mother, and pushed, the blood roaring in her ears. Someone was grunting fiercely, obscenely. *Now push, Rannei,* Mother said, and Rannei pushed with all her strength. She felt something warm and wet and slithery between her thighs, a heavy warm mass. Something hot and wet was running down her legs. She wanted to curl up in the hay and sleep, but there remained something else to do. *Rannei!* Mother said sternly, urgently. *The baby, the cord.* Rannei propped herself up on one arm and took in the wet shining mass between her legs. It did not look like a baby.

Then Kristin was gone, and Arne was there, an apparition white with snow, throwing off his coat, pulling back the pen gate, fumbling with a knife in his hands.

"No, Arne!" she screamed. For a horrible second Rannei thought he meant to kill her or the baby, then realized he was preparing to cut the cord.

"No, Arne, tie it first," she said. He nodded that he understood. Arne ripped a strip off the edge of her petticoat with the knife, and knelt beside her. He tied the cloth around the cord, seized the knife back from Tommy, who had somehow appeared beside Arne, and cut the cord. She floated back onto the hay, seeing above her Arne's triumphant face as he held the wet, red-streaked, yellow-ish, squirming object up by its feet and spanked it gently. The baby gave a gasping cry, like a swimmer who had taken too much water, then burst into a loud high yell. The ewe stamped her foot by Rannei's head.

"A daughter, Rannei," Arne was saying over and over. "We have a beautiful daughter, Rannei."

She held up her arms. "My baby," she said, "give me my baby, Arne."

Arne leaned down and placed the baby in her arms and wrapped her cloak around them both. The baby stopped yelling as she held it tightly against her breast. She dimly felt Arne pull her petticoat from under her and wad it up between her legs, heard him say to Tommy: "We must stop the bleeding."

Tommy's white face, eyes dark as coal, floated above her. A feeling of great power filled her and she smiled up at them both, seeing, just before she closed her eyes, the look of passionate love on Arne's face, naked and unde-fended. She spun away on that feeling of exultation like a leaf on the wind, rising, falling, whirling, dancing. Rising above them all, she looked down at Tommy's worried, horrified face, Arne on his knees beside her body, spread and bloody and triumphant on the hay.

IT'S THE MUSIC AGAIN, my own music, at last. Gently, now, so it won't go away. That tune — different, but I know it, always the same one, but how different each time. That instrument is a flute, but more like wind chimes, or a harpsichord, so soft and delicate — pine tree notes, spider webs thrumming in the wind from the fjord, fairy music — *but Rannei, there are no fairies. I know, Mother, but that's what it sounds like, always the same rhythm, blowing colors against my eyes.*

The greens, deepening and shifting and fading, like the waters in the fjord, icy green but warming into blue, blue, blue — the music is the color and the color is the music. That's what I never knew before. The blues and golds, the Catholic Church in Bergen — see how the pagans worship, Rannei, Grandmother says. Better the old gods than the Catholics. Music, fading into purple, red, purple-red, and strange ugly shapes, the wet red wound gaping at the edges and blood, blood, blood all over the hay.

OPENING her eyes from her dream, Rannei could not focus for a moment on the face bending over hers. It withdrew, then came back, closer this time, a face she knew; Sally's face.

"Drink this, Rannei," Sally's voice said, and Rannei sipped obediently from the cup. That smell was one she recognized. Drifting again into sleep, she remembered her mother giving her a similar tea when Rannei had sprained her ankle, and when she had a cold, and when she fell through the ice into the fjord that winter day. *But I'm not ill,* she thought astonished. *I've had a baby.*

"You're awake again," Sally's face beamed down at her.

"Here's some more tea for you. It's from your mother's case, and Arne says it will do you good."

Rannei tried to smile back, but her face felt stiff, caked in blood. No, it had not been her face, but Arne's hands, so red, holding the squirming thing aloft, the baby, the red on his hands her blood. She searched Sally's face and saw warmth and kindness smiling down at her. She said, "The baby?"

"The baby is fine," Sally said. "You have a daughter, a beautiful little girl, a hungry one, too."

"What day is this?"

"Almost evening on Friday. Your baby was born three days ago, on Tuesday. You've slept a long time." In the distance, Rannei heard a thin, high wailing, like a mewling kitten.

"See, she wants her dinner," Sally said. "I'll bring her to you. I've been giving her a sugar pap and soaking it in cow's milk, but she wants her mother's milk."

"Of course, she does!" Rannei said. "I can feed her."

The very thought of sugar pap made Rannei anxious. Kristin always said they were dangerous.

The baby was brought, still mewling, and laid at Rannei's breast. She felt the tiny mouth fumbling at her nipple, so taut and swollen. The milk must have come in; her breasts ached, painfully full. The bundled baby was surprisingly heavy lying against her. Rannei's arms felt like logs. She could not lift them, could hardly hold them around her daughter. The baby cried in gasping wails, her eyes squeezed shut, her mouth incredibly wide open. Her fists were clenched, waving wildly. One flew into the gaping mouth and the baby gave a sobbing, angry gasp, sucked frantically for a moment on the fist, then it flew out again, and the mouth resumed its loud wailing.

Rannei looked down at her daughter. She had not expected her to be ugly. The scrunched-up face was a brilliant red. Strange lumps showed through the thick long brush of golden hair sticking straight up all over her pulsating skull. The minute ears, flat against the head, were crimped at the edges like a pie shell.

"Sally," she said helplessly and Sally was there, adjusting breast and mouth, firmly trapping the angry waving fists. Miraculously, the baby stopped yelling as mouth met nipple. Suddenly its tiny mouth clamped down hard, and the baby began to suck with all its strength.

"There," Sally said with satisfaction, and stepped away.

Rannei closed her eyes, concentrating on this odd new sensation. It was not like Arne's mouth, caressing and tender. This grip was demanding, uncaring, primitive. The baby made little satisfied sounds, and curled its fist tightly where it lay against her breast. Hers. Her daughter. How strange. Her daughter's skull was not quite as red as it had been, but the face was so pink and splotched. Did newborns always look like this? She tried to remember. If only Mother were here. Rannei felt herself begin to sink away and opened her eyes quickly. She did not want to go back to her dreams just yet. There was only the moment, now, that she could think about.

Even as Rannei gazed down at her, the baby sucked less vigorously and her head lolled back, milk dribbling from the open mouth. She was asleep. Rannei looked up inquiringly at Sally, then felt a sudden tug. The mouth clamped down again, only to release its hold a few seconds later. This time Sally took the bundle from Rannei's leaden arms, and Rannei closed her eyes gratefully, the color patterns beginning again. The music swept her into a sleep as deep and seamless and blue-green as the ocean.

VOICES AGAIN. Sally's and Arne's. The strange, warm sensation, at her right breast this time, the almost painful clasping of the mouth, and then the strong, steady pulling. The feeling of relief was almost pleasant. She felt herself smiling, drifting back to sleep.

"There! Now you're awake. Try to drink some of this tea."

Sally held a cup to Rannei's lips, and she sipped, her eyes still closed. The herb tea again, warm, soothing, but she smelled mutton broth too, and it sickened her. She turned her head away. If only they would let her alone! She was so weak, and sleepy. Sally's voice insisted: "You must eat, child. You must keep up your strength. You don't want to lose your milk, do you?"

Rannei forced her weighted eyelids open. "No," she said distinctly, and Sally slipped a spoonful of broth in her mouth.

STILL LATER, Rannei again swam slowly to the surface

and lazily opened her eyes. Arne's face was close to hers. He was talking steadily, the sound that had awakened her. He was holding the baby in his two big hands. The tiny bundle barely filled them. "Our daughter, Rannei. We will call her for you."

"No, no," Rannei said, so loudly she made him jump. "I want to call her Kristin, for Mother."

"If you like, Rannei," Arne said, his voice filled with joy, perhaps because she'd talked to him. "Maybe Kristin Rannei Bergstrom? She is so beautiful, our daughter."

Rannei looked at her husband in astonishment. How strange for Arne to say that. "She is ugly," she said, and closed her eyes.

IT WAS dark when she awoke again. The coal oil lamp on the table provided only a small circle of light. *If they would only let me sleep,* she thought peevishly, but the voice was insistent.

"Mrs. Bergstrom, Mrs. Bergstrom, can you hear me? I'm Doctor Tom Winslow."

"Of course, I can hear you! But I don't need a doctor, I've already had my baby," Rannei said crossly. Reluctantly, she opened her eyes to take in a young, earnest face peering down at her in the dim light.

"Perhaps not, but let me examine you, since I've come all the way from Minnesela for that purpose." His voice was young, too, but sure and professional. Well, really, what did it matter now, after all that other business?

"Bring the lamp here, if you please, Mrs. Porter."

Sally brought the lamp and held it beside the bed. Rannei saw how tired and strained she looked and felt a twinge of conscience. What trouble she must be causing. The doctor pulled the curtain, shutting the rest of the room out. His hands probed gently here and there, but she fell asleep before he was through. Later, she heard them again, behind the curtain.

"She has lost a lot of blood," the doctor was saying, "probably from the baby coming so fast. She is torn a bit, but she is healing well, and no sign of infection. There is nothing I can do about the blood — it will just take time to build it up again. It is why she is so weak and disoriented. She must have rest, and all she can eat. The baby is a good healthy child, not a bit premature, I would say. Perhaps she miscalculated."

"Ya, perhaps," came Arne's voice. "She works too hard, with the lambing. I do not take proper care."

"You must not blame yourself, Mr. Bergstrom. A few weeks and she will be strong again. Then, too, the shock of having the baby under those conditions — but when one thinks of the Indian women, giving birth in a field or wood, then going about their business, one realizes that women are really extremely strong. Your wife is young and healthy, and she will recover."

"Thank you, thank you, doctor," Arne said, his voice thick with emotion. "There is no bed, but there is a buffalo robe, and a quilt for the floor. The lady sleeps here on the straw mattress."

"The robe will be fine, thank you. I always bring my own bedroll, and now if this young man will see to my horse? Already done? Perhaps I will retire, then."

Young man? Rannei remembered then for the first time that Tommy had been in the barn with Arne.

For a moment an image nagged at her mind of Arne, and Tommy, too. With the small house full of guests, they must be sleeping in the sheep shelter on the hay. But how wonderful, Rannei thought, that she could have this bed all to herself. And how cool and clean the sheets felt! She stretched her feet to the far corner of the bed, comforted by the thought of the doctor on the other side of the curtain. Drifting off to sleep, she thought how she hadn't needed him. She had done it all by herself.

MORNING AGAIN, the room filled with sunlight streaming in from the open kitchen door and pulled back curtain. Earlier, Rannei remembered, she'd been half-awakened by Sally putting the baby to her breast. Now the doctor and Sally were seated at the table. Rannei heard the clink of cups. They were drinking coffee. Lying very still, she listened as they talked.

"You're becoming quite a nurse, Mrs. Porter," the doctor was saying. "You'll have to hire out to me. First Cal Willard, and now this. But it's a good thing for Mrs. Bergstrom that you could come. That's the most wonderful thing I find about this country, people do help one another. It would be a hard life, I guess, if we didn't."

"Of course, I want to help her all I can, poor thing," Sally's voice was warm and cheerful, as always. "When I think of one of my own daughters doing what she did, all alone, I shudder."

"Has Cal Porter left for the east yet?" The doctor asked. "I thought Tommy, the other night, said something about him being back?"

Hearing Cal's name, Rannei slowed her breathing to hear.

"He started out east all right," Sally said, her voice settling into a comfortable, gossipy tone. "My boy Henry drove him to Pierre, but Jeffrey, you know, from down on the Belle, talked him into being his ranch supervisor, to train his horses. Cal's good with horses."

"But wasn't that how he got his hip broken?" the doctor asked.

"Oh — yes," Sally said after a slight pause. "But that was just an accident. He doesn't have many of those."

So that's how they all explained his injury, Rannei thought. *Protecting Arne, protecting me.*

"I see. Well, it's good news for us that he's staying."

"He'll always have the limp, you think?" Sally asked.

"It depends on whether we got the bone set properly," the doctor said slowly, as if thinking it through. "As you know, by the time I got there it was already very swollen. He should be able to have almost full use of it, however, even with a limp."

As Rannei listened, silent slow tears seeped from her eyes, and she turned her head so they would run into the pillow.

SOMETIME LATER SHE awoke from an uneasy doze to

find the doctor sitting beside her, holding her wrist in his hand, and talking earnestly.

"You must eat now, Mrs. Bergstrom. You will recover if you do, but in your weakened state you might catch a cold or other illness, which would be hard to shake off. I recommend plenty of milk and meat broth."

His voice was so earnest she couldn't help but smile at him. It was gratifying to see his quick response, to know that after months of ugliness, she could still make men smile.

"Stay in bed a few more weeks, and let Mrs. Porter wait on you. Take care of your baby and enjoy her. I'll look in on you on my way back. I'm on my way right now to the Fisher ranch, near the North Dakota line — do you know them? They are neighbors of yours, and not so far, either. Their children are all down with something."

Still the doctor lingered, and she saw that he wanted her to say something, so she smiled again, and said, "Thank you for coming, Doctor Winslow," and held out her hand to him. He pressed it warmly between both of his. He was quite good looking, with dark wavy hair, brown intelligent eyes, and a warm, pleasant manner. She would like to talk to him some more, if only she weren't so tired.

"I will do my best to get well," she whispered, and was surprised to find that she meant it. The next day, she did feel stronger, and she began to eat a little, because she knew she had to, for the baby's sake.

Sally fixed invalid's food for her, broth and mashed potatoes, and all the milk Rannei could get down. The baby nursed greedily, and hardly cried at all now that she had plenty to eat. When she did cry, Sally rocked her in the rocking chair, crooning to her.

One day as Rannei was growing more alert, Sally chose a time when Arne and Tommy were out and the two women were alone to give Rannei Cal's written message. It was simple and straightforward. He merely wrote a few sentences, saying he wished Rannei and the baby well, and that he sent his regards to Arne.

Rannei read it under Sally's inquisitive eye, then thanked her and said she would send him a letter, too, when Sally went home. When Arne was not around, Sally talked freely about Cal, but Rannei learned little more than she'd overheard in Sally's conversation with the doctor.

After a fortnight, Rannei was sitting up and walking around the house, venturing as far as the back step to sit a minute in the sunshine, bathing the baby and tending to her feeding. Now that Rannei could manage the baby on her own, Sally declared it was time for her to go home.

Saying her farewells, she set off across the prairie in the buckboard. She carried with her a message Rannei had written to Cal, which Rannei left unsealed, so Sally could read it if she liked.

Chapter Twenty-Eight

*C*al carried his trunk, the last of his possessions, from his buckboard into the cabin that would be his home for the foreseeable future. "Cabin" was hardly an appropriate name for the building, which was a small replica of the ranch house, a massive and elegant structure, built with logs from the Black Hills, as was his cabin. It was quite an upward leap from his shack on his Gumbo claim, Cal thought wryly. He had to admit to himself he wouldn't mind a little luxury. He and Henry Porter, who would be his assistant, would live in the palatial cabin and eat in the cookhouse with the rest of the crew.

The main room of his new abode had several big windows that gave perfect light for his art work. Best of all, Jeffrey seemed delighted to have an artist living on his ranch and encouraged him to spend all the time he wanted painting and drawing. Cal had immediately sent an order for more art supplies, including oils and pastels. At last he would be able to realize his dream of painting

Rannei. First, of course, he must finish the Dakota sketch-book and get it to his New York publishers.

As he stabled the team and Jubal, who had of course come with him, the stable boy, Dickson, came out from his quarters to introduce himself, and greet Cal, as they had been expecting him ever since Stuart Jeffrey had arrived home from his trip to Pierre and informed his hands they would have a new horse boss. The breeding, training, and care of the horses were all to be under Cal's supervision. Right now, Cal's immediate plans included dispatching several of the ranch cowboys to the Porter station where they and the Porter boys would round up his horse herd from somewhere out near his abandoned homestead, and bring them to the Jeffrey ranch.

Cal, however, would not go with them. Not only was he unable to sit a horse comfortably yet, due to last winter's hip injury, but for the moment, he did not want to go near his former claim, or the Bergstrom's either, much as he ached to see them and how and whether Rannei had survived her childbirth ordeal. The last he had heard, at the Porter's just before young Henry had driven him to Pierre, was from Tommy, who had arrived right after the sudden May storm that had brought Rannei's daughter into the world, to fetch his mother to care for Rannei. For months he had carried in his mind the scene as described by Tommy and embroidered in his own mind in truly horrifying detail: "And Rannei, she had the baby all by herself in a sheep pen with an ewe and lamb, and Arne cut the cord, and Ma, there was so much blood. . ." and Sally's not-so- comforting reply. "'Course there's blood—there always is."

He had had to sit there, unnoticed and unwanted, hearing this and knowing there was nothing he could do, except say febbely to Sally, "Shouldn't we send for Doctor Tom?" and hearing her call to Jimmie to do just that.

Henry arrived at the ranch the following day, and brought his few possessions into their quarters. Thrilled and excited by it all, it took him but a few minutes to hand Cal Rannei's note. Cal tucked the note into his shirt pocket and made Henry relate every bit of news his mother had relayed to him. All the details of the birth in the sheep pen, Rannei's recovery, the "darling babe" (his mother's words) who looked like Arne, and Arne's infatuation with the child. Then Cal left Henry to unpack and went to visit Jubal in the horse pasture. Leaning against the railing, with Jubal nuzzling his ear, he read Rannei's short note.

Dear Cal,

Thank you for your message. I have a daughter now. Her name is Kristin Rannei Bergstrom. Kristin for my mother and Rannei because Arne wished it. She is ugly now, but I hope she will improve. I am happy you will remain in the Dakotas.

Your friend,

Rannei

"Thank God," Cal said huskily to Jubal. Rannei, at least, was still his friend. Perhaps, in time, it might be possible to repair the breach in his friendship with Arne. Perhaps. Jubal nickered throatily into his neck in sympathy, as Cal dried his tears on his shirt sleeve.

❄

As Rannei grew stronger every day, so, too, the baby grew and became less ugly in Rannei's eyes. She lost the red splotches on her skin, and it turned gradually into a fair, rosy pink. The ugly lumps on her head diminished with time, and the golden fuzz, Arne's hair, did not fall out, in the manner of most newborns, but instead began to grow longer. Her eyes, a baby's dark blue, slowly lightened and became the gentian blue of Rannei's own eyes. Little Kristin had tiny feathery beginnings of eyebrows, but no eyelashes yet.

As Rannei regained her health, she liked to imagine her parents receiving the letter she'd sent them, which Sally had taken with her to mail from Porter Stage Station.

It had been a long letter, telling Kristin and Lars of the baby's birth in the sheep pen. Rannei had thanked her mother for helping her through the ordeal in spirit, although of course it had been much more real than that to Rannei. Her mother would understand. "Our daughter is named for us both, Mother," she wrote, "although she looks like Arne, with all that yellow hair. But he says she has my eyes, so she has some of us both." Rannei sent loving greetings to all the family, but did not mention her failed attempt to leave the Gumbo, nor the dreadful winter that followed, nor her dislike of her new home. That could wait. For now she must mend in both body and spirit.

It was a strange waiting time. The baby thrived and grew, and cried no more than she should. Arne, fascinated by his mite of a daughter, was always stealing in from his chores to stand over the cradle and look at her, and would take her in his arms at the slightest murmur. He rocked her in Rannei's rocking chair, looking enormous with the tiny infant lying on his broad chest. When he resumed sleeping on his side of the bed, he put the cradle where he could reach it in the night and rock it if need be. It was Arne who reached out with a sure hand in the dark and brought the baby to Rannei's breast, never sleeping until the baby was fed. After patting her back to bring up the wind, he laid her gently back in the cradle.

Rannei was amazed at this, and then wondered why she was. Arne was always tender with young things, and her own little brothers had adored him. He never showed disappointment that the baby was a girl instead of a boy, and when Rannei mentioned this to him, he looked incredulous.

"Oh, Rannei, we will have sons! I am glad this one is a daughter, for your sake, and mine too. I am only disappointed that she looks like me, not you. Thank goodness she will have your eyes."

Arne, she could see, was almost wild with happiness. He had his Rannei back and a precious daughter he adored. To Arne the baby was a miracle, and Rannei the giver of miracles. She could not help but respond to his joy. They were not lovers yet, but Rannei found herself more impatient than Arne, waiting for her body to heal.

The first day Rannei, coaxed by Arne, ventured out into the mild May sunshine, holding Kristin close, she saw the Gumbo as she had never thought to see it again. Green and verdant with new grass, covered by the soft blue sky, she remembered last May's trip to the Porters and her delight at each new discovery. But it also brought memories of Cal and the friendship they had all shared, and never would again. The merciful numbness of the winter months had long since faded and been replaced by an almost too acute awareness of all she had lost and a despair that she could ever make it right among them again. She pulled her sunbonnet further over her eyes to hide her face from Arne, and vowed silently to make Arne understand Cal's part in the whole affair.

Arne pointed to the horse pasture where Freya had come to the fence at the sight of them. Together they walked to greet the horse and introduce her to little Kristin. Rannei leaned her head against Freya's cheek as the mare snuffled at the bundle in her arms and brought forth the wrinkled, last-year's carrot in her apron pocket. The new ones were just showing feathery greens tops in the garden Arne had planted in early May. Freya gummed the carrot politely, then spit it out. Rannei longed for the day when she could leap into the saddle and fly across the prairie on her back.

May ended, a beautiful month of flowers and sun, except for that one unseasonable storm. Every time Arne came in from tending the sheep, he would bring handfuls of little yellow buttercups that grew along the creek bank, or the pasque flowers from the bluff, or the orange mallow roses that rambled low along the ground on the burnout banks.

"For my ladies," he would say with a flourish, courting Rannei all over again with his ardent looks and tender hugs.

But Rannei felt different, uncertain of being courted,

even. She was grown up and a mother. She would never be that girl who adored Arne with unquestioning self-abandonment.

Sometimes, she still thought of her dowry money that Cal had given her, hidden where Arne would never find it. She could not tell him about that yet. The trip to Minnesela for supplies, which Arne had made in May while Sally was here and she was recovering, had taken almost the last of their supply of money in the Minnesela bank account. They would have to make do with what they had until the wool money came in, but Cal would have to be repaid somehow.

Arne had told her he would give her the dowry money back at shearing time. When he made good on his word, she would tell him she had the dowry money still, and would give him half of that back to pay Cal. The rest of the balance owed to Cal would have to come from the shearing money. This would show Arne, she hoped, that she considered them partners, something Arne would have to understand if they were to continue as man and wife. She had learned she could survive here now but if she wanted to leave, she and her daughter, she had a right to do so. Arne needed to do his part.

So much had changed in how she thought of herself, yet Arne continued to act as if everything had returned to normal, and she was the same young girl who adored him so blindly. One day as Rannei was passing by the gilt-framed mirror on the wall, she paused and stared at her reflection. She had hardly looked in the mirror the months before the baby came, and not at all since, and she had almost forgotten what she looked like. The image struck her full force. The girl in the mirror was startlingly, almost embarrassingly, beautiful. The shining black braid framed her white oval face. Her huge, blue-purple eyes were set off by thick black eyelashes. Even her lips looked a healthy red, a sign of her rapidly returning health. Rannei's ordeal had marked her not at all, she realized, except to make her more beautiful.

She remembered again how aghast the Porters had been when she'd suggested cutting her hair. Her family, too. Everyone always loved it so. But it was such a nuisance, and she'd always felt as if her long hair belonged to others, even more than to her. Seizing the scissors from her sewing basket, she unwound her single fat braid and sawed through the thick hair. Then it was done. She undid the braid and shook her hair free. It fell to her shoulders, wavy from the braiding, thick and lustrous. How strange it felt, swinging around her shoulders.

Rannei looked in the mirror at the soft hair framing her face. It made her look younger, and less regal, perhaps. For a moment, she felt like sobbing with grief and sorrow, but then she smiled. Now her hair truly belonged to her alone. Not yet willing to part with her hair entirely, Rannei wound the severed braid into a circle and tied it with some yarn. She put it into her dowry chest wrapped in a soft linen cloth, feeling as if she were laying part of herself away, the other Rannei, the careless, happy girl who had grown up in Norway, forever defined by her long, black hair.

Arne and Tommy, coming in from the evening chores, both stopped and stared as one, mouths hanging open.

Tommy only gasped, but Arne strode over to her, looking behind her back as if somehow the shorn hair might be lurking there.

"Rannei, your hair."

"What do you think?"

"Your beautiful hair! But why?"

"I was tired of it," Rannei said simply. "I don't have time anymore for all that washing and brushing and braiding."

There was grief in Arne's face. Then, his face cleared. "Well by golly, it looks pretty too that way, only you look different, Rannei."

"I am different," Rannei said, and something in her face made Arne wrap his long arms around her and kiss her long and tenderly. Tommy slipped back out the door, scrubbing his hand across his eyes.

"You don't think I love you for your hair only, Rannei?" he whispered, holding her close.

WITH THE LAMBING over at last, and Rannei feeling better every day, Tommy was impatient to go home for a few weeks. Arne handed Tommy his wages cheerfully, even though he now would not have enough cash for the windmill he wanted to buy for the well that had yet to be dug. That would have to wait until after the shearing.

Coming over to Rannei, Tommy bashfully took her hand, and blushed as she kissed him on the cheek. Arne clapped Tommy on the back. Then Tommy, swung aboard his horse and loped away to the west, over the track that was fast becoming a road, through the beautiful June day. Rannei stood beside Arne in the yard, shielding the baby's eyes from the sun, her hair blowing freely about her head, watching the horse and rider until it was nothing more than a black dot on the horizon. Then it too was gone.

A Conversation with the Author

Is the Big Gumbo a real place? Where Is it? Did you live there?

Yes, the Big Gumbo is a real place in northern South Dakota and southern North Dakota, but it is not on any map. It is a local name in that part of the Dakotas. It is a large area of land with mostly 'gumbo' soil, a heavy soil that turns into clay-like mud when wet.

The ranch where I grew up was in the southwest area of North Dakota, not far from the Montana line on the west and the South Dakota line to the south. Later, my family moved to my father's partner's ranch, on the edge of the gumbo area, close to South Dakota, and I herded sheep there in the summers, during my college years.

Are you Norwegian? Have you spent time in Norway?

My DNA test shows that I am almost fifty-eight percent Norwegian with English, Irish and a mixture of other nationalities. My husband is one hundred percent

Scandinavian, first generation, with a Norwegian mother and a Danish father. We have traveled to Norway and Denmark several times and met some of his relatives there.

Is this book fiction or is this a family story—your family?

The nucleus of this book began with stories my father told me about his Norwegian grandparents, who raised him on a horse ranch in western North Dakota not far from the Big Gumbo I write about. I have read many books about Norwegian immigrants on the western plains, and heard stories from other members of my family and my husband's relatives. So some of it is suggested by family stories, and my own experiences as a shepherd, but it is all fiction.

When and where were you a shepherd?

My younger sister, June, and I herded my family's flock, starting when we were six and seven years old until I was fifteen and we moved to Missoula, Montana. We started with a hundred head and eventually had about one thousand. Later, I herded sheep during summers on my father's partner's ranch on the edge of the 'Big Gumbo' area. The sheep episodes in *The Big Gumbo* are all based on my own experiences, including the wolf episode.

What was your main reason for writing this story?

I was fascinated as a young girl by the Big Gumbo stories I heard from my father's partner, who lived on the edge of it, just over the North Dakota line. His ranch was much more isolated than the ranch where I grew up, and neighbors were sometimes ten or more miles apart. Women were so isolated that I was told by the mail lady that she was often late on her route because the ranch wives would wait for her by the mailbox just to visit with her. Several mail boxes grouped together was a gathering spot for ranch women as they waited for the mail. In 1891, of course, there were no daily mail deliveries and no cars, so women were even more isolated.

I loved the stories of Willa Cather and Edna Ferber and the pioneers who settled the plains, including my Norwegian great-grandparents who made a success of their Dakota horse ranch, and my maternal great-grandparents who tried to farm and failed in the dry years. I saw how hard my mother and grandmother and the neighbor women worked without running water and electricity or telephones. Although I loved the ranch and the prairie, I did not want to live my life like that.

Rannei seems pretty modern for the time. Were there really Norwegian feminists like her in 1891? How unusual was her perspective even in Norway?

Rannei was probably unusual even in Norway, but Norwegian feminists were ahead of American feminists. From 1854 to 1879, formal equality for women with men became almost universal, although not without resistance. The vote was not achieved until 1907. In Norway, suffrage was more of a class thing. Rannei was raised by liberal, educated parents from the wealthy elite, and her entire family was very well educated. Arne's family, although they owned their small farm, were poor. Arne attended the village school and then had to quit and help his family survive by fishing.

Women expressed themselves through literature, and with her liberal parents and grandparents, Rannei was exposed to the writings of Camilla Collette and Aasta Hansteen and saw plays by Henrik Ibsen, all of whom dealt with the conflict between conventional society and the feelings and needs of the individual. It was the wealthy elite who could afford books and plays.

Is Rannei's relationship to God and her Norse Gods unusual? How does she compare to the average Norwegian immigrant of the era?

Rannei loved the Norse saga literature and the tales of the golden age when Vikings ruled the world. These tales were often retold by the older folk in her village, most of whom had not gone beyond the village school. Norwegians were proud of their Viking heritage as they still are today, even as they adhere to the Lutheran Faith, as many of them do. Rannei's parents had a town house in Bergen, where Rannei and her older brothers attended secondary school, or college. Rannei's mother was Christian but her Bergen grandmother, the wife of a wealthy trader, made sure Rannei was exposed to sailors and people from all over the world, who told tales of other cultures and gods. Nobody considered Rannei's beliefs unusual in her family although her mother tried to gently persuade her of her own Christian beliefs.

Acknowledgments

My utmost gratitude goes to Laurie Rockenbeck, niece, author and independent publisher, who saw a promise in my rather unwieldly thesis and offered to publish it. Claire Gebben, my wonderful editor, also an author, helped me organize it in novel form. Her invaluable advice and corrections taught this former journalist how a novel should be written.

Along the way, the enthusiasm, and suggestions given me by Marg Rockenbeck kept the process going, and I thank her sincerely. I also am grateful to the three authors who kindly endorsed my book, Dr. Jane Healy, Robert Lee and William Kittredge. Kittredge was an inspiration and mentor at the University of Montana when I was working on my MFA in Creative Writing.

I owe my inspiration for this story to stories my father told around the supper table about his Norwegian grandparents, who raised him, and to my mother, who always encouraged me to write my stories. As a child, I devoured books about early immigration, especially about western North and South Dakota, and the struggles of women pioneers in the plains where I was raised, on a sheep ranch in western North Dakota.

None of this would have happened without the support of my husband, Jack, who always made sure I had a room to write in, and the patience and enthusiasm of my sons, Kriss and Eric, who always liked the stories I told them better than the ones in books. When I was writing this as a thesis for an MFA, my boys, still in grade school at the time, learned to cook and prepare meals with their father, and put up with my long hours of typing (on a small portable typewriter), and research at the library (no internet then).

Now adults, my sons, husband, my extended family and friends continue to provide the invaluable enthusiasm and support every author needs.

Thank you all.

Jean Herbert Winthers

Jean Herbert Winthers was raised on a sheep ranch in western North Dakota, not far from the Big Gumbo area she writes about in her first novel, *The Big Gumbo*. She herded sheep with her younger sister when she was seven years old, and many of the incidents she describes in her book occurred to the two of them.

Jean moved with her family to Missoula, Montana when she was fifteen. There she finished high school and graduated from the University of Montana with a degree in Journalism. Her first job was as Associate Editor for the *Alaska Sportsman Magazine*. Later, back in Missoula, she married and earned an MFA in Creative Writing with an early version of *The Big Gumbo* as her thesis novel.

With her forester husband, Jack, and their two sons, Kriss and Eric, she moved around the west, always near a ski area, working for various newspapers as reporter, photographer, and columnist. Winthers was also the editor of the *Selah Valley Optimist*, in Selah, Washington. In Colorado, she wrote magazine articles for the *Vail Beavercreek Magazine* and stories for the *Vail Daily News* as well as serving as the Public Relations officer for The Jimmie Heuga Center.

Although she wrote non-fiction, her first love was fiction and through the years she continued revising her thesis story, writing short stories, working on a ski novel and her memoir.

Jean Herbert Winthers lives in the Bitterroot Valley with her retired husband. She is currently working on the second book of *The Big Gumbo* planned as a trilogy, where she continues the story of Arne and Raneid Bergstrom as they struggle to make a living in the inhospitable land of the Gumbo.

CPSIA information can be obtained
at www.ICGtesting.com
Printed in the USA
FSHW020502190819
61184FS